QUEEN OF MISFORTUNE

By Peter Carroll

COPPERHILL MEDIA CORPORATION
http://www.copperhillmedia.com

QUEEN OF MISFORTUNE
By Peter Carroll

Published by
Copperhill Media Corporation
158 Log Plain Road
Greenfield, MA 01301
USA

Cover Design by Copperhill Media Corporation.
Image: Hopeful Prayer
Copyright: iStockphoto.com - Contributor: Aldo Murillo
Image: Chetwode window
Copyright: BigStockphoto.com - Contributor: Sybille Yates
Image: Chapel
Copyright: BigStockPhoto.com – Conributor: Yury Aldanau

Disclaimer: While inspired by historical events and persons, this work is based solely on the author's imagination.

ISBN-10: 0-9832800-2-9
ISBN-13: 978-0-9832800-2-6

Printed in the United States of America

http://www.copperhillmedia.com

ACKNOWLDEGEMENTS

I would like to express my appreciation to my wife Daphne for putting up with my living in the past for three years, Janet Hunter, who inspired and introduced me to Bradgate and Jane, and Sue Holford, who read and edited for me.

PREFACE

Pick up a history book covering 16th Century Britain and one will find numerous accounts of the monarchs but very little indeed about the very well educated and astute Lady Jane Grey, who became the nine-day Queen.

When researching my book I sensed the presence of Lady Jane in the confines of the tower named after her in the ruins of Bradgate House where she lived. I felt myself conveying to her that I so much wanted to tell the world of her, to make it more aware of her place in history. But she would have none of it, even though I suggested she may be visiting her former home on earth in spirit form.

"But I have no reason to return. Generally, my childhood was painful there and I do not believe it is a good idea to write about me more than has already been said."

"But I must, Jane, and I will and I think you know that."

Then the presence was gone. I felt it chill the marrow of my bones, yet something urged me to write the account of this remarkable girl as I have it, through research and a little more, the certain feeling that a romance did aspire between her and her beloved tutor, John Aylmer.

Bradgate House in Leicestershire with its beautiful country park, where grazing deer can still be observed, was where Lady Jane Grey spent much of her childhood.

Alas, it was not always a happy time for her. One would think that being brought up in such wonderful surroundings would be perfect, but she was constantly the victim of her parent's very strict regime, preparing their daughter in readiness for high society and eventually the contender to the throne.

Perhaps there is much more to Lady Jane. This is the purpose of my book, to envisage what may have happened. There are ominous gaps in her life of which we have no record. There are reports of an unknown personage who visited her when she was imprisoned in the Tower, a 'true friend' who frequently conversed with her in the privacy of her apartments, somebody who held authority and was accepted by Jane's gaoler, Mr. Partridge, as well as the Lieutenant of the Tower, Sir John Brydges.

We know Dr. Feckenham the monk visited her upon Queen Mary Tudor's instruction, in an unsuccessful attempt to persuade her cousin to convert to Catholicism.

But the kindly stranger was somebody Jane knew intimately. Why was his identity unrecorded?

There are well-documented reports of Jane's last moments upon the scaffold when, blindfolded, she lost her presence of mind, as if her God deserted her at the last moment; she asked for assistance to locate the block but those surrounding her seemed unable to move, perhaps overwhelmed with the feeling that a truly innocent young girl in her prime was due to meet her end; that they were unable to assist her passage to the ghastly death awaiting her.

This could not continue, Jane crouching on the boards, reaching out.

But the stranger appeared again. He climbed the scaffold and guided Jane, spoke softly into her ear. She calmed once more, found the block and knelt. Her God was with her again. Her head dropped down to rest upon the curvature in the block and she said loudly and clearly:

"Lord, into thy hands I commend my spirit." Her arms were outstretched - the signal to show her executioner she was ready. Slowly he lifted his axe.

But who was the stranger? I think, I have an idea…

When Jane was at Bradgate in 1545 and because of her parent's cruel upbringing, the only people she could turn to for love and affection were her younger sister by three years, Katharine, and her nurse and governess, Mary Ellen. That was before a young clergyman called John Aylmer came to Bradgate to be her tutor. He gave her much warmth and understanding and she felt here at last was a person she could trust and in whom she could confide.

When she was nine, Jane was despatched to Chelsea Palace, under the auspices of Katharine Parr, the sixth wife of King Henry VIII. They were happy times, Elizabeth the future Queen was one of her playmates and Jane felt she could treat Katharine like a mother.

When proclaimed Queen, Jane was unpopular because of the reputation of the family she had recently joined by marriage to the powerful Duke of Northumberland's son, Guildford Dudley.

Given the right timing she probably would have made a great Queen and if we look more closely into the events leading up to her execution, she portrays a very strong willed noble woman in line with Elizabeth, who missed the swing of the axe because of her great popularity and cunning. Bloody Mary Tudor, as she came to be known, knew she could easily dispose of Jane, but Elizabeth? She would be treading on very dangerous ground indeed.

How cruel our titled ancestors were. To behead a girl of sixteen, an innocent girl at that, unwittingly, caught up in the greed for power, after she and her husband Guildford, were charged with high treason.

Earlier she had been accused of conspiracy to gain the throne but she never wanted to be a Queen. Jane protested that the rightful heir was her cousin, Mary, but the seed had already been sewn. She had no option and the crown was already hers.

The main conspirator was the Duke of Northumberland. Mary knew Jane was not a conspirator and once enthroned, planned to send her to a remote estate where she would be entrusted to a loyal noble.

But we are told of Northumberland's hunger for power and how he and Jane's parents, Henry and Frances Grey, the Duke and Duchess of Suffolk, plotted a passage for Jane to be Queen of England.

The boy King Edward VI knew he was dying and, anxious to ensure a Protestant succession, drafted a memorandum bequeathing the crown to Jane's mother Frances Grey, niece of Henry VIII and unborn male heirs. But realising time was catching up with him he changed the wording, bequeathing the realm to Lady Jane, his plan being for her to marry his son, Guildford, assuming he had the power to leave it to anyone he chose. But Henry VIII's 1544 Act of Succession remained on the statute book, which made Mary Tudor the rightful heir to the throne.

It was as if Northumberland was assuming ignorance of the fact and hoped he might just get away with it. Perhaps he miscalculated the power of his position.

Here we see how poor Jane had absolutely no control over the might of Northumberland and his formidable Government. She was caught up in his web on a path, which eventually led to her early death. His reputation of cruelty to anybody who crossed his path, even for the most minor offence, was common knowledge. His declaration that Lady Jane should be Queen was a non-starter. She would never be accepted with open arms.

We know of how Jane was proclaimed Queen in London on July 10th, 1553 but we can never know just how much she fought against this. Northumberland knew in pressing Jane's claim that the way was tenuous. But his son Guildford's claim was non-existent. However, when Jane was proclaimed Queen, she was in the position to make use of her unwanted power and told her father-in-law that she would never make his son King. Instead she made her husband a duke, which caused a huge family row, such that Jane was never to live down.

Well, she never wanted to marry Guildford in the first place, but was forced to do so by those who chose to know best the most suitable partner for a future Queen.

Princess Mary Tudor was to be a formidable match for Northumberland. When she directed the council to oust Jane and proclaim herself Queen, Northumberland banded together three thousand men to capture her. She retaliated with an army of loyal supporters and numerous friends. Many of Northumberland's men changed sides and no battle was ever fought. Northumberland was beaten, Mary was proclaimed Queen and he was led to the hands of the executioner.

Mary imprisoned Jane and her husband in the Tower and, at the beginning, did show some leniency. But it is strange how Jane's father and his brothers somehow got tied up with a rebellion led by Thomas Wyatt to oust Mary in favour of Elizabeth, the Protestant.

This was bad timing indeed. Mary was liked by everyone including Protestants who had been sufficiently brainwashed into the belief that their new Queen would not deny them their religion. The rebellion was bound to fail.

Although Jane had nothing whatsoever to do with the rebellion she was family and Mary, listening to those who wanted Jane dead, despite the torment she often displayed of having to execute one so young, grew hardened. This and the accumulation of discontent about Mary's unpopular marriage with Philip, the King of Spain, led to a war with France and hysteria in England.

Now Mary, too, had become unpopular and she discovered plots against her. Her closest advisor, Simon Renard, an able French diplomat from the Court of Charles V, pressed that she needed to show her people severity in the punishment of all those who chose to revolt against her. She must immediately get rid of Jane and her husband should they find an opportunity to rise against her.

"You ask me to dispose of Jane who has royal blood," the new Queen anxiously protested. "She is my cousin, I simply cannot allow this, the very idea is repugnant to my soul."

But her advisor was cruelly adamant, his eyes opened wide, staring straight into hers...

"You have no option, Your Majesty," he pressed. "Already the people begin to despise you, you have to be rid of anyone who can overturn you, you must destroy anything you find appertaining to her and finally her life, too."

"But I have it from Elizabeth, my half-sister, that truly Jane is innocent and was tricked to take the throne."

"You have no absolute proof, Your Majesty. Your sister is wrong and I would query that indeed," snarled Renard. "But your sister may also have been misinformed in a vain effort to rescue the precocious Lady Jane."

Mary had little option other than to submit to the extreme pressure, she knew there was one light of hope if Jane converted to Catholicism, but the action would not be resolute and to add fuel to Renard's fire, Jane emphatically said she would not convert at any cost. The Queen eventually and reluctantly agreed to Jane's execution, and so the Queen-for-nine-days' sad fate was set, but not before there was a final attempt to secretly give Jane a way out. In her heart of hearts she did not feel at ease with the decision bestowed upon her and suggested Jane should admit her shortcomings and become a good Catholic.

Many a soul would have welcomed the option to save their heads but Jane, always stubborn, was belligerent when it came to her beliefs. She scowled that even the Queen should suggest that her own faith was lacking and Catholicism was the be all and end all and immediately rejected the option. Before her death on February 12th, 1554 she watched from her window as her husband was taken to his execution on Tower Hill and was still watching when a cart, bearing his body, his severed head wrapped in cloth, returned to the

Tower.

She asked if she could have a private execution on Tower Green, which was granted. She bravely gave a farewell speech and forgave the executioner asking him to dispatch her quickly.

The stranger watched.

Looking into Jane's childhood at Bradgate, although unhappy, she was a gifted student, having mastered two difficult languages, Latin and Greek. She was an enthusiastic scholar and needed to be. Her parents made sure of that. There was nothing coming from them by way of affection. In fact she confided in the great scholar and writer Roger Ascham when he visited Bradgate, that she was constantly taunted and physically abused by her parents because she was not putting her all into her studies. She vowed she had 'pinches, nips and bobs' besides things she could not mention.

She preferred to sit in the house reading the Greek philosophers. She claimed she gained much more pleasure in reading Plato's Phaedo than joining the rest of the household in outside sports and pursuits.

She was much akin to John Aylmer, her 'schoolmaster,' who showed her a kindness scarcely encountered.

It is difficult to imagine how she must have felt when she lived at Bradgate. If only the broken walls could talk. Looking at the ruins it almost seems apt that this beautiful old mansion should be so, as if in keeping with poor Jane's broken life. Local farmers and villagers started plundering stones and bricks, carting away the life of the place, as the misguided plotters in the royal palace took away Jane's life leaving the burial party to cart away her remains.

Perhaps the unrecorded stranger was the only person in the world she loved as a woman loves a man, her beloved tutor, John Aylmer. And she, too, meant everything to him. This was probably realised when she was fifteen and they would have discussed their impossible situation. Their true love for each other was unknown because of their standing.

Although there are reports that Aylmer fled to the continent during Queen Mary's reign, to return when Elizabeth was on the throne. It is likely he waited until the execution was over. It was important he was there to calm Jane with his love and strength in their mutual beliefs. Somehow, he managed to persuade both the gaoler and the Lieutenant of the Tower to let him see her and also gain admission to witness her execution. That it was important to him, even though it meant taking risks. If Mary had discovered the intrusion of a Protestant when her own Catholic followers abounded, Aylmer, no doubt, would soon have lost his head, too.

Although I felt a spiritual presence at Bradgate, I feel it was not Jane. I could not envisage her wanting to return to Bradgate with all those unhappy memories, unless she was seeking her schoolmaster. The presence I felt therefore of Jane was conveyed from another place in the depths of the ether.

But there is something there in the remains, something of Jane's childhood perhaps. I have walked along the long lane leading to Bradgate House only twice, between those famous pollard oaks, taking in the landscape as Jane must have done many times. Wondering if I could pick out something unchanged that took her eye, so I could get a glimpse into the person that was Jane.

Examining her assumed portrait, an engraving from the 19th century, I doubt if it is Jane. There is no proof. She must have sat for a painting as most noblewomen did, but why has it not survived? Yet the eyes show suffering, sadness and torment and there is a glimmer of determination and hope, which could be mistaken for the stubbornness Jane is thought often to have shown.

I wonder if, given different circumstances and the right opportunity, she could have made a great Queen. But then we may not have had Elizabeth who seemed to be right for England.

But Queen Jane? Well she was a Queen for nine days but it meant the forfeiture of her life. How sad it was to have lost one so talented and so young.

During my research I visited Bradgate again attempting to pick up those mysterious vibes recorded somewhere in the ruins. I would like to believe that Jane has gone to another place where her talents will be truly appreciated. She certainly received a raw deal here on earth in the sixteenth Century.

Sincerely yours,
Peter Carroll

CHAPTER ONE

It was Monday, 12 February 1554 when one of the most callous and horrifying episodes in English history took place in the Tower of London. First, the young Guildford Dudley suffered the headman's axe on Tower Hill. Then came the turn of his wife, Jane, formerly the nine-day Queen, in the confines of Tower Green.

A mysterious stranger appeared from the crowd to assist Jane upon the scaffold as her time drew to a close. But he was much, much more than just a stranger. He was John Aylmer, Jane's beloved 'schoolmaster' as she called him.

This is his story as relayed to his eldest son, Samuel, telling of his very special relationship with Lady Jane Grey.

***

"What shall I do? Where is it?"

They were almost the last words to be uttered by my sweet, sweet Jane and I could not bear to watch that which was imminent. It was a dark and dismal day and the morning mist hung low over the roof of the Chapel Royal of St. Peter ad Vincula beyond the scaffold site. The air smelt of sweet-smelling herbs befitting the stance of a noble woman, customarily sprinkled upon the boards with a light dressing of sand, moments before the arrival of the execution party. I remember, too, the sweet pungent aroma of freshly sawn wood used to build the scaffold the day before, and the smell of fresh hay strewn into a basket underneath the head block. Jane asked one of her loyal waiting women, Mrs. Tylney, to blindfold her with a handkerchief she had carefully chosen beforehand and held it out to her.

She made her own handkerchiefs, all personally embroidered with images of nature's gifts to the world-wild plants of all descriptions, animals of the forest and the wonders of the heavens, and always bearing her initials "J G." She told me it was good for the comfort of the soul, that she could also be mindful of her studies

My mind flashed back to the time I first realized her dilemma, when I discovered a bloody handkerchief left in her desk. When I handed it to her the next day she said absolutely nothing. But her expression was tort as she quickly banished it into her pocket, and made me realize all was not well, later realized through the deep concerns of her nurse, Mrs. Mary Ellen.

Although I understood her request for a blindfold, I wished she had not. It was nothing sadistic, but I wanted to grasp the final moments of life in those beautiful brown but persecuted eyes, entrusting they would gaze my way in hope that I could somehow ease her ghastly predicament. Her fair red tinged hair was neatly tied in a bow at the back. I shuddered at the thought I would never again see those familiar freckles that she hated, this wonderful girl I had hardly loved completely. She looked gaunt, tiny and so fragile standing there alongside her executioner, so pale and so thin. But despite her predicament she appeared as graceful and pretty as ever. I wondered just what was going on in her mind now, for that moment she appeared so cool, so tranquil and that alone was a blessing indeed, if only I could enter it, her soul, to be with her completely. If only it were possible for my head to be severed instead of hers. Her words again kept running through my mind, "we live to die." Jane's strong faith was constant, despite the attempted efforts of Queen Mary Tudor to persuade her to convert to Catholicism. Jane would have none of it. "I will die first!"

Her words again, the wonderful softness of her voice whispering in the sinews of my mind: "I will take your love with me, John, in my soul, my spirit. So fear not when I reach my end, for that is how the Lord would have it I feel certain. We shall meet again, my beloved, and when we do, we shall both be absolutely free to share our love without fear and discrimination and to know it is right because God will know it to be so. I shall always love you, John Aylmer."

I wanted to tell her all the things I wished I had before. I felt, if I could catch her stare, my feelings for her would instinctually be implanted into her soul, that no matter what happened to her physically now, the soul would sustain. But instead, my eyes were fixed on the large bulky figure of the executioner who stood there looking down clutching the axe beside him. I knew as soon as he lifted the axe I could watch no more. She forgave the executioner and bravely requested that he despatched her quickly. Never shall I forget the time in my life when I stood helplessly watching that terrible murder on Tower Green, for that is precisely what it was, a cold merciless murder. Yet, even now there was some hope in my heart that the stern Queen would pardon her cousin, a girl of such culture and intelligence. Could she live with the thought that she had murdered her own kin? Surely not, indeed, any moment a message would arrive to halt the terrible proceedings … But nothing could stop it now, nigh a miracle.

I prayed in earnest to the Lord, asking to speed her passing, that she may suffer no more, that ultimately the reason why such a gifted human being, who could give the world so much, was called to the other side so early and so abruptly. The reason known only to him but his kingdom would as much be the richer for it, as it was the earth's sad loss.

The cruel misinformed Mary Tudor would have much to answer for regarding her terrible deed having been ruthlessly persuaded to allow the execution. And in life she would undoubtedly reap the consequences. God rest her soul, for she cannot be of sound mind to have authorized the murder of Jane and Guildford.

Neither of the waiting women could bring themselves to take the handkerchief offered by Jane. Mrs. Ellen, her beloved nurse and governess, was saturated in tears, her hands covering her face, and Mrs. Tylney just stood there as if frozen, like a statue. She could do nothing. John Feckenham, the monk, watched silently clutching his bible. He had attempted to gain a pardon for Jane, in badgering her to simply convert to the "true" faith.

But time and time again, he realized she was adamant and told him that, indeed, to forego her true faith would be worse than any form of punishment the Queen could procure. She will have lived to die in the knowledge that she had betrayed her true conviction. But to convert to another faith in which she did not believe would indeed procure a passing to hell rather than heaven. She could not bear that!

And unlike her contemporaries, she would not accept the stringent conditions in converting to Catholicism.

Sir John Brydges, the Lieutenant of the Tower, whom Jane had befriended, stood in the background, his towering figure rising above the rest. Despite my earlier reservations brought about by Guildford Dudley's unsavoury remarks regarding Jane and the Lieutenant, this fine gentleman became an ally and a true saviour.

Perchance, Jane would see and recognise me, amidst the small crowd facing the block. I concentrated on her every move, but she did not seem perturbed, she just gazed downward scanning her tiny velvet prayer book cradled in her small hands, which looked so white, protruding from the sleeves of her black dress. Secured between her fingers her open handkerchief fluttered in the gentle breeze, in a flash of light, and when the sun shone through in a brief break of cloud, I saw the image of an angel embroidered thereon, but as quickly as it appeared it was gone again. Her guardian angel? She, unaware of my being there to comfort her, to replenish her soul.

I pleaded to our maker: "Oh! Lord, please let this innocent soul know that I am present. Let our eyes meet for just the second I need."

But perhaps I was being presumptuous as she showed no outward sign of needing any spiritual guidance, having conducted herself with absolute calm in narrating, with clear precise speech, the 51st Psalm, The Miserere, in its nineteen-verse entirety. She was already at one with her maker.

Visiting her for the last time the day before in the confines of her prison apartments was a deeply moving experience. When I should have been comforting her, she was the one who took it upon herself to ease my depression in the light of her ghastly predicament.

Her words still rung in my head: "They may destroy my timid body but never my soul. The head by this tiny neck will be separated from the rest of me but the soul will remain intact. I look forward to tomorrow, John, that I shall once more, after just sixteen years, be in the hands of our Lord. Please do not cry for me but rejoice that I will have left this cruel world, that, no doubt,

9

we shall meet again, my beloved schoolmaster. That we all live in rehearsal for the passing from this world to another, when our Lord so chooses."

Then there was the magical touch of her lips upon mine, the kiss that said everything, of her true love for this humble being, and we were instantly immersed with each other when, momentarily, nothing else mattered, we were as one, body and soul combined and whatever happened physically, our souls would remain forever together.

What extraordinary faith she portrayed. She looked radiant; her charisma was infectious. Soon I was sharing her joy. We were in our own world...

***

"Dear Samuel, in this year of our Lord 1594 forty years have passed since Jane's death and soon it will be my turn to meet our blessed Lord. I still remember her as if it was yesterday.

"But I am blessed with seven sons and two daughters and it is absolutely right, that you being the eldest, should be told certain truths regarding my early life and concourse before I die. Now that you are here, Samuel, beside me as I rest upon my deathbed, I will tell you I have been assured by my physician that the end of my long life is imminent. I will pass on to you my memories, which have been concealed for many years. For the spirit of Lady Jane now beckons me to convey the truth to you, my son, who will, she assures me, preserve my notes carefully, that eventually the time will come, God willing, that the truth is known to all...

"Here, Samuel, in this manuscript, is the true story of my association with Lady Jane Grey."

The frail white bearded old man passed a leather bound folder, from which he had been reading, to his son who took it graciously and placed it upon his lap. Samuel's expression was full of sadness but there appeared a faint smile as he responded to his father:

"That was before our good Queen Elizabeth made you Bishop of London in 1577, Father. And who was this John Aylmer who, by example, famously persuaded the Queen to have a very nasty tooth extracted?"

"That is another story, Samuel. The Queen trusted me, perhaps because I have known her for so long and she too remembers Jane. She has told me so on many occasions, Elizabeth, who knew Jane so well.

"You will discover something of your father you may find difficult to forgive. But I urge you as, indeed, I urged our Lord to understand the circumstances in which I freely submitted to this sin. I must suffer the consequences when I am adjudged, but I hope the Lord has forgiven and I hope also you will, too."

"I will read it now to myself, Father, whilst you rest. And, at the same

10

time, I will remain here at your bedside."

Looking up, John responded quietly: "I am fortunate indeed to have sons and daughters so loving and devoted to their father now that your mother has passed on. I have remembered her as well as I do Jane. Julia was a wife who was always there to calm me. I must hope that your brothers and your sisters will not lose the respect they have always shown to me, even when I am gone. In this vein, dear Samuel, I must leave it entirely to your discretion if you will let each and every one of them read the book in its entirety."

Samuel continued to read where his father had left off as the weary author smiled contentedly and dropped into a slumber. Yet as he read he felt it was his father who was still the reader and he the listener.

***

Although I constantly remember the time I was so close to Jane, and the tragic circumstances of her death, I am uplifted by the manner in which she conducted herself during her last moments. That a girl so young had confidently attained the wisdom of a saint, accrued during her constant studies of the great philosophers to whom we owe so much, and her steadfast religious faith, a true Calvinist at heart. I was at a loss to understand how she openly accepted the premature end of her precious life so easily, welcoming her death in that to enter into it would replenish her soul and show why her ordeal upon this earth was warranted.

Yet, she had gracefully shown me the path to take, knowing I was meant to know her in life as in afterlife, for she is constantly there, like a guardian angel, to mark my way. Always her words recorded in my mind: "We live to die." Loving her forever and cherishing her sweet soul. I found myself questioning and doubting my faith that day, but, as if assured by Jane's sheer courage, I knew how our Lord works in strange ways indeed, ways which as humans we could never understand, but at some time after the passing from this earth we would. We live to die indeed and maybe we die to live? Who can tell? We can only surmise and ponder and trust in our Lord that he will do what is best for each and every one of us. But I strongly feel that Jane and I will meet again in another time and another place.

Being there, when her life was soon to end and as the seconds passed by, I remember I prayed that a messenger would appear with instructions to halt the execution. Her mother, Frances Grey, was uncertain about asking Queen Mary for a pardon, because of her husband's ruthless yet pathetic and disastrous involvement in joining Thomas Wyatt's attempt to oust the Queen - without doubt another reason why the Queen agreed to the execution of his unfortunate daughter, Lady Jane - and knowing that her daughter had the option of living if she obeyed the Queen and became a Catholic. But that was not to be. Jane would have none of it. Frances was a harsh, grasping, cruel woman who dominated her whimsical husband. These characteristics were shown comparatively early by her attitude towards her daughters, especially Jane

As her tutor, I had known and loved her. As she grew into womanhood I realised the love I held for her was much more than I had dared to imagine. Now I felt the torment and frustration in the need for her as a lover as well as a pupil, and as soon as she reached adulthood it soon became evident, although not realised fully of one so innocent, that she felt the same towards me. I will always remember those eyes looking up at me, reminiscing, too, how I wanted to hold her so close, to pacify her trauma and fears, to calm and take her, comfort her being, as if to protect her within, our souls combined where she may be out of harm's way. Plainly, I was in a hopeless position, being unable to express my true feelings for her wholly. I could only be her tutor, her 'schoolmaster' as she preferred to call me. Anything more and I would have the Lord to account to, because it would have been pure abuse of my cloth, given the circumstances we could never marry and the danger of being discovered and the consequences thereof did not bear thinking about. I would instantly be dismissed and almost certainly executed, leaving my beloved Jane in an impossible situation. Yet I loved her, how I loved her. If only life was simpler and straightforward. But Jane was of Royal blood through her mother Frances, which, of course, meant she could never be free to marry whom she pleased. Yet could I, a mere human being and a male at that, resist the natural flow of my love for her?

She was absolutely innocent of any form of conspiracy or treason, in as much she never intended to steal the throne. She would not have been capable of so contemptible a deed. Her life was devoted, absolutely, to her studies, to the extent that what was happening in the world around her meant nothing.

She was merely the tool of those hungry for power – a puppet – bullied, abused until she so reluctantly succumbed, knowing full well the risks bestowed upon her in the tenuous position as Queen of England. Sharing her doubts and suspicions at the time, most of which have since been verified in the years of Elizabeth's reign, one could do nothing except guide her in the solace of her deep spiritual faith.

I had been entrusted with information, which might have halted her execution. This information Mary Tudor could have used as ammunition to offset the enormous pressure from her adamant advisors to be rid of all those who might incur a future threat to her, that she had been too lenient by far and must alter her ways if she were to be seen as a strong monarch.

I wanted to shout out what Jane had told me for all to hear. But that would have been a betrayal. After one last glimpse before turning away, I closed my eyes. She waited for slaughter like an animal.

Earlier, that same depressing Monday, 12th February 1554, after her

12

husband Guildford died on Tower Hill, some folk were saying it took two blows of the axe to finish his life. The news spread like wildfire, how the doomed young man cried hysterically, how he had to be held down and how he moved his head on the block at the wrong time, causing the blow to slice through only one half of his neck. A long excruciating scream was heard which came to an abrupt end as the executioner quickly made a successful second swing.

Many of the facts were misconstrued regarding Guildford's execution. Mrs. Ellen told me: "The Queen did not wish it to be known that one so noble suffered the clumsy efforts of an executioner who afterwards was punished and dismissed. The records show that Guildford died bravely without fuss. I feel surely, both executions will haunt our Queen. They were so very young with so much to offer. We know how Jane despised Guildford but his life was as young as hers and he died like our Lady Jane because of his predicament and the struggle for power of his own father. In truth, Dr. Aylmer, the poor wretched young man was beside himself with grief and cried and cried, yelling for mercy but to no avail. They had to hold him down in the end, apparently by his ankles and hands, and someone holding his head in place by his hair. It was devastating. He just did not deserve that upon everything else, even though he was of evil Dudley stock or not. But now he rests in peace and the Lord will truly guide him now, as he does our Lady."

One hoped, Jane did not hear of that. She had already watched from the window of her lodgings facing the White Tower, her husband being brought from Beauchamp Tower at 10 o'clock and escorted to his execution upon Tower Hill. She was still there when a cart, containing his body and head wrapped in cloth, returned twenty minutes later to the Chapel of St Peter ad Vincula for internment.

The fact that Guildford was interned in the chapel there suggests that, despite his proclamation that he was not given the opportunity to convert to Catholicism, he did so, Queen Mary being adamant that no further protestant internments would take place in the chapel. For other reasons she objected to Lady Jane being interred there. Her bodily remains were secretly taken to another place and, no doubt, Queen Mary arranged that.

Mrs. Ellen, her nurse and governess, later told me, she and Elizabeth Tylney, her lady in waiting, were prevented from removing the body from the scaffold whilst John Feckenham pleaded with the Queen, that by God's law it was correct that Jane's body should be interred alongside her husband's in the chapel there. But the Queen was belligerent and resisted.

Mrs. Ellen also informed me with repulsion, it was four hours later that the French ambassador in passing, noticed the body still upon the scaffold paled in blood. It was all too much for her to bear and she broke down as I took her to my shoulder, comforting her that at least Jane would be in peace now, the trauma of all she had suffered had gone and she would be with her God.

The ambassador bitterly complained to the Queen's envoy. Shortly afterwards, Feckenham returned with directions that the body be placed in sacking and buried secretly in un-consecrated ground beyond the boundaries of the Tower.

Mrs. Ellen, beside herself, promised she would do her utmost to discover where her body was buried. She could not bear the thought that she be buried without the proper reverence she deserved.

"She didn't even scream, Dr. Aylmer. I vowed I could just not endure to watch the executioner, but despite all that my eyes were as if glued to the axe sweeping down, my inner self wanted for the axe to veer away from its target, poor Jane's tiny neck. But as quickly as the thought came it went again, because it simply would prolong the agony for the lady, that he would have to make a second swing of the axe or maybe a slight contact, how it was with Guildford. Not enough to sever the head with one clean cut. Did he feel that? Was he alive until the second stroke completed the job? I could not bear this. I wanted, I actually wanted it to be a clean cut to instantly deliver the poor Lady to her maker."

"Do not repent, Mrs. Ellen," I plead. "You simply wanted whatever was best in the dire circumstances."

Only months before, Guildford's father, the once powerful Duke of Northumberland, met a swifter end when his head rolled off the block despite his conversion to Catholicism the day before. Londoners cheered as the executioner picked up his head and, clutching it from the hairpiece, declared that it was the head of a traitor.

What was going through Jane's mind as she waited for life to abruptly leave her? A strange silence ensued, broken only by the sobbing of her women. I remember turning again and looking upwards. Jane had bravely secured the blindfold herself and Mrs. Tylney, her hands shaking profusely, now held the little prayer book. The awkward silence continued as Jane, awaiting a reply to where she should go and what she should do, stretched out her hands for guidance. It was as if the whole world had stopped right there. Feckenham, the waiting women, two guards and the headsman – even Sir John Brydges who had escorted Jane, arm in arm to the scaffold – stood still like statues. Perhaps at that moment it had come upon them how wicked and unjust was the execution and none wished to be seen to condone it. Alas, the general public, because of Jane's attachment to the Duke of Northumberland who they had hated so much, did not feel such sentiment. They had been coerced into the belief that it was better to be rid of all those who had anything to do with the attempt to deprive Queen Mary of her rightful crown.

Although the Queen was a devout Catholic and many Londoners were Protestant, they still backed her in the knowledge that she was the daughter of King Henry VIII and the sister of the late King Edward. She had given the impression that all Protestants under her jurisdiction would be free to continue their faith uninterrupted.

If only poor Jane could have moved to make herself more familiar with the people as did our present Queen Elizabeth. One felt Queen Mary in that predicament would not have dared sign Jane's execution warrant. But part of the character that was Jane was a recluse and, unfortunately, this fact assisted her demise. Perhaps the torture and punishment she had received from her parents had made her so inclined. Had she been more aware of the world about her, perhaps she would have realised before it was too late, she was being used as Northumberland's pawn.

I remember how my heart bled to watch Jane bend and fumble, seeing her hands not quite reach the block. Despite this I held onto the notion, perhaps like those on the scaffold, that Queen Mary's conscience had pressed her to induce a late pardon and a messenger would appear with the joyful news.

But it was never to be. Perhaps I knew it in my heart. If Mary relented, then she would be seen to be too lenient a Queen, according to her adamant advisors.

Then, upon the scaffold, Jane lost control. Her body twisted and turned as though she had suffered a fit. Whilst before she had been in constant touch with her God, I felt she had lost her guidance of him. I knew her enough to realise she was suddenly aware of the horrible death immediately before her. This was my chance to finally be with my beloved Jane, to let her know I was there. Nothing would stop me clambering onto the scaffold to take Jane by the arm.

I felt her shudder nervously. Then something happened: She relaxed and I saw her head move upwards. It seemed she knew it was I although the blindfold shielded her eyes.

"Be with our God, for he is with you. I am with you also, body and soul. We are taking that trip to our heaven, remember? Time is not of the essence and soon I will follow as if there has been no time between us at all and we shall be as one, for our love is so complete body and soul, all to take, everything to give, feeling your heart beat with mine, like a dance, swirling, gliding so free, but now just you and just me. Be not afraid my love," I whispered.

She lifted her head and nodded, her eyes now hidden but the spark of her spirit flowed and the squeeze of her tiny hand, after she had reached out to find mine, she consoled me she was no longer fearful, that nothing could mar the very special relationship we shared and she would be waiting where there would be no more hurt, no more misgivings, and no more bad karma. Just utter perfection, our souls entwined eternally. As her hand clutched mine, her thoughts flowed through and I felt completely as one with her again.

She cried: "Oh! But that I could escape from all this and just ride off with you. My mind is warm but my body cold as if already passed to the next world. Perhaps it is right, John. I leave now, for we have known and shared our love, something we can both cherish, something that is ours and can never be taken away."

My thoughts responded, remembering the most intimate times I have ever known body and soul, whatever injustice has been committed upon Jane, we both had the strength of purpose given by our love and our faith in the Lord our God.

I believe, Jane would have been pardoned if she had relented to convert to the Catholic faith, but such was her dedicated commitment she would never allow herself to be humiliated or drawn into such a thing. Everything Jane did in her short life was absolutely committed. As her tutor I have never known such a devoted student. Indeed she was something very special and there could never be another Jane Grey.

CHAPTER TWO

Mrs. Mary Ellen was always close to Jane at Bradgate. She was employed as governess and also nurse responsible for Jane and her younger sisters, Katharine and Mary, at Bradgate. She was a pleasing, strong-willed woman in her early thirties and was both respected and well loved by the children. There were many times she told me she had to keep tongue in cheek, especially regarding the strict discipline which was expected of her towards the righteous and correct path the children must be taught to follow at all times.

She had known Jane since her first birthday, when she started her employ at Bradgate House. As we became more known to each other, Mrs. Ellen confided in me regarding much of Jane's life at Bradgate during her childhood years, that she was a lonely, reserved, introverted girl finding solace in her studies. Mrs. Ellen reiterated Jane's dreams and how she spoke of them.

"I am prone to the most horrible dreams, Mrs. Ellen. I awaken myself frequently with a vision of a tall dark shadow standing over me. I can never see the person whose face is masked. Yet, he is always gentle despite my screams. I have been having the same dream over the past month and it frightens me. It seems so real and, despite the fact the figure is calming, I feel the presence most alarming."

"This was just one of the dreams she mentioned, Dr. Aylmer, 'dreams that pierce the darkness of the soul' were her very words. Another involves her being poisoned in so many ways. All I could offer was to be a good listener and a frequent shoulder on which she knew she could cry upon."

Following the sad death of Katharine Parr, Henry VIII's sixth and last wife, the woman Jane confided to as her substitute mother, Jane eventually returned to Bradgate in 1549 at the age of twelve. She had been the chief mourner for her beloved Lady Katharine and she was truly devastated by her passing. Days passed after her return to Bradgate before she could adjust, such was Katharine's influence upon her. She received no comfort from her mother who scorned her for being listless and not paying due attention to her parents. Later that year I had the rare opportunity to befriend Mrs. Ellen. It was then that the duke and duchess took the reluctant Jane to visit 'fine and noble' friends.

Usually, Mrs. Ellen, along with Mrs. Tylney and other ladies in waiting, would accompany the family, but because of a slight fever the physician ordered her to rest for a few days.

I looked forward to a break. I was happy to walk the tranquil country trails surrounding the house. Mrs. Ellen approached me and asked if she might accompany me. The fever had left her and she said that she, too, adored the loveliness of the countryside on such a fine sunny day that it was. I was well spoiled that day. She brought a picnic basket, the contents of which we both heartily enjoyed, having discovered a beautiful spot on the riverbank.

We squatted down and Mrs. Ellen placed the picnic basket between us. Then she looked up thoughtfully and talked calmly, her eyes filled with feeling:

"I have wanted to speak to you since I realised how much you mean to my dear Lady Jane. From the picture she paints of you, Dr. Aylmer, I can tell you, there is not a finer tutor living. When her late majesty, Lady Katharine, died, she claimed if not for you she would have truly killed herself. She is very fond of you and I know, I feel, you are likewise with her. I would not be so bold to tell you this if I did not share the same fondness and love for this poor girl, who deserves so much more than that which life has given her. But my faith is deep and I trust in the Lord that she will be so rewarded in due course. I know we are akin to the same beliefs that the 'new learning' is positively the way forward.

"Lady Katharine encouraged this, as we know, but what great love and comfort she issued to Lady Jane, who must have endured great sorrow when she was the chief mourner at her funeral. Jane often recalls her memories of her. How her faith very much complimented certain aspects of eastern beliefs. She wanted to intelligently accept that, no matter what was one's faith, each should be respected and it was not correct to blemish anyone because of their religious following. To discuss, yes, but not to be bigoted. If questions were asked of one's faith, then, by all means, reply but never in a condescending way. Lady Parr strongly believed we all have what she called the Karma within, but it was up to each and every one to find their own Karma."

It soon became apparent that Mrs. Ellen was truly anxious to discuss her deep concerns with me, something she would never dare do in the confines of the house, because if her true feelings were relayed to Jane's parents, she would receive such punishment as she would never work again. To be in the employ of aristocrats was something sought by many. Out there in the tranquillity and calm of the country air she declared she could dispel her thoughts to one she knew and could trust, because it was apparent we both shared similar concerns for Jane and her sisters, but especially Jane because we were both aware that she was continually scolded significantly by her mother, than ever were her sisters. The problem was not so apparent when Jane was last at Bradgate, but since her long stay with Katharine Parr and her third husband, Thomas Seymour, she was not the quiet timid girl of times gone by when she agreed with absolutely everything her parents decreed of her.

She was still anxious to please her parents in every way. She was that sort of girl and truly believed it was God's wish that she should always be subservient to her parents and those of equal nobility. But having shared part of her childhood with the young Prince Edward and Princess Elizabeth at the Royal Palace before the death of King Henry VIII, who were brought up with far less restraint under the guidance of Katharine Parr, and afterwards at Chelsea when the widowed Queen dowager married Thomas Seymour, she had discovered more of herself, that it was right and proper to discuss differences of opinion. This was openly encouraged by Katharine, who was akin to the thoughts of the great philosophers who themselves often disagreed in some way with one another, yet continued to debate their differences in an attempt to arrive at a feasible solution to a given problem, knowing always, the wisdom that such a solution could never be confirmed absolute.

In my view, Katharine Parr was the most placid of Henry's wives. A very beautiful woman adorned with a fair complexion with stunning auburn hair. Those eyes, so expressive, her voice soothingly soft and her kind and sunny disposition remained constant. We both shared many interesting discussions regarding her keen interest in all the latest developments given to the growth of the New Learning, and I was also well advised in the correspondence with my contemporaries, both at home and abroad.

I had heard much from Roger Ascham that whilst visiting the Court any day of the week in 1546, a year before King Henry's death, one could meet up with a Bishop or two, or a famous writer or scholar. There was always something going on, some talk or discussion. Katharine encouraged the interest of many noble women who dropped in by way of passing as it were, to be delivered of good tidings and information about the New Religion as well as discussions regarding social issues. Fashion was always on the agenda, talk of how the new Farthingale could enhance and compliment femininity, richly embroidered costumes with wide skirts layered over the wired Farthingale hoops. The women of class proudly displayed lavish hair styles held in place by wired head rails decorated with pearls and jewels. Pomanders and small purses hung from the hooks attached to the girdle. Large round or square bonnets, complimentary to one's hairstyle were also fashionable.

Queen Katharine was enthusing men like Nicholas Undall, master of Eton College, who had edited a number of volumes translating Greek and Latin for those who unfortunately had not discovered the wonderful languages for themselves, and to which Princess Mary was herself contributing. Katharine also displayed great enthusiasm for gentlemen's dress and once persuaded Nicholas Undall and Roger Ascham to wear more colourful less drab clothes, insisting that certain styles and colours were much more agreeable to the feminine eye, just as well dressed ladies were to the male. She introduced wives of noblemen to patterns and illustrated drawings portraying numerous examples of fashionable clothing they may like to see worn by their husbands, the fashionable falling collar with matching cuffs, short gowns with fur facing and paned trunk hose. Shoes, similar to their own made of *Cordwain*, Spanish leather, silk, or velvet brocade with flat heels. Beards and moustaches were popular, too. Hair was closely brushed up from the sides and held in place with gum. *"Coppin tank"* hats were also encouraged. Swords,

19

rapiers, and daggers were slung on chains or belts, as were perfumed purses, sometimes carried in sleeved hose. All appeared very colourful. Children wore clothes, which replicated those of their parents.

Katharine absolutely adored children and it was to her credit that, when Henry was alive, she gained permission for all the royal children to live under the same roof which, in itself, was a great achievement and an indication of her determination that such an arrangement would ensure each child would receive her full loving care and attention, as well as the best spiritual and intellectual education, each child given the benefit of equal and shared opportunities. I know she gained the appointment to Chelsea Palace of the leading Greek scholar, John Cheke, who was well known as an intellectual at St. John's College, Cambridge, I recall, and the services of William Grindal – also from Cambridge – to tutor Prince Edward and Princess Elizabeth.

Some of Jane's happiest childhood days were spent at the Royal Palace and also at Windsor, Hampton Court, Greenwich and Richmond Palace. One of the most joyful letters she wrote to me was during this period. She told me of sentries holding arms, rows of corridors, hundreds of windows and dozens of gardens. Statues of Roman emperors, and stern gothic figures, seemed to be watching her from every building. She had seen beautiful tapestries from Flanders and Italy and talked of a huge one, which told the story of Abraham, a vivid tapestry with threads of gold and silver in the King's Guard chamber at Hampton Court.

She remembered Katharine Parr once accompanied her into the Privy Council room at Whitehall to see a great fresco painted for the King by Hans Holbein.

The furniture there was made of carved ebony, cedar wood, walnut, oak inlaid with mother of pearl, ivory or Florence brocade fringed with gold. Persian carpets adorned the walls and floor of the corridors, gallery hall and bedchambers. Dozens of attenders, musicians, ushers, carvers, servers, cupbearers, singers, and so on, were always on hand.

It was an awful lot for a young girl to absorb but she thoroughly enjoyed the experience.

She later confided, she liked the King and sympathised with his ailment that he suffered badly from gout but the Queen was keen to comfort and nurse him. She had spoken with him on several occasions and he had commented on her good scholarship. Although she later had reservations when she learned the King had a priest killed for not accepting he was head of the church.

"Surely, God knows and that is all that matters," she bravely declared to the King regarding the issue. There was a short silence, and then he erupted in a roar of laughter.

"You will learn, young lady Jane," he bawled. "You will learn that sometimes such actions have to be sanctioned in order to protect the realm."

But Jane confessed to me, she would never condone such a deplorable act. "How could he implement such a killing merely because of a mere difference of opinion?"

"You are a brave girl, indeed, for taking the King himself to task," I told her. "Not many would dare. He has a huge ego."

I loved her for her courage and her sense of justice. "It is just all so cruel, John, this world of ours, all the ugly killing and bloodshed, one human being to another. You must particularly feel it because of your conviction, that Jesus was so much against this, you must feel terribly frustrated you are unable to stop it."

"If but I could, dear Jane, if only. I begin to think we live in a world where killing one's own kind will never stop. I pray to our Lord constantly that one day, perhaps one day, we shall all see the absolute shame of it."

She came to me, her head resting on my breast, her hands gently circling my waist. "I guess, we all have to hide many of the things we would like to shout out", she whispered, her eyes looking up at mine. At that moment I wanted to hold her so very tight, I wanted to kiss her. Something was happening to us both. We almost seemed to be as one, that it was perfectly right for us to be so. But she was still comparatively young, and it could never be.

After being widowed for the second time, Katharine had reluctantly put off Thomas Seymour, the man she loved and intended to marry, because of the demands made upon her when Henry decided she was to be his new Queen. In truth, she did not have an option in refusing the honour. As Seymour's wife she would never have been in the position to achieve her religious ambitions and it was unlikely, indeed, that she would ever have been permitted to marry Thomas. The seal was set but she had her just reward, when she married Thomas after Henry's death. To Henry, she was always a loyal and sympathetic companion during his troublesome declining years. After his death Katharine moved to her dower manor at Chelsea and took Princess Elizabeth with her to complete her education. Jane was instructed to join them.

"I am overwhelmed by this very clever, young lady," Katharine told me. "I am informed that she could read the Coverdale Bible at the age of six. The King was most impressed. You, of course, will know that it was the first Bible to be completely translated in English, Dr. Aylmer."

I replied that I was aware of the fact and complimented the work of Hans Holbein who contributed to the design of the title page. His woodcuts illustrated beautifully the King surrounded by Bishops and nobles, Adam and Eve hearkening to the serpent, the risen Lord, Moses, Christ with his disciples, the reading of the law and St. Peter preaching the gospel.

Jane herself treasured one of the first editions.

Katharine was thirty-four when she married Thomas Seymour.

This fine Lady had served me well in recommending me to Lady

Frances Grey, given the backing of Roger Ascham, who tutored the royal children at Chelsea, an ideal tutor for her children, Jane, Katharine and Mary. I was summoned by the duke, who showed real interest in seeing me once again. Some years had passed since I served as a domestic in his Bradgate house and he spurred me to go to Cambridge, where I gained my Doctorate. When the King died in 1547, Katharine Parr, remembered as Lady Latymer of Snape Hall, had been widowed three times. Then, in her early thirties, she was still a most desirable woman. Given the happy disposition already described, Roger Ascham confided that in his opinion, Katharine Parr was a mature and well educated person, a very knowledgeable lady indeed, knowing much about the world and hardly had a disagreement with Henry who was experiencing extreme mood changes when she was married to him.

I felt honoured to have known Katharine who, despite the trauma she had suffered with the passing of three husbands, and the knowledge that her last husband, whom she loved most dearly, was often unfaithful, maintained her admirable characteristics throughout her life, especially noted by Lady Jane, and it was so sad a day, when she lost her own life in childbirth, just after it was thought she would recover. But she had made a great contribution to uphold the New Religion and had encouraged many new souls to follow the path.

She would not have had any idea in my view, and that of Roger Ascham, that there was any likelihood of Jane becoming Queen. Certainly, if she had, or if she had been blessed with a longer life, she would have undoubtedly realised the route for Jane was dangerous. She would have known at once Northumberland's motives and had the power and the authority to guide Jane in another direction. She was already well versed in the devious ways and methods of gaining power to the demise of many an innocent in the most horrible blood. Letting way, she could not convince Henry that this was so. In his world, politics were his affair. The attributes given to a woman were better directed to the social order and bringing up his children. But she could not help but continue to let him know of her concerns and, during his last days, according to John Cheke, he sympathised with Katharine's concerns and much must be accredited to her for achieving just that without offending the King, which she would never want to do.

Alas, it was too late for Henry to muster appropriate enquiries and actions. His days were numbered and soon the Kingdom would be ruled by a new boy King under the close watch of Edward the Protector, Edward Seymour, Thomas' brother, and this laid the path open for the Duke of Northumberland's device that would seal the eventual demise of Lady Jane.

CHAPTER THREE

After Katharine's sad passing, her widower, the Lord Admiral
Thomas Seymour, wanted Jane to return to his home. He was keen to arrange a
marriage between Jane and Edward VI. But there was no response from the
new King and I knew Jane was not interested. They were friends but,
scholastically, incompatible. He often teased her about always having her nose
in a book and having no time for anything else.

"Edward and I would have been a hopeless pair, John," she recalled,
"and heaven knows why The Lord Admiral ever envisaged that we could be
paired. I just wish I could be free to choose my own future. I have thought long
and seriously about how it would be with you and I, if it were possible, dear,
dear schoolmaster of mine."

She looked sad, as she entwined her fingers together looking up at me
so sweetly and demurely. "I do not think I could ever love another the way I
love and adore you, a love that grew with me, and now has reached fruition,
that now besides my deep respect and friendship for you I have grown into a
compassionate woman. Nay, more than that, much more than that, but I fear
my true thoughts if mentioned now would only discomfit you, kind Sir."

I was absent of words to describe my deep feelings for her. She was
still so young and I always harboured the notion that, as far as her feelings for
me were concerned, they were merely the feelings of a girl who had not
discovered what true love between a man and a woman was.

But how could I have known how a woman feels indeed when Mrs.
Ellen confided in me Jane's feelings I never realised.

"When she told me how deeply she felt for someone," Mrs. Ellen
whispered, "someone who must be unnamed, I knew it could only be you. A
woman knows and sees these things of another woman, you see, Dr. Aylmer.
She is growing up fast and begins to feel the strong pangs of her emotions and
how physically arousing that can be. She is but a young healthy woman
growing into maturity.

"Jane enquired of me, 'Is this how it feels to be in love, Mrs. Ellen?
That I must also be deprived of true happiness because I am of royal blood?

"'Sometimes when I am near him I almost want to run my fingers over
his body just to show him how deeply passionate I feel, and to feel his reaction,
it is truly so wonderful.'

"'I returned that it is true, a growing woman feels these things and it is
all but part of the wonderful process of nature, to want to give and take, to
share all, 'You are simply growing up, my Lady and need your love to be
fulfilled.'

"'But how, Mrs. Ellen- tell me how?' she enquired.

"I could not answer; it was not my place to answer, Mr. Aylmer. Oh!

23

What will become of this sweet, sweet girl who knows of the love between a man and a woman for the very first time?"

"We must trust in the Lord, Mrs. Ellen," seemed to be the right thing to say for this so delicate matter.

Later, I thought much of that which Mrs. Ellen had said as I sat watching through the window, the shadows of clouds wafting across the full moon, the light struggling to come through likened to my inner thoughts about my beloved pupil Jane.

Looking up I felt it seemed as though the moon wanted to shine its reflected light clearly and without hindrance. Then I realised how it was, as if my feelings for Jane, remembering always she was of royal stock, were hindered because of her stance. Knowing those thoughts would forever be like a shadowed moon, not able to clearly give out all its light, to shine brightly. The shadow would always remain because I was a commoner and could never hope to naturally realise my true feelings twofold because, too, I had to strictly abide to my cloth.

So, in that mode it was alright, and if Jane had those feelings for me, as Mrs. Ellen hinted, they could never be realised. Yet I wanted to pretend there could be a future for Jane and I, but shaking my head when such thoughts came through, knowing that such thoughts and pretence were preposterous.

Furthermore, it would not be fair to show Jane how I felt because it would only endure pain and heartbreak for us both.

Then the clouds thickened and the light from the moon was no more. As if signalling the end of any imagined romance, it must always, like the moon behind those clouds, be hidden.

I was unaware of forthcoming events, which would severely test my ability not to show my true feelings.

Back to the time Jane lived with her guardian, it was known that Thomas Seymour strived to approach the boy King regarding a marriage with Jane, but the constant presence of Edward, the Lord Protector, the brother he despised, prevented him from doing so. If Jane was obliged to marry the King and he could be coerced into accepting her for the good of the reign, Thomas's future would be assured and he could easily dispense with the brother he hated.

Thomas apparently planned to act as Jane's guardian until the matter was resolved. But as Jane had not reached maturity, he was compelled to announce that "she should not be married until such time as she is able to bear a child and her husband to get one." Jane was not aggrieved when her father consented she could return to Seymour. She conceded it was better than staying with her parents.

But two weeks later I received a very distressed letter from Jane, which made me restless, worrying about her. I was well aware of the philandering of the bustling Thomas Seymour who, on more than one occasion, excited Elizabeth during early morning frolics in her bedchamber.

But she was that much older and physically mature than young Jane. Jane wrote to say she had heard ridiculous rumours about her own forthcoming marriage to Thomas Seymour when the time was right and wondered who could have started such idle gossip.

But it came to pass that he was spending some time in her bedchamber without a chaperone. Jane, in her innocence, could not understand why. It was something to which she was not accustomed. She assumed, he was merely taking interest in her studies and her musical diversions.

But why did he insist on her sitting obediently on his knee? I discovered this occurrence during further letter exchanges and casually enquired into her on-going relationship with the Lord Admiral. Now, there were certain things she conveyed that worried me intensely.

I was at a loss as to know what to do. I distrusted the lusty Seymour.

Jane's present tutor, Dr. Cheke, was away for a while. I imagined Seymour was biding his time until he gained favour by means of his charm. That Jane, innocently supposing he was genuine in his tender caring, and his continued recollections regarding the qualities of his dead wife, telling Jane that he enjoyed the closeness of the girl who Katharine so adored, that Katharine felt for her as she could have been her very own daughter and he would also treat her as such. And Jane believing all that, tucked up into his lap, his hand doing things down the nape of her neck.

"He so likes to tickle me and set me in good humour, and he looking so deadly serious which confuses me. Then I think of his great loss and realise his lack of humour at this time."

I crunched the letter in my hand and threw it into the fire grate in disgust.

What was I to do?

The solution came the next day and it was all so simple…

I was beckoned to call upon Jane's mother at Bradgate. She wished to discuss with me the prospect of my tutoring her daughter upon her imminent return to Bradgate. This was an opportunity not to be missed and I was genuinely flattered.

She ruled she wanted only the best for a possible aspiring Queen Regent and trusted the Lord Admiral Seymour would soon have some news regarding a 'royal suitor.' That she had heard nothing but the best of me and would I consent to being Lady Jane's resident tutor. I let it be known that I was duly honoured so to be but, curious to know when I should start, I asked if the Lady Jane would be returning in due course.

The Marchioness paused looking speculatively at a large painting of the Lord Admiral perched high above her. Her broad face and heavy shoulders very much resembled the features of her uncle, King Henry. She spoke deliberately.

"I think so, else the lusty Admiral, known for his games with Lady

Elizabeth, will surely take my unsuspecting daughter for himself. A very reliable member of my household, whom I sent to Seymour's house to be her chaperone, advised me that the Admiral would have none of it and had the audacity to transfer her to housemaid duties, which would be of better service than perching upon her seat in the presence of Lady Jane, 'likened to a hen hatching its eggs' were his words

"That he and the Lady Jane must have absolute privacy at all times in order to precisely follow her studies and their common interests.

"I asked my husband to look into this and to approach the Admiral on this matter, that she should at all times be chaperoned. He seemed satisfied with the Admiral's assurances that he had kept in employ all his wife's maids and could therefore provide suitable attenders for one who is so important to us all and soon, the country as well. But I was not convinced and neither was my spy who informs me all manner of things. I have now insisted that Jane return in haste and that be the end of it."

But it was not to be. The Lord Admiral was a powerful man and was able to persuade Frances that all would be well, that his mother, old Lady Seymour, had arrived. So my services were not yet to be called upon. I wish I could be as confident as Lady Frances about her daughter's honour. But Frances was ambitious, her aims political, and her disposition was that of an impatient, permanently dissatisfied plotter. She was constantly on the move, in order to keep in touch with her richer friends and her Tudor relatives. She was much more geared up than Henry Grey to adapt herself to the ever-changing patterns of religious and political movements controlled by Henry VIII.

Of course, I later learned that a sum of money had been passed over by the persuasive Lord Admiral to continue his ward ship of Jane and the greedy duchess relented without further argument.

"Maybe the duchess may see it fitting that I may also be installed temporarily in the Lord Admiral's household," I suggested speculatively and continued: "If I am to tutor the Lady Jane upon her eventual return to Bradgate, it may not be a bad thing for us to get to know each other on a scholastic basis."

This was a solution to the dilemma. I would be in a perfect position to watch over Jane, to ensure that she would not be *snared* by the cunning Thomas Seymour. I hoped the duchess would take the point of my request.

"That is an excellent proposal, Dr. Aylmer, but you will know, of course, the Admiral employs a tutor of his own, despite his insistence to take such duties upon himself where Lady Jane is concerned. It may be difficult and the course may not be smooth. Are you sure, if I am able to convince the Admiral, you would be prepared for this?"

"My absolute concern, my Lady, is directed to the Lady Jane, her wellbeing and her education, which, as you have advised, is of utmost importance for one who may be Queen Regent."

"I despair, Dr. Aylmer, that this may now not be so. The point of our agreement with the admiral in sending Lady Jane to him was that he acted as her guardian and duly arranged for a bond with King Edward when both were of marriageable age. This has not come about and I feel there is much the wily admiral has not told us. But one of the reasons the duke and I have agreed to the extension of his guardianship is that he has assured us a match will eventually be arranged, when the time was right. But I will write immediately, Dr. Aylmer, and insist he takes you on as a matter of urgency."

I bowed to the duchess and made my exit. Two pages opened the doors for my departure. I hoped the duchess would succeed. Immediately I wrote, too, advising Lady Jane of the news and ensured the courier took my letter in order that Jane received both communications simultaneously.

The reply was good and I was asked to proceed forthwith to the Lord Admiral's London house.

Now I was in constant touch with Jane. She had an abundance of papers to show me and eagerly she told me, she was glad I was to be her new theological tutor. It is true. Her parents and Thomas Seymour were right. Jane was already showing there was another side to the quiet exterior. Her strength of character was coming through in abundance. Apparently, her new guardian had realised her potential and had the ability to properly bring her out, to dispel of her inhibitions and lack of confidence kept formerly at bay by the severe discipline received of her parents.

"My parents have complained to the Lord Admiral about my recent behaviour, that I have lost my manners and dare to speak back to them," Jane announced.

"But in confidence, Dr. Aylmer, my guardian has proclaimed it is proper that I should spend time away from my parents because I was too close to them. They could not appreciate I was growing into a talented young woman, that I was not still the small child who would dare not offer fair criticism in the way they treated me. He could not conceive how I am brutally treated by my parents, but when my father complained that I had been spoiled whilst under this roof, that I had lost all sense of respect, and that, for lack of the bridle, I had taken too much the head, he suspected I was so treated. My Lord Admiral declared that he would have none of that under his roof and Katharine would not have ever condoned such abominable treatment."

Jane gave the impression that she adored the Admiral. In consequence I decided to tread cautiously, remembering the things her mother had told me.

"I understand the Lord Admiral has taken his own time in which to join you with your studies," I remarked.

"Surely, he does. He is everything a guardian of a 'special young lady,' as he calls me, should be. Mother is probably correct that the Lord Admiral does spoil me but I do not take advantage of this."

"A special young Lady, indeed. You are surely that, Lady Jane," I spoke with carefully chosen words. She turned her head to meet my glance, her eyes querying. I wanted to ask if he was taking advantage of her, but on account of her innocent ways it would not have been fitting at that time. I would find such devices to see for myself that the Admiral was a gentleman, always remembering his reputation as a rake and seducer, a man who had enticed many women with his certain charm and enviable understanding of them.

As afore mentioned, it was well known that Princess Elizabeth had been made aware of the dawning of her womanhood when the Admiral frequently visited her bedchamber in the early hours. It was never assumed, however, that a sexual union was established. Elizabeth showed no despondency when she was removed from his household, apparently after Katharine Parr discovered her husband in an embrace with Elizabeth and following reports from Elizabeth's lady in waiting about the morning romps. Perhaps Elizabeth had grown tired of his philandering.

But I was relieved to discover Jane was safe and had not reached puberty. For, as much as Thomas Seymour was promiscuous, I realised his integrity was such that he would not stoop to such lowly levels of behaviour. Mrs. Ellen confirmed Jane had not reached maturity.

I discovered for myself, Lord Admiral Seymour was a ferocious man with an enormous sexual appetite, which indulged many fantasies. His ego was such that he openly boasted of his conquests with me as if failing to recognise my cloth; he was in an exalted position where he could take almost any woman he desired and I feel sure, from the titterings I had overheard, that he had taken advantage of many of his female attenders who, of course, were prudent in as much that their livelihoods would be at risk if they were to resist. I could not hide my indignation when we came face to face. But Seymour was not prepared to rationalise his ways, stating he could still be a good Christian person who was simply entrusted by God - for want of a name - he added, to play his part in implementing good sound stock in the name of England!

"And indeed, who am I to resist a certain smile and pleasure a woman, for that is all I do, it is nature. I would never dream of taking a woman against her wishes. Most women just want to be loved for what they are, they need comforting in knowing they are wanted, to be told they are beautiful and very desirable."

As if to endorse his statement and whilst I was there, he called for a courtier to render him several of the most beautiful maids at his earliest opportunity for such pleasing reward that he, the courtier, too, would enjoy the pleasure of their charms after his Admiralship.

Without fail, Seymour's request was granted the same afternoon when I encountered a host of chuckling ladies led by the same courtier, heading for Lord Seymour's private chambers.

But, for all his lusty ways, I do not think the Admiral would have risked his high position or, certainly, Jane's respect for him, in an attempt to infringe her honour. Yet I felt he was secretly waiting to pounce when the time was right.

"You plainly are a God fearing man of the cloth," Thomas Seymour acknowledged, "and I respect that, by the same token you must strictly abide by the rules given under your Lord and I equally respect that. But whilst I believe there is a worldly creator I do not know who or why we are here at all. I cannot commit myself to a faith without more proof you see."

Perhaps I was under-estimating Jane's morals. Certainly she was a changed girl as said. Probably, she was quite able to control her emotions. "When adolescence arrives, it is a confusing time," Mrs. Ellen advised.

"But the Lord Admiral was careful not to encounter myself," she added, "and nor would I give him the encouragement. I would add that he was a charming man and it would be hard for any woman to resist his charm. His disposition was such that he would smother a woman with flattery and one felt he was being his most sincere, he told me once he just adored woman, that he simply could not resist."

Jane was vulnerable when there were men like the Admiral around. I would assume constant heed. But I knew the Admiral respected my deep faith, "despite what you may believe" he assured and applauded my encouragement in showing the way of our Lord to Jane. But she needed no encouragement. Her faith was already set without my example.

My worries were unfounded. For a few weeks the Admiral was absent and I found gratification in the teaching of the very academic Jane, constantly enthralled and surprised with her obsession with the works of the Greek philosophers. She could now write legibly in Greek, Latin and French and spoke each language fairly fluently. She was a veritable genius and my only concern was, that she was missing out in some of the normal activities of a girl her age, because she would rather use all her daylight hours in devotion to her scholastic ambitions, given small time set aside in the evenings, towards her musical and embroidery hobbies.

"My life is full, Dr. Aylmer, as you well know. I have no need to follow the path of my parents in their obsession to socialise. I crave for the time I can choose my own independence and not to be forever tied, along with my sisters, to the selfish pastimes of my parents. We seem to be forever bored, tired, and exhausted with having to travel hours on end to their friends, especially the Willoughby's of Tilty in Essex, even to their insistence that my sister, Mary, with her severe ailments, travels, too. And when we arrive, what then? We are almost ignored, expected to sit there like stuffed dolls, to speak only when spoken to and listen to how mother claimed to have wasted £2000 on my guardianship by Lord Seymour and returned to them much the worse for the gross disrespect they claim I now have for her and how I had changed, not the sweet quiet girl she had once known, meaning I was no longer willing to accept her disdain, having learnt from the Lord Admiral that the time had come. I was growing up fast and needed the independence of a modern young lady of high standing.

"I am sorry, it may seem unethical but I begin to loathe my parents as they surely show no real love for their children."

I saw tears appearing on those gaunt cheeks. I simply wanted - and it seemed natural to want to - hold out my arms for her comfort, sensing she knew this but always, always trapped by the ethics of a proper and right tutor/pupil relationship, yet in my heart I knew my feelings for Jane were constantly nurturing my concern for her welfare. I felt it would be good for her to mix with friends of her own standing and age. She looked up now with those eyes that could be piercing finding mine, questioning eyes, almost pleading of me. But all I could offer were words and a smile. But then a hand reached out and I found myself clutching it warmly. She squeezed, and instantly I felt her anxiety as her fingers trembled in my palm, then that so sweet smile as she began to speak with soft enticing words.

"And you, John Aylmer, so very good for me and my sisters, too. They both enjoy your company. You are always the perfect tutor. But for me, much more, so very much more."

Then her smile left her face, which was solemn again. It was as if we were both aware emotions between us were growing, but I had to contemplate it was simply an overriding emotion that so many students experience of their tutors, the pangs of first love so innocent and immature to consider seriously.

Her hand left mine almost as quickly as it had joined. If only I could read her thoughts. But then what good would that do? I was merely her tutor and a commoner at that. She had royal blood. Yet is seemed, as we sat there, silently and undisturbed, her thoughts were mine.

"That I could share my true self with you, dear John, but just know, I have an enduring love for you, a love that binds my very being to yours, as though souls shared and free to flow without disruption, that we could be free of all social standings and commitments. If only we could be in another place, another time, another ..."

Those thoughts again, running through my head. No doubt, Jane was a deep part of my life now if I was to be honest, yet even such honesty has to be shielded.

We were to soon learn that Lord Admiral Seymour had done great mischief whilst he was away, when he was caught red handed in the King's bedchamber. Determined to gain more power, he apparently intended to kidnap the boy King Edward, thus depriving his brother of the King's guardianship and taking it upon himself. Perhaps this was always his intention, telling Jane's parents that, eventually, the time would be right to arrange marriage between the King and Lady Jane. If the King was under his guardianship, and if he snatched the power given him as such from his brother, this would be easier to achieve.

But it was not to be so, to the Lord Admiral's peril. The King's dog was alert and his growls threatening. In panic, he killed the dog, aroused the guards and was doomed to an early execution in 1549, it being proved his intention to put the King in harm's way. Jane was immediately called back to Bradgate. She wept over the Admiral and could not understand why he had been so stupid but, that if his intention was thus, then he deserved what was coming to him.

I have always doubted the story. The Lord Admiral was an intelligent man. I fear his elder brother, Edward, may have contrived the unlikely tale to be rid of his troublesome brother forever. Thomas was never allowed to stand trial and perhaps be proven innocent. Edward saw to that. As Lord Protector he was adamant, Thomas had committed treasonable offences against him.

In the meantime, Jane had grown up and the fearsome Duke of Northumberland was the new Lord Admiral.

I will mention how Jane entrusted me with information regarding King Edward. Although it had no direct bearing on Jane herself, it did involve the powerful Duke of Northumberland. If the information could have been made public at the time of Jane's trial, it is possible that Queen Mary may have been more inclined to spare her, knowing the evil in the duke's mind and to what extent he was prepared to go in the pursuance of power.

She told me of a note written by Northumberland to her father. How, in the winter of 1552, she had discovered it partly burnt in the hearth of the fireplace in the study. She assumed her father had meant to destroy it by throwing it into the open fire but it had been screwed up like a ball and rolled onto the hearth.

"He took it upon himself to disclose the fact to my father, expressing his plans," she proceeded. "That to be rid of a weak King would open the way for a Protestant Queen."

What has passed is history, but how often my mind is pounded still, that I should have disclosed the information before the axe came down upon Jane's head, but the heart refused and the tongue froze. That was the promise to Jane and one could never betray her trust. Until this day the secret remains steadfast. Her tutor has grown old and his end is imminent. But the content is of no further significance because with God's mercy, we shall meet once more. I will then leave it to fate whether or not to tell the world of its substance but the note will surely perish in the mortar at Bradgate House, her childhood home in Leicestershire.

"If it is meant to be found, God will ensure it be so," Jane wistfully advised, "for only I know the place it is hidden in Bradgate and I understand no good or revenge will come from it, because my father's head will be at stake."

Although I queried, this she would not go into further detail at the time. But I realised why Jane was adamant that the contents of this note held

31

information, which could involve her father and understood why she was so secretive.

It was ironic that, because of the part he played in attempting to dethrone the Catholic Queen, her father was also beheaded later in the year of his daughter's execution.

The new Queen was also being pressed to execute Princess Elizabeth, with whom Jane, in her younger days, had spent many joyful moments under the roof of Queen Katharine Parr. Again, the fangs of her French advisor, Renard, were showing. Elizabeth, as well as Jane, was Protestant and as ever a threat to her rule.

But at the time of the uprising, and the eventual dismissal of Northumberland's army who had, according to Queen Mary, "fantasized" about bringing her down before she could make her claim to the throne, it later came to my ears that no one in allegiance to the precarious Duke of Northumberland thought that the then Lady Mary Tudor could survive at Kenninghall. It was as if a miracle came forth and not a single shot was fired when she rode out of Framlingham. Somehow, the hearts of his army softened for Mary, maybe because she was better liked and respected than Northumberland who was always unpopular by his cruel deeds.

Now Mary was convinced that the hand of God had come down on those who dared to try and prevent her becoming the rightful Queen and she, as a staunch Catholic, was the right choice. It was absolutely right that England should return to Catholicism.

She was known to invite her half-sister to her coronation to hopefully show the people that Elizabeth was not denying her the crown, as indeed she was Henry's eldest daughter. It was right that she should next be in line, but more important, by showing herself alongside her sister showed that, indeed, the fact that their beliefs differed, Elizabeth was willing to maybe lean toward Catholicism and maybe one day succumb. This notion, not necessarily denied or agreed by Elizabeth, gave the new Queen a reason not to go with her advisor and execute her. But clever Elizabeth, by her popularity and cunning alone, was able to offset her own execution and became Queen in 1558. If only Jane could have achieved that, but it was not in her nature. Elizabeth was outgoing and always inquisitive, always watching and listening. Indeed, she was nobody's fool. But Jane was content to descend into her beloved books, almost to the extent that the world outside seemed irrelevant.

Also, her unwanted relationship with Guildford Dudley and his powerful father, the Duke of Northumberland, did nothing to better her popularity. The uncrowned nine-day Queen Jane had to bear the strife of her father in law, then the head of Government, and was ill equipped to dispel the reputation dispersed upon the Dudley family. The country was coerced into thinking that Jane was part of the conspiracy and the treachery. But that she was not.

I feel honoured that she confided in me. The memory of her words, similarly expressed to my valued friend Roger Ascham, will be with me for the rest of my days.

"And you, my dearest friend and schoolmaster, whom I have always cherished, you, John Aylmer, who has taught me so well and so complete, you have no need to become so involved, for surely you also will be branded a conspirator. You are in good favour with Elizabeth, who will become a strong Protestant Queen and I am sure you will be a bishop one day. You must never divulge the secret of the note for surely your life rests upon it whilst Mary reigns."

My mind tormented my heart, realising now just how deep I felt for this so very brave woman, for that is what she was now, no longer the girl I knew and loved at Bradgate. I thought then, as a beam of sunlight shone through the window of her apartment that, like the morning sun and the rolling waves of the ocean coming into shore, loving the one that you love, dreaming of being with her with overwhelming passion, sometimes gentle but all times, wonderful and breath-taking, soul searching too, those beams of sunlight shining into the soul, above all the love remains like the sun rides the sky, the rolling waves moving the largest shingles, ever constant, drawing the heart, taking and giving, sharing of the passion and lust, the joys of exploring like the glittering of sunlight on the rolling waves, then the storms grow, like the passion in Karma, reaching it's crescendo, its wonderful finale, the indescribable sensations of the climax soothing and satisfying the soul then love is fulfilled and all is calm again..

Now to share the joys of gentle romance as the sea becomes almost still like glass, souls share the warmth of holding, they gently caress, the stroking, the wonder of each other in a way only lovers understand, like the storm now passes, the fire of passion temporality dimmed, until the strong winds blow anew, like the sinews of our bodies, the passion renews and again the morning sun rises, the waves roll and once more love is complete.

When love and passion meet and the flame burns so strong the wild imagination plays wondrous tricks upon the mindset, almost as if it is real, wishful thinking indeed, a passion and love shared so deep with my Lady Jane…

During her last days she seemed to hold an inherent knowledge of what the future would bring. A future, which she would not know, she accepted that Mary should rightfully be Queen. But now, Mary was showing her true self, already bearing the reputation, which would induce her to be known as the 'Bloody Queen.' Her cruelty showed no mercy. Especially for those heretics not willing to convert to what she pertained as the true faith.

She ordered that they be burnt at the stake, sometimes slowly, and by the time Elizabeth was crowned Queen, no less that 283 heretics had met their most horrible and atrocious end.

CHAPTER FOUR

Upon my arrival at Bradgate in March, 1549 I was delighted to take up my new residential appointment in the tutorship of Henry and Frances Greys' daughters, Jane, Katharine, and Mary. Jane was approaching her twelfth year of age. I was honoured and privileged to be called upon by Jane's father Henry, who was then the Third Marquis of Dorset, later to become Duke of Suffolk. He was gracious and heartily greeted me upon my arrival. He spoke to me as one friend to another and I was much drawn to him for the help and encouragement he had given to me in gaining my entrance and doctorate at Cambridge.

He urged me to be seated when we arrived at his richly furnished apartment on the first floor. There was a distinct odour of lavender in the room. I remembered how His Grace emulated his wife in tidiness and cleanliness at Bradgate. Lady Francis had a habit of running her fingers along shelves and ledges and woe betide the cleaning attenders if she discovered a mere speck of dust.

But I was soon to discover her grasping nature. Her ambitions were political. She had a restless temperament, which reflected on her husband's moods, who normally was placid by nature. She was constantly scheming and her soul was restless to the point where she would explode into roaring fits of temper and woe betides anyone who got in her way.

She was forever visiting to keep in touch with her richer friends and her Tudor relations. It was as if her husband, Henry, was like a mere puppet and she pulled the strings because she was more apt to adapt herself to the changing times that her Uncle Henry VIII had controlled politically and religiously.

"So you have come back to the fold as it were," the Marquis said warmly taking a place opposite me. "And I know you are the right person to educate my daughters in the manner to which Lady Frances and I would expect."

"I, too, am proud you have so chosen me, Your Grace," I acknowledged. "I will be eternally grateful for the appointment and your splendid support in the past."

He smiled and declared he envisaged I had great promise as a boy.

"I am in my thirty fifth year now and you must be...?"

"Twenty eight, Sir," I replied.

"That is correct. I remember there was about seven years difference in our ages. Academically speaking there was nothing in it," he esteemed.

"I have been advised by Roger Ascham, who, I am told, has become your good friend, you are indeed a great divine and the politest of wits. You are addicted to good literature and excellently well learned both, in Latin and

Greek. So be it, I do not so mean to flatter but I would find it very difficult to find your equal in virtue or trust. Those whom I dare trust these days come very few and far between. Roger tells me you went on to Oxford after Cambridge to take your degrees of divinity?"

"Yes, Sir. In fact, it was Roger who advised I would be best tutored there."

"And, like Roger, you also aspired in humanist studies?"

"Yes, but Roger leads the way in that field and is, I believe, presently writing an essay on such."

"So be it, Dr. Aylmer, for that is how I must now address you. We are thus academically equal - nay, I must not flatter myself, my achievements in the knowledge of languages are grossly inferior to yours."

"We all have our diversities, and for good reason in the Lord's way of things, Sir," I submitted.

"I like you, Dr. Aylmer, and I trust we shall continue to be the good friends we once were. We are even similar in appearance, short, stubby but well proportioned, aye? And I have heard about your sense of humour. I hear you like bowls. We now have an excellent course in the grounds. In fact I had it especially designed and built in time for your coming. Lady Francis will probably tell you differently, that it is just my excuse. But I will openly admit I long to share a game or two with a fellow who apparently is renowned for his great skills in the game. I should add, however, when time permits. Presently I am overwhelmed by social responsibilities and am absent from this beloved place more than I would like."

"I am most flattered, Sir," I acknowledged gratefully.

"The privilege and the pleasure of gaining your appointment here are shared by Lady Frances and I. My wife was most impressed that the late Queen Dowager herself had good things to say about you. You will of course remember my eldest daughter when she shared some time with Lady Elizabeth and Prince Edward in Court. I believe, you often visited whilst Jane was there?"

"Indeed, Sir. It very soon occurred to me that Jane was indeed a bright girl and she was interested in my views about the Queen Dowager's favourite topic, the new learning. We have since shared some correspondence regarding her continued studies."

The Marquis then went on to express concern regarding his eldest daughter, saying that since her return from the guardianship of Thomas Seymour, which he had secured after the death of his wife, Jane had become increasingly difficult to understand. But he felt reassured that my influence would do much to correct her manner, which was not befitting to him and causing much disturbance with Lady Frances. He claimed, she had become solemn and moody, spending most of her time in her chamber and was lately not the sweet, kind daughter she once was."

I decided to take what His Grace said in my stride. It was my first task to befriend my new pupils and gain their respect if I was to achieve the best education one could muster for them.

The Marquis introduced me to Mrs. Ellen as the children's indispensable nurse and governess, a charming lady with a kind, yet firm appearance I imagined to be in her early thirties. And then Mrs. Tylney, "the children are much like waiting woman" who greeted me with a welcoming curtsey and smile. In fact, all the servants and attenders to whom I was introduced similarly curtsied or bowed and greeted me with equal enthusiasm.

Already I felt I belonged and was an important addition to the household.

Mrs. Ellen then beckoned me to follow her upstairs.

"Lady Jane will be in here," she advised gently knocking at the first door along the corridor.

"It is she to whom I am obliged to introduce you first, Sir, because the duchess places her children in order of importance according to their ages. Jane is the eldest, of course."

"I have met Jane, Mrs. Ellen," I advised. "Here at Bradgate when she was only three, and the duchess was still carrying her second child, Katharine. But Jane will remember me from our meetings when she was staying with Lady Katharine Parr and, more recently, when I was her tutor under the guardianship of Thomas Seymour."

"I do beg your pardon, Sir. I did not know but I think you will see a big change in her. Our Lady Jane is almost a young woman now."

"I fear she is not within," I suggested when there was no response to Mrs. Ellen's knock.

"Surely, she is," Mrs. Ellen laughed as she turned the knob and opened the door.

"She will be into her books oblivious of the world about her. There you see?"

Lady Jane was seated on a bench, both hands grasping a large opened book on the table before her. When we approached, she turned slowly to us and the concentration in her expression changed to one of surprise.

"Dr. Aylmer," she exclaimed loudly, her whole face opening to a welcoming smile. "I forgot you were arriving today."

"You look different," I gasped. "It has only been a few weeks since I last saw you. You are a young woman now."

"It is surely I, Dr. Aylmer."

Mrs. Ellen was obviously surprised and delighted by Jane's reaction, jumping up from her bench and running to me with open arms.

"Lady Jane, remember, Dr. Aylmer is now your tutor and you must treat him with some diligence," she asserted. Then turning to me she continued:

"I have never seen the Lady behave so!"

"Do not be concerned so," Lady Jane chuckled. "John Aylmer does not."

"But you are still a very young lady," Mrs. Ellen corrected.

"I am, Mrs. Ellen, but in two years I shall be old enough to marry and bear children. I am near enough a woman!"

She twisted herself in a full turn, her crimson dress swirling as she lifted her arms joyfully upward.

"I certainly remember you, sweet John Aylmer, from the time when I was very young and how you spent so much time talking to me and telling me wonderful stories. I cannot resist this happy and joyful gesture, Mrs. Ellen, to encircle this wonderful man with open arms. You will forgive me, Sir?"

"I will indeed, Lady," I confirmed.

"You must continue to address me by my Christian name, John Aylmer, as I will address you."

"My Lady, you must remember your station and that of the Dr. Aylmer," Mrs. Ellen gently advised.

"When we are alone then, Mrs. Ellen, I will call him John but in company it will be Dr. Aylmer. I hope, too, that you, John will likewise address me?"

That wonderful inspiring smile enlightened her whole face as she looked up at me. I loved her as a tiny child. I still loved her. My expression was obviously sufficient to confirm her request, which she acknowledged freely, kissing me upon each cheek. It was good to know Jane again.

I had already discovered that Jane had two sides to her personality, the smiling open-faced adolescent who had everything before her and the down side she obviously portrayed to her parents, the side described by her father only moments beforehand.

Her nurse was openly startled by Jane's reaction, taking me aside she whispered:

"You, John Aylmer, are the tonic this poor girl so desperately needs."

Jane then accompanied me to the nursery where I met her sisters, Katharine and Mary.

I remember, Lady Francis was with child when I left Bradgate that would have been Katharine, so this was my first meeting with Jane's younger sisters. Katharine was nine years of age and was generally fairer in complexion than her elder sister. One could tell they were sisters. But Mary, poor Mary, she was so small for her age, just four and she appeared to have a badly formed spine, bending as she struggled to walk towards me. But she greeted me with a warm smile and I felt at ease with the sisters.

Jane introduced me as their fine new tutor and how they must learn at all times during study to be astute and keen to learn from one so wise. That they would develop into wonderful ladies as befitted to their station.

I thanked Jane for her kind and warm introduction and was delighted the girls appeared to like me. I was keenly looking forward to teaching each of them, not least Jane who showed so much willingness and virtue.

I shared dinner with the family on a table placed in the corner of the great hall, and was advised there would always be a place for me at their table.

As, expected, table manners were strictly adhered to and the children were not allowed to converse whilst at the dinner table. Outwardly, there appeared no tension between the family but I would learn that this was not the case. I would learn a lesson or two about diplomacy when I needed to keep on good terms with my employer despite my disagreement regarding their methods of punishment, which was more expressed upon Jane than her younger sisters.

Upon her return to Bradgate, Jane had become a much-learned twelve-year-old, blessed with the good sense and knowledge only Katharine Parr could purvey. Mrs. Ellen observed how much Jane had changed, how much more confident she was, and how most of that was due to the great care and attention given her of Katharine Parr. Jane realised her parents were not the be all and end all in the opinions they held. It was apparent that the new spirited young woman was heading for a conflict with her parents, especially the duchess who still treated her daughter as she had always done before. That she should never question or appear to disagree with anything she or her father said or did.

The day Mrs. Ellen accompanied me in the park at Bradgate she told me:

"I have written in my diary that I constantly feel for the girl who is so physically and emotionally abused. I find difficulty trying to control my emotions and being put into a position where the duchess orders my obedience in taking greater heed to control the manners of her impudent daughter. This in the presence of Jane who knows under her tears that I could never scold her so. I must then pretend, always pretend, that I will do as the duchess commands.

"I am loathe to mention these disconcerting times, how I, with the duchess watching, placed my hand sternly on Jane's shoulder and conveyed her to her chamber. Once there, I closed the door behind with Jane simpering at my side. I reversed back to my true self, not having to pretend, encircling her tiny form in my arms whilst she shed any tears she had left, all the time feeling the vibration in her body, that of a girl in terrible pain. Again, the duchess had used the dreaded horsewhip and poor Lady Jane was ravaged with pain, unable to lean or sit, lest it be with the greatest of discomfort on a chair I have padded. Sometimes it is her father who administers the punishment, though I feel he is under the dominant instruction from the duchess. She tells him that Jane will not heed her, that she needs the firmness of a man's strong arm."

Mrs. Ellen paused for a while, and then continued hurriedly, as though she was bursting to tell somebody of her obvious concerns:

"How can she be so cruel to her own daughter, Dr. Aylmer? Jane is but a gentle fragile girl, sometimes arrogant but I know that to be part of her nature. She is constantly obsessed in her studies and if, whilst in deep concentration, she is disturbed, her arrogance unwittingly comes through. But I feel she can take only so much. I saw her eyes glaze over; I saw her leaning halfway over the window in her room recently. She looked so sorrowful, almost as if she would … But I must not harbour such thoughts. Why is the duchess so excessively strict with her when she is her own beloved daughter? Even her sisters, Kathleen and Mary, do not have to suffer the same ordeal of physical punishment and pain though she is equally as forbidding with them."

I tried to comfort Mrs. Ellen as she sunk her face into her hands.

"God made women to be of two sorts, Mrs. Ellen, some of them wiser, better learned, discreet, and more constant than a number of men. But another and a worse sort of them, fond, foolish, wanton, 'Flibbergibbs,' tattlers, triflers, wavering, witless, without counsel, feeble, careless, rash, proud, dainty, nice, tale bearers, eavesdroppers, rumour raisers, evil tongued, worse minded and doltified with the dregs of the devil's dunghill. Lady Frances is fraught by her own demands upon herself. Eager to maintain her stature as expected of one in the royal bloodline. She expects and strives for absolute perfection. It is as if she is unable to accept all humans are fallible."

I comforted Mrs. Ellen by placing a hand on her shoulder as we sat there upon the grassy bank. She looked up at me, half smiled, but with a tear or two trickling down her cheeks.

"The master is like putty in her hands, I say to you, Dr. Aylmer. The duke is far too lenient with the duchess. I have been there when that hard loveless woman; I'm sorry, I have to say this but if you have witnessed that which has become a regular torment, you would surely say the same; when she orders the duke to take the poor girl sternly across his knee which he does in a manner exceedingly embarrassing for a girl growing into maturity, whilst she, she who calls herself a true Christian mother, pulls up her daughter's skirts and instructs the duke to thrash her into submission of good and true conduct to those who brought her into this God forsaken world, for whom she had known severe pain and hardship; that she could have sacrificed both their lives if she had not struggled to shed her child promptly, before the blood of her wounds, her being such a stubborn birth, would have drained her dry. That this misguided child should know what real pain was if she was ever to find her place in the world as a fine and exceptional noble woman. A woman fit to be Queen were her words as the duke mercifully came down with the seventh and last stroke.

"Poor Jane could hardly move; she stood there, motionless, tearless. Her poor tortured face crimson, her eyes glazed, her whole being numbed.

"Then the loud command from the duchess ordering me to take the wretched girl who, she complained, was unfortunately deemed to be her daughter, away into the confines of her bedchamber so she may suffer the pain for the rest of the day, to let that be a lesson for her not to upset her parents further.

"I remember too, a month ago, walking in the garden near the lakeside. It was a beautiful quiet afternoon, hindered by the sound of a girl sobbing, near the vicinity of the south facing boundary wall. The sobs were familiar. I had heard them before. I walked to the spot and discovered poor Lady Jane huddled up against the wall, almost hidden by bracken, sobbing her heart out after a former beating by her cruel mother. I just kneeled with her. That is what she wanted. Not for me to fuss, just to be there until she recovered from the pain and humiliation cast upon her.

"You will surely understand why I have such difficulty in controlling my emotions, Dr. Aylmer, and God knows, one day, if this goes on much more, if Jane is so mistreated, then I will be bound to do something absolutely disgraceful in the eyes of our Lord and I so earnestly ask for his guidance through your good self, Sir."

I was astounded by this good woman's observations, although not entirely surprised by the method in which Jane was punished. It explained why she often appeared uncomfortable in the study when we went about our daily lessons. Although I was quite aware she was constantly suffering the physical torments from her parents, she often talked about the slaps and pinches, I could not imagine her receiving so torturous a beating or understand why this was so.

Mrs. Ellen served Jane and her sisters diligently as their governess at Bradgate. A well cultured woman from a good family known to the Grey's, she endeared pleasant looks, dark flowing hair and a rosy oval face with soft brown eyes. She was a woman who could be both gentle in her manner yet firm in her ways. I immediately took to her open personality.

Even today I am constantly appalled regarding the accepted intolerance towards children and support Roger Ascham in his efforts to strive for a more humanist approach to child welfare. But when torture and execution are abundant in our times, it will truly be a difficult if not impossible conquest.

One would think the daughter of nobility, such as Jane was, would receive less stringent punishment than shared by the commoners' children of our time. But, if anything, so much more was expected of her.

"It is not that Lady Jane is careless in her studies," I advised Mrs. Ellen. "Indeed, she constantly tries so hard to aim for perfection. But in the eyes of the duchess, even this is not good enough. What more can this girl give in order to satisfy her parents' demands?"

"Verily, Mr. Aylmer, I see a light in Jane that never extinguishes – despite the hard life she must endure, and this she constantly reminds me is given through the Lord. Thank heaven, she, at least, has a gentle and sympathetic tutor."

"And you too, Mrs. Ellen, and Mrs. Tylney, must never forget that you are equally as important in Lady Jane's life, for she never fails to regularly praise your combined kindness and understanding. Think of that when you are at your wits end. We have spoken of this before and my prayers are with you that you will resolve to control those actions, which do Lady Jane no good at all. Think of how it would be for Lady Jane if you were instantly dismissed, how she would cope without your support? You cannot jeopardise that special kindred relationship, ever."

Mrs. Ellen's expression lightened and she held out her hand to mine:

"We all need the support of a good and dear friend, Dr. Aylmer, if I may be so bold as to address you as such. I feel, you are truly a friend, somebody who knows the right thing to say at the right time. Of course, I realise you are absolutely right. Lady Jane is paramount in both our lives. The most we can do is to continue to comfort and support her through these difficult times, that soon she will be happily married to a fine suitor, whom I hope will be Prince Edward. She will certainly make a fine Queen Regent."

"It does not look too hopeful now, Mrs. Ellen. The young Prince seems to have aspirations for a French wife called Elisabeth."

"Then I wonder who Jane will marry?" Mrs. Ellen asked bleakly.

I had inkling, the way the wind was blowing. Walls have ears and it has been suggested that the Duke of Northumberland's son, Guildford, was in the running, although Jane detested him. This had apparently come from Northumberland's own lips and knowing of his devious ways, I feared what his motive might be. It would, of course, have been imprudent of me to share this knowledge with Mrs. Ellen at the time. Certainly Jane herself was unaware of Northumberland's notions.

"Whoever is the lucky man, Mrs. Ellen, I pray it will be a love match."

"Indeed, Dr. Aylmer, indeed."

"Now that we are friends, may I be so bold as to enquire when you are to be married, Mrs. Ellen? Or have the rumours I have heard been false?"

She looked up at me with a scornful look in her eyes. I immediately apologised if I was out of order in asking such an impertinent question. I knew she had lost a husband several years before, who died of sweating sickness. But I had seen her in a passionate embrace with Prince Edward's valet at Chelsea and had a whisper from Elizabeth Tylney that they were engaged.

"You have heard correctly, Dr. Aylmer. Forgive me, but it is just that I must be careful not to let the duchess know of my plans. When I became governess, she implicitly stated that I must not remarry whilst Lady Jane was in my care. That her daughter would require my exclusive attention twenty four hours a day, and I could not achieve that if I had a new husband in my life. I love Robert, surely I do, but I must give the Lady Jane my full attention – even by risk of losing Robert, who is being difficult. He demands I marry him soon but he cannot see that we would both likely lose our respected positions. He is so blind, Dr. Aylmer. He cannot see that."

She looked at me despairingly and I tried to reassure her.

"I suspect, he loves you so dearly, he demands a good part of your attention rather than come second to those expected of you as Lady Jane's governess, which is normal. Love sometimes is blind, especially for men folk, Mrs. Ellen. Women are always more practical when it comes to matters of the heart".

"Can you perhaps have a word with him, Dr. Aylmer, that he has patience and wait my readiness when you see him? He writes to me every day. I have told him not to as suspicions may arise if the duchess notices I receive so much correspondence. He is a tenant farmer near Lyn ford; occasionally we dare to meet, when we are able and have the time to spare, our relationship must be strained. I think so very much about him and look forward to the time we are together again. When I lost my first husband, I imaged I could never love again but the Lord has been kind to give me another chance. For now, the only time we can be together is if we can match rest periods, which are extremely difficult, for we must both meet away from our places of work. This week, with Lady Jane being away with her sisters, would have been an ideal opportunity, now that my health is improved but Robert is taken up with the demands of his work. I have bad dreams that Robert will tire of waiting. I love him dearly. I do. I cannot imagine living the rest of my days without him, yet I must stand by my Lady Jane and her sisters. I must therefore take the risk that dear Robert will continue to understand, but I do feel he becomes despondent."

I extended my arms, placing a hand on each shoulder easing her.

"I suspect Lady Jane will be married by the time she is sixteen," Mrs. Ellen continued after a brief pause, acknowledging my concern, shrugging her shoulders as if to denote she would be strong.

"And she will have no further need for my full attention. Her sisters will have their own nurse but, as we have spoken, the Lady Jane is in dire need of the time and the care both you and I can devote to her.

"Robert and I became close friends when, as an employee of the duke, he worked as a stable hand in Bradgate. A year past, the duke took to him and recommended his post as the King's valet, which was a great honour, but he could not bear being distanced apart from me. He was impelled to resign the exalted position for that of an opportunity to take up a farm of his own. He was thinking of our future, you see. It was not long before we both realised our deep love and affection for each other. He is a good man, Dr. Aylmer, and I would so hate to lose him. Can you help?"

This was an unusual request but I agreed to talk lightly to Robert whom I remembered when he was at Bradgate. She handed me a slip of paper.

"Will you give Robert this?"

I took it and she said I could read it if I wished. It was a poem…

Ripples of time

It's just the way you are
Something special to me
like the brightest star
Glowing, shining so lovely

You are the sky
I am the sea
The horizon joins us
So perfectly

The ripples of time
Forever ride the tide
Just for you to be mine
That wonderful feeling inside

You are the sky
I am the sea
The horizon joins us
So perfectly

It's something so real
Something so good
That's the way I feel
And it feels right I should

You are the sky
I am the sea
The horizon joins us
So perfectly.

"I love to send him poetry. It seems to strengthen our love and sometimes he sends poetry to me."

I complimented her on the writing of the poem and told her, I would be sure to hand it to Robert.

It was time to return to the house. I had some correspondence to deal with and escorted Mrs. Ellen back by way of the stream. We had cemented a friendship, which would become constant and, on my part, quite necessary to keep me in touch with those things Jane would consider inappropriate for my ears.

As Jane grew into a young woman I wanted so much to tell her that which my heart confessed. That now I loved her deeply, as a man loves a woman. But it could be of no consequence, she of royal stock and I, a commoner. My foolish heart has caused me to dream such and in that dream her reply was significant:

"Our dear relationship must not develop so. I see you only as my schoolmaster, John. For that is, as it must be. I will thus be honest and admit to you that I am but a woman. You are truly most agreeable to me in every way a man could be to a woman. But I must think not. I must not even imagine such a thing, for surely your wonderful exemplary reputation would be at stake and, if our love were consummated, what a secret we would bear and the Lord would know, too. And what lies we would tell if suspicions abound. In my surroundings I know not what is truth and what are lies, in the pursuit of power and good favour every member, save few in this household, has succumbed to mistruths. I would not wish the scourge of dishonesty to reproach my heart and disarray our special association with each other."

I had to contend she was absolutely right and it would have to always be so. If it were another time, another place! Oh! How I wish that could have been. But nothing could stop me from loving her and I imagined constantly her true feelings were mutual, that, in real life, she could never divulge those feelings for I was simply her teacher. I would always be so and she, always, my pupil. Yet I fought the mind's logic, put aside principle and argued that when the time was right, she must be assured of the feelings I hold for her, if I was thus to return the devoted trust and honesty she constantly purveyed to me.

Yet life sometimes changes things - and we change, too …

CHAPTER FIVE

The large stately home of Bradgate with its Great Hall, hexagonal towers, large mullioned windows, surrounded by high walls built with locally kilned bricks looked elegant in the winter snow of January 1550. I remembered the beautifully coloured windowpanes set in Small Square and diamond shapes within lead encasements. On a fine sunny day, as the sun moved across the sky, the interior would be amassed with elusive jewels of dazzling sunlight beaming through onto the facing walls, the murals, fine tapestries and painted cloth which adorned the wainscoted surfaces, the panels formed by plain stiles and uprights. The duchess was very diligent, indeed, in keeping the mansion an elegant place for any Monarch or dignitary to visit. Even the huge oak doors were decorated in a running design reflecting the area in which the house was built. Engravings of deer and rabbits surrounded by leaves of oak and horse chestnut filled the panels; climbing roses appeared on the surrounding uprights and horizontals.

The furniture was equally luxurious. Polished oak tables and box chairs covered in red leather and velvet black feather cushions adorned the living rooms. Large beeswax candles were in plenty to illuminate all quarters and were set in wood supports with circular grease pans below. The Great Hall had three great candle beams, which were suspended from the ceiling and operated by a pulley. Huge carpets adorned the large rooms and the family sleeping quarters, but elsewhere, especially in the servants and attenders quarters, rushes were spread on the floor and regularly replaced. The duchess insisted sweet smelling herbs grown in the knot garden were daily sprinkled over the floor rushes to ensure freshness. That was one of my tasks when I was a servant in the household. The duchess also had the gardener make up posies of herbs and scented flowers, which were worn by the gentry to "offset nasty smells given off by the peasants and the like." Most rooms had a fireplace, and a good supply of logs and peat was at hand during the cold winter months.

Lady Frances insisted bedrooms were furnished to the latest standards equal to the best houses in the land. Beds were of the new design; rope mesh tied into holes on the outer frame supported warm eiderdown mattresses. Some were fitted with suspended canopies for family and important visitors. The front panels were engraved with the family coat of arms in white and green to match the popular Tudor colours.

As she approached her thirteenth birthday, Jane was despondent. She did not relish being back under the auspices of her parents again.

Dr. James Haddon, an esteemed Minister of Religion joined me to share the tutorship of Lady Jane and her younger sisters, Katharine and Mary.

He was an older man in his forties with a stern expression, tall with greying hair, a keen disciplinarian but Jane liked him for his 'patience and understanding.'

He told me of his earlier tutorship at Bradgate when Jane was only eight. A classroom was set aside for the girl's lessons and, every day, Mrs. Ellen brought in clean smocks for each of them.

"I noticed, Jane especially was silently distressed upon our first encounter, and I realised my first task was to show the shy girl trust before I could teach," Dr. Haddon recalled.

"I taught Latin one word at a time; saying it, asking her to repeat several times until she remembered its meaning. Gradually her apprehension disappeared when she came to remember several words to form a phrase or sentence, which she came to enjoy. Then, within a year, she was forming the letters of the Latin and Greek alphabets, proudly putting them together to make words and expressing them to Mrs. Ellen, who, indubitably, was dismayed."

I could sense a change in Jane's mood when she joined me in my study for her lesson one morning. As always she was enthusiastic to proceed but she had a certain aura of depression about her. Of course, I realised her earlier disappointment in having to return to Bradgate and the confusion, which had been stirred up by her former guardian. She liked the late Lord Admiral and the young King and simply could not understand why Seymour had acted so stupidly.

I was concerned for the ordeal she had suffered and thought the course of our mutual enthused interest in the writing of the Greek philosophers and, indeed, her Calvinistic faith in God, despite the continued bullying and intimidation given of her mother and, occasionally, her father, too, she was quite able to cope and calm herself. She began to confide in me, telling how that her parents blamed her for not taking the fine opportunity, when she was with Seymour, to encourage conversations with the King, that if she had done so, a betrothal may have been set and she would have been honoured one day to be his wife.

"It seems my Lord Seymour made no mention that the King was interested only in the pious Princess Elisabeth of France," Jane ventured.

"In fact the idea of such a match truly never occurred to me, and was never discussed with me. I would have to say also, that although I deeply respect and care for the King I think it would not be enough for a marriage union. I have told mother that, as far as I am concerned my studies presently demand everything of my body and my soul and I am not ready to partake in such arrangements concerning my future spouse, that time would come when I was ready, to which she called me an ungrateful imbecile, and it was just as well I was back at Bradgate under their bridle. But I will rebel against their cruelty, I surely will. I am so tired and sickened by their bad attitude and their physical abuse upon me. Truly, through God's eyes, one must respect and obey one's parents, but I find that increasingly difficult so to do, Dr. Aylmer and seek the guidance of our good Lord through yourself."

46

I asked her if Dr. Haddon knew anything of this. She simply looked up to me with a slight frown making me feel that I should not have asked such a question, because the answer was obvious.

"Dr. Haddon is a good tutor, but his ways are not your ways, Dr. Aylmer. I respect him as a great teacher but I could not confide in him on such personal matters."

I felt her trust developing now. Jane, I knew, was reluctant to talk about the abuse she suffered from her parents but I felt there was something more, beyond the boundaries of comprehension, which restricted her.

"You do me great honour, Lady Jane, and I am glad to be a good listener."

"As I have mentioned before, you may call me Jane when we are alone, Dr. Aylmer. You feel to me as a friend, and, momentarily, I am so lacking of good friends. I need someone like you with so strong virtues, someone whom I feel I can trust absolutely. Not since Katharine Parr have I found such calming ways as those which are evident in your good self, Sir."

"You obviously miss her so very much, Jane - she was adored by all her friends and subordinates alike. I will always remember her for the joyous gentle woman she was and have not doubt at all she was King Henry's best Queen."

I was thinking how she selflessly sacrificed her forthcoming marriage arrangement with Lord Seymour to marry King Henry as his sixth wife - it was surely a great honour to become his Queen and she served him devotedly. But as if by providence meant, after the death of the King, she was reunited with the Lord Admiral.

Jane recalled the time at Sion House when Lady Katharine gave birth to a daughter and of the sad time of her death just a few days later. "She was so very happy, John. And then..." Tears appeared as she brought her hands up to her face and I instantly comforted her, firmly moving my hand on her shoulder. "She felt happiness at least in as much as she bore a new life, even though that was blemished, too, for those few moments she was happy. We must trust in the wisdom of our Lord that he felt it time for her to move on to his domain and we know now she is at peace with her maker.

"I remember asking her if she had loved the King after she had married Thomas Seymour..."

" 'I loved him in my way, Jane,' she responded willingly.

" 'Is it possible to love two men at the same time?' I remember she smiled so warmly - the woman who had sacrificed marrying her lover Thomas Seymour to please the king as his bride, yet to be rewarded just four months after the King's death in marrying her beloved Tom as she called him. He was almost six years older, strikingly handsome as much as Katharine was beautiful with her gorgeous auburn hair and so fair complexion so very feminine.

" 'My true love is clearly Thomas, Jane, but to marry a King is honour bound and I simply had no option other than to cast my relationship with Thomas aside but with a promise I would marry him when and if the time came. This was our pact, now with child I am a happy woman indeed. Jane, when you one day find true love you will understand why so soon after the King's passing I felt it absolutely right that I should marry Thomas as soon as possible. Never was I unfaithful to the King, indeed if I had and it was discovered we both would have lost out lives.

" 'But, my Lady, I do feel I am in love, my heart bleeds so and I have longed to share my truest feelings with someone I know I can trust to be prudent.

" 'My sweet, sweet Jane, for one so young how can you be sure?'

" 'Is being sure not being able to sleep, not being able to get him out of my mind, feeling ones whole being shudder and tingle and one's heart pulsate every time I am close to him?'

" 'Should I ask, who he is, Jane?'

" 'I am in turmoil, my Lady for he is a commoner, there is absolutely no future in it - I know it but love does not account for that, does it? And I despair, cry myself to sleep, unable to release my true feelings to him, I know not how to cope with the deepest of feelings I have ever known for another, feelings that taunt my body, my very soul, feelings that tell me all is right and natural when in reality those same feelings can never be set free, to be allowed to flow.'

" 'You have obviously thought a lot about this, Jane and will know your position as one who is privileged to be of royal blood, yet can never be free to marry a commoner, you can never be free to marry outside your cast - you will need to be strong and banish thoughts of any such relationship both for the good of the one you love so dearly and yourself.'

" 'But just some time together, Lady Katharine, to show each other our feelings, to vent our passion - something to hold at least, to cherish and to share ones love and I do wonder if it is healthy and natural to withhold and restrain what your body and soul yearns for.' "

But although Lady Katharine did not again ask who was the one with whom she had fallen in love she issued comfort and Mary Ellen was there, too, realising her need, and she, in turn, was able to confide in me at a proper time and when poor Jane had died. But, of course, I always knew that she loved me as much as I her. Mrs. Ellen insisted that it was her substitute mother, Lady Katharine, who found a way for Jane to accept what had to be.

However, she was constant in her studies, always questioning philosophically and methodically; this was a time when she turned passionately to the great works of the Greek philosophers. She was especially enthralled by Socrates and his pupil Plato.

For a while all seemed to go along smoothly and I, as much as Lady

Jane, looked forward to study times, which, as far as I was concerned, took place in the afternoons at Bradgate House. My contemporary took the morning classes with Jane. At other times Dr. Haddon and I would take classes with the younger children of the family. But Jane's parents, particularly her mother, stressed that we must allow Jane prime time for it was she who was most likely to be the future Queen, something we could not comprehend at the time, assuming it was just wishful thinking on the part of a very ambitious Lady Francis.

Dr. Haddon and I shared doubts over this issue. How possibly could Jane become Queen when Edward had his eyes focussed elsewhere? But we respected her parents' hopes and ambitions. Little then did I realise the other route by which Jane would become Queen. The idea that the young King would die was, of course, never realised and even long after his death I found it difficult to accept that the plan to poison him - of which her parents were aware - was true. I simply refused to believe that the Greys would stoop that low in quest for power and status and at their daughters expense, in order to agree with Northumberland's scheme to murder the King in his prime under the guise of his illness. It was all so repugnant to me but, of course, that is exactly what they did, and the plan was already in motion …

In this mode the Suffolk's were keen to show off their eldest daughter given the least opportunity and were generally socialising with those who mattered, as Lady Frances put it. In the summer of 1550 Jane had to suffer the discomfort of travelling the many miles to the Willoughby's in Tilty, Essex, then to the King in London followed by a long visit to Princess Mary at Newhall in Essex. There would be grand dinner parties and balls, a little too much for Jane who fell ill and was obliged, much to her parents annoyance, to return to Bradgate for a rest. She was simply exhausted but her parents showed no sympathy. It was that which was expected of her and she must be prepared to give her all in the quest for her future role.

"She simply had stop feeling sorry for herself," her mother snapped.

I pitied Jane immensely. For one so young and prone to sickness, an awful lot was expected of her. Yet she bravely attended her beloved studies despite her sickness and was cruelly scolded for doing so by the duchess. She argued that if she was well enough to take on her studies then she was well enough to travel. In the matter of days her parents had dragged her off to Newhall again. It was imperative, they told her, that they should keep on good terms with the Princess Mary at this time. Jane knew very well her parents desperately wanted to keep their options open, that if the princess did one day become the Queen of England, they would be in her good stead. Of course, what they really wanted was for Jane to become Queen but there was much connivance to be done before that could be achieved and the possibility was tenuous indeed.

When, several days later, Jane returned again to Bradgate, she was still having difficulty with her health and was prone to a nervous disorder, which concerned me.

I spoke about my concerns with Dr. Haddon who agreed he had noticed some nervous tension in Jane. But his main concern was given to the knowledge that the duke and duchess had taken up the craze of "hideous gambling" for reward and the House was becoming more like a gambling establishment. Even the servants and attenders had been recently taken to the habit, and he was determined to put a halt to it, one way or another.

He argued that, on the one hand the duke and duchess magnified the importance of true Christian thought, the well-being and proper religious upbringing of their children – yet, on the other, they invited all in the realms of aristocracy to join them in their unchristian pastimes. The same, too, as was befitting for the Lady Jane to spend as much time as humanly possible following her studies, she was constantly deprived of such time because they chose to drag her off to regular jaunts around the country – some of which he had no doubt, was in the pursuance of their gambling habit.

Dr. Haddon asked if I would join him to protest against such ungodly pursuits in the House of Bradgate. I was aware of the trend towards gambling but assumed it was carried out without the induction of reward. I was therefore shocked and dismayed that such a high family could openly partake in the habit and, indubitably, it was right and proper that it should be halted. I told Dr. Haddon I would, as a matter of urgency, support him and he made the required arrangements for council with His Grace. My support was twofold, that I could, in consequence, bring up the question of Jane's wellbeing.

Dr. Haddon was a plain, down to earth man, devoted to his deep calling, a true protestant of the old order but willing to discuss the new movements in which Katharine Parr played a large role. His great wisdom ordered that changing times call for changes in direction and he was generally akin to the new thinking. He had a very authoritative manner about him, which was complemented by his age. Indeed, I would have found some difficulty in approaching the duke about that which could become a very controversial matter. The duke and duchess were quite set in their ways and I imagined our proposals to alter some of those ways would be difficult indeed. But I knew Dr. Haddon was very capable of taking very gentle and diplomatic steps. Having achieved this, he was one to suddenly proclaim his message with clenched fist and fervour – as was well known in his sermons. On more than one occasion the carpenter was called to repair the pulpit stand.

During this time Jane and I befriended John Ulmis, a prominent young academic in his early twenties who was visiting Bradgate upon invitation from Henry Grey. His Grace was sponsoring his studies at Oxford and we shared some wonderful conversations. Although he was merely a guest, he was adamant in backing our gambling protestations.

But the mood of the duke was much to be reckoned with when we attended his counsel.

"God," he bawled at us both. "Would God have it that we all led uneventful lives, devoid of a little excitement? You are both men of God. You chose to be so and that is your prerogative. The duchess and I would employ no other for the important task of our children's education."

At this point his voice mellowed and his mood changed. Dr. Haddon looked calm. He stood there like a huge statue and I stood several inches lower to his left. He was tall and bestowed with a well lived in face. His charisma was magnetic and the duke knew him well enough not to underrate his intelligence. He asked us to be seated opposite him and started again:

"What I am saying, you are both invaluable to us. Lady Jane and her sisters do well indeed in the pursuit of their studies and I know much of that is due to your selves. But I feel, and I am sure I speak also on behalf of the duchess, I feel it is not your place to suggest which pursuits I should encounter in my own home."

I wondered if there was an unspoken threat here. Was the duke attempting to put us in our place? Our positions could easily be replaced by others who would cherish the honour.

But Dr. Haddon was unmoved. He diligently defined his deep concern that the servants and attenders also had taken up this "ghastly" practice, which, especially under the roof of one so noble, should be regarded as degrading. The duke remained silent and bore a stern expression. But Haddon was still to deliver his "ultimatum" – that, unless the practice was immediately halted, his next sermon would define the extreme dangers akin to the unchristian gambling habit and he would be bound to link this with those who have fallen into degradation in the House of Bradgate.

The duke halted the meeting at that point stating he had not the time for discussing the trivia of such absurdities but, in view of our deep concern, he would discuss the matter with the duchess and would be asking her to draw conclusions and further discuss this trifling matter with us.

Dr. Haddon had shown his weaponry. He knew his sermons and his writings were well regarded in all corners of the land and the duke would be unlikely to treat this matter lightly, even if he gave that impression.

Unfortunately, because of the duke's sudden departure, we were unable to put forward our concerns about the health of Lady Jane but I concluded perhaps a meeting with the duchess would be a better time to discuss this.

Jane informed me that after our meeting her father was furious. It came as a surprise when she pointed out that our concern was hers, too, that she had never liked her parents atrocious gambling habit, which, she confided, they continued during visits to their friends of times into the early hours.

"I will gladly therefore back both Dr. Haddon and yourself in hope of dispelling the practice in Bradgate House," she advised.

"Do you think that will be wise, Lady Jane?" I ventured. She was still very young to partake in such a controversial protest direct against her own kin. "Would it not be better to just leave it to us?" I suggested as an alternative.

She would have none of it. "Old habits die hard, Dr. Aylmer, and I also tire of my parents bullying ways. If I am to be a woman of high esteem it is well time to let my parents know that I do have a mind of my own. I have put it that it should be a condition of employment that gambling be prohibited under this roof and, in fact, have put it to my parents that you and Dr. Haddon will have no option other than to leave their employ because, in the deep confines of your faith in Our Lord, it would unequivocally be incorrect for you to continue, knowing what is happening here."

"That could well mean he may, in the circumstances, ask for our resignation," I speculated.

I saw her brow stiffen and her brown eyes met mine defiantly. She wore that arrogant expression that I remembered from her childhood.

"I have already expressed my extreme concern if that was likely," she smiled.

" I have become so knowledgeable, so enthused under the direction of your teaching and that of Dr. Haddon. I should be loath and unwilling to be taught by anyone else. Mother and Father are discussing the matter as I speak. I expect you and Dr. Haddon will shortly be summoned for further discussion on the matter. We are winning, Dr. Aylmer. We are winning! "

I had a feeling though that the battle we fought was not the same battle. She obviously detested the gambling habit but her main battle was just about to begin.

The following day I noticed Jane was upset. She still spoke of Katharine Parr, of her deep religious thoughts. She undoubtedly missed her terribly. She missed the time she spent under her roof. She now despised Thomas Seymour, having learned that he was not the loving husband he pretended to be but also for his atrocious behaviour in the attempted kidnapping of the King. Her opinion was such that he truly deserved his horrible fate under the headsman's axe on that fateful 20th March 1549.

"Why do things upon this earth change so rapidly, Dr. Aylmer?" she whispered bleakly.

Noticing her tears I rested a hand on her shoulder and advised her to trust in our Lord, that only he knew the answers to such questions. There probably was good reason why we have to suffer both joy and torment upon this earth.

"I do search for the abundant faith both you and Dr. Haddon have and trust in what you have taught me."

I encouraged her to further study the Greek philosophers and suggested she would find comfort in their writings. The confident lady of yesterday had changed. The next day Jane was merely a girl again and there was something else. Those tears were physical as much as emotional.

"Why are you in pain? I see it in your face, Jane, and I am deeply concerned. Have you not called the resident physician?"

"The pain I bear, Dr. Aylmer, will go of its own accord. I need not a physician as I have suffered many times and will go on doing so whilst I remain in this house. But I thank you for your concern, Sir, which is greatly received. Only the mere touch of your lips upon mine would ease the pain I endure, sweet schoolmaster."

She glanced upwards, her cheeks flared as her eyes met and became affixed to mine, She was truly a young woman now, looking wonderful but solitary as if craving for my embrace and I simply could not resist the kiss she wanted. A gentle warming kiss as our lips met. I sensed the perfume of lavender, she always kept a sprig of it upon her person. My whole being seemed to fire up instantly as the kiss grew stronger until it came to a point when I knew mind over heart would cause me to cut short the embrace. As I stood back her eyes were closed and she was full to overflowing of passion. How I wanted her. But she could never ever be mine. When she opened her eyes again she seemed to accept the predicament and gently whispered "thank you," I wanted to know more about the cause of her pain but she would not tell me anymore. Indeed she seemed reluctant to do so. I was merely her tutor again; I could never be her lover.

The following day I received a message to see the duchess later in the morning, and Dr. Haddon had received one, too. Perhaps the time was right to put forward my concern regarding her daughter's general health.

Good sign, she received us well and, after being invited to join her in the drawing room, she asked that we be seated and instructed the kitchen maid to fetch refreshment.

We exchanged the usual fineries and she was in good mood, not at all what I expected, having seen the other side of her many times. Dr. Haddon glanced across to me with a speculative smile. All seemed well.

Then she got down to business and her voice changed from the quietly spoken tone of hostess to the firm distinct sound of a woman of stature, talking to her lowly employees. "I have it from His Grace that you both wish to challenge our gambling habits – as you call them?" Her eyes were hard as she looked directly at us; I could see nothing of the sweetness of Jane in her.

Dr. Haddon was acutely ready for her:

"They are indeed such, Lady Frances, and you must know of the Lord's displeasure."

She did not instantly respond. Haddon's statement was advisory, not a question.

"I take it that you both would prefer us to cease the pleasure forthwith?" she eventually announced, her fingers crawling crab-like upon the wooden arms of her chair.

Dr. Haddon was quick to reply, stroking his long white beard as he did so:

"It is the word of God. As always, Dr. Aylmer and I are simply his messengers."

"And my eldest daughter too I see!" she barked. "Well, it would appear that we have no option. I take it the Lord would rather us not play for reward. In future, we, and such special friends we choose, will join us in a closed room and will always be discreet. We shall immediately make it known to all and sundry that, forthwith, no gambling of any description among all remaining persons will be permitted under this roof. How does that suit you, Dr. Haddon, and yourself, Dr. Aylmer?"

I nodded to Haddon's questioning glance and he advised the duchess that it would be more fitting if the habit was completely dispensed with but she became stiff and pardoned us saying that we may leave and she would consider this in due course. Dr. Haddon advised her that, of course, he must accept her decision but desired it would be in the Lord's favour.

Now it was my time to speak and I advised her of our concern regarding the health of the Lady Jane. She asked if this was affecting her studies and I had to reply that her efforts were exemplary.

"Well there, Aylmer, your concerns are unfounded. The girl is growing into a woman, that is all."

She rose from her seat and chuckled:

"But you men would not understand such things."

That was all she said and I could see there was no real concern as befalls a mother to her daughter, another reason why Jane missed the mother figure she had discovered in Katharine Parr.

It was during that year in 1551 Henry and Frances Grey became the Duke and Duchess of Suffolk and they spent more time at court, having taken possession of Suffolk House on the Thames at Southwark and numerous other mansions. Their status had been increased tenfold and at Bradgate there was much coming and going. High-ranking dignitaries were commonplace and the general style of the Grey's family life changed considerably.

In the course of the following months, the household reluctantly obeyed the new instruction given to gambling at Bradgate. But Dr. Haddon and I were very aware that the practice was still taking place behind closed doors as far as the duke and duchess were concerned. The duchess made no further comment on the subject.

Whilst at Bradgate I enjoyed teaching the children there given the inspiration of the Protestant religious reformer, John Calvin, who lived in Switzerland. I had met him on more than one occasion and we shared correspondence regularly. Although it was always presumed the Lady Jane, because of her stature, should receive privileged tuition over that of her two younger sisters, I persevered to rationalise equally my time with them.

CHAPTER SIX

I remember so clearly how Jane reacted. Her father had just told her that it had been dutifully decided that she must marry Guildford Dudley, the good son of the Duke of Northumberland, that it was an honour that one so noble should be chosen toward his eldest daughter. She was fifteen years old.

"For one thing he is a year younger than I. He is of no liking to me and I wish not to marry him. Even by my own parent's heed I will not marry until I am ready to marry."

Mrs. Ellen had heard the commotion in the master's study from her quarters further along the corridor; she hurried to the area and listened, then relayed to me the news.

"I know it was uncouth of me to listen through the keyhole, Dr. Aylmer, but Lady Jane has been poorly in the night and, as my duties here include being nurse to the master's children, I was concerned for her wellbeing.

"As I approached I saw Lady Frances enter the study. I assumed she had heard the commotion and would calm things but she did not. In fact I heard her shouting, too.

"I stood by the door and listened. I wanted to enter but remembered my place. I hoped and prayed the excessive argument would stop.

"The duke must have just told Lady Jane that she was to marry Guildford Dudley. I heard her repeating to her mother what His Grace had declared and appealing with her that it could not be so, that she was contracted to Lord Hertford. I have never known my young lady to be so excessively distressed and it bleeds my heart that, that..."

Mrs. Ellen was distraught and her whole face tightened. She was having difficulty in expressing herself, most unlike the usually strong willed woman whose charisma and confidence was known to all at Bradgate. I told her to try and calm herself. I felt she was upsetting herself to the brink so much it could have repercussions. I suggested she should remember Lady Jane needed her strong support, that if she was going to let this get her down too much she would be of no use. She lifted her face from her cupped hands and her eyes met mine. I sensed she also had suffered the torment of some excessive trauma in her life; her eyes, although kind and caring, showed it. I knew about her late husband dying so young and realised how deeply upsetting that must have been for her, so very sad, but I felt there was something else, too, that maybe she had been abused, there was just something about her aura and how she reacted to Lady Jane's abuse.

For a moment our eyes froze. She said nothing, she had no need. It was as if our minds were joined as one, something we shared, a certain charisma that somehow did calm Mrs. Ellen. She paused a moment longer and was able to continue.

"Lady Frances stressed the contract with Lord Hertford was never confirmed. That he was of poor means now that his father was imprisoned and it would not be appropriate for a lady of her standing to marry into the Hertford family.

"I know that Lady Jane had no love for the boy Hertford but she quickly responded in no uncertain terms that she despised Guildford and his stock. Her parents would have none of it and accused her of being the most ungrateful child that she spoke so badly of the charming Guildford Dudley to whom she should honour to be his wife.

"I heard Lady Jane shouting that she would never marry Guildford, that she would rather die first. The Lady Frances became hysterical and was instructing her husband 'to beat the bitch into submission.' Then I heard her screams of pain, Dr. Aylmer, which I could not bear. I could not stand there any longer, I opened the door and saw how the wretched girl was being ruthlessly beaten, expecting at the same time to be scorned by Lady Frances for my intrusion. Instead she ordered me to take the unruly girl out of her sight. That she never wanted to cast her eyes upon her until she saw the good sense and logic of her parent's wishes.

"I took Lady Jane in my arms and escorted her to her chamber. She was so distressed; she was beside herself with emotion saying she wished only to die. That even the thought of changing her name to Dudley sickened her.

"It took me the whole afternoon to calm her. She wouldn't eat anything and wanted just to be left alone. I later respected her wishes and left the poor girl crouched upon her bed. Occasionally I returned to her chamber and was grateful to note that she had fallen into sound sleep. She had her little black prayer book clutched in her right hand. I trusted and hoped the content had finally eased the pain she must have felt both emotionally and physically.

"You see, Sir, I feel what she feels, the pain and the torment, the anger that another, be it a parent, has the right to punish another in such a gruesome and severe manner. I feel I cannot stand by much longer without having to give Lady Frances a piece of my mind."

"Don't!" was my instant reaction. "For the same reason your health, mental and otherwise is important, and so is your position here, your responsible position would immediately be dashed because Lady Francis would dismiss you without remorse, aye, without realising your unique value to her children."

I prayed she would not take such drastic steps.

For a whole week Jane's reaction remained constant. Each day she told me she would not do something, which was so detestable to her.

Mrs. Ellen confided in me again during that week, that Lady Jane had told her, "I simply love another, someone who cares for me of that I am abundantly aware. What does Guildford think of me? Without caring there can be no true love, Mrs. Ellen.

"Tears streamed down her tiny cheeks. I fear for her heath more each day, Dr. Aylmer. She loves you, does she not? You are the one to whom she refers. You need not say a word; I would never ever or dare mention it to anyone - yet she needs you at this time."

"I am but a commoner, Mrs. Ellen, as well you know. As her tutor I can help her by way of my faith, which is accepted and acknowledged. And I have the advantage of seeing and being with her regularly. I simply have to consider that because she has come to trust me as a true friend as well as a tutor. Her affections have become confused and will pass given time, but as my position acknowledges, she does not have choice or option to marry as she would like, but what the others would like, and I suspect there are reasons behind the Duke of Northumberland's wanting his son to be her husband which will become clear. We must remain as mere bystanders, Mrs. Ellen, of course, and I thank you for your prudence. But I can assure you I am not about to take any advantage at all regarding our dear Lady Jane."

I was trying to hide my surprise in fact that the relationship, the special relationship Jane and I shared, had been learned but, of course, Mrs. Ellen being so astute would know, she an intelligent woman and so very aware of the needs and concerns of her charge, but by the same token she would also be discreet. I believe she was relieved that she had an ally in me in as much that she knew I was akin to her concern.

"You love her I do believe, John Aylmer, but my lips be closed, let's just be there for her."

The fact that she addressed me by my Christian name assured me of her absolute trust.

***

Spring came early in that year of 1553. It was Friday, the end of the dreadful week when Jane was informed of her forthcoming marriage. The weather was gorgeous, the May blossom was in full display and the bountiful trees of Bradgate were beginning to break bud. I usually tutored Jane's sister, Katharine, in the afternoon but she was suffering from a mild stomach disorder and could not attend.

Mrs. Ellen could not have chosen a better day when she knocked on the door of my rooms and openly invited me to join her for another picnic:

"I hope you will accept the invitation, Sir, because Lady Jane is joining us on this occasion. I have enough food in this basket for three. There is home cured ham I know you like and some of cook's homemade bread as well as a splendid variety of fruit and cakes."

She paused for a moment as if she was checking that no one was around, and then whispered:

"The Lady Jane, who waits downstairs, will enjoy a picnic at this time, and I know she will enjoy your company as well as mine."

"Of course I am delighted to come, Mrs. Ellen. I shall be with you in two minutes!"

The horses were waiting and Jane looked appealing in her long sweeping beige riding dress. I had not seen her in the saddle before but could see she took particular delight in taking her mount to a slow canter. Mrs. Ellen and I followed behind.

"We are heading for Jane's domain," Mrs. Ellen advised.

"She adores riding but rarely has the occasion to do so. If she takes to the saddle when her parents are at home she knows they will take her hunting and you will know how she hates the sport. But she used to ride much more when she was a child. We often took this route towards Cropston then. I do not know if you will recall, for you did serve His Grace in Bradgate House at the time when Lady Jane was only three, she was presented with a Spaniel as a birthday gift from her parents."

"Yes, I do remember the dog," I recalled. "Lady Jane was never without it."

"That is right, Dr. Aylmer. She named him Henry after the King. We regularly exercised the animal in this area and when he sadly passed away the Lady wished for him to be buried here - thus the wooden cross you will see in a few moments."

Jane looked back and pointed ahead.

"That's the spot," Mrs. Ellen announced, "as indicated by Lady Jane. See up there, just below the sloping rocks. You will see there is a wonderful view of the county to behold."

On our arrival I tethered the horses to a tree as Mrs. Ellen took the picnic basket from her side pack and some coverings, which she had strewn across her animal's back, which she spread over the grass.

"We shall sit and enjoy our picnic here, Dr. Aylmer, I think you will acknowledge why this is Lady Jane's favourite spot in all of Bradgate."

Truly the scene was a treasure to behold, rolling hills and winding streams. Fallow deer in plenty and, just to the right, Bradgate House, looking more like a dolls house in the valley.

Mrs. Ellen prepared the picnic, laying out utensils for three and Jane stood quietly, hands clasped behind her back, scanning the view, sometimes raising her head and closing her eyes. I have rarely seen her looking so relaxed and especially of late, given the pressures recently put upon her.

I approached and stood beside her quietly. It seemed, for those few tranquil moments, dialogue was unnecessary. There was a soothing atmosphere about the place, serene and beautiful, as though, for those few moments at least, the world with all its torments had frozen in time. She seemed to belong there, as if she had been there forever.

I shuddered, not with despondency or fear, but with absolute calm of wellbeing. That this was also God's special place. He was there, too, watching, watching, absorbing and acknowledging the sublime peace there. Our hands touched as if by instinct as we stood there. My first impulse was to quickly take my hand away but our fingers were entwined, hers squeezing mine fervently. I felt a wonderful flow of warmth rise up my spine. My whole being seemed to quiver, then her head turned, and our eyes met, hers seemed to be saying ...

But at that moment Mrs. Ellen called.

Eventually, Mrs. Ellen broke the silence in advising us the picnic was ready. She smiled beautifully. I had never seen so radiant a smile and instantly responded as we both returned to enjoy the refreshment.

The three of us were content to sit quietly and enjoy the nourishing picnic. It was as though we belonged there, in that place, at that point of time. I felt no awkwardness, no feeling that one should break the silence. Indeed, any conversation at that time may have spoilt the absolute calm. It was enough simply to enjoy the good food and the beauty of the surrounding countryside. Indeed, if time ever stopped, it did that day, for just those precious moments.

After all the food and refreshment was consumed it seemed right that we should converse. Mrs. Ellen asked if we had enjoyed the picnic and then retracted her question with a joyous chuckle. It was an unnecessary question because there was not a crumb left.

"I adore the springtime," Jane sighed. "It is a season of restoration when everything comes to life again after a hard winter. There is no doubt in my heart, John, that nothing less than our God would have created all this, that we are all akin to the ways of nature, that we all replenish ourselves after we die whether it be in another form or whatever. We sleep the long sleep, to awaken again like the buds of spring, bursting open to show vibrancy and colour, fresh and untainted."

She paused a while to inhale the fresh sweet smelling country air - pulling a blade of grass from its socket, tasting the white stem between her teeth.

"Oh! That I could remain here forever in this beautiful place," Jane declared joyfully, "with both of you as my companions eternal, you, John Aylmer, my superb schoolmaster and spiritual guide and yourself, Mrs. Ellen, whom I cherish as an excellent governess and friend, who has often kept me in my place without the need for strictness. Your charisma has always sufficed since as far back as I am able to remember."

I smiled and suggested she should not let us take all the credit. "I am sure Mrs. Ellen would agree; you have achieved so much by your own resilience and standing. I am sure we both feel that it has truly been an honour to serve you."

"Indeed, we are both very proud of you and...." Mrs. Ellen hesitated, pulled a handkerchief from her pocket and wiped her cheeks, then continued:

"I am sorry. I should not spoil such a wonderful day with such wonderful company."

Jane comforted her governess, placing a hand on her shoulder.

"You both speak as if this is the end of an era," Jane sighed. "You are both mistaken that, if I am pressed into this unwanted marriage, your services will be deemed no longer required. I shall always seek your advice, Mrs. Ellen. I trust after this marriage, which I will do my utmost to prevent, you will be available for me to call upon as a dear friend.

"And you, my esteemed tutor, I know you, John Aylmer, are thus committed with your new archdeaconship but I will make it my business to call upon you and join your congregation, listen to those deep felt sermons such as the ones you have oft times delivered here in our small chapel. And I sincerely hope you will continue to visit me, even though I shall be many miles away. I cannot imagine living with Guildford at Durham House and should ask to return."

Oh! What a ridiculous situation. Jane being pressed into an unwanted marriage to someone she didn't love. Just for a moment her eyes caught mine and it seemed she read my thoughts, that she knew how deep my love was for her and how very precious she was to me and how I wanted true happiness for her.

"If I could but marry the man I really cherished and loved," I swore her eyes were telling me. If only we lived in a different time that she, like me, was a commoner, so that I could fully express the true love I held deep inside, as I knew she felt for me. My mind wondered once more… I was sitting on the shore, watching each wave coming in to rest and dissolve into the sand, constant, sometimes rough, sometimes gentle, but always finding calm at the end of its journey.

Like the emotions of love, the feelings we all share – complete - to restore and regenerate into the calm waters, which, eventually, will stir again, as the sea pulls back and returns with each tide. Like the passion shared between lovers and the deep, deep fusion of souls combined remain like the waves and the tides, forever.

Sometimes the sea evaporates in the heat of the sun, like a love lost, hidden in the clouds above, seemingly never to return, our hearts become vacant, our minds confused: How can our love be shared? We search and sometimes find that, which we try to substitute for love, but the chemical fusion is unbalanced, it is not love but lust, which flashes like lightning and ends with thunder and afterwards abandons us, until another storm brews.

But real love, suspended in space, sometimes returns. The climate is right and the clouds turn to rain, each droplet to fall into the ocean as a minute part of a new wave, and the process starts all over again.

The love is constantly there, but there is no recipe for finding it.

But when you have it, when you finally recognise it, you will know it can only be true love.

I was suddenly aware again of my surroundings as Jane continued:

"But perhaps we assume too much. I will resolve to put off this marriage and, if I am forced into it, I will make it conditional that I continue to live here."

Jane seemed confident in her tone but I felt it was most unlikely that she was in a position to resist her parents command, who themselves had been tempted with the fortunes of power by Northumberland whose son she was to marry.

"I will never lay with him," Jane continued with a forceful dominant tone, which seldom she used. "I do not love him. I would be committing a gross sin in the eyes of our Lord if I were so to do. I know I could not bear him to... to touch me. It would be despicable for him to do so for he does not love me. We have rarely met, and when we have, we have never spoken with each other. I doubt if he even noticed me as I hardly noticed him. Guildford Dudley would be the last person in the world I would want to lay with."

I expected Mrs. Ellen held the same doubts; the way in which she glanced at me seemed to confirm this. Jane was by blood a royal descendent and she would have no personal choice in the matter of marriage.

But Jane was determined that this should not spoil the day. She was an intelligent girl. She would have realised our doubts. In her heart of hearts she would know, too. But she seemed to put her concerns behind her as she stood and asked if we would like to join her in a ramble.

We walked for two to three hours, exploring the flora and fauna of the countryside. We straddled rock faces and clambered over course ground. But Jane was happy, and so we were, too. When we returned to the picnic area, we rested again and Mrs. Ellen produced a jar of very refreshing indeed homemade lemonade from her pack.

Jane turned to me: "There you are, John. You have seen 'Lady Jane's Place' here in the middle of nowhere and over here are markers which, until now, only Mrs. Ellen and I knew of. Since I was a small girl we have come here so many times. There, you see?"

Jane pointed to a young oak tree, which she declared she had planted as a sapling when she was only five years old.

"I love oak nearly as much as I love ash. I used to love collecting the acorns in their small cups. But I agreed with Mrs. Ellen when she said there was an abundance of oak here, which would be befitting.

"May I be so bold as to ask you, John, in your ecclesiastical capacity, if you will consecrate this area for you will have noticed the cross it bears and the name of my wonderful childhood companion who rests beneath? It will be wonderfully fitting if you would do that."

Of course I was happy to do so and was delighted it made Jane so happy. She so sweetly kissed me afterwards, just a warm touch of her lips upon mine. From that precious moment in time I knew I no longer loved Jane as a child but as a woman. It was as if the world around us froze as her eyes were fixed upon mine. She must have loved me, too. How could I tell her what I felt? My feelings for her were destined to remain dormant.

I wanted to return her kiss, to hold her so close, never to let her go. I needed her body and soul completely but sadly knew that could never be. For a moment her hand clasped mine. Then gently she pulled it away, her joyful smile had gone, and her look was serene. It was as if we were both waiting for the other to make a move, hesitant to show our natural instinct and expression. Everything was suppressed. There was no release. From then onwards my feelings towards her had changed. I was deeply and hopelessly in love with Lady Jane.

I was looking into space, feeling the electricity of the ether, realizing it was she, my beloved Jane, the vibes of her love, her passion creating a spectacular wall around me, enclosing my soul.

Thousands upon thousands of orbs were sprinkling my being like pepper. The feelings I sensed for her were as nothing before. They completely submerged with her feelings, like our souls, our very beings, in my dreams.

Unbeknown to me it was the last time I would see that place in her company. But I had a premonition that I would return - one day.

We mounted our horses and made for home. It was a day I will remember always.

The following Monday, Mrs. Ellen approached me with some haste. She was tearful and had difficulty in finding her words. Guildford Dudley visited the weekend, apparently to be formerly introduced to his betrothed.

"That awful father of hers had inflicted the most terrible pain to the Lady. What a poor sorrowful young lady she is, for one so young to have been beaten like a stable boy is degrading. I can understand her objections, if she hates Guildford Dudley that much. She protested saying that if she was betrothed to any man it was Lord Edward Hertford. She was simply looking for an escape. I remember when she met Lord Hertford, she liked him very much and supposed she would marry him, but she was only six at the time. They sometimes played together when the Hertfords visited. But it was simply the wish of a child and as such, a betrothal was never confirmed. Poor girl, she is surely meant for better things."

Mrs. Ellen did not know that I was keenly aware of Guildford Dudley's visit, and, although my services were not required over the weekend, I decided to stay in my room and read. When I heard a resounding knocking at my door and the tortured sound of Jane's voice I immediately let her in. She was beside herself with stress screaming not to let that idiot touch her.

"Guildford?" I asked, comforting her in my arms, trying to calm her.

She was just in the mode of replying when the figure of an irate

Guildford appeared at the open doorway.

"So she prefers her tutor, does she!" Guildford scorned. "Now I wonder if Lady Frances is aware of this, perhaps she should be told?"

I was at loggerheads wondering how to deal with the situation but Jane was quick to respond to Guildford begging him not to say a word, if that was what he wanted, she would yield to him and no more said.

I reminded Guildford that Jane's mother trusted me implicitly and there was absolutely nothing to hide, that her affections were natural as they would be for any pupil who respects and likes her tutor, and he would therefore be grossly mistaken to assume anything detrimental and, looking sharply at Guildford, I suggested that he knew this very well and if anything, he should treat his future wife with respect and not attempt to force her into anything in which she would feel sinful or unclean out of marriage.

Later Jane told me that I obviously impressed Guildford because he seemed to admit his remarks were unfounded, that they were simply said in the heat of the moment; and she thanked me, too, because obviously my telling him to respect her wishes worked, too, that he settled for just to hold and kiss her softly. She did wonder if his earlier attempt to take her by force was simply that he was trying to prove something, that was the feeling she had about him, but whatever it was remained uncertain in her mind, she would never trust him and realised she could never ever bow to him as a lover would. These were tenuous times indeed.

I did not see Jane on Monday. That is what Mrs. Ellen came to tell me – that her mistress was so distressed and so bruised she reluctantly would not be attending her studies. I immediately knew that for Jane to forego her studies was extraordinary, she must be in a wretched way. I wanted to see her but, of course, that was impossible.

When Tuesday came, there she was. Sullen and quiet, it was as if her spirit had suddenly diminished. She took her usual place before me and gently lowered herself on her black velvet cushioned box chair, using her arms to steady herself as she did so. That was after she removed her study books from the panelled cupboard beneath, as was her habit. She'd had the chair especially made to her specification and design, linen fold carving ornamenting the back with chip carved roundels on the box. The panels were hand painted. A mythological figure of Plato adorned the front. Vine patterns were beautifully carved into the side panels entwined with hand painted flowers.

"Are you sure you want to study today, will you be able to take heed for you appear tormented and ill at ease, Jane?"

"I am as much frustrated that, here am I, now a young woman nearing my sixteenth year, still being punished like a child. That he who is my father has course to punish me so, almost as if it was his pleasure so to do, that I should be subjected still to such gross punishment simply because I express my true thoughts. My 'fine' mother, too, who holds me down whilst he

65

thrashes me, all due to the wicked, wicked Northumberland who has persuaded my parents to permit my betrothal to his gruesome son. I am no beauty I do admit. My freckles constantly bother me, my red hair is atrocious and my nervous debility is always disturbing. Yet I feel I am of superior maturity – I am told often - that of a woman several years older than myself. To me, Guildford is simply a boy with no particular charm, with no intellect and absolutely no good looks. The marriage is obviously doomed not to work. I would certainly not share the same bed with him. His breath is revolting and his habits are disgusting."

Jane had hardly spoken to Guildford but she seemed to know all about him.

"He had the audacity to insist on visiting my chambers and his inquisitiveness was intrusive. When I complained he said that if I was to be his wife he needed to know all about me. He ventured into the corner tower, climbed the spiral stairs and told me to follow, entering the small room at the top, which I hold most sacred. My sisters and I have played there many times in the past but now I use it to follow my studies in peace.

"He asked what I did in there and I told him. He replied that he had heard I spend most of my time in study and hardly ever joined in the pastimes of my family - that, soon all that would change, that there was a time for study and a time for recreation and enjoyment, that he did not want a recluse for a wife.

"Then he bungled around the room, moving things of my attire, advising that which he would not have me using or wearing in his presence. I felt at the end of my tether and loudly proclaimed it was not my wish that I should be his wife and asked him to leave.

" 'Then who would you propose to marry, do you know of another who would, even if he could?' He grimaced.

" 'You will never ever know the secrets of my heart,' I returned but he abruptly ignored me and opened the secret cupboard, the contents of which were only known only to me and my sisters when we played hide and seek. He looked inside and saw my playthings and my dolls, which I hold so dear. He grabbed them and threw them out saying I would have no further need for them and why did I need a secret cupboard anyway.

"By that time I was in tears and terribly upset and told him that is where I hid from my parents. The questioning continued: Why did I hide from them? Why this and why that? Then he dared to say I was indeed an altogether displeasing girl, obviously spoilt and that he would change all that.

"I hated him for what he did and what he said and I shall never forgive him, John.

"That I should so thoroughly and painfully be thrashed because of that feeble minded child and furthermore, be threatened with more severe thrashings if I did not condescend to marry him, is beyond my understanding, dear John, but here am I in a hopeless situation."

She knew that a person of her standing did not have an option. She must marry Guildford.

The next day was set for another portrait by Lucas Horenbout, the third in a series of three ordered by the Duchess to celebrate her daughters forthcoming marriage to Guildford Dudley. Jane loathed and hated being painted and was quite uncooperative with the renowned artist commissioned to do the work. Such was her dislike for the first painting she secretly burnt it in the gardens to the rear of Bradgate House which caused a storm with her parents, especially the duchess who was keen to have her daughter's portrait join the other members of the family in Chelsea Palace. Jane needn't have worried, I have it on good source that the portraits were subsequently burnt by the catholic Queen Mary - all except one, which I hold so dear and cherished in my church and will forever more remain …

Later, I saw her run out of the house screaming out that she could endure no more; she was beside herself to a degree I had never before known. Mrs. Ellen sped to my side at the doorway watching the fleeing girl in disbelief.

"Oh my God!" Mrs. Ellen yelled. "What if she…? Look she is headed for the stream."

I removed my jacket and gave chase, yelling aimlessly, knowing she could not possibly hear me, the wind was in the wrong direction and already she was well ahead, but somehow I felt I needed to reach her without delay, the warning in Mrs. Ellen's voice made me fear the worst, knowing, too, how Jane had recently suffered the torment and abuse of her parents and now burdened with the knowledge that she must marry against her will. Had she come to this, that this was the only option, to escape sacrificing her life to end it all?

When I got nearer I slowed to see her hovering over the wooden log bridge staring into the deep moving stream. I feared for her life now, the stream was merciless and the water, almost overflowing the banks after a night of storms, was flowing strong, I saw the wind fiercely blowing her skirts and the rain was still pouring down, and it was so very cold.

"Jane, Jane!" I yelled instinctively. "Hold on, let us talk, please?"

But she seemed not to hear me; the wind was too strong and in the wrong direction. I needed to be nearer and moved up a pace wondering if she now realised I was near.

I was about ten yards away when I caught her glance; I tried to ease her trauma, telling her I loved her, that she could not do this, that she must not do this. She said nothing. I could see she was breathing deeply, catching her breath in the strong gust and wiping her eyes of the fearsome spray.

"Jane. Jane, let us talk …"

She still stood as if frozen when I approached and then I was with her, grabbing and holding her shoulders firmly, she cried so much: "If it was not for you, John Aylmer, it would be easy. It is *you* who keeps me alive in this God forsaken place, in this hopeless position. My faith and my deep respect and love for you prevents me from ending my life. It is you I should be with and it would be right, I know it. Why does it have to be like this, John? Why can't we just run away and be just us, you and I together for ever more?"

I led her away from the danger of the stream and held her there for a while under the shelter of an oak. There was no need for words; all I could do was comfort her best I could, holding and caressing the back of her head as she nudged into my shoulder still whimpering and shivering now. I persuaded her that she must get back to the house and change out of her wet clothes before she got her death of cold. She held her head back, her eyes staring directly into mine, and there was almost a smile there in her eyes as I realised what I had just said and then, like something had changed her mood, she responded with a strong kiss upon my lips.

Then she whispered: "That would never do, my schoolmaster, for what would life be without you."

Soon we were back in the house, Mrs. Ellen running to us as soon as we arrived, guiding Jane to her quarters, to help her remove her soaking clothes.

Mrs. Ellen pressed two fingers to her lips. "Best not mention this to the master and mistress. The Lady would not want that at all," she whispered. "And best you change, too, Dr. Aylmer. You are drenched, also. Look at you, shaking like a jelly. But what you have done is wonderful indeed."

Then, unusual for Mary Ellen, she closed to me with a warm embracing hug.

"I have done nothing, all I did was to console her," I responded.

But Mary Ellen indeed was no fool, her warm smile said everything, but she did add she did not mean that, she meant...

But she didn't finish her sentence. She heard voices and quickly banished me off to my quarters. She did have one final say, though: "Thank you for loving her, for without that, she surely would have perished."

Now I was the one pressing fingers to lips.

Later, I heard a gentle knock at my door. It was Jane, looking so small and fragile wrapped in a blanket, courtesy of Mrs. Ellen, she said, "I simply wanted to thank you, John, for comforting me. I felt I just had to tell you that as soon as I possibly could. I felt I just had to be with you, to show you how much I cherish you. I could just not go back to my room and sit there, stewing and not seeing and thanking my so dear tutor whom I love so much. I just don't care anymore. I want the world to know it is John Aylmer I love."

Her eyes were glistening and if I had ever had any doubts about the eyes being the windows of the soul I was certain now, for at that moment seemed as if our souls had fused and we were as one, our spirits truly joined, our simple desires were flowing, so strong, so wanting. The spirit within reminding me my allegiance to God and what was right in his eyes. But I was merely human with all the emotions and natural desires given to me, given to any man with his heart so full of love and wanting so very much to share that love with the girl who was now a woman.

For all that is in heaven above there must be a shred of forgiveness, to complete a union that is flourished with true love, if social stigma stands in the way, it is manmade and not made by God, for in his eyes we are all but equal. This union was so vital, so needed to replenish the body and the soul. To confirm a bond never to be shed, no matter what the future may bring.

"We are here and now, dear John. We cannot let this very special moment pass. It is meant to be; I feel that. I feel it has to be now - I simply love you so very much."

I felt her hands brush behind my neck as her blanket slipped to her feet, this figure of beauty closing to me, my feelings prompting me to clasp my hands behind her tiny waist, to feel the utter vibrancy of this woman, so very wanting, so very… The impulse was there.

"Just love me, John - just take me and all will be alright."

Heaven was open, surrounding me and I was there. It happened as, of course, it was meant to, and it was wonderful. And when it was over we knew no matter that would be, we would always be with each other forever.

CHAPTER SEVEN

If I had ever had bad thoughts about the Duke of Northumberland, they were never more prevalent than in May 1553, when Jane had no sooner been instructed that she must marry Guildford but also that the wedding had been set for May 25th. She had just two weeks in which to prepare herself.

Her parents advised me that her life would temporarily continue as before, that she would return, immediately after her marriage, to their house in Suffolk Place, London where the family would reside henceforth. As my tutorship would continue, despite earlier rumours to the contrary, I was delighted I would therefore regularly see Jane. I later learned that this arrangement was initiated by her as being a conditional requirement if she agreed to the marriage; also, that she would not be required immediately to live with Guildford.

It seemed that Jane, despite the horrendous treatment given to her, still had the strength and initiative to win over certain issues. For this I was relieved and grateful indeed.

On our return to the house on that beautiful memorable day and after Jane had departed to her chambers, Mrs. Ellen and I were confronted by Mrs. Tylney who was overcome with emotion. She beckoned for us to follow her into the pantry where we would be alone. Her speech was accentuated with rapid breaths taken between each sentence; she could not divulge her news quickly enough:

"I do not think the Lady Jane is yet aware that her sister Katherine is to marry Lord Herbert, and the Duke of Northumberland's daughter, also Katharine, will marry Lord Hastings on the same day at Durham House."

Mrs. Ellen and I shared confused glances. This could not be true. I asked Mrs. Tylney where she had heard the surprising news.

"From the duchess herself all but an hour ago. It seems she is anxious to marry her eldest daughters off and betroth the youngest one to her cousin, Lord Arthur Grey, to be sanctioned when she is of marriageable age. She has asked me to inform all the servants and attenders and yourselves to gather this evening at six o'clock in the great hall when we shall be given full details and instructions regarding the necessary arrangements."

It was definite then. Despite her protests Jane would be married accordingly. "Her sister Katharine was overjoyed about marrying the very handsome Lord Herbert," Mrs. Tylney added, "although young Lady Mary was not pleased with her match."

During the next few days there was no time for scholarship at Bradgate. Poor Mrs. Tylney often ended her days in tears with the coming and going of those who were immediately concerned with the preparation of the marriages. There was no time for rehearsal; only those who knew the families would be present at the weddings, which would be officiated by the Dudley's chief chaplain.

I occasionally caught glimpses of a very unhappy, young woman during those two hurried weeks.

She seemed happy to acknowledge me as her attenders bustled her and her dressers anxiously measured and made. Jane made several suggestions regarding design but to no avail. The duchess was dominant in decision-making and poor Jane had no option but to accept her mother's choices.

It was all too much for Mrs. Tylney who recently suffered a severe bout of fever; her expression was taut, she looked drained. Usually a strong wiry woman, she was now but a shadow of herself. Following prompting from Mrs. Ellen the duchess instructed the resident physician to see her, and when afterwards he advised that Mrs. Tylney should rest for a few days the duchess snapped that one day would be more than enough, that no matter what, during this special time the services of her head lady in waiting were indispensable.

Next morning the duchess came storming from Jane's chambers in a great fury and immediately dismissed the entourage. The Duchess of Northumberland had made an unexpected visit to oversee the preparations. It soon became evident that she was unimpressed; everybody in attendance that day would have known it. She was a self-opinionated grasping woman with a loud commanding voice that even Lady Frances could not equal. She nervously looked up at the tall overdressed snapping woman. It was as if she, Lady Frances, was the subordinate and not the higher-ranking woman of royal stock

"If you are unable to properly dress your daughter, Frances, then leave it to my attenders. I will only have the absolute highest quality workmanship as befitting to Guildford whom your daughter will be privileged to marry."

Lady Frances scowled at her tall, buxom accomplice and remained uncharacteristically subdued offering no resistance. Despite her lower rank the Duchess of Northumberland was the most powerful woman in the land and even Lady Frances knew her place. But she whimpered that in so short a time and with two daughters to prepare for marriage it was an almost impossible task.

"Then your daughters will immediately accompany me on my return to London where I will personally see to it that they are properly prepared, Frances. Frankly, I am disappointed in you and trust you will ensure that the remainder of your wedding entourage will be adequately dressed befitting to this great occasion."

Lady Frances could only stand back and accept the duchess's command but made no amends in coming down upon the household staff afterwards, blaming them for everything.

She stormed to her quarters in distress and was not seen for at least two days. The good that came out of this was that Mrs. Tylney was able to recuperate in peace.

Poor Jane and her sisters had no option other than to reluctantly comply with the demands put upon them. But as Jane departed she looked at me and waved sorrowfully, I sensed a temporary calm that would later change.

I took this opportunity to talk with Margaret Tylney. She had always shown loyalty to the Grey's family and deserved better treatment when her sickness prevailed. My sympathies went out to her but she would have none of it. However, she welcomed me to her bedside and was obviously pleased to see me.

"The mistress is in deep distress and I feel I should forgive her for the way she spoke in the company of Lady Dudley. What a bombastic woman she is to behold. If I had been Lady Frances I would have certainly put her in her place, Duchess of Northumberland or not. She had no right to talk to my mistress like that, as if she was an imbecile.

"I later received good account from Lady Frances herself who chuckled in telling me of the numerous problems Lady Dudley accrued in deciding the wedding apparel which, due to the short time left, had to be borrowed from the Royal Wardrobe."

Mrs. Tylney looked a little uncomfortable propped up in her bed so I helped in adjusting her pillows until she found the right position.

"Trouble with staying in bed for so long is pins and needles," she complained. "I hate it, Dr. Aylmer. Much rather be doing things."

"I can see that you will soon be doing again. What's that shiny substance covering your face?"

"It is what the physician prescribed, a herbal liniment substance which, he advised works wonders. Don't like the smell, though. It stinks, especially when it's been on for a while."

"Then I will ask the gardener to bring in some flowers to freshen the air, Mrs. Tylney."

"I am being thoroughly spoilt. Mary Ellen in her capacity as nurse ensures I have everything I need and makes sure I keep warm. That's what all these covers are about - heaven forbid - I look twice the size of the woman I am. I need to sweat the fever out I am told with plenty of fresh air circulating."

"You are smiling, Mrs. Tylney. That is a good sign I'll be bound."

"Shame is, and I know Mary feels the same, we should both be with the children and should have accompanied them to London, but Mary declared the visiting duchess would have none of it. Her attenders were well able to cope sufficiently well. Thing is, at a trying time such that it is, especially for Lady Jane, Mary understands the Lady's debility and how she should be best treated. None of us would cherish the thought of being under the same roof as the Duchess but the children would have always to come before our own preferences.

"Poor Jane. Having to marry a man she doesn't love. At least Katharine is happy with her Lord Herbert but it's awful for any woman having to submit to someone who means absolutely nothing to her."

Mrs. Tylney seemed to be speaking from experience and responded to the question in my mind:

"I can tell you this now, Dr. Aylmer, because the so-called gentleman is dead. But I must not speak too badly of him because Lady Katharine Parr was devoted to him, despite his many wanderings. When I was serving Lady Jane at the time of his guardianship of her he demanded of me something in excess of my usual services and, unless I submitted, he made no bones about replacing me for a more willing and loyal Lady in Waiting. The fact is, although I bear the title of Mrs., it is simply the way in which I have always been known. I have never been married and, in fact, until Thomas Seymour, had never been with a man. "

I could not believe what she was saying, a man of his repute fraternising with a servant. Or perhaps it was my naivety in finding that so hard to accept. Truly this misused woman of gentleness had been put into an impossible position that if she did not submit to his demands she would be deprived of her position. She looked at me with embarrassment reflecting in her eyes, I noticed tears too as she obviously struggled to tell me more.

"Truly you must not blame yourself, Mrs. Tylney, you did what you thought was better for Jane no matter what the consequences and I admire your courage and prudence for that."

"He laid with me on several occasions," she continued, "and each time I was repulsed, angry that my body was used in such a way, that there would be no probability of my becoming pregnant.

"I too was alarmed to hear certain things that must remain unspeakable for consequence they may be wrong. The Lord Admiral was sometimes a restless sleeper and many times spoke out loud in his sleep. I pray to the Lord, some of the things I heard were simply a result of his imagination, something he would never esteem to do in real life. I must be discreet at all times but I fear the worst for what may happen if all I have heard is true."

I told Mrs. Tylney I respected her fortitude and she must abide by her own rules that God, too, will know and He is always there to call upon.

She paused and continued: " He is determined to keep Mary Tudor away from the throne. I do believe he has wicked deeds in mind - along with that very wicked and nasty Duke of Northumberland and his son Robert Dudley, too, is involved. He made no bones about telling Lord Seymour that if Mary became Queen he would have to burn his books and flee the country for dear life saying that she would have the whole country made Catholic again.

"I am afraid, Dr. Aylmer, that since Lord Seymour had me against my will I have never thought of any man in prospect to marriage, not because I have been subjected to the selfish needs of man but mainly because I feel dirty that I permitted such an unnatural and, in the eyes of our Lord, a sinful act even though I am fully aware that if I had made any objection, as primarily I did, he would have taken me with even more gusto, because that is what he wanted. That was his particular pleasure.

"I was relieved when, eventually, he tired of me and discovered others who would satisfy his huge appetite. I hope, given my explanation, Dr. Aylmer, you will forgive my atrocious sins."

Of course I forgave her. Truthfully I was not surprised. Margaret Tylney was a naturally attractive woman whom the lusty Seymour would have found difficult to resist. She had an abundance of curly red hair with a parting in the middle. A most pleasing and pleasant face with a fresh complexion with soft kind looking green eyes and smile lines around her small mouth. She stood about five feet two inches tall and was always ready to help the children; they all liked her and she was always at her ease in their company yet, when they were sick or depressed, she was the perfect shoulder to cry on. She spoke with a soft appealing voice with a slight nervous stutter

"But what did surprise me," she continued, " I imagined most of Lord Seymour's successful encounters with the opposite sex were gained by his notorious charm and not, as I had thought, by blackmail. I concluded that such an action was a last resort to get his way."

She said she was relieved she could confess to me, that keeping such a secret hidden was more than she could withstand, but she trusted me like she could no one else.

"I do forgive you as God will forgive you, Mrs. Tylney, and you must not bathe a sin you unwittingly committed. Simply let it drain from your mind and pray for God's forgiveness. For the man who treated you so badly, he will have already been adjudged and sent to the dunghills of hell. Hold that in your mind that he can be no more, for the gates of hell remain forever open to souls like that, for those who ruthlessly use their position to take advantage of their subordinates to such extremes."

She looked thoughtfully and her face brightened. "We must think of the happy times Lady Jane spent with the fine Lady Katharine Parr at Chelsea Palace, Dr. Aylmer, and as her lady in waiting I was privileged to share those special times with the woman she adopted as her substitute mother."

"We surely must," I agreed.

Jane and her sisters were fortunate indeed that they were endowed with two very remarkable devoted and loyal servants and I felt that really was a blessing to offset many of the unhappy events in Jane's life.

But there were the sad times, too, later at Sudeley Castle and Mrs. Tylney quietly recalled them and how Jane was devastated after Katharine Parr's untimely death.

"Apparently, after early concerns, Lady Katharine seemed to recover after the birth of her daughter child?" I asked Mrs. Tylney. She replied that it was all so very sad and Jane was absolutely beside herself.

"Indeed she loved her, like we all did, but Lady Jane, well, for her Lady Katherine was always a substitute mother and she had lost someone so very dear to her, someone who really cared and wanted her for herself. She was devoted to her and spent much time sat beside her bed, sharing thoughts about their deep faith and poor Lady Jane was still present when she was unconscious. It seemed odd that after her almost complete recovery she so quickly developed puerperal fever. I shall always remember the date, it was September 15th 1548.

"But I must tell you, now that Thomas Seymour has departed, how uneasy I felt. Something was not right. I know that. It is just something I heard when the master was laying with me, sound asleep though he was, that he had keen intentions to marry Lady Elizabeth whether she knew it or not, that the reason Elizabeth left after Lady Katharine discovered them in a compromising position was because she, like Jane, respected and adored Lady Katharine and she would never deem it to be right and proper to lay with him, a married man. Then I heard him say it, Dr. Aylmer, that his intention was to poison his wife so he was free to marry Elizabeth, and not because he loved Elizabeth, far from it, he made no bones about her being one of the ugliest women of high standing but the status she could offer by way of marriage was attractive enough to put looks aside."

"You deem this to be true?" I asked Mrs. Tylney with some trepidation.

"It is amazing what secrets can be discovered in the presence of a lover, and even though his words were uttered whilst he slept I can believe they are true. I assumed at the time it was just a horrible dream but the way things became I feel sure he did succeed in poisoning his wife after his daughter was born; that would explain why the Lady's recovery was halted and she died so soon after the birth of her only child the birth date being August 20th. You may think I say these wicked things because of the way he treated me with disdain, but not so. I feel sure that the Lady was murdered, by her husband!"

"Did Lady Jane learn of this?" I carefully asked Mrs. Tylney who seemed relieved that she had confided further in me.

"My Lady Jane adored the man, Dr. Aylmer. I dared not share my suspicions with her in fear that it may have harmed my relationship with her. He was a charming man and Jane, like other women I saw in his company, was devoted to him, nay, even besotted by him. Although my personal feelings are that this was also because of the way he treated her in the stance of her guardian so much in contrast to her own parents. I do not think she would ever have believed Thomas Seymour would do such a thing to the woman he outwardly loved. Certainly I, too, would have found it so if I had not heard it from his own lips."

"Were you also besotted with him, Mrs. Tylney?" I asked gently,

She seemed lost for words for a moment as she seemed to reflect. "If the truth be known, Dr. Aylmer, and I will be absolutely truthful to you I was indeed, otherwise I would not have made it so easy for him to lay with me."

She sighed and again I felt that sense of relief that she had cleared her mind of these things.

"Reflecting on the happy times shared with Lady Katharine I remember so vividly the conversations shared with our Lady when I too was allowed to join them. I remember how they both seemed to be completely compatible about their theological views. Lady Katharine also recalled how, when she was Queen, how she so enjoyed the atmosphere of those wonderful gatherings at Court when there were an abundance of supporters there and, also, how many weaned away because of what the Queen considered, was a travesty because of the bigoted views of the Catholic fraternity who considered themselves to be above all other thoughts and religions, that they even attempted to have her tried for heresy, but thanks to the good nature of the King and given certain conditions which she was obliged to adhere to. The attempt failed, of course. The Queen also contributed much to the upbringing of Edward and Elizabeth and gained good stead from the King, also how she took in Lady Jane when she joined her cousins at court and how wonderful they got on together, least with the future Queen Mary Tudor who was not much younger than she and a Catholic, a devout Catholic, too, yet this did not deter their kinship. It was just something about the charisma of the Queen that put differences of religious thought aside and accepts that differences were inevitable.

"Although a wonderfully refined and caring woman she could be strong and talked much with the King himself about the New Learning. So much I believe that she was considered to be impressing the King in a direction not considered ethical for the Head of the Church and that was the problem, she was so enthused by her faith and could be so convincing that all other things regarding her safety and future as Queen were put aside. She had such clear ideas about her beliefs, strong enough to argue the fine points with the King himself and could not see the possible threat to her life when he began to become agitated by her 'constant babble,' so much was her loyalty affixed to the King that she thought their strong bond assured her safety, but even though that security was taken away from her when she was very nearly removed from Court, she still remained constant and loyal to her husband which, Dr. Aylmer, said so very much for the then Queen.

"It was wonderful to hear such inspiring conversation at Chelsea, with the then Lady Katharine and indeed - and I did not know this - Lady Jane also played a part in an effort to protect her when King Henry was considering her trial. She went up to the King who towered like a mountain above her and told him to save his beloved Queen from such a wicked end. Lady Katharine recalled how she heard Jane telling her Uncle King Henry and how she feared the consequences. But her adolescence saved her.

"And I remember, oh, so clearly, how after the tragic death of her substitute mother, Lady Jane was adamant she would continue her most righteous and important work. They both had so very much in common - Lady Jane being such a bright and intelligent girl, found it easy to understand Lady Katherine's language. One could see her natural flair and enthusiasm oozing out. I realized then, our Lady was a very special Lady indeed, almost like an angel and she, like Lady Katharine, extruded a certain ambience and well being to others regularly invited to the Queen's seminars.

"It was truly a wonderful time and I will cherish the memories for the remainder of my life. "

Having spoken with Mrs. Tylney it did seem evident that the outwardly charming Lord Seymour was indeed a wicked soul and deserved the awful fate bestowed upon him by his brother who, no doubt, knew his downfalls more than anybody and was obliged to have him executed without proper trial in the knowledge that if such a trial was arranged many a foul deed would come out.

CHAPTER EIGHT

I will recount those wonderfully inspiring days at Chelsea; Jane was just nine years old when, in the spring of 1546, Queen Katharine skillfully arranged for the three children to come together under her auspices. This was no mean task because the king was constantly moving the prince's household in order that he should avoid the extreme cold at various times of the year. The Queen implied the sickly prince would be constantly watched over at Chelsea and it would also show to all those who opposed Henry that the royal household demonstrated strength through unity. Prince Edward was the same age as Jane but princess Elizabeth was thirteen. The eldest of the three royal children, however, was Princess Mary, who, at the age of thirty, was just four years younger than the Queen.

She wanted to stay at Chelsea, too. Despite their religious diversities Mary bonded with Katharine, perhaps she thought at the time the bringing together of the family unit was more important.

Mrs. Tylney recalled her time with Jane at Chelsea:

"It was not long before Queen Katharine came to be so popular and loved by the royal children and Lady Jane, too, was kindled by the Queen's warmth and open sincerity for their wellbeing, their health and their devoted learning. I cannot remember a time before or after when Jane suffered no sickness or debility. She constantly looked to the Queen as her guiding light and indeed the Queen herself had the knack to give each of the three children as much care as she could muster, always watching over them, ensuring every need was satisfied, yet never did she spoil them. Indeed, if any of the children became demanding she would firmly but diligently put them in their place - and that went for everybody in the royal household.

"Everybody respected her, liked her in so much that her nature would bring out the best in them and this was very apparent with the King. Often his most horrendous moods, when his voice was heard bellowing in most corners of the court, ranting on about the business of state, the way he had been let down, abused and the like by his so called advisors, but most times complaining of the atrocious pain in his leg that only his sweet, sweet Katharine could make better.

"When summoned, Queen Katharine would stop whatever she was doing and depart briskly to the King's chamber, as she walked, placing her arms stiffly downwards with her hands spread out and moving in upward and downward motions, she advised everybody present to remain calm and continue whatever they were doing.

"Then, when the Queen departed onto the King's chambers the incessant shouting stopped. In due course Queen Katharine reappeared with a gratifying smile and resumed whatever she was doing.

"We soon discovered the Queen was as much a nurse as she was a wife, perhaps more so because it was known that the once lusty King had lost all his appetite for sexual discourse and the Queen was grateful for that. Although she was plainly loyal to her husband and cared for him a great deal, he was no longer an attractive man and she often complained about his beastly habits, some of which she had delicately scalded him for, to such degree that he often teased her when he was about to pass wind, giving her fair warning that a gust was on the way and she should hold down her skirts. At least she made him aware of his indelicacies and, in so doing, he was able to refine them."

I prompted Mrs. Tylney to tell me more about Queen Katharine. There were still many gaps in Jane's life at Chelsea as far as I was concerned. I wanted to know of those times and her relationship with the Queen.

Margaret Tylney laid back her head, her eyes glancing at the ceiling as she relayed her memories, the magnificent drawing room at Chelsea Palace where Queen Katharine warmly welcomed them upon their arrival. The princesses Mary and Elizabeth and prince Edward, too, were present. Mary, being the eldest was the tallest of the three.

"We are so pleased to meet you, dear Jane. I have heard all about you and your Mrs. Tylney, who, I am glad, will continue to serve you here at the palace."

Queen Katharine asked them to be seated and beckoned an attender to bring some fresh scones and suitable refreshment. "You must be famished after your long journey from Leicestershire. I want you to make this your temporary home, Jane. I have one of the finest scholars in England to further your studies, a Doctor Cheke whom you will meet tomorrow. In the meantime I have some business with which to attend regarding the poor King's ailment. So, I will leave you children with Princess Mary to become acquainted with each other and if you, Mrs. Tylney, will come with me I will show you your rooms."

The rooms were such that Mrs. Tylney was overcome with esteem.

"Am I to take this room, Ma'am? Surely it is fit for a princess, not an attender such as I?"

A beautiful, furnished four-poster bed with red velvet embroidered upholstery adorned the centre of the room. Wide displays of tapestries were hung upon the high long walls. The aroma of Tansy produced certain freshness everywhere.

"You must not underrate yourself, Mrs. Tylney. Like myself you are the daughter of a comparatively modest country squire. You come with an exemplary recommendation from Lady Frances herself who thinks much of you, otherwise indeed, you would not be here accompanying Lady Jane. Now, the servants will bring your baggage and you can settle yourself in and afterwards you may escort Lady Jane to her room. No need to hurry because I

79

want Lady Jane to have a little time to become acquainted with her new companions first.

"Later you will all meet our great King Henry. But I must tell you that presently our King is suffering great pain with his ulcerated leg but the good thing is I am honoured to nurse him through these difficult times and am glad to be useful. We must all pray for his return to good health."

Margaret Tylney recalled how she was overcome by the great honour bestowed upon her, to be living in the same home as the great King Henry VIII himself!

After Queen Katharine left the room, she unpacked her things and tucked everything neatly away. Then she gently lowered herself down onto the edge of the bed, sinking deeply into its duck feathered mattress and sat there quietly taking in the wonder of the beautiful place, not quite believing this was happening to her, thinking how much Lady Jane would relish living here. Bradgate was grand enough, but nothing compared with this wondrous place. She rose and walked over to the large window seat and was entranced by the view through the leaded panes of the oak framed windows. She saw roses and rhododendrons, all neatly planted in round, oblong and square beds with twisting paths surrounding them.

There were avenues of oak and willow trees as far as the eye could see. She had never ever seen anything quite like it. Although beautiful in its own setting, Bradgate served primarily as a grand hunting lodge and park, because of the rocky terrain cultivation was limited.

Yes, she would enjoy her stay at Chelsea and she felt sure Jane would too.

***

Margaret Tylney's instinct proved happily to be right. In a matter of hours the children had grown accustomed to each other. Elizabeth, because she was the eldest child, sometimes took charge and was prone to some light bullying. But Jane would have none of it and showed how defiant she could be. Edward was the most timid but they were always made aware of the fact that he would be the next king and should be treated with extra care and respect as befitting to him. Sometimes the personalities of all three clashed but Queen Kathleen or Mary Tudor were always near at hand to calm things down. Generally they all seemed to grow fond of each other and happily shared play and lessons together.

Princesses Mary and Elizabeth became Queen Katharine's ladies in waiting and for a month or so everything seemed to be right in the royal household. The Queen took an active role in Jane and Elizabeth's musical interests and often they enjoyed playing the spinet to each other; her caring sensitive nature continued to work miracles with the King's incessant bad tempers and her sympathy for his ailment was genuine.

Her interest in Protestants grew and she often talked about the 'new learning' in as much that she believed it could achieve much to reform the tedious methods given to the traditional ways of learning. She envisaged that this could bring both standard religions closer together and dispel much of the sensitivity between the two beliefs, that, after all, they all worshipped the same god.

It must be recognised that the Princess Mary was a strict advocate of Catholicism. Queen Katharine skilfully took this into consideration when discussing the issues with Mary and her friends who were keen to take part in the regular discussions. Mary showed no diffidence and continued to treat the Queen as a stabilizing mother figure, even though there was only four years age difference between them.

The twice-weekly gathering grew as many of Queen Katharine's acquaintances called to discover what all this new learning was about. They talked not only of religion but also of new fashion trends and the like. Embroidery was close to the Queen's heart and she seemed to impress everybody with her designs. Often the children took part and even Prince Edward decided to try his hand, until King Henry rebuffed him, saying that was woman's work. The affairs of State were the work of men, not fiddling with a needle and cotton. He would be King and no King should be seen to be doing womanly things, he would never live it down:

"The only embroidery you need to concern your head about, my son, is how to embroider your monarchy, how to keep all factions stitched together as it were, you will learn, my son. You will learn."

But Queen Katharine's popularity almost proved to be her downfall. There were those seeking to destroy her, who were deeply anguished about her influence over the king.

They linked her with the so-called religious reformers who, they argued, could do the monarchy more harm than good.

Margaret Tylney recalled the surprise that went through the court when, one morning without warning, a group of King Henry's avid advisors descended upon Kathleen demanding her arrest, that she was openly planning to create a conflict in the church of England and, as head of the church, interference would bestow alarming repercussions upon the King himself. She was outwardly distressed. She declared that she knew nothing of this, that she had only been with the King a few moments before and he would surely have mentioned something.

Could it really be she was so near to losing her life when her enthusiasm for the new learning offended the King? She really did seem unaware that he had been cleverly and deviously persuaded by the catholic fraternity that his position as head of the church was being put in jeopardy by his own wife.

The Queen was beside herself finding her life threatened because of her passionate interest in theology following debates in the court with many companions who took avidly to her views and her teachings.

Then Margaret Tylney's face tightened. Her eyes widened as if she had been deeply disturbed.

"One could almost hear the sighs of disbelief as one of the party took the Queen firmly by the arm and escorted her away to the King's chamber," she continued, her voice sounding strained now. "An eerie silence followed. The royal children, including Lady Jane, Mary, John Cheke, and myself, were in the Queen's study. We closed together fearing the worst, knowing the King's reputation regarding the treatment of his former wives. Would she be another Queen to end her life on the scaffold? We were all too shocked even to speak; ironically the Queen was discussing the new religion when she was so blatantly interrupted. Now we all huddled together but upon Mary's suggestion we prayed for this innocent Queen that, Dear Lord, she would come to no harm, that those who seek to depose her would fail in their attempt to arrest her.

"We feared the worst, that the Queen would reappear surrounded by the henchmen, to be transported to the confines of the Tower.

"Surely, King Henry would know that Katharine could never do anything that would result in harm to anybody, least the King of England.

"It was Princess Elizabeth who had broken the silence of prayer, who stood there rigid, her expression tight and foreboding. Her eyes fixed on the large framed painting of Queen Katharine, which adorned the room. A beautifully composed picture showing the Queen wearing a crown headed flower broach with two diamonds, one ruby, one emerald and three hanging pearls.

"The sharp sound of her anger pierced the nervous silence. I had not known this side of the red haired princess. She was set to be a very strong and formidable lady indeed, an ideal person to follow Henry to the throne.

" 'This cannot be! I will approach my father myself and tell him to immediately dispose of those treacherous men who claim to be his advisors.'

"She started to make her way forward with a look on her face that spelled trouble ahead. There was nothing anybody could do to hold her back. Even her half-sister, Mary, could not restrain her. It was unheard of that anybody should interrupt a meeting in progress, which unbeknown to the Queen, had obviously been sanctioned by King Henry himself. But Elizabeth was her father's daughter and nothing would stop her having her say. Soon she, too, had disappeared in the direction of the king's chamber.

"Lady Jane came to my side, her body trembling as her hand found mine: 'Oh! That I had Elizabeth's courage to approach that horrid man,' she cried. 'Surely, he would not bestow on his own wife so ghastly a sin for that is surely what it is in the eyes of God, is it not?'

"I reminded her that indeed he had done it before and Jane just looked up at me and cringed.

" 'Then I must join Elizabeth,' she cried making moves to follow her cousin.

" 'You cannot, you cannot,' I hastened to advise, 'Remember Elizabeth is his daughter, your presence would possibly do more harm than good.'

"Still trembling she burst into tears as I gently took her arm holding her back: 'We must pray and hope our King will be merciful,' I said.

"But the events which followed proved Elizabeth could be equally as foreboding as her father when she screamed and yelled at him, all of us hearing the shrill sound of her angry voice, that if he destroyed the Queen like he did her mother she emphasised that only more atrocious pain would encroach his body and soul like he had never know before, because surely, by killing her he would be also destroying the only person who seemed to have the ability to nurse and calm his pain, his mortal being, least the woman he loved better than his self, better than his soul.

"I saw that Jane's expression was aflame now, her hands clenched as if she was there with her cousin. The others there, including Lady Mary, were standing as if frozen looking aghast at what they were hearing. I myself, having often heard of the King's temper was fearful that Elizabeth, too, may be summoned to the Tower along with the Queen she was trying to protect.

"But then silence, one expected the roar of retaliation from the King but nothing, absolute silence…

"A few moments later the Lady Elizabeth reappeared with the henchmen. There was a sigh of relief from all present that the Queen was not amongst them. They appeared to be angry and confused as Elizabeth openly banished them away from Court, screaming that they would be truly sorry for their atrocious behaviour to the beloved Queen. To observe the small figure of Elizabeth compared with the bulky henchmen, she striding behind them was something I will always remember.

"We later learned that the King, following the persuasion of Stephen Gardiner, the Bishop of Winchester, had called for an investigation into the Queen's newly found beliefs. That she had chosen to take advantage of the King's poor condition in order to cast the same beliefs upon him. That she was attempting to guide him into the wrong direction, he being the head of his Kingdom and also his church. Katharine had made the mistake of undermining her husband and the bishop in taking it upon herself to preach the gospel according to Katharine and not the King.

"But the Queen had to gather all her strength and obediently submit to him, confessing that she had gone astray and should take learning from his superior knowledge, but she had inadvertently used her faith in hope and trust that the Lord God would see fit to cure her beloved King.

"Whatever it was that changed Henry's heart nobody could tell. Certainly Elizabeth demanded of her father that he should think twice before condemning such a wonderfully talented woman, a woman that had taken every opportunity to take the royal children and Jane Grey under her wing, to treat them like a mother figure, as one big family of which he was the integral part. Only Elizabeth was in the position to tell him that and she returned to us to keep us informed. I believe it was her charisma, her own karma that saved the Queen on that horrible day.

" 'I think my father will be honour bound to pardon the Queen,' Elizabeth confidently announced. 'When I left her she was in tears but still attending to the needs of my father's medical care. If he fails not to pardon her for such a paltry offence then it will be me he will have to answer to!'

"Although the King was disappointed that Elizabeth had been born into the wrong gender he loved her enough to care for her welfare and obviously respected her for sharing his fiery temper.

"It was not until the following morning that we learned that the Queen had been openly pardoned and a great sense of relief was experienced by all. The great Queen had won over the formidable power of Bishop Gardiner and his henchmen.

"Very memorable times they were, Doctor Aylmer. It is sad indeed that her life was quickly taken after her marriage to Lord Seymour."

***

On Whit Sunday, May 25th 1553 I attended the wedding of Lady Jane Grey at Durham House accompanied by my friends, Roger Ascham and Dr. Haddon. Jane looked calm and unmoved during the marriage service. When, earlier, she passed me with her entourage she turned and looked so meaningfully at me. It was as though our souls fused at that moment. The pain I felt, that she, the woman I loved, was to be married to another, was absolutely gutting, but that look, that certain something made it alright because, whatever, I knew her heart, her love would always be for me, our bond was tied and nothing would shift that.

I remembered her words the previous day: "I will not be weak in showing them my disapproval of a loveless wedding with someone I loathe and despise. In my heart I have discovered my true love and will focus on that thought, that, unlikely as it is, that one day, perhaps in another place, another time I shall truly be with the one I love."

She had no need to tell me who it was, for fear that the impossibility and illegality of such a marriage would simply create unhappiness and, indeed danger. Her true feelings would remain hidden but the mutual understanding was recognised: "Just your presence, kind tutor of mine ,will calm me, just your being there and knowing your feelings."

84

Her words, her thoughts expressed my thoughts as if our souls were truly bonded.

She wore a white coif, a green cloth gown embroidered with gold and a mantle of silver tissue. A headdress of green velvet set in precious stones. Her hair hung down her back, combed plaited and braided with pearls in an unusual fashion.

A host of dignitaries were in attendance

The young King, because of sickness, did not attend and neither did Princesses Mary Tudor and Elizabeth. It all came to pass that they disapproved of the marriage. But beneath the splendour of the occasion there lacked the wonder and joy of what should have been a time for rejoicing. For Jane and her waiting ladies it was certainly not an occasion to rejoice. There were no tears of emotion. She simply went through the motions as was expected of her, but I noticed the couple hardly looked at each other. Guildford sat closer to his mother than he did to Jane and she seemed as though she could not bear to look at him as the ceremony commenced. She looked paler than before and her eyes seemed to be red but perhaps made more prominent by the dark shadows under her eyes, she was plainly fatigued and looked as though she had not slept, and I could understand why. She declared openly it would be like a horrid dream to her, that she would just go through the motions as was dutifully required of her, but that was all. She would never kiss her new husband and when his father gave the call to raise goblets one and all, Jane was finding it difficult to raise hers; she seemed to sway but then straighten herself again as though an angel had passed over and helped her. It was surely obvious this was a contrived marriage and there was no love to be shared. Her new father in law callously yelled across the large hall that Lady Jane was truly a fortunate girl indeed to be married to such a grand husband. I heard the grooms brother, Robert, say before the marriage that truly he would have been in line to marry Jane had he not already been married, whilst he was aggrieved that he may miss out on what would be achieved, because Lady Jane was a cousin of the King, he felt he could not hold any real feeling for a girl set so much absorbed in her passion for books and learning, and who most times seemed to appear sullen and lacking in good spirit and humour. Of course this was of no consequence to the girl who already had discovered her true love and promised her love, despite the consequences of what happened that day, would forever be the same eternally.

"There could never be another to replace my schoolmaster," she whispered to me beforehand.

I did not see her again that day. Mrs. Ellen advised me Jane was suffering from a severe stomach disorder, headaches and sleeplessness and, after some heated discussion with her mother and the Northumberlands, had returned to the family's London residence in Suffolk Place.

"Dr. Aylmer, our Lady was rebelling, expressing quite candidly to her new in-laws and her new husband, Guildford, that she had no passion or desire to consummate a marriage which she considered void because their was no love shared.

" 'You will obey your new husband.' demanded her mother. 'Be eternally grateful that Guildford has chosen to take you as his bride!'

"I saw Jane scowl, Dr. Aylmer, barking back at her mother, telling her in no uncertain terms that she knew very well that it was not Guildford's choice but his parents and others for reasons she dreaded to assume.

" 'I have the same royal blood as you and that is the true reason, is it not? For you and father will know I am fully aware of it. My marriage to Guildford being very appropriate to a devious plan if, heaven forbid, our King dies.'

"The Duchess interrupted her daughter, raising her arm as if to strike her, shouting that she was a truly wicked girl and Satan will take her to his dungeon! As her arm came down her hand spitefully seared her daughter's neck, enough to bruise but Lady Jane grasped her mother's hand so tightly and pushed it away.

" 'You would not dare to abuse me anymore, Mother. I am no longer your little girl to treat as you wish. Remember, I now belong, as you say, to Guildford and you would have to answer to him if you were to plant any more bruises upon my body. I have taken so much from you, your horrid punishment which I consider now to be disturbing, to the extent that you both derived some excitement and sexual deviation with your own daughter which makes you incestuous by your methods.'

"These were indicative words that plainly shook the duchess, I have rarely seen the her lost for words, Dr. Aylmer, but she was then. Her daughter continued to tell her mother that Guildford had no passion, even lust for her; she knew that to be true for reasons she would not divulge and she adamantly declared she knew she would never ever allow the marriage to be consummated: 'Never, never! The thought is utterly repulsive to me!'

"I have never witnessed such determination in Lady Jane, Dr. Aylmer, yet I am frightened by Lady Frances' last words that no one disobeys the great Duke of Northumberland and when the time comes, she will want the marriage to be consummated. Whatever did she mean, Dr. Aylmer? Is our Lady Jane set to be in harm's way by that monstrous man with an evil reputation?"

I calmed her: "It is early days; anything can happen. Jane has truly developed a strong mind of her own and perhaps she will be a match even for the Duke. We can just pray, Mrs. Ellen."

That was Jane. She would not want to take part in the wedding feast or ceremony. She would find all method and means to forego that, which, like the wedding, was distasteful to her.

Afterwards, life carried on as before and, as arranged, I took up my position at Suffolk House to continue my tutorship there. Jane's ladies in

86

waiting and Mrs. Ellen joined us there. Dr. Haddon returned to Bradgate to resume his position as private chaplain.

During the next few days a good relationship grew between Jane, Mrs. Ellen, and myself. It was comforting to see Jane's health improve dramatically. Mrs. Ellen told me her headaches and stomach pains had gone and confided Jane had been experiencing 'growing problems' which probably were responsible for the recent upset.

We spent much time together discussing the works of the philosophers in which Mrs. Ellen was now addicted. If anything, we helped direct Jane's mind away from her new husband whom she despised immensely. Yet we all knew, that when Guildford's father commanded, Jane would be whisked off to Durham House, to live as man and wife with Guildford.

This happened sooner than any of us expected. Ten days later Northumberland sent a carriage for Jane's immediate dispatch and there was much discussion between him and Jane's parents.

For the second time in the short span of a month I waved goodbye to Jane as she was reluctantly bundled off to the awaiting carriage.

Imagining Jane with Guildford haunted my soul and I seldom slept. I cannot explain my feelings after the wedding; the thoughts of Jane submitting to a man she did not love tormented me. But she had no passion for him, my mind was telling me. She conveyed that to me several times. Jane was capable of being a very stubborn woman, indeed, and I calmed to think she would never wish to submit. Although I had absolutely no hold over her and could marry her, I felt she was still mine in body and spirit and my weaknesses were such that I imagined I was Guildford laying there beside her. We could never be complete as man and wife. In my heart of hearts, of that I was truly aware. But my masculine mentality wondered if Jane would act differently towards me, that without the warm cloak of everlasting love, her sweet body having been plundered by some weak soul like Guildford, her feelings for me would be different. She was devoid of knowing how it would be if the relationship were mentally and physically absolute. She so deserved much more than this but the fate of the monarchy dictated over all and Jane was unfortunately part of it. Ladies of such high standing are expected to succumb to the advice of those who proposed knew best and, truly, were limited when it came to choosing a suitor. Very rarely could it be a real love match and, certainly, Northumberland who dominated the scene, who, for his own selfish reasons, demanded for his son to be married to Jane, would not choose to take such trifling matters into consideration. The true allegiance of a Queen is to country first; her own needs must follow in accordance with that which was truly best for her country. It would have been more satisfactory for her to have married Edward, the boy King, an option that was earlier preferred but did not materialise. Although Jane never loved the King, she thought very much of him, more than she ever thought of Guildford. But she informed me Edward's heart was elsewhere, that he often talked about Elisabeth, Princess of France, and how he thought of her.

I constantly thought of Jane, wondering how she would cope in Durham House with Guildford and his formidable mother. I imagined it would be imminent when Northumberland initiated his instruction, as was customary, that the marriage would be consummated, whether Jane agreed or not this was mandatory to seal the contract. She had no option but to obediently submit to her new husband. I could not see how that could be avoided. I felt our close relationship was doomed. That someone, too, would surely notice my mannerisms, that I could not but help display my true feelings whilst in her presence, that my frustrations would be evident. But my concerns regarding this matter were unwarranted whilst Jane lived at Durham House. I was told in no uncertain terms that my services would no longer be required by Northumberland himself. But Mrs. Ellen stayed on as her nurse whilst Mrs. Tylney returned to the Grey's residence in London to be Lady Mary Grey's lady in waiting.

On leaving Durham house for the last time Mrs. Ellen confided that Lady Jane was now at loggerheads with the Northumberlands. She claimed she was being poisoned with a devilish substance to compel her body to rule over her head and her stomach pains were more frequent - if just a device to offset the consummation she rebelled against. Whilst I could not accept this I feared that Jane was confused. She wrote to me frequently saying how she loathed living there. She had many differences of opinion with her husband and her new mother in law and spent some time away in the Palace of Chelsea recovering from her spasmodic illnesses which I assumed, as Mrs. Ellen had thought, were to do with the business of adolescence and periodic complaints. But I understood from Mrs. Ellen that, besides the sleeplessness and headaches and stomach pains, the visiting physician at Durham House concluded that she had an accelerated heart rate and was losing some of her hair and her skin was abnormally dry. He assumed this could have been attributed to stress and advised that she should convalesce in more tepid and quiet surroundings. Jane was the first to admit that her visits to Chelsea were for "cure or recreation" but I was later to discover from her own lips the true reason and how she urged to stay with her mother in her sheer determination not to return to Durham House.

Although there was no love lost between her and her mother, she still preferred her company to that of her husband and his parents, which said everything. And, although I was barred from seeing Jane at Durham House because Guildford insisted she allocated all her time to their marriage, I was gladly accepted and welcomed at Chelsea and, indeed, Jane implemented this: "I shall still need your help. Just because I am married and not by choice does not mean I wish to terminate my studies, therefore, if you can spare me the time, it would be wonderful, John."

"You are welcome and I am your servant," I replied diligently with some relief. I so wanted still to be with her, even just for those few hours a week,

"You aren't my servant, John, you are my tutor - nay, more - my very special friend also." Those eyes so full of expression and the love I knew the special 'something' we both knew and shared - I was so very near to holding her in my arms there and then, wanting to cherish her for ever, to combine my soul with hers, it all seemed so right that we should, yet my heart was fighting my mind once more, if only, if only we were away from that place, that Jane, sweet Jane had been permitted to live the life she wanted and choose the lover she wanted. But again my mind won the battle and of course it was right that it should, there was simply no place for us together and never could there be. She was still looking into my eyes, she surely knew my thoughts: "Know, my dear schoolmaster, I am with you; you are as if but part of me. We share the same space but in time I know our hearts and souls will meet and we shall be as one, always another time and another place but I know you likewise feel the same." It was not a question, simply a statement, the question needed not to be asked for the answer was instituted deep within; we knew how our feelings for each other were so strong and so complete.

She indeed was so special to me. I imagined her life at Durham House must have been depressing indeed that she was willing to come back to live with her mother despite the earlier abuse she had known.

"She dare not touch me now, John. According to her I am now under the jurisdiction of the Dudley's and, to be more precise, my husband Guildford Dudley and she dare not mark me again ever.

"So you will always be an important part of my life, John, and I will make my wishes known to my mother in no uncertain terms."

I was glad for Jane in as much as now married she was considered to be a woman of substance and of course her parents recognised this, that her position demanded the respect expected, even of them.

But I felt I should frankly discuss my fears with Jane, that it would thus be diligent for me to severely limit my visitations, the reason being obvious – that I could be banished from ever seeing her again.

CHAPTER NINE

In the event of the distressing events concerning Jane's dilemma my mind often returns to memories of happier days. I remember with great joy the many conversations I had with Roger Ascham. We had much in common scholastically, and our hopes and ambitions were high. On one such occasion he was keen to discuss the special qualities of Lady Jane and how he had especially enjoyed meeting her again at Bradgate. It was in the summer of 1550 when he had just left the tutorship of Elizabeth. Jane was twelve.

He had first met her in Chelsea Palace when she was staying with Katharine Parr and had discovered her many scholastic talents. He was entranced by her sweet charm: "Equal to that of a noblewoman." But he was truly confused: "One would think, living in a superb mansion like Bradgate, surrounded by beautiful country, streams and woodlands bountiful with deer would be absolute paradise. Many a girl would cherish the thought of residing there. Food was plentiful, too. I remember being invited to the duchess' birthday celebrations last year. The duke and duchess were wonderful hosts. A hundred guests took their places at the huge dining table in the hall. Firstly, we were served with brawn soup, with a choice of stewed pheasant or swan followed by stuffed peacock, rabbit and egg fritters. Still there was more to come, enormous quantities of all manner of fresh conserves and fruits. Then the caraway seed wafers, which were delicious, tansy cakes and saffron buns. It was all too much for me." Roger passed a rueful hand over his stomach.

"I hoped you tried the hippocras, Roger? Especially recommended to wash everything down," I smiled.

"Of course!" he chuckled. "A Bradgate speciality, I understand. I am told the duke consumes the same after most meals. I must say this vintage did much for my palate. But what am I telling you all this for? You have dined and wined at Bradgate on many occasions."

"In moderation," I replied stretching my hands outwards away from my stomach to which Roger returned an understanding grin, knowing I was prone to some obesity if I did not pay attention to my diet.

"I do recall with some distaste, John, the passing of bottles underneath the long dining table. Although now the memory sometimes brings tears of laughter to my eyes, those attenders scurrying to and fro each end of the table, emptying and replacing the well used receptacles.

"When I dined there we took our places at three in the afternoon and lifted ourselves very cautiously from our places during the middle hours of the evening, some of the male gentry not once having left their chairs I might add. It soon became apparent why this was, the bottles of course. With all that wine consumed Mother Nature would often make her call. I remember hearing what sounded like running water. I knew about the building, how underground channels carried water and assumed that was where the sound was coming from. When my immediate neighbour nudged me, pointing downwards it rapidly occurred to me just how the gentry relieved themselves. A large, already half filled, earthenware bottle appeared between my feet. I could not bring myself to use it. I passed it along and used the latrine facility in the hall closet when nature frequently called.

"I am told this practice is readily accepted during the discourse of large functions. For myself I will not be enthused to attend another. It is a little off putting to say the least.

"One of the hard-pressed attenders was bitterly scorned and dismissed in tears by Lady Frances when he dropped a full bottle almost under her nose. She was absolutely outraged, apologised profusely to the guests seated at that end, who were requested to move to a smaller table, which was quickly set up in another part of the hall.

"The section was screened off whilst the area was thoroughly cleansed.

"However, returning to Lady Jane – I was rather sad to hear what she had to say but heartened by her overtures about you and what you meant to her life at Bradgate. I dare say I am about to flatter and probably embarrass you, dear John. But let the truth be out. You deserve to be told, even praised for your special achievement in making a very sad, distraught girl very, very happy."

I probably had good account of what he might say concerning the sad heart of Jane but I was bemused as to what this special achievement was. Roger continued:

"I noticed Jane was reading the Phaeton Platonis. I asked why, on such a beautiful day, she didn't join her family who were in the park. I shall never forget that smile. She replied that their sport is but a shadow of that pleasure she found in Plato. That they never felt what pleasure means."

I told Roger I was readily aware of Jane's interest in Plato. That sometimes after lessons, it was task enough to draw her from her books, but her unsociable disposition concerned me, how she tucked herself away for hours on end.

"In her future capacity she would require to take up the social attributes if she wished popularity with people." I acknowledged, I quite understood her fascination with Plato, how she was able to discover great faith and hope by his writings. But she was young and needed to live a little. She needed to participate in the world in which she lived, to take heed of that.

"But for all her good qualities, Roger, she is plainly stubborn and, for one so young, is plainly set in her ways. It is difficult to bring her out of her books."

"Well if anyone can do that, you are that person, John," he advised, his deep eyes peering directly into mine.

"But have no such concern over her enjoyment of life," Roger continued. "It took me a while to draw her out. I wanted desperately to know what allured her to this knowledge of pleasure. Now, John, you had better take note because this very much concerns you."

My senses responded. What was this he seemed enthused to tell me?

"Jane spoke with absolute freedom and confidently. She was clear in her mind and I think she really wanted to tell somebody of her deep feelings with regard to her accomplished tutor. She was quite open and honest with me and expected I would be much impressed with what she had to say. That one of the greatest benefits that God ever gave her was that He burdened her with sharp severe parents, but so gentle a schoolmaster. They were her very words, John."

Roger paused for a moment. He had noted my reaction.

"You appear surprised. That's not the end of it, John. She confessed that when she was in the presence of either her father or mother, no matter what she was doing, she was so sharply taunted and so cruelly threatened.

"If she is telling the truth, and I cannot imagine why she should not, she is truly being ill used in word and deed to the extent that some things she could not bring herself to tell me. I queried what she meant but she declared she would not describe for the honour she bore them. She continued that the abuse was so without measure disordered that she thought herself in hell, till the time comes when – now this is it, John – till the time comes that she must go to Dr. Aylmer."

I told Roger I was flattered. I told him I had sometimes noted her tears and, although I had never witnessed a mark on her face, I had noted with some concern her limitations in movement, her inability to comfortably sit and the hurt in her expression. Yet, when I saw her at Chelsea Palace she was a different girl, always talking of her substitute mother, Katharine Parr. But then on the 7th of January 1556 the Queen Dowager died in childbirth at Sudeley Castle and her husband, Thomas Seymour, seemed unmoved. It was a horrible loss for Jane who was chief mourner at her funeral.

"Her tears are of sadness, John. She hates the times when she has to leave your tutorship. Her great pleasures are unequivocally in her books and the gentle method by which you teach. She endows you with nothing but praise, that without you, Plato, and her many correspondents, her life would be unbearable. I am most impressed, John. Your methods of tutorship I feel are much more fitting to the aspirations of the pupil. It truly grieves me to note the general attitude adopted by many tutors these days. I feel, given careful and sympathetic teaching skills, pupils will gain so much more than by having a subject too harshly taught. Presently, I am writing a thesis on the subject."

Roger was truly a great friend and he seemed enthused in advising me of Jane's most detailed expressions of my worth to her. His eyes had sparkled and his smile was constant. I was thus surprised when his expression changed.

There was an almost forbidding look in his eyes.

"I have, no doubt, embarrassed you enough today in conveying to you the compliments of our Lady Jane in regard to yourself but I do sincerely hope I will not embarrass you with my concerns regarding such deep feelings she has for you. Of course, she is not yet a woman but you will be aware of the dangers."

"What dangers, Roger?" I asked.

He paused, his broad cheeks stretched, and he sank his left hand into his full beard thoughtfully. Then he carefully replied: "Infatuation can sometimes be compelling in a girl of twelve. Perhaps, in Lady Jane we have an exception because of her disposition, her natural ability to question everything of herself, why, how and wherefore. And then knowing in balanced mind that which is correct. Whilst her admiration for you is complementary, the danger is always there, that she may become overwhelmingly infatuated by you, which, obviously can lead to all manner of complications."

I thanked Roger for his astute observations of which I was unaware at the time.

I treated Jane no differently from my other aristocratic pupils except, perhaps, to acknowledge her greater depth of learning. She had already learnt Latin and Greek to incredible standards and she was now keen to learn Hebrew. Her first tutor, Dr. Harding began her Greek, Spanish, Italian, and French lessons. She loved music and composing also but scarcity of time prevented her from following this course. But, occasionally, when her parents were absent, she took a few moments off to play the cither and harp, sometimes the lute and was interested in melody making.

If only I could have saved her enthusiastic musical compositions for eternity, so the world would know just how intelligent and versatile she was. Add to that her observations taken with Katharine Parr and the New Learning, all this and some portraits, too, all destroyed after her execution, probably because then no credit could be bestowed upon her talent. I can still remember like it was yesterday her playing a song on the lute she called simply 'Green Sleeves' which, although attributed to her Uncle I believe was her own competition.

Roger meant well and, at that time, I felt everything was under control. Jane and I shared a love of learning and her interests were mainly academic and, as far as I was then aware, were directed solely to her studies. She had an abundant appetite for learning, so the fact that, as Roger assumed, she worshipped me was just as much as she worshipped her studies and, simply, the two went together.

Jane told me about Roger Ascham's visit: "I did not know he was a friend, Dr. Aylmer. I was fascinated by his conversation. I do indeed enjoy indulging, as you know, in wholesome conversation and he being a staunch humanist, too. You are fortunate indeed to have such wonderful friends but it is easy to realise how you and he do get along so well with one another, as if to complement each other."

"And if you are curious," she smiled with a knowing look, "he spoke highly of you in every respect. Friends, good friends confide in one another, yes, Dr. Aylmer? So, I guess he probably mentioned my true thoughts about you?"

I found I was lost for words and instantly Jane recognised she had put me into a very awkward position.

"Jane. You are a wonderful young lady and I absolutely adore you, but …"

"Of course, I recognise there has to be a *but*," Jane tactfully interrupted. "I am very young, yes? I am confused and growing up too quickly for my age and, if that in itself was not difficult enough, I am of course of Royal blood. I am fully aware that my feelings must remain harnessed. I won't embarrass you in asking your thoughts but whatever you think and assume, I do know my own mind. I am certain of that, and I also know in my heart my feelings true enough."

I examined my conscience. Would I have overstepped my position? I would surely be aware of it and I would never have dreamed of taking advantage of such a young girl even though it is true to say, she had the intellect and mentality of a girl perhaps three to four years her senior. But, nevertheless, she was a pupil and I was merely her tutor and I had never thought of her in any other way then.

"I am truly sorry but I cannot help my feelings, Dr. Aylmer. But have no fear. I will remain just your pupil, for I am not so foolish a young girl as to not realise anything else would cause turbulence and possible dismissal if any scandal accrued from rumour or otherwise. Let it be then that I will be utterly prudent at all times."

It was indeed an impossible situation and I was relieved that Jane was fully aware of the situation.

"We will work it out," I assured her and I would like always to be there as a true friend as well as merely a tutor.

When the lessons were over, she would bid me farewell until the next time and she and I would go our own ways.

Yet, thinking about it now, perhaps unwittingly, Roger had planted the seed in my mind and soon I would be asking questions of myself. In my case it would not be infatuation, something that could pass overnight. It was something more permanent. But a few months would pass before Jane reached a certain maturity.

CHAPTER TEN

When I tutored Lady Jane at Bradgate after the execution of her former guardian, Thomas Seymour, I observed the real Jane and also a great deal regarding myself, something I had never before encountered, being of the firm and ordered opinion that my life and soul belonged to God.

I had not envisaged that the girl, who was then rapidly becoming a woman, would give reason for me to doubt my ambitions in the Church. After all, I realised I needed the love of a woman in my life and could not give my absolute whole to such a demanding calling. I really believed that.

I became besotted by her. Because of her keen interest in learning and the heavy demands put upon her by the duchess, not a day would go by when I did not see her, except on those few occasions when she had to join her parents on social visits. Her mother spoke to me about her and the duke's disappointment that, since she returned from Chelsea, she was no longer the quiet calm girl they knew before. She charged, that I must instil into her the importance of respect for one's parents and elders and take no nonsense. But for me everything I saw in Jane was in her favour. She had simply grown up a little and was coming to the age where she wished to assert herself. I was glad for her, that, at last, she was dealing with her parents' intimidation and bullying. She was starting to learn how to resist.

Though her parents had noticed her arrogance of late, I assumed this was not meant to be expressed as being disrespectful but simply an expression of confidence in a girl who had gleaned so much during her time at Court, albeit the new learning, too, dispensing many of the old ways regarding religious trends, encouraged by Katharine Parr who had achieved much in the formation of a new protestant movement.

She seemed in constant touch with her maker. She often gleaned that she did not have to ask for Him. He was always there, when needed. We had so much in common and sometimes her spiritual and emotional maturity seemed daunting to one who had taken a doctorate at Cambridge. I was the teacher but also the pupil and discovered then that one could never stop learning, not least from those who looked to you for knowledge.

I have since had to question my deep faith, confused and despairing, that a woman able to absorb so much knowledge was called by her maker at such an early age, when so much goodness would have come forth for the good of our country. A young woman who was pure, honest and of such disposition that carnal thoughts were easily put aside, that such considerations apparently never came about in such measure as could sway her. Here was a young woman in the prime of her youth, taken from life, as if her learning meant nothing.

If anything, my faith was immediately strengthened. I did not possess the natural power Jane always sustained right to the end, to be absolutely sure in accepting the ways of our Lord, trusting in Him and knowing His was the right way. Truly, I jested with her on many occasions, that our God was so well ordained, he must be an Englishman! She always returned a smile but we both knew He was much more than that. I accepted that, truly, He would name the day of our departure from this world and something Jane repeated several times was absolutely right.

"Live still to die." Life was merely a rehearsal for that which must come after death. The knowledge and lessons we learn here in our world will undoubtedly go with us; it is only the material body that dies. I remember the deep discussions we shared, her thoughts flowing like still they are, through time, through her spirit.

"We all live, love, and survive because of the spark which was ignited at the beginning," I whispered and immediately she returned, as if something was coming through her very being, that one so young could be armed with so much knowledge has always fascinated me.

"And until the end of our tenancy here on earth, John, we live to die to live again in rebirth, so our bodies return to dust and our souls reincarnate to fuse and spark again in another place, another time."

She looked up at me, those eyes so deep and so very appealing.

"Indeed," I followed. "What goes around comes around in the circle of life."

"It does make me wonder, John, what we will be in our next life? Whatever, I feel it will be with you because our spark is always alight and the flame burns so strong. I think we both know that very well."

"Then, Jane, what is the lesson in life? I think it is to learn in life how to develop and make the very best of our talents and how we apply them in life. You seem so enthused in everything you do, you have always seemed to be basic, thorough and leave nothing unattended."

I spoke to her softly. We had so very many conversations of this nature. She called it her Karma, that we are all, each and every one of us are blessed with it, but some will never recognise it, according to our diversities. There was good and there was also bad Karma. We knew that, for some unexplainable reason, the days which followed yesterday and today were never quite the same and that was like Karma. There has to be a balance, for us to appreciate one from another, else being human, we would be bound to take it for granted.

"I wonder if I knew you, John, in a past life. I think we are truly soul mates." That was one of the most wonderful things Jane said to me. Now I live to die in the name of sweet Jane and all those executed who, like her, were truly innocent of any violent crime, like our saviour himself, Jesus Christ.

I was so pleased Jane found peace and understanding in my tutorship and I was later astounded, when Roger Ascham published a full account of everything Jane had confided in meticulous detail about me, as part of a thesis on education.

Looking further back to the Queen Dowager's untimely death and before Jane returned to Bradgate, her father sent for her to go to his London House and we were constantly in touch by way of correspondence. She sent me full accounts of her progress. Her increasing knowledge of Socrates and the Greek classics astounded me. It seems uncanny that the writings of Plato inspired her to change her outlook in matters of life and death. As if the Lord, through that great philosopher who combined his thoughts with Christian attitudes, was preparing her for her premature passing from this world. That we should fear not death; that we simply live to die, the important thing being; how we choose to live which would determine our soul's existence after death.

Perhaps, as the months went by at Bradgate, I was getting too close to the girl who was rapidly becoming a young woman, never realising at the time that my feelings were more than they should be. She was of marriageable age. Although small and petite she had already acquired the graceful and beautifully proportioned body of womanhood.

She was keen to read the works of Johann Heinrich Bullinger, chief pastor of the radical church in Zurich, having heard of him from John Ulmis. She came to look forward to Johann's letters and was keen to show off her knowledge of the Latin word when corresponding with him. It was as if she had a tireless appetite for absorbing, not only languages but also the real issues relative to what had already become her deep beliefs.

"I truly believe, John, that we do live merely as tenants of the Lord upon this planet so very precious, that we are each under the close scrutiny of our Lord and are constantly being monitored regarding our behaviour - that upon passing this planet we are returned reincarnated to undergo a fresh experience and so on until we reach the ultimate time, those of us that can make it, some will always fall by the wayside, and in the eyes of God; fit to become part of the 'whole' which truly is the Kingdom of Heaven."

That one so young as Jane has come to such profound and all inspiring conclusions of why we are here at all truly fascinated me and I spent many free evenings in deep thought and meditation examining the findings of my astute pupil. Indeed, I asked her if together we should meditate, to share our deep thoughts and inspirations to which she openly agreed.

"Truly, your Karma is my Karma too, John Aylmer, and I am blessed and privileged by your company. The law of cause and effect is so evident here I do so believe, and we shall surely please the Lord in sharing our meditation."

I was falling even more for Lady Jane and couldn't hold myself, our thoughts aspired to join souls and it did seem almost as if we were one.

As we took our places before the alter in Bradgate chapel I caught her glance as she kneeled beside me, she turned her head to me, so trusting and so complete - it seemed it had all happened before, that it was all written out for us and that is how it should be, at least for this time around, perhaps in another life, another time. Another place? It seemed as though it had all happened before and it was right we should be there together to pray and to meditate.

As Roger Ascham told me, after his visit to Bradgate, she seemed oblivious to worldly events. Her life without books would have been depressing indeed. It was almost as if she was quite happy in being a recluse, so long as she had the implements of studious design about her.

Her obsession for learning did not always go down well with her parents who were more content to while away the days in the pursuits of open air activities in the large park surrounding the house, or to socialise with 'their kind.' Many arguments ensued and Jane was determined to get her way, which sometimes she did. I know not how because the duchess was a formidable woman and usually got what she wanted.

CHAPTER ELEVEN

I must record that there was a time when Jane strayed from her diligent course. It was during the time of John Ulmis's visit to Bradgate. Jane became associated with Mary Sidney, daughter of John Dudley, the powerful Duke of Northumberland, and she would sometimes visit Bradgate. She was a very attractive lady with an exuberant disposition. Lady Frances adored her and openly encouraged the new friendship with Jane. Mrs. Ellen recalled the time when, concerned with Jane's vulnerability, she really wanted to intervene but her post denied her. As briskly reminded by the Duchess, she was taking on too much and should remember her place.

"My daughter needs your expertise in the approach of femininity," she heard her saying to Mary Sidney. "She is plainly a stubborn girl who, although exceptionally clever with her studies and has a first class tutor in John Aylmer, she fails in the scholarship of not knowing how to improve and cultivate her rather subdued personality. Obviously, she is not blessed with your beauty but I am sure your advice and assistance will help her pay more attention to her best features."

Mary Sidney, a tall woman, wore an abundance of rather gaudy jewellery, her flowing brunette hair brushed across her forehead complimenting her best feature, her eyes wide, oval, and brown. Her extroverted nature created a stir in the house and she was extremely attractive to men, although she made it quite plain she would only converse with those of her class, given perhaps the exception of an 'underling' she occasionally lured with her grasping ways.

"I shall do my very best, Frances, you can be assured. She has plainly been neglected by her guardian of late who plainly had eyes for our jaunty Elizabeth with one thing in mind, neglecting the ethics of the girls."

"Indeed!" scowled Frances. "Jane's attitude and changed mannerisms have been evident which must put blame on Thomas Seymour. It seems, he lacked the need for respect, which has reflected upon Jane also. This is a matter to which I have been at loggerheads with her but, I fear, to no avail."

"Leave your daughter to me, Frances. She is growing up and I seriously don't think you recognise that. Fortunately, she is at ease with me, enthusiastic methinks to discover her true sexuality which will work wonders for her."

"Does the presence of your handsome brother Robert bear any significance to this? I do wonder, Mary."

"Then you have seen him. I trust you will welcome him here. He wanders in the magnificent walled garden. He adores the peace and tranquillity, you know, having recently quarrelled quite substantially with his wife. He will be along soon to greet you, Frances dear."

"Will he now? Well, I am sure he will be absolutely charming. It has been some months since I have seen Robert and, to be honest, although not to put down your younger brother, Guildford, I would have been delighted indeed if Jane and he bonded. Think what a wonderful pair they would make - almost heaven sent."

"But would Jane think that?" Mary questioned. "From what I gather, she has her heart set elsewhere."

"If you are talking about Lord Herbert, he is a wimp no less and is not at all suitable for her. She will know of my wishes and will have to abide them, for she has no option, Mary."

"I was not thinking of Lord Herbert. Surely, you have noticed the look in Jane's eye when her tutor is present?"

"Impossible!" Frances was adamant. "She simply adores him as an adolescent who adores her tutor, simply that. And, plainly, he's a commoner, and Jane knows her position would never allow such a bond and ..."

"Such a shame Robert is married though, don't you think, Frances?" Mary interrupted with a knowing smile. She teased Frances to be sure, for Robert had already mentioned quite categorically that he would be indeed desperate to bond with such a recluse, that his idea of a woman was one with ingenuity, beauty and an abundance of natural energy.

Mrs. Ellen said she held her breath hearing of Mary Sidney's scandalous suggestion regarding Lady Jane and her tutor, but was truly relieved that the mistress did not take up on it. She found solace in being able to share her concerns with me, as also those conveyed to her by Mrs. Tylney.

"I believe Lady Frances deliberately arranged this in collusion with Mary, her intention being to bring Jane out of her introvert disposition. Mrs. Tylney served me well in keeping me informed, although it was not until later that I heard about conversations between Frances and Mary Sidney who later openly flirted with John Ulmis. It was even to the extent that she declared she was tired of her present marriage and was looking for a new husband. He seemed clearly embarrassed by her flaunting and whispered something into her ear. She immediately stopped and, like a naughty child, placed her arms stiffly down each side of her but noticeably, teasingly swaying her hips.

"I noted the open-eyed expression upon Jane's face as she observed intensely, which made me angry that this was a bad influence on her. I felt that John Ulmis, a man of high principles and character, would not be taken in by all this.

"Although, on one occasion I apprehended them embracing in the corridor, John afterwards assured me that he was not at all interested in the very persuasive lady who had merely caught him off guard."

Of late Mrs. Ellen confided in me, "I am sure a man of his high standards and morals would not be coerced by this brazen lady."

I said, I noticed the change in Jane's habits. Formerly, upon my arrival for study she was always in class, dressed in her clean smock and heavily engaged in study, her books opened upon her table. But presently, upon my arrival, the classroom was empty and sometimes I waited five minutes upon her arrival and on one occasion up to fifteen minutes.

During studies I noted her mind was not entirely on her work. It was most unlike Jane to be preoccupied because her studies were so very important to her. But she was giving less time to her studies and more to music and a new found interest in luxurious clothes and jewels, which annoyed me intensely. I realised, of course, she indeed was growing up and fast but everything in moderation. I approached her, carefully issuing my protestation, that she must give due time to her studies and less time to her wardrobe, that an accomplished scholar did not need an excessive wardrobe with which to succeed, that her studies must exceed nearly all else excepting health problems and bereavement.

I reminded her that her cousin, Lady Elizabeth, refused to alter any of her plain habits while all the other ladies were dressed and painted like peacocks, that it was not becoming for one who embraced the new religion. Also, I reminded her, that she herself, who made reference to Elizabeth when she received a present of tinsel cloth and velvet, laid on with parchment lace of gold from Lady Mary, complained what should she do with it? Clearly she was unimpressed.

"But that was as much to do with our faith," Jane inferred. "When Lady Sidney proposed that I should wear it at my marriage, I refused because it would be a shame to follow my Lady Mary against God's word and leave my Lady Elizabeth who follows God's word.

"I am indeed blessed, John, with Lady Sidney's assistance in helping me overcome my awkwardness - as my tutor you do me well - but there are some things better taught by another female."

Jane's lack of tact concerned me at times. She did not consider the effect of what she said. She tended to judge herself from a detached point of view, exactly as if she was condemning anyone who exploited her or denigrated her ideas. I approached her and she replied:

"At this time, Dr. Aylmer, I am merely following the instructions of my dear mother who proclaims to know best, that I quickly grow into womanhood and must make the best of myself in exultation of our great and noble family. But I must and do confess, I have a leaning toward the new fashions and beautiful wonderful designs adorned by spangles of glittering jewellery as formerly encouraged by Katharine Parr and now my dear new friend, Mary Sidney. You would surely not discourage my new born interest, Dr. Aylmer?"

"But Katharine Parr was never excessive, for it was not in her character to be so," I argued. "She was always guided by her faith, which tempered moderation in everything. You are plainly excessive, Jane. Look at your fingers, your hair. I have never seen so many glittering diamonds upon the person of one young woman."

Jane's face reddened, she frowned and began to sob as she remarked angrily:

"For the first time in my life I can recall, I have achieved something to which my parents truly aspire. For once they withhold their abuse and praise my actions. But now, John Aylmer, I offend you, which pains me more than words can tell. You must understand this is no longer the girl you teach but the young woman who has, with your great experience, achieved such excellent standards. I was expecting, at least from you, great words of exultation, of admiration, of joy that your scholar has become a worthy adult. Please do not turn against me, Sir, for it is you I have loved and trusted these past months of strife."

She met my gaze eagerly.

I appreciated her explanation but not her excess and politely advised, submitting to temptation in the eyes of the Lord, such excess would not be gratefully received.

"Could it be, John Aylmer, you are jealous? For surely, our Lord would give precedence to those of us in such high standing, that we above all, should inspire and command our due respect from those below our standing."

It was almost her mother speaking. Not quite Jane, the Jane to whom I had become accustomed. What had come over her? And why that question? I puzzled.

"You fail to reply, John, because you are jealous, are you not? Jealous that I have lately been paying too much attention to John Ulmis and not enough to yourself?"

I chose not to reply but she seemed taut and annoyed with me. "It is Robert Dudley, too, isn't it? You don't like me talking to him. I have felt it in my bones."

"Don't you see, Jane, it is obvious something is afoot. Why the sudden nurturing from those who have almost ignored your presence before?"

"Robert is a delightful charming man whom I have come to adore and respect very much. I feel sure that he has no ulterior motive in giving to me some very well accepted attention. I lament because he has to leave so soon but he has assured me he will be back."

I could see her cheeks flush as she spoke of Robert, who I knew to be a woman's man, and now was he luring Jane with his charms. I tortured myself with my thoughts.

For the first time in my life I turned away from her. I was lost for words. Stupidly, I chose to walk away and I shall never forget that for the rest of my life.

She was absolutely right about my being jealous but I felt strongly I was right about her personal excesses. I wanted to impress upon her that which was in bad taste, that which suddenly she seemed to have inherited from her grasping mother with the outlandish encouragement of Mary Sidney.

It soon became obvious she was not prepared to alter her ways. This became apparent. Two days later, when the duke and duchess were away for a short time, and Mary Sidney was still in residence at Bradgate, she approached me with some gusto, telling me I was wrong to advise Lady Jane against that which any young lady, approaching womanhood, would find quite natural to do.

She looked at me with piercing brown eyes as she spoke:

"You must be congratulated for being a fine upstanding tutor and the Lady has surely benefited from such. But there are certain lessons no man can teach a woman. Only a woman can do that. I have spoken with the duchess who agrees. You should refrain forthwith from advising Lady Jane regarding her personal preferences. She must have every freedom to do as she wishes on the proviso it meets with her protocol, as set by her parents and it would not be in your interest to pursue this course. Do you understand what I am saying, Dr. Aylmer? Remember your services to the Lady Jane will shortly terminate. It could be sooner than you think. I understand the duchess already has someone in mind to continue the tutorship of the Ladies Katharine and Mary."

"The duchess has informed you of this?" I asked irritably. "She has not mentioned anything to me."

"Do not be insolent with me, Dr. Aylmer. I remind you of your place. I am the daughter of the most important man in England. You, who was once a servant here, are merely an employee and you must not forget that."

She was making it clear that, as the daughter of John Dudley, the powerful Duke of Northumberland, her rank was far in excess of mine. Her manner was precocious and obstinate. She did not reply to my question but continued to patronise me:

"You will learn, Sir, in due course and when my father sees fit, of the true reason of my being here. Then you will not choose to vent your anger upon me lest you gamble with your life."

"Does Lady Jane know of this reason, Lady Sidney?"

"She will know when is befitting for her to know and I instruct you until then to keep silent. I have unwittingly already said too much in responding to the anger you have dared to display to me and I would not forgive you for that. For all the charm and gentleness you have apparently shown to Lady Jane I have brought out your true self and shown you for what you are. In future, kindly remember your place and speak only if you are spoken to. Do you understand, Sir?"

It was as if her foreboding of me was brewing the more we spoke. I realised my best course was to show the respect she demanded of me. I nodded and bowed gracefully with my hand upon my chest and made a hastened exit.

But even as I left the room she chose to further intimidate me: "And remember, Dr. Aylmer, you have encountered more than your match with me. I am not your beloved schoolgirl. I would prefer that you keep away from me."

I decided not to dwell on what Lady Sidney had said, although I wondered what was the extent of her influence upon Jane. I assumed she had already persuaded Jane in luring her to extravagant ways, that one could not make the excuse that it was just her age. I could not accept that the true Jane would neglect those studies she had always treasured.

But for the time being, I was out of favour with both Jane and Mary Sidney. I was incensed by melancholy but above all, above everything else, whatever my selfish feelings, I was truly disturbed regarding her negligence toward her studies.

In this vein I asked John Ulmis if he would write to Heinrich Bullinger and other correspondents with whom Jane communicated, if he would ask them to write to Jane, stressing to her the importance of her studies.

In the meantime I suffered the indignity of Lady Sidney's treatment of me, often passing her in the corridors as she scuffed her skirts, pretending I was not there, that I did not exist. But I was more than aware of her, the rich scent of lavender as she swept by and if I was absolutely honest I perhaps should admit that, although I detested her extremes, she made me realise my sexuality on more than one occasion to a point no other woman had done before. She had a certain charisma difficult to ignore and she was quite aware of her sexuality and how to use it best to her advantage, a veritable tease for most weak-minded males. I scorned myself for letting my lust slightly overcome my senses and immediately remembered I should act in a manner fitting to my cloth and do my utmost to correctly guide my pupil Jane, who was now in the process of growing rapidly into womanhood.

For a short time, Mary Sidney seemed involved with the master's valet, Richard, a handsome young man to whom she was apparently greatly attracted, and she was careless in discretion. Oft times he was observed, I was told by various members of the household, to be entering the lady's chamber late in the evening and, sometimes, leaving in the early hours.

Concerned in reference to her uncouth influence on Jane, I felt it my duty to approach her realising the probability that my advice would be badly received.

She pouted at me and scoffed in her inimitable way and was vulgarly free with her words: "Perhaps you would like to visit my chamber, Dr. Aylmer? You, a man, who presumes to be the advisor with good intent. Perhaps it is deep in your mind that you would like to change from tutor to scholar and be taught a thing or two by a well-learned lady. What must a man do in your position to express his natural feelings I query? You are not an unattractive man, a little portly around the hips but I am sure some virulent bonding would help remedy that and I could so easily succumb to your masculine charms. You, so agile and so bustling a man whom, I observe, plays bowls with great zest and vigour. I have watched the way you swing the wood and accurately align it. And you come from a fine family, too, I am informed. The Aylmer's of Norfolk are well respected. I may have underestimated you yesterday. You will be most welcome in my boudoir, John. Come tonight. I will be as prudent as you wish and I am sure a little soothing pampering would be good for the soul as God only knows, and you of course, too, if you were to be honest man of God. If it was the Lord's intention for the sexes to intertwine, that He alone made us that way, then this is surely a taste of his heaven. And in the interest of survival of the stronger species, it is natural for a woman to prefer good hardy stock."

I was unable to hide my profound distaste and shuddered, as I stood there, unable to find the appropriate words in response.

"You need not be too shocked, John Aylmer, for I conceive the way you are with Jane in contrast to the way you are with me, for I am a real woman of essence, truly aware of my femininity and my effect on the opposite sex whether they be of high nobility, the lower class, or, indeed, men of cloth. You would not be the first one, Sir, whom, entrenched in the word of God, has chosen temporarily, yea, occasionally, to submit to temptation, and feel the better for it, to disregard the cloth for a brief rehearsal of what it may be like to be in heaven. I have that ability, John Aylmer, to give you an exclusive rehearsal of what heaven may be like."

"If, indeed, you choose foolishly to decline my invitation," she continued, "be careful not to report my indulgence to those fine aristocrats who attend this house, for they, too, may have enjoyed a little time in my heaven."

I was revolted by her manner and her vile tongue but chose to remain silent, not to be drawn into such conversation.

I later discussed the matter quietly with Dr. Haddon. I was desperately in need of good advice and explained my fears regarding Lady Sidney's unfavourable conduct and the impression she may have on Jane.

I could not understand his response:

"I am sure our brightest pupil will not be effected by one who stoops so low. Do not be concerned, John. You know God always works in mysterious ways."

I lightly quarrelled with him suggesting that, nevertheless, we should discuss the matter with His Grace. That it was surely our duty to uphold certain moralities.

"Such are the female of the species, we know not how their minds work, which is probably a good thing. You are surely more involved in your student's welfare more than becomes your place here. Sometimes I feel you are too possessive of the girl and it is high time she should indulge in other interests, which will eventually compliment her wellbeing.

"Regarding Lady Sidney: We know these things go on, John. Such is the way weak men are, that they encourage the immorality by their degrading actions. Given those temptations by an extremely attractive woman such as Lady Sidney, any sense of morality is rapidly surpassed. If no harm is done then we must remain silent. If we break the rule the harm will come, I have no doubt. Lady Sidney is a very formidable woman with an equally formidable father. She is also a grasping woman who will brazenly take what she desires without recourse. I have heard that her sexual appetite, like her father's, is enormous."

"Yet she is married to Henry Sidney, Dr. Haddon. She is breaking her vows to God?"

"That is correct but the Lord will be judge of that and of her husband who, on the last count, had three mistresses, I understand. It is the way they live, John. Your naiveté sometimes astounds me, it really does."

"I prefer not to think of such things, Sir. It is surely not good for the soul."

"It is only bad if you yourself doubt your cloth, John. Look deeply into your soul and ask yourself this: You are made of flesh and blood and, even in your capacity, you are prone to the natural feelings of man to woman. Let us be quite truthful about this. The Lady Sidney will catch the eye of any normal man."

I have to admit I then had a terrible, degrading thought that Dr. Haddon himself was one of the men of cloth to whom Lady Sidney made reference. It seemed rather odd that on the one hand he was passionately adverse to gambling, yet on the other, he seemed almost to condone fraternisation and adultery

I was fighting a lone battle. Perhaps even the duke himself enjoyed the services given of the whore of Bradgate, for, in my mind, that is what she was and there would always be a hidden price to pay for her services.

Low and behold, I became like a jealous lover, extremely concerned when, quite openly, as if to intimidate me, Lady Sidney talked about Richard to Jane in such a way, in that tone of voice that borders on sexual suggestion, even teasing her in asking her had she noticed he was a boy with charm and was handsome with an outstanding disposition.

She then assumed to whisper to Jane which was not a whisper at all, tantalizing me, because it was too defined and clear enough for anyone close by to hear, that she thought it a terrible shame that Jane could not take Richard to her bosom, for there was nothing better for the learning of so primed a young lady than to share those new growing up feelings with a young man of such a wonderful stature.

But that which she whispered next was truly a whisper. Lady Sidney knew quite well just what she was doing. It was as if she knew more about me than I did myself, or rather the secret feelings I kept shut away. In effect, she was now tantalizing me to the extreme as she continued to speak so very softly now and directly into Jane's ear.

I noticed Jane's cheeks flush and all sorts of notions entered my mind. Could she be persuaded to befriend Richard secretly, for I felt Lady Sidney, a woman full of secrets and sexual prowess would feel no inhibitions at all in making such a suggestion, most possibly arranged with Lady Frances in the strong belief that her daughter needed to have that first experience to help her mature, in order to prepare for the responsibilities which later would be expected of her.

I shuddered at the thought but trusted that Lady Jane would not hear of it. And yet, she was young and fertile and I had sensed in her manner of late her hormones were causing her stress. I would have indeed been too vain to think maybe her attraction to me, her newfound adult attraction, would spark hidden aspirations. Of course, all these thoughts were quickly dismissed because of my standing. Yet they were there, always there, my carnal aspirations for the woman I loved.

On the one hand I accepted that I could never love Lady Jane openly, yet on the other, the thought of another loving her or be it just toying with her, was absolutely repugnant. It could never be a love like mine for her.

Surely, she would not be influenced by Lady Sidney in that direction, and yet, I saw her nod and smile when Lady Sidney concluded her secret talk with her, the Lady turning devilishly to meet my eyes with hers and I knew there was something going on. It was as if she had won a battle with me, to show me how disadvantaged I was. She was, I felt, like a woman scorned that I had not taken up her offer to join her in her room. She was testing me to the limit and she knew it. Whatever she was up too was not good news and I just did not know which way to turn. It seemed I would have to suffer the torment maybe - although I hoped I was wrong - that indeed Lady Jane may just be interested in the young man, in as much that knowing because of my disposition could never serve her as a man should regularly serve the woman he loves and cherishes.

Later, I was again approached by Lady Sidney. She knew exactly what she was about: "You cannot stop what is nature, John Aylmer. I have arranged an introduction for your pet pupil whom, I feel sure, would simply love to befriend Richard in a way that may obviously be repellent to you, but I will encourage that, bearing in mind the poor girl needs a release from all the hard work she puts in with her studies."

"But Richard is merely a servant and a commoner at that, my Lady. And you cannot truly believe that a person of Lady Jane's integrity could allow herself to be involved in such a hopeless position. Think of what her parents would say if such a thing happened."

"You are indeed naive in so many ways, John,' she said. It was later significant she now called me by my Christian name.

"I would have you know that indeed her parents, as knowledgeable as they are of worldly matters, whereas you are not, being ruled by your cloth, they would indeed turn a blind eye in the hope that their daughter may become a more mature and less awkward young lady. Indeed, from your present reaction I can tell that you yourself would not be adverse to a more close relationship with Jane. A woman can tell these things, especially of late. I believe, although this notion may not have tampered with your mind, it has done so with your heart. I think you, too, are in need of some meaningful instruction in this vein and you know you will always be welcome to visit me during my stay here. In the meantime I will indeed encourage a union between these two well-matched people. However, if you would like to discuss this matter more fully, I would suggest again that you take up my offer in a real effort to please me, in order that I may properly chaperone the young Jane who, I can tell you, is quickly coming to fruit and could well discover that her body will occasionally rule her mind."

I noted a mischievous glint in her eyes. She, indeed, knew exactly what she was doing and apparently would stop at nothing, least of all blackmail, to sustain that which she wanted. Yet I felt it more egotism than physical need.

I could not think of a time, since I had known Jane, so strained. Indeed, we had come to a stage when we hardly conversed, save upon the progression of her studies. I had never known Jane to be like this. Perhaps there was a part of her she had never had cause to reveal to me. I felt ill at ease about her manner, which was so very uncharacteristic. Indeed, I felt the influence of Mary Sidney was doing her no favours at all.

Yes, philosophically the new Jane I could easily fall out of love with, and when I thought about this perhaps it was progressing God's way in cooling our impossible relationship, which maybe was too much of a strain on us both.

God does work in strange ways but perhaps I was underrating the true character that was Jane.

CHAPTER TWELVE

It is with some repulse, I feel obliged to include the time I was led into the vault of temptation when Lady Mary Sidney came to Bradgate. This chapter was originally not intended for inclusion but as much as I held the whole episode back from Lady Jane it has to be recorded. Despite that which I have said before, that I was not exactly free of sin in the eyes of my Lord, and therefore I feel it right the whole truth be known that the spirit of Jane might also learn and hopefully forgive me. The truth is, I was tempted against my better judgment and pray the Lord will be lenient in judgment of my soul.

As tutor to the ill-fated Lady Jane Grey at a time when Henry VIII ruled and was married to Katherine Parr, I should have known better because discovery of my affair with Lady Sidney would truly have resulted in my dismissal by Jane's parents. I had watched my star pupil grow up from girl to young woman and unwittingly fell in love with her. But of course both our positions denied fraternization, Jane being of Royal blood and mine because of my cloth and position.

When Lady Mary Sidney, who was married to Sir Henry Sidney, visited Jane's home at Bradgate and took a short spell there to educate her niece, the teenage Jane, into the ways of womanhood, she did not hide the fact of being immediately attracted to men in the employ of Jane's parents. I never envisaged I would be one of them.

I knew Lady Mary, a woman of some means, her father being John Dudley, the powerful Duke of Northumberland, was an intellectual, passionate about everything she took on, especially the opposite sex and had the advantage of being in a position to procure an affair with any man to whom she was attracted. For although married, it seemed to be generally accepted both her and her husband were at liberty to enjoy extramarital affairs. She quite openly verified this during our many conversations, which started seemingly under the guise of her wanting to learn about the educational standards of Lady Jane and my method of teaching.

The first male to catch her eye at Bradgate was as already mentioned, the Master's valet, Richard and of course John Ulmer, then the young Ned Steer, the assistant keeper of horses, and finally, whom she clarified was to be a far bigger challenge, there was myself of whom she would attempt to seduce "because you, John Aylmer, are the more amiable," adding that the conception she could win over a man of the cloth exited her tremendously, for, in her thinking, a man who supposedly resisted carnal practice was being entirely untrue to himself, to the real red blooded man inside, whom God intended, given the survival of the species, to deliver the seed of life to woman.

"So, why should it be that one of his servants be denied as you, John Aylmer. What a veritable waste!" the latter of which she was heard to

109

announce in company, too.

When she came unexpectedly into the small chapel in Bradgate as I was preparing mass, she pounced on me, no holds barred.

"The truth and nothing but the truth, " she proclaimed. "I am in a house of God! John Aylmer, I have noticed your look when we pass in the corridor. A woman knows these things. Perhaps we should share some special time, some quality time together? I have attempted, John Aylmer, to gain your attention and have said things to you, which I admit were unwarranted. Please, accept my apologies and let's start again, shall we?"

Feeling utter astonishment and disbelief I explained: "You must not talk of such things, my Lady, for I am a man of God, as well you know."

"But you have no heed what it is like for a woman in my genre, who needs the comfort a man can give, and you are an ecclesiastical man of God. Is that not part of what you are all about, to give comfort and help to those in need? Well, John Aylmer, I am in need, sensually and mentally. Love is not enough, although I love my husband, I do, but a woman so highly passionate needs more than just love. She needs physical love. You glow with charm and grace and attractiveness, John. So, please, help me to understand the blessings God can give in a way only His servant can relay."

"I promise you," Lady Mary continued, almost touching me, she was that close, her eyes searching mine. "I know the cloth tells you not to be concerned with reward, but the reward I can give you surmounts all that is good and human, all that a woman can give of her true femininity. Come, John. Let me feel that which you must desire within. I can see the glow in your eyes when you look at me. Do you think I do not notice? You have as much need for the carnal as do I and you will have to hassle with your God. Show him that, that you are indeed human, a man, simply that, and a man needs the comfort of a woman as much as a woman needs a man. It is natural and right and I cannot see how a God can deny you of that! Come share your God's heaven with me, and you shall find it sooner than you could ever imagine."

I was speechless. She seemed to have the key to my most private innermost feelings. But clearly, I had to come to terms with the fact I was utterly aroused, there was no denying that, and Lady Mary was astute enough to realize that. She suggested, I should examine my conscience, be honest with myself, that I could still serve my God, and her, too!

The invite was open. "Do not think, John, my welcome comes easily. I have a particular leaning to this man of God, being you, and that is the only reason I attempt to gain your attention, knowing full well that you cannot attempt to gain mine in such a mode. But I can assure you, my cathedral will show you an alternative way to heaven and once there, once inside, you will hear all the angels imaginable sing, you will hear the sound of choirs and the music of love and lust. For that is what you desire, you are denied it with Jane. I sympathize with you both, especially you, because Jane has not yet reached the peak of her womanhood, but you, you John, are well and truly there. Do you think I have not noticed? You are not denied it with me. I am open to welcome you, so when your mass is done, remember me, take time out to please consider and I shall be here, in Bradgate, waiting ..."

Of course, I resisted Lady Mary's advances, which continued over the next few days, trying to resist her suggestions to share her heaven, that if God was so kind and understanding, he would be all in favor of our joyful union, unless he, God, was jealous of that heaven she could share with me, that somehow he felt he was being denied.

"Could that be, John?" she flared. "Surely not. You need to come to terms with yourself, share the deep passion hidden inside, the passion as I have already told you, I know you have for Lady Jane."

My mind was in turmoil. How could she be so cruel to bring sweet Lady Jane into it, into the same breath as her seemingly lecherous advances? But I took a deep breath and simply acknowledged her in repeating I was in the Lord's hands, He who understood such things. But the Lady Mary Sidney was like her father, determined. She said she had seen the spark in the expression of the man of cloth. She had seen that time was on her side.

Lady Frances Grey made it known, she was truly grateful for Mary Sidney's time in preparing her daughter for adulthood, but it was rumored that she aspired her daughter may soon become the Queen of England. We were obviously unaware of Northumberland's plan, but that was another story, to do with politics, the death of the King Henry and his son, Edward.

Besides her motive for gaining the favor of Jane's virtuous tutor, as she often addressed me, Lady Mary, I feared, harbored other reasons that would eventually be exposed, if she did not get her way. Although she never confirmed, I felt the suggestion was there. But as promiscuous as she was, she seemed basically a caring and considerate woman of Christian merits. She had done much along with her husband to help the poor, so perhaps I was wrong to judge her so harshly.

She told me she had spoken carefully with Jane, who had now reached puberty, regarding her feelings for the opposite sex and, in fitting with Tudor values, inasmuch that a young lady was ready for marriage when she reached puberty. Jane had been a late starter, but Lady Mary discovered she held strict morals and would not be inclined to stray aimlessly into the arms of a perspective mate. Also, the small boned girl was not exactly the most alluring female of her genre. So, there was much to do by way of nurturing her, showing her the way she should use cosmetics, and by so doing making the most of her best features, her eyes, and her high cheeks,

She was satisfied that the womanizer Seymour, who had been Jane's guardian and rumored to have excited Lady Elizabeth, the future Queen, had never touched her, perhaps relieved that his advances were made more towards the more sexually mature Elizabeth.

"If she cared at all for her tutor," Lady Mary ensued, "other than the admiration she openly confessed for you, if indeed she loved you, she showed no obvious feelings in that direction, maybe knowing the consequences, that if any were directed to you and discovered, you would instantly be dismissed."

But I felt differently. I had known Jane long enough to realize her feelings deep in her soul, the way she had lately looked at me, the tenderness and caring in her eyes, that was love, indeed.

Perhaps that is what Lady Mary wanted, to be rid of this influence in Jane's life, once her education was completed. But for what reason, what would be her advantage? It was obvious she never had any inclination to be more than a passing lover as far as I was concerned. I knew that, she made it abundantly clear, and to achieve that ambition would be a triumph indeed!

I soon realized, she made it her business to be present as much as possible when I was around, although not obviously so, and I assumed her plan was to lure me gently and snap when the opportunity came. She had that much charm and confidence and was to become renowned for her many male acquaintances with whom she had a relentless flair.

In just a few days, Lady Mary had influenced me to a point I became confused. I knew, I had feelings for my pupil, once just plain and simple but now, since she had reached womanhood, much, much more, and a certain passion that had almost come to the fore if it had not been for the Jane's integrity who, no doubt, realized my need for her. No doubt, she was confused, too, but being a woman she was more practical. Remembering recently, when our lips had touched, and we kissed passionately, she managed to resist, and we both agreed just to let the water flow under the bridge and see what would prevail, that God may have reason in having drawn us together that way, and we should trust in him for guidance. Maybe simply a rehearsal for the next life, she knew the law of Karma and we had oft times discussed it.

The astute Mary Sidney had sensed her man of cloth held a secret love, a secret lust that needed to flourish. I was more than fully aware of that. She planted the seed, that in my mind she could be Jane for me and in so giving my passion to her, I would then diffuse the sheer frustration of holding back and not being able to give to the woman I truly loved, adored and cherished. She would come to me in such a way, that I would lose my senses that I would reach that point of no return. She would see to that with no hesitation, and she would have achieved what she wanted, to take a man of the cloth and show him a short cut to heaven. All the time she was whispering these things to me, making me quite aware of her innermost thoughts, and I was like the proverbial lamb waiting for slaughter as it were. For the second time she invited me to join her privately. Then, silently, she lured me onto her den, guided me to her bed, and laid my head down upon her bosom. She continued to gently talk to me, whisper the things I wanted to hear, the things I would really like to hear from Jane. She would be her voice. The love between us would be the absolute love lust and be transmitted soul to soul through the surge of passion.

"Just close your eyes, dear John, and it shall be. Your prayers will be answered and you will be so much more a happier and contented man."

I was slipping as if unconsciously into another world, a world within my secret self, the deep self that harboured sensual desires to complete the love I had for Lady Jane.

"I can feel you have suffered so much in consequence of your love for Jane. It must be sheer frustration for you in being utterly unable to consummate your love, and would your God be right in having you go through that sheer torment? The agony must be awesome."

"I do love her so," I heard myself confessing as I felt the comfort of her breasts against my brow. "I want her so. I have been unable to sleep, to think properly. It has been sheer hell on earth."

She whispered for me to shush as she comforted me. I felt the warmth of her caress slowly fondle me in a way I had never realised could be so wonderful. Looking up, it was not Mary kissing my brow and feeling my passion, it was Jane, wonderful beloved Jane, and then my mind sensed a perfect peace. I wanted her so much.

"I have longed for this moment, my beloved Jane. If only you knew how much. I do love you and need you completely. You are my reason for being, my urge to live and be forever there by your side, for each of us to comfort one another, to arouse and satisfy the passion our love ferments, the flame that burns, to feel that which is truly you inside, to sow the seed of life itself."

I was there, almost there, feeling the heat of our passion grow, the absolute yearning of what a woman can give a man, to her lover. But then, she was not my lover, the senses sparked and I came back down to earth from that place that seemed to be heaven. It was Mary. My mind was playing tricks with me, and all the time I was being adjudged by the Lord, my Father.

As if reading my thoughts, Mary clamed me: "It is God's will for all his children to use the gifts given of him. To withhold such deep feelings is truly a recipe for sin, that which ferments the soul of man to take some God forsaken woman against her will, and in so doing, to make her suffer emotionally for the rest of her life. And if a child is born as result, what of that child to think her or she is the result of a horrible rape. Truly, love is the only course."

"But, Lady Mary, I do not love you. I love Jane!"

"Of course you do, John, but we are adorned to each other. That is obvious, and I would be a pleasing substitute, would I not?"

"Because you taunt me so much and take full advantage of my predicament," I replied in some haste, but then realising I was wrong to cast the blame upon her. It was as much my wanting her, wanting the love she could give, if not by way of mind but through the passion of her being, knowing how deep and fermenting was the pulsing of my soul. But it would still be as substitute for the love of Jane. But how could I explain that?

It was not right. I opened my eyes and saw ahead a man rejected, a man who had forsaken both his God and the young woman he loved, and he would have to live with that.

"This is not the way forward, Lady Mary. We must be sensible and put aside our feelings. Let us take time to reconsider and reflect. Let me pray to God for guidance."

I then discovered how no woman likes to be rejected and Lady Mary was no exception. She exclaimed, very loudly, that she had never been turned down like this.

She shouted, she tore away the bed covers, stamped her feet wildly, and knocked things off the bedroom cupboard. She rendered words unheard of to me, words which shocked and astounded, and I responded, telling her she was a devil woman, she was the most wicked woman I had ever encountered, that in the course of my duties I had met many who had come to me, come for God's forgiveness for the things they had done, so blatant and so nasty. And now this woman was showing her true colors.

But when she calmed, as if to realize that way not the way forward, she claimed she had one more pawn to play. Passion and lust and hate can come together in the most extreme way, and when she stripped, portraying her all to the man standing like a statue before her, when I lavished my eyes upon the full beauty of her charm, her womanhood, it was like a magnet. I was howling with torment, fighting with my conscience to resist the sheer determination of this woman before me and she was howling, too, as if the anger and annoyance had returned. But I was also taking her in my arms, struggling with her, one part of me saying I should let go and leave, the other submitting to her strong persuasion and desire. The glass that had been half empty was also half full, and when we clambered relentlessly onto the thick goose feathered mattress, even God could not stop me. I was at that point of no return. I was an animal, and was still howling out at her. What a wicked woman she was as I took her completely and without inhibition, fired with the energy of passion and all that entailed, thrusting, heaving, feeling the heat of her body, the body I wanted now to explore, every fissure, every part of her femininity, and soon she was thus primed, so utterly ready for me, her fingers clawing the thin skin over my back, drawing me closer to her. I could not hold back now. I had to go all the way until the climax and the heaven came with a burst of reoccurring energy, both of us meeting the surge of our passion until we were still again.

Now we were lovers, the seed sewn, and that was just the start ...

Later, when we had calmed, when we both just laid together, like it was after the storm, she said: "John Aylmer, you have so much to give, all that pent-up and restrained energy now released. For a man who has never made love before, you were absolutely wonderful, and I do feel proud, no matter what you think of me, I do feel proud and honored that I have been your first lover."

For a while I was happy to remain still and silent, feeling calm and at ease, until I came down to earth again, realizing what I had done.

It was as if almost she knew my thoughts. I had to come to terms with myself. Lady Mary was a truly sweet intellectual woman, despite her overriding passion. She was flirtatious to the highest degree.

Her eyes caught mine once again as I lifted my head from her bosom. She touched her lips with her index finger, then placed it on mine, teasing it along my lips sensually, assuring me of her absolute discretion.

"You are alright, John. You don't have to relent. It was the most natural thing in the world you have just done, nay… accomplished with me. You are indeed a wonderful lover and have so much to give, and I hope I have the opportunity to share our heaven together more in the coming days, and then you won't feel so bad. I know, it must have been difficult for you, not being able to release your true sexual desires with the one you love."

"I am unsure, Lady Mary, if God will accept me, now that I have done this deed, that I have done it without love, that it was purely lust of one's carnal misgivings. I am not at all sure if it was right, that it would have been correct if I should have restrained in the faint hope that one day I might have shared my first time with hers, my sweet, sweet Jane."

"But, John, your love was duly shed in her direction. It simply came though me, the spirit of your being, and hers, too. Remember, she must have had similar feelings of guilt perhaps when she slept with my brother, Guildford, whom, my father demands, will marry her."

I was aghast by what Mary had said regarding Jane and Guildford sleeping together. I questioned without words. How that could be?

"Of course, I should not divulge such private matters but my father's plan will include a marriage between Jane and his son Guildford. You will realize all in good time, and I am afraid you must accept. You are merely Jane's tutor and have no hold whatsoever upon her. When my brother visited last week, it was at my father's command, that they both get to know each other."

"But Jane would not have slept with a man she had just met. I know it."

"Well, you have slept with me, John, and we have known each other for only a week. Is that not the same? And the reasons why… Would she not feel equally as frustrated as you because she could not shed her sexual lust that was part of her love? Could it be that like you, her passion was bursting at the seams and had to be released?"

"My God! Jane and Guildford together that way, and both so young. I

115

cannot even begin to think of it, she and he. It does not stand to reason. It is so unlike Jane."

Much later, in my mind, there was the image of Jane telling me how Guildford repulsed her, that the marriage was not consummated, so it was very unlikely she could have slept with him before.

"Sometimes our deep sexual desires change us, bring out the true feelings we need to declare. The passing of time was with Jane as she has reached puberty. It has changed her from girl to woman. You were unable to fulfill that purpose. Come now, it is time for us to return to our heaven and now you will feel more at ease so to do, won't you?"

I did not resist. Somehow, my trust in Jane was diminished and my raw passion was utmost as Mary eased me into our heaven. Now, knowing Jane had relented, that why not me too, or was it a cunning plan by Lady Mary to gain more from the man of the cloth she said she found so irresistible? And could it be that maybe learning about Jane's bedding with Guildford would ease my guilt? Now I was learning to love the games we played in Lady Mary's bedroom. It was like entering into a fascinating new world. Now I was the pupil and my bed partner the very well qualified tutor. She loved to pamper and tease, tantalize and torment, until my senses, the spirit of my being were aflame and I became that mad animal again, taking her in many ways.

"Roar like a lion for me, my man of cloth, be rough and demanding. I want that, I need that. Do what you must with me, share your bread and your wine and confirm me with your passion and all. And you, John Aylmer, you have endowed me with your heaven. My cathedral is aflame with many candles of lust and desire, and I feel the spirit within as you nourish me with your blessing."

Now I could not get enough of her, and she of me. The sheer togetherness, the heat of passion, the sensations of oral delights, the deep kiss that never ended, the feel of the soul, combined with the body, all coming together to ferment our carnal desires, until finally we were expended, exhausted and utterly fulfilled.

But how long could the affair last without word getting to Jane? I still could not believe that Jane had indeed slept with the repugnant Guildford Dudley and envisaged that it was just a scheme on Lady Mary's part. I just did not know. I was confused, yet I did not want dear Jane to discover my affair with the woman who had been guiding her into the ways of womanhood. And just how would Jane feel about her tutor doing something, which she would never, ever dreamed? And what about Holy Father, how would he perceive all this? Such were the thoughts attributed to me who had never before been with a woman. Could I be excused for the torment of the flesh in having to restrain my true will to be with Jane, and to let it escape into the bosom of the illustrious Mary Sidney?

"You will never ever tell Jane, Mary. Please?" I asked her the next day.

She caught me playing my favorite game of bowls with the master of horses, Ned Steer. She seemed to have ignored my whisper as my companion collected the bowls for a new game from the other end of the playing pitch.

"I have been watching. You play your game so well. You intrigue me how you play. Perhaps you could teach me, or better your companion? Introduce me to him and I will ensure our little secret remains just ours."

I did as she asked and realized soon after she had lost interest in me. Her eyes now turned decisively towards the younger man. It soon became obvious to me that our brief affair was at an end, and so I was able to gather my thoughts once more, or so I assumed, with the help of the Lord who knows best.

But later Lady Mary confessed that her assumptions about Jane and Guildford had been proved absolutely wrong and without foundation, because her brother Guildford came bleeding to her, that his forthcoming bride would not share his passion.

Now I felt I would have to bear the cross of the guilt that I had given myself to another, but I could in no way tell her of my weakness. It was not the right time. I would not have wanted to upset her when she had to suffer the torment due to the hunger for power of her family and the Duke of Northumberland.

CHAPTER THIRTEEN

Several weeks later, after John Ulmis had left, Jane approached me. She had been unable to continue her studies because of sickness. She was having "feminine problems," Mrs. Ellen informed and "far in excess of normality" in her opinion.

But her excesses for her wardrobe and expensive trinkets were no longer apparent when she simply came to me, kissed my forehead and apologised.

"I have been a foolish girl, John, and seek your pardon. During my sickness I have had time to think, access my true feelings and values. And, for your information, John Ulmis is quite a gentleman but could never surpass you, my schoolmaster!"

There she was, kneeling in front of me as I sat at my chair, her small hands entwining mine, her gorgeous brown eyes staring wistfully up to me.

"I think, we have both learned from our recent disagreements, Jane. I must accept that you have truly grown into womanhood and Lady Sidney is right, I am not in such exalted a position that gives me precedence over your personal needs."

She gently smiled.

"I would much take your advice than that of Mary Sidney. She is a fair friend but her ways are flaunting, sometimes atrocious. Did you see the way she spoke with John Ulmis? And to my great embarrassment I declare, she is a married woman, too. I perceive, she had better be careful, indeed, and expressed to her my concerns that she should not be so foolhardy. She is but a mere woman who would flaunt her wares as appropriate, enticing any fanciful male into her web, and you, John, being no exception. It was John Ulmis who told me to listen to her advice but not necessarily to take it, that Mary Sidney had the thunder and determination of her father, John Dudley and will seemingly stop at nothing to gain her own ends. She is but temptation as it were, an extraordinarily attractive and beautiful woman who it would be difficult to pretend was not there."

"You were absolutely right about my inexcusable neglect of my studies," she sighed, " and I trust you have already realised this no longer be the case, Sir. I could never be like her and told her so."

I was wholly relieved and despised myself for believing Jane could be so easily persuaded into such temptations as those procured by Lady Sidney. Another lesson learnt from so wise a scholar. She never failed to astound me.

Although I was exceedingly pleased and happy Jane decided to revert back to her true self and put her mind wholly upon her scholastic studies and responsibilities, I felt never the less, guilty that I had failed to give credit to her integrity and bowed silently to her in my mind's eye, for her sheer determination not to be succumbed by the intentions and ways of Lady Sidney. And yet, all of this, all that had happened recently had the effect of compelling me to love her even more and, for my part, I knew I would love her forever.

As if acknowledging my inner thoughts, Lady Sidney came to me before she left for London, whispering in my ear that the young Lady Jane was besotted with her teacher and that is why she declined the charms of young Richard.

If I had unanswered questions in that regard, they had now been confirmed to my relief. It was almost that Lady Sidney had conceded and yet I continued to feel this very devious lady was planning something else

"But you should be very careful, my esteemed John Aylmer, not to take too much upon yourself, for there are those who would destroy you, given the opportunity. The slightest whisper, if there was something there between you and Lady Jane, would be your end."

The next day, I was approached again by the formidable Lady Sidney. I thought she was going to wish me farewell but she said she had decided to wait until her father, the Duke of Northumberland, had visited, that she had not seen him for some duration and there were a few things she felt he needed to know.

Whether or not she was attempting to unnerve me, I was not quite sure, except the way she looked. I suspected, there was something she was about to discuss with me. She looked stern and forbidding and prompted me to follow her into the garden.

"Away from certain ears," she whispered.

She had noticed how Jane came to me and was blaming me in not discouraging the "headstrong girl" and what she said next could only have come from a very perplexed woman indeed, that I had drawn Jane away from young Richard for my own ends because I was jealous and the rest of it. That I should find someone my own age, or was it that I preferred them young and untouched, that maybe I could not cope with a worldly woman, but how would I know if I had never had one?

"You know, that is not true and with respect, Lady Sidney."

"But there is unrest in your soul, Dr. Aylmer, is there not? I can see that, being a woman of my experience, you know!

Men of the cloth, like you, forever amaze me. There you are, normal red-blooded males by all accounts, yet you resist the satisfaction of soothing your soul with the opposite sex, lest it be Jane because to ease your conscience. She would be pure and clean, unlike me who did crave your attention and you chose only to ignore my favors and perplex me thus. Perhaps, John Aylmer, I understand you more than you may ever think because maybe, just maybe, I was looking for someone untouched, too. You were, were you not? A virgin, I mean. Or is there some dark secret that is harbored in your dark soul? I doubt it. I doubt that very much because everything for you must be absolutely right and proper and I should think your mind is playing bowls with your heart because of how you would dearly like to have Jane, for your very own, forever. But foolish thinking, John, and you know it. So why not come to me, get the dregs of longing out of your being? I did see to that in more ways than one, you could count on that, John Aylmer."

Of course, she was aware of the untenable circumstances regarding Jane and I. I believe it was another ploy to prompt me to take up her offer, that we could be indiscriminately ruthless and irresponsible as she was promiscuous. And now the mention of her father, and what she thought he had better know of. What then was she insinuating and just how much damage she could do to my reputation and me? Yes, the way she was interpreting, but more so for Jane, she did not deserve that and I didn't want to be the cause.

In some ways I could understand her thinking, of course, but she had grossly misjudged me. During the next few days, and with the continued luring of this remarkable woman, the thought did enter my mind that perhaps she was right, that I should please her desires, intending to steer myself away from any further temptation with Jane and also to veer Lady Sidney from certain statements concerning Jane and I. I could not bear that, for Jane to be embarrassed in such a way. Rumors grow and I was now in a very delicate situation. It could work against me but God would know the truth, no matter how prudent Lady Sidney promised to be but more importantly, he would know my circumstances, too.

I fervently remembered what Lady Sidney had said and speculated about the outcome. Nothing regarding the termination of my scholastic duties as tutor to Jane and her sisters was mentioned by the duchess, and she showed no distaste towards me other than the occasional remarks about the gambling dispute, which was still unresolved.

Yet, surely, the duchess was very aware of Lady Sidney's reason for frequently attending Bradgate of late, but I tactfully made no enquiry.

Jane's recent excessive display of expensive jewellery was noticeably absent when she attended class. She wore only her pendant and a gold cross given to her by Katharine Parr. Only in the company of distinguished visitors did she continue to wear lustrous accessories but more in keeping with her mother's insistence.

During the end of the year, the presence of the Duke of Northumberland was felt at Bradgate. If only we had known the true reason for his call upon the duke and duchess at that time. If only Jane had known. She was about to become the main pawn in Northumberland's plan to ensure the next monarch of England would be truly a Protestant.

The occasion was perhaps bigger than anything that had been laid on at Bradgate. The tables were full to capacity and the distinguished guests numbered 150 or more. Jane discussed with me the forthcoming event a few days before. I asked why Bradgate was so privileged to host the great duke himself.

"I do not know the full facts, Dr. Aylmer, and yet I know the reason for his visit, given with such short notice, involves the King and I. I am not particularly drawn to the duke whom I have already met in London. He is a ghastly man with very high opinions of himself. But for some unearthly reason my parents are excessively rejoicing because he chose to visit Bradgate."

"Perhaps he plans to make an arrangement for marriage?" I wondered aloud.

"You mean the King and I," she scoffed. "I think not. If the late Lord Admiral could not manage it I doubt that even Northumberland could

"Of course, I would be prepared so to do for the crown of England, if I had a choice that is, but the King is betrothed to his beautiful Elisabeth de Valois. But I fret not. After all she is French and I have French blood on mother's side."

"But is there a problem relating to her faith, which is not in keeping with the protestant faith of our King?" I asked Jane freely.

"Knowing what sort of man is Northumberland, that could be overcome if his persuasion saw fit. He is a hypocrite. I know it. He would change his faith to suit the occasion, so it would not be hard for him to presume it would be the same for Elisabeth."

"Then we must wait and learn," I ventured. But I was quick to correct my statement: "Rather, you must learn, Lady Jane. Please do accept apology for my impertinence."

"John Aylmer," she smiled openly, "you are my close friend and I cherish your thoughts, which I know are in my interest. You can never be impertinent as far as I am concerned. You will certainly be the first to know of this, you have my heartfelt word."

She kissed me lightly upon the brow and my hands neatly cupped her soft cheeks before hurriedly she left the study. This show of light affection was becoming normal after each parting. But this time, it was not just the kiss, it was something more, the way she clutched my shoulders as she reached for my brow and the way she hurried off, but not before her lips sought mine in a frenzied turbulence.

"If you have any doubts whatsoever, John, I did not bed Richard." She had told me what I already knew, of course, but coming from her sweet lips meant everything.

"But all experiences are valuable," Jane whispered looking thoughtful. "And I have to be truthful and admit, yes, the handsome young man was charmed with a pleasing disposition and I was moved by him. But I knew deep in my heart it was not enough to allow myself to be coerced into a union which, because my heart and my mind were directed to another, would have caused me to be very uneasy and guilty afterwards.

"John, you see, I have discovered a little more of myself, my developing maturity as Lady Sidney would have it, and I feel fervently I should save myself for something much more meaningful and special to me."

Then she was gone, scurrying away. We were both falling deeply in love and I could not prevent that. It was something that had been developing for a few months, neither of us realizing, because we had known each other for so long on a tutor, student relationship, and her changing from girl to woman, almost complete now, and the changing love, too.

Yet we both realized our impossible dream, like a veritable spirit within us both, which would forever join us, in spirit if not in body, we could cope with that, couldn't we? The question in my mind unanswered.

Now, with the impending Northumberland's visitation and whatever the Duke had in mind, I hoped, for selfish reasons, it would not disrupt our kinship.

I knew at that moment what Roger Ascham meant. That there was something about the relationship between Jane and me. It was deeper than I had envisaged. She had unwittingly displayed it and my reaction was instinctively responsive. She did love me as I loved her. I know that to be true.

In the evening Dr. Haddon joined me in my study. It was our habit to meet frequently to discuss the progress of the children's education and all things that involved our presence at Bradgate. It was clear he was still not happy about the fact that the duchess had not ventured to advise him further since our meeting with her some two months earlier, and he was deeply upset about this. He advised that on several occasions he had mentioned it to the duchess, but she simply responded with an "all will be well", or "I am too busy now, Dr. Haddon" which was just not good enough.

"Do you feel the practice still continues, Dr. Haddon?" I enquired. "I have not seen anything that suggests it does. Certainly the members of the household have responded well. They respect their jobs too much."

"As I speak, John, I am aware the Duke of Northumberland himself joins his hosts in the games room and I distinctly heard him order his man to fetch, from his room, a set of playing cards fit for a king, that he felt lucky and presumed his hosts pockets were substantially filled." He paused, looking distraught.

"This behaviour is in contempt of everything we stand for," Dr. Haddon continued. "I will surely mention this in my forthcoming sermon and show our employers that, above all, the word of the Lord should, at all times, be honoured and respected."

I looked silently at him. He was an angry man but I felt wary to support such action that may warrant bad tidings. He was not indispensable. New preachers were coming to the fore and, if the duke and the duchess were stifled of their pleasures in this way, his position could be in jeopardy.

"That is not the end of it, John. You have heard the news regarding the Lady Jane, of course?"

122

My ears immediately pricked up. "What news is this, Dr. Haddon?"

"Well, I am sure most of us would have liked the Lady to marry the King himself. We would have been delighted and honoured to witness such a happy event. But, there you are, the King is betrothed to the French girl, Elisabeth, and we all know the problems that could emerge if she were not willing to transfer her faith. But for the Lady to marry the fool Guildford is more than even my ageing heart can stand."

"Lord Dudley is to marry Lady Jane?" I gasped.

Dr. Haddon nodded wistfully. That is why the Duke of Northumberland felt it necessary to visit this house. And I immediately searched my mind for the reasoning behind the Duke's inclination. For it was surely his idea for such a marriage to take place and he had obviously convinced his hosts that this should be so. Not as if they would have needed to be persuaded in that direction, such a marriage would mark well their place in the social order. And then something else occurred to me. If Lady Jane were likely to attain the crown, then Northumberland's son would be the Prince Consort. Of course, everything would become abundantly clear in the course of a short period of time.

But what of Lady Jane? How will she succumb to all of this? For succumb she must. The Duke of Northumberland was the most powerful man in the land. For whatever reason the Lady Jane was to marry Lord Dudley, it would be agreed, without question, that the arrangements were for the best. Poor Jane was already being taken by the snarl of Northumberland's devise but she could not have known of the trap, which was to beset her.

"Like me, you seem astounded?" Dr. Haddon asked. I stammered for a moment having been submerged in my thoughts.

"We can only pray that it will bring our Lady happiness," I optimised.

But I think we both knew the consequences. Dr. Haddon, who was closer to politics than I, possibly knew better.

"Well, my boy. Do listen to my sermon on Sunday. If we don't act now our position here will be hopeless. The fact that Lady Jane may be the next Queen has convinced me that such action should immediately be taken. It should be particularly stimulating because I have been advised that the great Duke himself will be in the distinguished congregation."

Dr. Haddon meant business and I was sceptical of the consequences. But my heart was with his and so my support. My mind was akin to the present feelings of Lady Jane. It was late when Dr. Haddon left my company. I endeavoured to sleep but it was difficult. I wondered if Jane was sleeping. I longed for the morning to come when I would see Jane. At least then I would be able to access her true feelings and offer her some comfort.

But she was not present. Lady Katharine came and advised me her elder sister was terribly sick and would not be attending her class. "Mrs. Ellen is in attendance and assures that my sister will soon recover."

"Thank you, Lady Katharine. Well, then perhaps it will be better if we first complete your daily duties in place of your sister."

I needed to occupy my mind in the pursuits of Lady Katharine's studies, whom I usually saw later in the day, and then hopefully I would later have the opportunity to see Jane.

"That is what mother suggested, Dr. Aylmer. She is not happy with my sister because she thinks Jane is play-acting. But Jane is sickened, I know it. I have never seen her like that time before and mother should know that. Poor Jane. I do hope Mrs. Ellen is right and she is soon better."

I quietly sympathised with Lady Katharine's feelings. She was a twelve-year-old caring young lady now. She was different from her elder sister and I felt that one of Jane's faults was that she seemed not to give Katharine much of her time. Perhaps this was unintentional, most of Jane's time and energy being engaged on her abundant desire to study. But Katharine seemed not bothered. She was a good girl, the most attractive of the three sisters. She was very aware of her younger sister, Mary, who was born with a humped back and wished a fairy would come and make it straight.

Again, Jane did not show any obvious affection for Mary and I was concerned about this. I hoped I could put this to rights with some tactical guidance, advise Jane that it was fine to follow her studies but it would be God's wish that she put aside a small amount of her time for her family as well as herself. Her lack of interest in anything external was also worrying. She had no desire to be advised of worldly affairs unless they involved the lives of her correspondents. In fact, as she approached her fifteenth birthday she had become almost a recluse, hiding herself away within the walls of her private apartments, as long as she could continue to correspond with her favourite clerics and study the works of the great philosophers she seem contented.

A future Queen would need friends by the score. She would need the utmost support from her people, their loyalty, too. She had not the inclination or desire to meet the people, at least to give them an insight of her. She was just a name and, furthermore, a name connected with the duke they detested, Northumberland.

Later she apologised profusely for missing her morning lesson. It was so unlike Jane to be absent. I assumed her sickness was brought about because of the new pressures being put upon her but she would not excuse herself. She vowed to work extra hard to make up for her inexcusable negligence and confirmed it would never happen again. That she must be strong. She must not languor in the self-pity that had almost tarnished her soul. "The Lord is strong and we must all follow His example if we aim to be true followers."

It seemed every day I was confronted with growing concerns regarding the future for my Lady and I felt it my responsibility to guide her auspiciously. But she seemed unaware of the importance of this issue and announced metaphorically she would never be privileged to be a Queen unless

124

she married Edward, and, since he had eyes only for his beautiful French princess, there was no likelihood of her wearing the crown. She had not the slightest notion that she could become Queen via another route.

"Apart from which, as you well know, I am now promised to Lord Dudley and am told I must, in consideration of the realm, be contented with my lot. Oh! To be a simple girl, to choose one's husband at will."

She looked up at me, those eyes sparkling the way they always did when she was going to pay me a compliment or give thanks for the way I 'teacheth.'

She also grinned mischievously:

"I would choose you, John Aylmer, so that you could teacheth me for the rest of my living days, that we relish in the work of Plato and the rest of those wonderful, exceptional scholars who take care to discuss the real meaning of life. And today, I have a letter from Bullinger who informs me of the scoundrel Copernicus who, you may have heard, has the audacity to suggest that our planet rotates around the sun. John Calvin, says Bullinger, has condemned him for daring to print such utter rubbish, which contradicts the teachings of the Bible. The man is a coward, too. He waits until his passing before he allows his book to be published. Bullinger goes on to say that now the ministers of God are left to restore the faith in all Christian belief and put right the damage Copernicus has done."

This energetic girl was more concerned with her correspondence and her deep faith than her own forthcoming marriage and what that might mean. Her wish that she would rather marry me did not go unnoticed, although I was not naive enough to believe she meant it in connotation to a gesture of love, more that she recognised that we were always at one scholastically and, in that vein, she could forever approve of my company.

"Copernicus was born a simple Polish peasant, Jane, and then became a churchman. I would doubt that the planet on which we live, so full with life and energy and the planet of Jesus' birth, could be anything than the centre of the Universe. But the debate apparently continues and it is surely dangerous to condone such erratic assumptions, but that is the way philosophy has led us. If his theory is proved valued I suspect that there is an explanation in the Bible."

"There is always so much to learn, John Aylmer. How can one find the time to live and learn? After dusk I spend time looking through my windows searching the skies, watching those stars which move around us. But one can never see them actually move, unlike the moon, especially when full. Watch it slowly disappear as it floats past the windowpane. There is so much we do not know, so much we have to learn. I am quite happy just to do so for the rest of my life, with someone of like mind as yourself. I am not at all bothered with marriage or children, least becoming a royal personage. I wish simply to devote all my time to the study of everything God has provided and, truly, I believe it is God's intention that I do so. Otherwise, why would He have given me the deep satisfying desire to learn? He is truly so wonderful, John, and I especially thank you for your teachings of our Lord."

We sat there, in the study, in perfect unison. Here was the delightful girl whom I wanted to hold so close. I almost wavered, turning to her, catching the sparkle of life in those startling eyes, almost as if they were telling me to hold her, to cherish her being, then questioning why I did not. Then her whisper broke the silence of our togetherness.

"I think I will love you for the rest of my life, John Aylmer. Please hold me. Just hold me. That it is God who holds me, who cherishes me, who guides me to Him."

Her lips came up and met mine and I simply could not resist. I was a man of God but I was also just a man and the feel, the sweet touch of the wonderful Lady Jane engulfed my very soul. Our lips moved and moulded in unison, immediately taking in those sensuous wonderful feelings a man cherishes in the woman he loves.

I whispered softly, so softly into her ear, words, which simply flowed …

"This mountain high up in the sky, just a speck from down under in the mind's eye. I can cover the speck with my little finger, but it is always there like the love I feel for you, like the way you make me feel through and through. Remove the finger and the speck reappears, move on and it grows throughout the year like our love, and all we have learned about each other.

"One day we will reach its peak, standing so high up there in the clouds, like our love so proud and strong, the way we like to express the way that we belong, wanting you all day and night long, feeling the warmth that is in your heart, looking to a new day, a new year, a new start."

Then it was over. Jane backed away, murmured how enthralling that was.

For me it was the most intimate thing that ever had happened to me. But I was frustrated that my God should allow me to become besotted in Jane is such a way that could never be made complete in His eyes. It was almost as if He was testing me to the ultimate. I was truly wrong to blame the Lord for what I did, but what had just happened, for me, and I know for Jane, was a true display of our deep love for each other, come but may. Of course we both knew our love could not be ripened to make us complete forever. But, nevertheless, there was that something we had both discussed, even the way our eyes met and we just looked at each other for long periods of time, enhancing and realising our understanding of our mutual Karma, that our feelings were meant to start in this life, to be completed in the next, when there would be nothing to deter us and there would be no fear about all the things that could happen if we openly declared our love for each other.

I came to the conclusion that this was just another of the Lord's mysterious ways that merely as humans we can never hope to understand. We can only surmise and trust in the Lord that we are doing our very best to follow the code of conduct according to His code.

Smiling, she rose and whispered that she would look forward to seeing me tomorrow. She knew love but she was still naive regarding the consequences.

It seemed all my concerns with regard to her blatant unsociability were put into the background. Her shortcomings, if she were to be Queen, somehow seemed unimportant. Even Dr. Haddon had made no further comment. She was a unique girl, so taken up in her own obsessions. She had no time or energy for social events. She made that quite clear when she was still forced to go out occasionally with her parents. Nothing would change that. Dr. Haddon and I agreed on that. We trusted that when the time came our Lord would make the right adjustments that she might win popularity in every quarter.

Dr. Haddon did not have the opportunity to deliver the sermon he intended, which, given the new tensions at Bradgate, were best put aside. He suffered what the resident physician, Dr. Huckley, described as sporadic heart murmuring and was ordered to rest a few weeks. Those vividly remembered final days at Bradgate passed only too quickly.

CHAPTER FOURTEEN

July 9, 1553 brought ghastly news that the King was dead. Even though we knew the young Edward has been critically sick there had been news of late that there had been an improvement in his health, and it was generally assumed that he had fully recovered. Jane was heartbroken and in tears. The sad news was brought to her by her sister-in-law, Mary Sidney. She had been recovering in bed from her continued spasmodic health problems at Chelsea at this time and I was present following Jane's invitation.

I knew she had been close to Edward and he was very dear to her and assumed the tragic news would come as a great shock to her. Yet, it was as if she expected the worst would happen. "That was how it had to be," she groaned bleakly. "I have known and dreamed it lately. It was as if it had already happened. My premonitions have been very strong!"

We later discovered that she was right. The King had died three days earlier and Northumberland chose not to announce his death immediately because it would not have fitted into his scheme.

Immediately after Mary Sidney informed Jane of the sad news, she proclaimed that Jane was summoned to Syon House and should immediately return with her upon the barge, which had brought her along the Thames to Chelsea Palace.

"But I cannot come today," Jane cried. "I am but so poorly I can hardly stand."

Mrs. Ellen stood close by Jane and ventured to support her statement:

"As the Lady's nurse, Madam, I would prefer she delay any activity for at least two days on the advice given by her physician, especially taking into consideration the tragic news you have brought her."

It was true and her paleness portrayed her bad health. It would have been better that she remained in bed until her sickness had cleared. But Lady Sidney was adamant. Ignoring Mrs. Ellen, she looked directly at Jane and spoke firmly to her:

"You can take care to dress warmly, but the weather is fair and not too cold. The freshness of the air may be beneficial to you. You look as though you could do with some sunshine. Your face is so very white."

Then she turned to Mrs. Ellen.

"Your kindness to the Lady is admirable," she complimented.

Then, she continued, turning to me:

"You, Dr. Aylmer, her tutor, who seems never too far away, comforts her, too. But we must not molly coddle when affairs of state are urgently to hand. Lady Jane's presence at Syon is commanded at once."

Eventually Lady Sidney persuaded Jane to come on the advice that her presence at Syon House would be seen as a mark of great respect for the poor late King.

Mrs. Ellen helped Jane to dress suitably for this auspicious occasion. She wore her long black dress, which gave her the appearance of being even thinner than she was. Her hair, because of her sickness, did not compliment her form yet, in her grace, she showed good spirit in making the best of what she could muster at short notice.

Jane requested that I accompany her and Mrs. Ellen and we both assisted her onto the waiting barge. I remember that it was truly a beautiful day with a very gentle breeze wafting down the river. Jane looked so tiny. She sat between her sister-in-law and Mrs. Ellen, looking upwards and slowly inhaling the afternoon air.

Upon our arrival at Syon House I watched Jane carefully climb the steps leading from the riverbank up to the entrance. In the great hall there, Jane was outwardly astonished to see her parents accompanied by her husband and his mother and a host of high-ranking dignitaries, some, unknown to her, stood in line like statues, but she did recognise the Lord Mayor of London whom she remembered visiting her parents at Bradgate. He and others waiting to be introduced, were the Marquis of Northampton, the Earls of Arundel, Huntington and Pembroke and the Earl of Shrewsbury. Dismayed why they all showed excessive courtesy and respect she called to her father-in-law, the Duke of Northumberland, who explained he was there in his capacity of President of the Council and everything would soon become evident.

Each of the distinguished gathering greeted her with an overwhelming pleasantness and, to her obvious embarrassment, proceeded to curtsy and bow before her in a manner to which, one could readily observe, she was not accustomed.

Her father-in-law responded immediately to her second bewildered call to which he expressed, so that all may hear, the sad news of the King's death had come as a shock to everybody.

Then he continued:

"Everyone has good reason to rejoice, least our new Queen who knew the King so well, in the virtuous life he had led and the good death he had died. We should take heed and comfort that at the end of his life he had taken such good care of his kingdom, that he made provision to ensure his successor may continue to uphold the responsible position in like manner."

The tall richly bearded man graciously led Jane to a raised platform, beckoned her to climb the three steps and be seated upon a splendid looking wooden high-backed chair, which was richly carved to display the royal sceptre and the coat of arms.

I watched her comply with his grace's wishes as she awkwardly placed herself down, held the arms to pull herself properly onto it but leaving her feet a good six inches above the floor. Obviously, the circumstance was envisaged because an attender quickly placed a small wooden box underneath her feet, so as not to deplete her elegance.

But she was not condescending. "The Lady Mary is the rightful heir," she lamented and there was a dreadful hush amongst all the dignitaries present.

She looked so small for one to be Queen but her strong concern regarding her qualification was obvious. She then continued: "That the laws of the kingdom, and natural right standing for the King's sister, Mary Tudor, she would beware of burdening her weak conscience with a yoke which did not belong to them, that she understood the infamy of those who had permitted to violation of right to gain a sceptre, that it were to mock God."

She paused and surveyed the gathering there. "Besides," she declared, " I am not so young, not so little read in the guiles of fortune, as to suffer myself to be taken by them."

The Duke was now looking up to Jane and explained how the late King had taken that great care of his kingdom in so much that he announced the terms of 'His Majesty's Devise,' how he had so wisely and profoundly come to the decision that neither of his sisters, Mary or Elizabeth, was worthy to succeed him and, after great thought and consideration and talking to the Lord Himself through prayer, he had nominated his cousin Jane to follow him, to take forth this great realm which was rightfully hers.

"Then you would have it," Jane followed, her cheeks glistening with tears, "that I follow the misfortunes of Catherine of Aragon and Ann Boleyn when they wore the crown. Do you really love me so little you would seek to add my blood to theirs?"

In remorse she stood up and then kneeled there in front of those gathered to pray to her God for guidance, and upon receiving no sign of disapproval from God and receiving the constant reassurance that it was right and correct from the noblest voices of the land, she had no option other than to accept the crown.

It was all like an unwanted dream Jane told me afterwards:

"Yet it was not so much of a surprise as disbelief. That my mother-in-law had told some of her high ranking guests that her new daughter by marriage would be Queen one day, too. I scorned her for untruthfully boasting. I even perceived that my hasty marriage to Guildford was part of Northumberland's plan but put the notion aside as preposterous."

I watched Jane freeze and shudder on the spot, noting equivocally she could not bring herself to either believe or accept the news. One could see she was still surprised and embarrassed when Northumberland turned to the gathering, his right hand held high, then turning back to Jane as he clearly and distinctly announced:

"Behold, the Queen."

Everybody, including the Duke, knelt before her.

Jane collapsed and sobbed bitterly, pronouncing she was not fit to be Queen and she had not the right to be so, that Mary Tudor was the rightful heir to the throne and she would be as an impostor.

But the Lords of the Council solemnly swore to shed their blood in defence of her right. She was dominantly persuaded by Northumberland to accept her throne with dignity and honour in that it was what the King desired, that is what the Lord desired and that is what was best for her kingdom.

I saw her response. It was if a sudden change had come upon her. She wiped the tears away with a handkerchief and pressed her hands together, asking everybody to join her in prayer, that, if to succeed to the throne was her absolute right, nay! Her duty to England, God would help her govern the realm to His glory.

The following day Queen Jane was received into the Tower for her coronation and their were a great number of lords and nobles following behind, sworn in to obey their new Queen. She looked glorious in a green and white bodice and kirtle. The duchess of Suffolk, her mother, bore her trains with many ladies and there was a firing of guns such had not often been seen between four and five o'clock. By six o'clock on the same day came the proclamation of Queen Jane, with two heralds and a trumpet blowing, declaring that Lady Mary was unlawfully begotten, and so went through Cheapside to Fleet Street proclaiming Queen Jane. Northumberland gave strict instructions for immediate denunciation of anyone who dared display contempt of the new Queen and there was a young man taken at the time for speaking certain words about Queen Mary, that she had the true title. His punishment with all watching was for both his ears to be cut off and on the same day the young man's master, dwelling at St John's Head, and another master, who was a gun maker, were drowned for similar offences.

The 12th July brought by night to the Tower three carts full of ordinance such as guns and small bows, bills, spears, Moorish pikes, armour, arrows, gunpowder and stakes, money, and tents. Later followed a great number of men at arms for a great army near Cambridge and two days later the Duke of Northumberland, his son, Robert, with various lords and knights went with him and they were accompanied by more men and gunners, too, with many men of the guard towards the place where Lady Mary stayed, to destroy her grace. But the army had not the heart and turned against the Duke. The battle failed and Lady Mary prepared to make her way to London to take the crown, which she insisted was rightfully hers, and not for that sprat of a girl who had not the makings to serve such a great country.

"Queen Jane indeed!" she was heard to have exclaimed angrily raising her arms in defiance that as the eldest daughter of the great Henry she could only be the rightful contender to the throne. That Jane's blood, although royal, given from her mother's side, her weak and stupid father was apt of the right content and so her blood was diluted as would be her hold of the throne of such a great country. She could never qualify to hold the keys to the Kingdom.

Ironic that later Robert Dudley openly admitted to Queen Mary, that he was a fool blinded with ambition to join his father in a hopeless situation as to arrest a woman so respected and admired by the people. This statement along with his conversion to Catholicism and his ability to charm any woman, least Queen Elizabeth in later years, probably gained his pardon from execution.

He had also declared he wanted to keep Lady Jane safely out of the plots his father had concocted but could not do so. Of course, the contents of Northumberland's note to Jane's father implied the King would soon die but she did not know that the devious duke would have conspired and persuaded the boy King to illegally alter the terms of succession, to make certain the Protestant Jane would follow his reign. The legal document, drawn up during the reign of Henry VIII , denoting his children would be heirs to the throne, was fixed in her mind. She later told me she would not have known the reasons Northumberland put forward to the boy King that both Mary and Elizabeth were illegitimate, that Mary was a devout Catholic, which would mean an end to the protestant church and so forth.

By the same ends, to ensure his status would be assured thus exalted if his son were King by marriage to Jane, he used the document, signed by the late King, to assure and persuade Lady Jane that it was perfectly in order. I know that she was not entirely convinced and her doubts were verified nine days later. Henry VIII's 1554 Act of Succession was still in the statute book. Edward's alterations were not put through the proper channels and were thus null and void.

It was hard enough for me and dreadful for Jane that her parents, influenced by Northumberland, forced her to marry Guildford Dudley only weeks before. That she cared not for her 'unpleasant husband' and cared much less about wearing the crown for which she was persuaded to take a fitting.

But when the time came and she was Queen she urged me to stay, speculating that she would always need my advice on matters of scholarship and religion. She could correspond with me, yes, as with others she respected, all great scholars and writers like my friend Roger Ascham who was Princess Elizabeth's favourite tutor as well as an intrepid humanist, a subject I was later to ensue. A charming and graceful man who, perhaps was just as respected and liked by the Princess Elizabeth than another mentioned, for, as much as he taught the Princess about scholastics, she was equally the tutor in subjects unknown to him as later I would discover.

But Jane needed more than ever to pray with me in the Chapel and she was still able and keen to learn from me. At least I would be able to speak with her without interruption in the solitude of the Chapel there as we had oft times spoken in her childhood in the chapel of Bradgate House.

I was naturally delighted that the new Queen wanted me to stay in residence and immediately changed my plans. It was an honour and, for very selfish reasons, a relief that I would still see sweet Jane.

Very soon, too, I discovered all my sleepless nights had been in vain. She told me of her silent prayers to the Lord that had excused her the torment of a physical relationship with Guildford, that she needed to be in love with the person she must share in body and soul, that, otherwise she could well do without. She grew to like Guildford Dudley, but not in such a way that she was physically attracted to him.

"These were my prayers, John."

She turned and glanced as if knowingly into my eyes as if she was fully aware of my recent torment. Then her eyes softened and she smiled, as if to announce that my worries were over. It seemed she was saying to me that she could be with no other man, except the man now in her presence, if that were possible. But she must have noticed my puzzled expression:

"Do not be alarmed, John. Guildford has other callings. He is not interested in women. He simply married me because that is what his father wanted."

My immediate response was an overwhelming sense of relief. I knew the man Guildford had effeminate mannerisms but had never envisaged him that way. For Jane I felt both pity and joy and when I hesitated to find words she gesticulated by placing two fingers to her closed lips and, again, those sparkling brown eyes looked into mine, were they perchance telling me instinctively that she understood completely my feelings. Her small but prettily shaped form, those arched eyebrows, a little darker than her red hair much adorned her graceful gentle movements. Then she simply dropped her right hand and found mine, rested on the arm of my chair beside her. I felt her touch on the back of my hand and I felt overwhelming warmth radiating into my soul. I envisaged this was how it was to be, nothing more and nothing less. We both must honour the majesty of her position and direct all our passion into the pursuits of her scholastic ambitions and pray that the rightful heir to the throne, either Mary or Elizabeth would soon replace her as Queen and that the passage to that end would come without bloodshed. She was just sixteen but was endowed with the maturity of some women twice her age. Indeed, the fact that I was twice her age did lately enhance our close relationship.

The next two days were to be difficult for Jane. I was present when she announced to her parents and the Duke and Duchess of Northumberland that she refused to make Guildford King of England. She already knew it was highly unlikely that Parliament would want it too. She was now in control and able to make her own decisions in Court and when they asked why, I heard her quietly say: "Who would be ruled by an effeminate King", and when requested to speak up, she had no need because one of her courtiers who had heard, implied with roars of laughter, that England would be ruled by two Queens? The silence that followed indicated that Northumberland and his gathering were unaware of Guildford's failure to consummate the marriage. He was obviously reluctant for the news to spread and Jane, in her anger, was determined that no more would she to be bullied into decisions. A furious row ensued. The Duchess of Northumberland was almost hysterical but Jane was adamant. "If the crown belongs to me, I will be glad to make my husband, the Earl Dudley, a Duke, but I will never consent to make him King."

The new Queen would do nothing unconstitutional and as the duchess continued to rave, Jane dominantly repeated her promise. Northumberland had quiet words with the Queen. With her approval, given that he accepted the decision regarding Guildford, he ruled that his son's sexual preferences should never again be mentioned in Court or out of it. He promptly walked out of the assembly with his retinue announcing that he must immediately find Mary Tudor, that if this got out she, who would have it that she is entitled to the crown, would have a case indeed. He would be the laughing stock and they would all end up on the scaffold, as would everybody in the assembly.

I later discovered Northumberland's conclusions that, after the scandalous news was confirmed by his son when a lengthy delicate conversation ensued, Jane would not last a year as Queen and all his ambitions for Guildford were thus destroyed, because she refused to make Guildford King and following her crucifying announcement concerning his son's "depravity".

Northumberland urged that "Mary must be put in irons and such scandalous whispers would be considered an act of treason. Jane will not suffice as Queen of England so we must go for Elizabeth. The Catholic, Mary Tudor, has no place here".

I talked to Jane whom I expected to be distressed but she qualified her actions saying she knew quite well now that if Mary became the next Queen, she, along with Northumberland, would be tried for treason. I was concerned that it was not in her best interest to incriminate her husband. She had no need. Her position as Queen qualified her refusal to share the crown with Guildford and even the most powerful man in the government could not change that. But her naiveté, her honesty, and her determination to exercise her new authority to the full, overshadowed her common sense. She had inevitably stirred the hornet's nest.

"But it is right, John. I want everything to be out in the open. I am sickened by the dishonesty and the secrets I have been forced to endure. That I have, by Northumberland's devious desires and lust for power, unwillingly been planted in this precarious position. It will be my intention to create a more worthy monarchy and government for my people, that which they have never known before".

"And what will happen to those who deny you?" I enquired with concern. "Will you punish them by taking their lives? How do you propose to quieten those who, by their very nature, will jostle for power and attempt to gain your favour by devious ways, only to betray you when their own selfish needs are satisfied?"

"I will simply ask for our Lord's guidance, John" she graciously replied and continued: "Guildford's mother has already had the audacity to instruct her son not to further come to my bed. She truly believes that this will suffice as punishment for my unworthy accusation of Guildford. She protested that every mother knows her son and she knew Guildford was a normal man. But I submitted that there are some things a wife knows more by deed of sharing a bed. I know very well I have embarrassed Guildford and I should imagine the last thing he would want to do is share my bed. But I advised them both that to a Queen her monarchy must come before everything, least one's own desires. That Guildford, the Queen's husband must be at her side, even if he did not share her bed."

Perhaps Jane had all the good virtues to make a good Queen but she needed much more. I was keenly aware of her shortcomings. It was as if I knew by instinct that her monarchy could not last.

But if Elizabeth ruled, Jane's future would look better because of their early kinship and the love they shared for Katharine Parr who treated them both with the care and attention of a mother. Elizabeth would surely not forget that. If only it could have happened like that, things could have been so different.

CHAPTER FIFTEEN

By the 18th July, 1553 the devious Northumberland plans were in jeopardy. During the short time I spent in Queen Jane's Court, this became very apparent and my concerns grew. At the time none of us were aware that he had concealed the death of the young King Edward for three days, that he had sent a letter to Mary Tudor after Edward's death advising her that her brother was seriously ill and had asked for her presence at his bedside, apparently to make an easy capture and dispose of her before she was able to lay claim to the throne.

I often wonder how things would have been if Mary had not received word of the duke's real intention as she hastily made way for London praying she would reach her brother in good time. But instead she turned and fled to her residence at Newhall where she gathered much support. Northumberland's response to lead an army in an attempt to capture her was doomed to failure.

In the meantime Jane's health had suffered immensely. She was constantly suffering from diarrhoea and sickness. She had always been prone to a nervous debility, which, I believe, was brought on by her parents' constant emotional and physical abuse during her days at Bradgate. But now in her palace in the Tower her rank had been extended above that of her father who was now custodian there. Yet, despite his atrocious treatment of her in the past, she still respected him foremost as her father.

She summoned me to her bedchamber shortly after having reluctantly agreed to be Queen. I really think she thought she was going to die but the attending physician assured her it was just a temporary disorder.

Mrs. Ellen drew me up a seat beside the Queen's bed and she looked so tiny wrapped in huge blankets, her head resting in a nest of white cloth pillows. But she managed a smile when she saw me:

"You are my tonic, John Aylmer. I thinketh no need for the physician's terrible concoctions if you are here at my bedside."

She looked pale white but her complexion was generally so. Mrs. Ellen commented happily that this morning she had noticed a glow in Her Majesty's cheeks.

I took heed that Jane was now Queen and remembered my etiquette. I stood beside the chair, bowed and bid Jane in a manner befitting her:

"I bid thee good morning, your Majesty."

"Please be seated, John. I am still unaccustomed to my serving ladies calling me that, least my beloved tutor, but I am bent on learning that it should be so in the presence of a Queen, though I do not accept myself to be a true Queen, that I am still marauding as such, an impostor I think, when, clearly, it should be Mary's or Elizabeth's that presences this fine place. That is why somebody, the Duke of Northumberland or my stepmother I beseech thee, is

136

attempting to destroy by poison no less, this monarchical impostor who lies before you."

Jane's accusation starved my words. Why on earth would the duke wish to dispel with her after he had gone to such great lengths to make her sovereign? Was she that naive or was this simply a notion brought about because of her debility I wondered? She must have sensed the doubt in my expression...

"It is true, John. I have never felt so certain. Indeed, in early June, when I lived with the Dudley's in Durham House, I had my suspicions about his mother in this vein. Both my in-laws have motive to kill me since I refused their son a crown. Now the duke plans to replace me with Elizabeth but he still has Mary Tudor to contend with. She is a formidable woman. If he disposed of me the sooner, Elizabeth could take the crown. Since my marriage, and while I lived with Guildford and his mother, I often felt the stomach pains. I have come to the awful conclusion I am being slowly, methodically poisoned. And the attacks only seem to arise when Northumberland is present. Most times he is away days on end, going about his devious business I suspect. Now he visits me here, in the duty of the crown's business he affirms, and, again I am plagued with sickness." She spoke deliberately and was clearly suspicious of her father-in-law:

"I have thus ordered the cook and her servants to prepare and deliver my food with every care."

"Whatever has put all this into your head, your Majesty? This cannot be so. It would be a terrible thing, even for Northumberland. You must not reason in such tortuous terms."

"Please address me as Jane when we are alone, John. Anything other, relative to my unfortunate position, pleases me not. I was and am quite happy being just Jane."

I looked around and, truly, we were alone. Mrs. Ellen had departed Jane's bedchamber.

"Yes, we are alone, John. Mrs. Ellen knows my wishes when my teacher is present. I look to you for your guidance, John, in these distressing days. I have been advised that, even as I speak, Northumberland has made way with an army to arrest poor Mary before she claims the crown. No doubt he expects, upon his return, I will be dead, and with Mary imprisoned the way will be made accessible for Elizabeth."

Her eyes were wide and her fears were apparent. I asked what proof she had to establish that Northumberland was attempting to poison her.

"I do not know of any proof. All I know is that someone is trying to poison me. It cannot be the cook or my ladies in waiting or any of the other attenders whom I trust implicitly. It has something to do with Northumberland. I know it."

"But how could it be Northumberland?" I asked. "Why should he so

137

wish to destroy you, a Protestant? Surely, the fact that you refused Guildford the crown would not warrant so awful a deed."

"For the same reason he chose to kill the King perhaps, John Aylmer."

I gasped at what she was implying. I was absolutely shocked.

"Jane, you should not harbour these wicked thoughts. You know it is strictly out of context with our Christian faith, that you should even think as such."

"But I have proof, John. You will believe me when I tell you that Northumberland planned to poison the King months ago.

"I assumed, when Northumberland wrote the mysterious note to my father mentioning the fact that being rid of the weak King Edward would open the way for a Protestant Queen, he was thinking of Princess Elizabeth. It would never have occurred to me that he meant me. I have royal blood in my veins, yes, but the order of succession, accorded after the death of great uncle Henry, set me well down the ladder. I imagine the part of the note, which was destroyed, mentioned me by name. I would have been prepared for that but I wonder how I could have prevented it. But now I understand why my father, in his devout hunger for power assuming he would be the father of the new monarch, was completely misled by Northumberland's horrendous plan. I was reluctant to accept my own father was part of this and I shall never forgive him. But knowing he is my father I have a Christian duty to still accept him as such. At least I know he did not kill the King. It was Northumberland himself, just as he and his stock have tried to kill me, as he will try now to kill Mary Tudor. For now his intent will solely rest with Elizabeth with whom he believes he is able to coax to his means."

She paused looking up at me, her expression not quite so fraught now:

"I doubt even if the mighty Northumberland could achieve that, I know the Lady Elizabeth well enough. She, too, is a formidable woman, a woman not to be trifled with. Yet now, as we speak and while I would wish no harm to Lady Mary, I will know my life would be safer with Elizabeth. For, as I was strongly advised – and you will not know this John – if I had refused the crown I would, under the consent of my own parents, be sent to Spain where my life would be in fearsome danger. Now it stands, that if Lady Mary Tudor gains the title, I will be tried for treason."

"What about the note, Jane? It is your assurance that you are innocent of premeditated treason."

"I would not attempt to use the note to save my skin, for my father would thus lose his life, and he is still my father. If it is meant to be found, God will ensure it be so, for only I know the place where it is hidden in a leaden container at Bradgate, and I understand no good or revenge will come from it because my father's head will be at stake. The note, John, is forever hidden there and shall remain so. It has no other cause now that the King is dead."

"But Northumberland must be punished. He has committed a terrible sin, Jane."

"God will surely punish him, John. Is that not what we believe? That we must not adjudge what is right and what is wrong? That the final judgement rests with God and it is for Him alone to render the punishment He sees fitting? And you must devoutly promise to me this day, John Aylmer – and as a distinguished man of God I know I can trust you more than any other I know upon this earth – that you will never divulge the information I have passed to you this day."

I had no option other than to render my promise. If and when the note was discovered, if it has not rotted first, then such time would have passed that it would not matter anyway, lest the history books would be adjusted accordingly and there would be no doubt that Jane was innocent and did not deserve that early finality to her young sweet life.

The existence of the note has forever troubled me but now, since Jane's execution, I felt, despite my promise to keep secret, I should have made it clear to the new Catholic Queen that Jane had proof she had no wanting for the crown, that she recognised she was an impostor, that she was truly tricked and trapped into accepting it. But alas I was held by my promise to her that I would never divulge the existence of such a note, though I often tried to release myself of the promise with the plea that it felt right, that a life could be saved because of it, but it was to no avail. If the note had been found would it necessarily have pardoned Jane. I could not be certain.

Northumberland recruited his army to find Mary Tudor in order to banish her from the scene and thus prevent her from claiming the crown. Her father was to lead the army but Jane strongly protested. In her new position she manipulated her power, even over the mighty Northumberland who was forced to lead the army himself. A decision he must have later questioned of himself because whilst he was away. Those immediately under him were quick to show their disapproval of his recent actions. There was a general feeling in the country and in London that the rightful inheritor of the crown was Mary Tudor simply because she was the eldest daughter of the former King Henry VIII. As far as they were concerned the very unpopular duke had gone too far and because Jane was now a Dudley, she too was hated.

Jane knew of this, she told me so, but trusted in the Lord that He would find a way to turn the people's minds to her. I remember thinking how dreadful she had been trapped into this position. It concerned me that Mary would break through and claim the crown which, as Jane openly declared, was truly hers, despite the meanderings of Northumberland who, it came to pass, used his devious influences upon King Edward V to eliminate the illegitimate Mary and Elizabeth from the list of succession.

These were trying times indeed and with Queen Jane being so unpopular with her people, as much as she was not part of Northumberland's stock, I feared the inevitable would happen, that the Queen's life would be in jeopardy, that someone loyal to Mary Tudor, the eldest of King Henry's daughters - no matter what her religious following - would be warned of the devious Northumberland's plan to depose of her, and the outcome was significant.

CHAPTER SIXTEEN

Now in 1594, I am Bishop of London and forever will be, given the Queen's pleasure, so long as I live, beholden to my following and Queen Elizabeth. She is a noble Queen who, despite my shortcomings, pays homage to my standing. I wonder if she ever thinks of Jane, who is constantly in my prayers. But there is a truth, which, like Northumberland's note hidden by Jane at Bradgate, remains undiscovered. Yet, unlike the note, a recorded material document, this truth remains staunchly in the mind of the beholder and must for ever be so until death nullifies its existence of a time and place in the past, in Jane's past, in my past, in our past. No matter what I have said regarding the contents, and Jane knows this in death as she did in life, there can be no historic proof that King Edward was murdered without the evidence given in the note and, indeed, no evidence to support the true relationship between Jane and myself. If God decides the evidence should be known, then that will be so in his own good time.

But I humbly thank God that Jane and I were in absolute unison, that for a few brief moments our souls were combined.

I found it difficult to accept Jane's version of Northumberland's motive in destroying the King. It was well known that the duke was always most concerned about the King's health. I have put great thought into this and have since come to my own conclusion, which slightly differs from that of Jane's findings in that Northumberland originally wanted Edward to live. It may be that noting the King was growing weaker by the day after his grand tour of the southern counties, he showed signs that his health was rapidly deteriorating. This was the time when Northumberland approached the King and persuaded him to alter the line of succession. However, the King's health improved and his death was no longer imminent. But Northumberland was already set in his scheme. The time was right to set it in motion.

Mary Tudor was concerned about her future safety and was pondering on the prospect of fleeing to the continent. Now was the time to act but he had to be sure the King would die. Thus the poison was administered. Obviously there was no doubt in Jane's mind. I feel certain she would not have misunderstood the content of the note, but it had been partly burnt and therefore the message thereon could have been misconstrued, in that the intent to poison Edward was to be implied only if he married the Catholic French princess Elisabeth, because of the problems which would ensue.

In hindsight, Northumberland was devious to the extreme, whilst I pondered on the question in my mind: however should one so cunning, be careless enough to advise Jane's father by postal messenger of one's murderous intention to kill the King? He must have surely been aware that such messengers sometimes failed to reach their destination and the note could have been read by those who would dearly love to be rid of the dreaded Northumberland. But time was not on his side. Quite likely, he decided to take the calculated risk, probably advising the messenger. Failure to deliver the wax sealed envelope would result in his end by death in the most horrible method.

But I was to discover I was underestimating Northumberland, that the note was written in code. When Jane was younger her father tested her intelligence by asking her to decipher some sentences he had formulated. Jane commented it was comparatively easy. When she discovered the note, she instantly applied the procedure she had memorized and quickly made sense of the message therein.

Jane had been Queen for just nine days when her father, the Duke of Suffolk, went to her bedchamber and told her she must immediately relent her claim to the Throne, that Northumberland had failed in his attempt to procure Mary Tudor and she, with the backing of the people, claimed the title as rightfully hers.

The duke was leaving on my arrival and Jane explained his message to me.

"I told my father I respected Mary's position and would gladly relinquish the crown I never wanted in the first place," Jane proclaimed.

She stated she asked her father if she could now return to Bradgate but he advised it was the new Queen's wish that she should be held in the Tower of London at the Queen's pleasure until such time she was ready to deal with her. She was assured that the Queen intended to pardon her in due course, that it was a matter of formality.

"We must never meet again, my beloved John Aylmer," she told me before her sad departure. Yet she seemed strangely in good heart. It was if the world had been taken off her shoulders. But there were still tears in her eyes as she stood there before me. She quickly kissed my brow.

"Goodbye, John," she whispered as her bottom lip trembled.

"I will find a way to come and visit you in your new residence," I assured.

But I knew that was virtually impossible. As a Protestant under Queen Mary, who was a devout Catholic, I would have no such authority to render further my blessings upon Jane. Certainly, I was strongly advised by Dr. Harding, Jane's first tutor at Bradgate, either to alter my faith or flee to the continent. That if we did not submit, Mary would burn us at the stake and it would be in the Lord's interest if we continued his work upon this earth no matter which denomination. I never envisaged that Dr. Harding would disregard his true faith with so meagre an excuse, which sickened my heart. Surprisingly, and to Jane's disgust, he later chose to convert.

After Jane's removal to the Tower under open arrest in 1553 I knew I would have to find a way if I ever wanted to see her again. I could not imagine being so distant departed from her and I envisaged she would need my guidance more than ever before. There just had to be a way. I could never change my strong Protestant conviction and Jane would never forgive me for doing so. My good friend Roger Ascham had the answer.

Looking back, I cherish the time when Roger Ascham and I first became friends. We had much in common and both shared a mutual interest in Greek philosophers. I frequently corresponded with him and visited him twice at Cambridge where he lectured in Greek at St John's College. He was an incessant scholar and a prolific writer on matters relevant to humanism.

Henry VIII was unquestionably brought up under the influence of the new learning, which now abounds. His father was of the medieval thinking that the world was centre of the universe, a view now doubted by some philosophers and theologists, and universal monarchy under the Roman Empire was sacrosanct. The head of all was therefore the Emperor, whilst the universal church was ruled by the Pope.

But the great philosophers have showed us other cultures, which have led to the new way of thinking. Humanitus merely means the culture of things and how best adapted to the way we now live. The so-called Renaissance Prince was King Henry VIII himself.

Roger and I were strongly on the same lines and my Christian beliefs were well adapted to the new learning.

Although only five years my senior I felt Roger had achieved much more in his studies than ever I could in a lifetime. He was well respected by his contemporaries. He had the honour of being Princess Elizabeth's head tutor in languages. He also taught Edward VI under the auspices of Sir John Cheke who is truly a great man, having taught Roger himself. Somehow Roger achieved the unique position of being in middle ground regarding religious matters, which secured his position when Queen Mary ruled.

In 1553 I wrote to him further regarding the tenuous position of Jane and he replied with an invitation asking me to stay a while with him at Cambridge. On my arrival he mentioned he was writing a book on the method of teaching and complemented me by announcing that I had been a great inspiration to him. He remembered Lady Jane, before she was Queen, had been in constant correspondence with him regarding her scholastic interests.

"Of course, you will know that, John because she always mentions in her letters that it was through your inspiration that prompted her to discuss a philosophical theory of Plato or Socrates and how Platoism changed her life and her outlook on life and death. But you will not know how, since I spoke to her at Bradgate, she has aspired in glorifying your methods of teaching. You, John Aylmer, have restored my faith in human nature, that, in this day and age when severe teaching disciplines obstruct the avenues of learning, you take care to teach carefully and gently. You apparently have this charisma about you, which enhances the great joy of learning. You are exceedingly ambitious and hopeful. That is what Lady Jane says, and now I have thoroughly embarrassed you once again, for I am sure I did so at Bradgate. But I take great heed of what Lady Jane writes and your efforts are duly noted."

I discovered during my stay that Roger was one of the few who could beat me at my own sport, bowls. His energy was truly daunting.

I managed to take in some of his lectures at Cambridge and he gladly let me look through Jane's letters. In fact he insisted I did so, her being my most important pupil. He told me he had been intrigued by Jane's scholastic progress as, indeed, had some of his contemporaries who had lectured at Cambridge.

"As we know, she had been in touch with Bullinger, Ulmis, and other German Calvinist and Zwingliam ministers. It seems, her appetite is endless and, even now, imprisoned in the Tower, she continues to correspond, although this may become increasingly difficult if the new Queen has her way, her being a staunch Catholic. Not to underrate the girl, your influence, John, without ever intending to be patronising, has undoubtedly been significant and I feel, as you have indicated your concerns to me that this great young talent is on the verge of destruction. Queen Mary must pardon her, for something she never committed anyway. She had openly admitted her route to the crown was taken in the confines of Syon House, given the bad advice of the horrendous Duke of Northumberland, but, never the less, blames herself for having been coerced into the tenuous position in the first place. But we know the duke was executed on Tower Hill on August 22nd, 1553 and the people were glad to be rid of him.

"It has all been like a nightmare for the sweet young girl. At least Northumberland has now met his just end by the stroke of the axe, even though he tried to convince the Queen that he had seen the error of his ways and converted to Catholicism like many others are doing these days. But you, John, I think I know you well enough to understand you could not stoop that low, not like your contemporary, Dr. Harding."

Roger's expression looked grim as he glanced through Jane's latest letter.

"She seems to believe that Queen Mary will issue a pardon since she has written an open and honest declaration which she repeats here in a letter to me. I should like you to see this too, John. I fear for Jane, indeed. It is true, Queen Mary may be sympathetic but, clearly, she will be pushed by her advisors who dearly would like her to be rid of Jane and Guildford, even the Princess Elizabeth. All three offer a high degree of danger to her tenable position. You know Jane is loathed that Dr. Harding has converted to Catholicism. You may not know that he had the audacity to advise Princess Elizabeth that, if she did the same, Queen Mary would be more inclined to pardon her. But now, the monk Dr. John Feckenham, the master in the art of gentle persuasion, has been designated the task. But Jane tells me she is actually enjoying the challenge. That her faith is so strong that even the persuasive Feckenham will be reduced to cinders if she has anything to do with it. Yet there is another side of her, which I have never encountered and I wonder if you have, John. By her own admission she ventures to say that if she were in a similar position, but a Protestant Queen, she would be reluctant to issue a pardon to anybody who may cause such threats to the monarchy, that it may well be in England's interest to dispose of that threat lest they converted likewise and thus stop any claim they may have to the throne. It is almost as if she wants to die. She constantly refers to the words of Plato in her letters, to 'live and learn to die,' which is rather disconcerting."

I remembered the long discussions Jane and I had about those words of Plato. The concept that by living purely as tenants upon this earth our behaviour and devotion to the Lord would be adjudged after death and whether we were returned in another time, another place, and even perhaps another life form to prepare us for the final glory of heaven. That to die was simply a natural step to another stage in the development of our souls.

I read carefully through her letter and Jane wrote almost as she spoke. It was as if she were there, issuing those distinct words by mouth. I knew very well how her mind was working and that, if the worst was to happen, she would be prepared and would go to the scaffold diligently accepting that was the way the Lord had planned. I was frankly surprised by her overtures, that given the position, she too would pronounce death in a given circumstance. This was unlike Jane. I felt this view arose because of her intended forgiveness to the Queen. There was something not quite right and it was imperative that I should meet with her and discuss our thoughts together regarding her present position. I discussed this with Roger and he agreed. Where there is life there is always hope and I am sure even our Lord would agree with that. He may have prepared the way but we shall never know the way. It would be imprudent to accept a way merely predicted by man.

"Then it is evident you must discuss these matters with her. She looks to you for guidance, John, more than any other I suspect."

He paused a while and looked through some papers on his desk, rubbing his chin thoughtfully. Then he looked up with a speculative expression and spoke with enthusiasm.

"It is imperative that we arrange a periodical visit to the Tower on behalf of the humanists. We shall never get away with the religious alternative. The Queen relies only on Dr. Feckenham for that. She would never accept the argument that because Jane is a Protestant she should then be entitled to receive a Protestant Minister."

I felt myself frowning. What exactly was this highly intelligent man suggesting? If he had an idea it would have been thoroughly researched. But there was a catch...

"This will have to be a test of your faith, dear boy. You will be authorised to visit the Lady Jane at my bequest. Not as John Aylmer but as a colleague, John Palmer, a fellow humanist and a great writer of truths. He will be disappointed you will be taking his place but will take it in good part. You will be an impostor, John. I know not how this will test your faith."

I was confused, bewildered. Was this great man losing his mind?

"There will be a certain risk," he continued. "There always is in these circumstances, John. But you must consider if the risk overrides the reason. Nobody at the Tower knows you, I have already checked, only the other prisoners, Guildford of course and his brothers, Lady Jane's attenders, Mrs. Ellen, Mrs. Tylney, Mrs. Jacob, and a page. Lady Jane tells me she is lodged in a comfortable two-story apartment near Beauchamp Tower. Guildford and his brothers are kept in the Beauchamp Tower. Lady Jane has refused to see Guildford whilst she is there on the premise that she has completely rejected the Dudley's, and who can blame her for that? She also feels that her devotions need only to be turned on 'this poor wretched woman' who is herself suffering horrendous circumstances brought about by Northumberland and his stock."

"I can see you have put much into your plans, Roger, but is this going to work? Jane and her attenders are likely to react as soon as they see me. Also, I fear I may be turned away without a proper introduction."

"Well, of course, it would be dangerous if I were to advise them John Aylmer was visiting but I have thus written to advise John Palmer will be visiting her Gaoler, Partridge and his wife. Partridge will understand that his visitor is preparing an essay on the treatment of such distinguished prisoners and, of course, Queen Mary, anxious to endorse she is a fair and just Queen, has given me her full sanction. I understand, too, she has passed on an instruction to her Lieutenant of the Tower, Sir John Brydges, that John Palmer may also converse with other high-ranking prisoners. Of course, I will be there just to introduce you, you understand. The rest will be up to you or rather the distinguished John Palmer who does conveniently look like you in many ways."

I would never have envisaged that my friend Roger Ascham was so resourceful. But this became evident when he was appointed Latin Secretary to Queen Mary. I said plainly but in good spirit:

"If I did not know you better I would even say you had devious tendencies, indeed. Even in so much as you have assumed that I will be willing to execute this challenging task at the risk of losing my life if I am thus discovered. Queen Mary will have no hesitation in disposing of me. Yet you do know me, Roger. You know what my answer will be."

Roger grinned.

"Not quite, John. As I have advised, John Palmer actually does exist and the visitations have thus been planned with an essay in mind. You simply will have to complete the essay in his stead, and I know you are well capable of that. I have prepared a dossier for you with some supplementary notes. You

146

will be doing us and Lady Jane an invaluable service."

"What of disguise?" I asked. "What is the humanist wearing these days? Do I need to let my beard grow?"

"The clothes of a cleric will do fine, my dear boy. But we will find you something that, perhaps, is a little more comfortable fitting than your present attire. You are putting on weight John since you have been at Bradgate. But then, everybody knows about the huge Bradgate luncheons and those who survive the seven courses. They look as stuffed as the pheasant, swan and peacock they have consumed that is for sure.

"My stomach begins to rumble. We shall ourselves luncheon immediately. But thinking about the disguise, John, I know a very good mummer who was King Henry's favourite actor of traditional mime. He is an exceptional disguise artist. No need to grow a beard, John. That will take too long. My man will give you the most charming, distinguished and handsome beard you would ever have seen worn by the noblest of gentlemen. By the time he has finished with you, you will not even recognise yourself. Perhaps it is advisable that you adjust the character as an actor would. You will not be quite the high-spirited, bustling and witty person I presently see before me. Perhaps solemnity would go with the character I have in mind. That is not that you wish to depress the Lady Jane, heaven forbid, but perhaps everything in moderation.

"It is imperative you see the poor girl, John. You have my blessing. After lunch, I will put you in touch with Edward Vere, the man who will alter your look. I assume you will be free next week, John? I have it by ear that you are to be Archdeacon of Stow in Lincolnshire. It wasn't that long ago you were rector of Bosworth."

"That is so true, Roger, but with the new Queen at the reign the appointment will be postponed and, although she has indicated the Protestant Church will continue with her blessing, I have serious doubts. She has already put me to task be it through Dr. Feckenham because of my denial to accept transubstantiation. I must tread carefully for the present and have time enough to implement my forthcoming visit upon Jane. Next week will be perfect."

"So you have never met our new Queen, John?" Roger asked me.

I nodded that I hadn't.

"Well that is perfect. You see, John, she requires to see you as John Palmer. I had no option other than to arrange this before you could visit Jane. It will be in the noon of tomorrow sharp!"

I was completely lost for words but Roger reassured me that he would, as her secretary, introduce me to the Queen.

The next day I waited nervously and patiently until I was called. Roger accompanied me to the Queens chamber.

"You know the procedure, of course, John," Roger whispered. "The bow and not talking until you are spoken to by our sovereign lady. Do try and let it flow. She is a formidable woman but she will listen to anything you have to say but pay particular attention to your reply, always with care, John. Remember, you are John Palmer. One slip could mean your life, but urgent matters sometimes require risks. I know you will agree."

On arrival Roger presented me to the Queen's lady in waiting who quickly greeted and guided us through a second chamber and announced us to the Queen seated very regally and imperiously bolt upright upon a dais.

After the anomalies, the Queen graciously asked me to be seated and beckoned Roger to leave us, and promptly took visual account of me as I sat motionless hoping she would soon speak. Her auburn hair was neatly laced and her pock marked complexion made her look severe and forbidding, the eyes sunken and almost hidden as she began to speak. Thoughts ran through my mind as I imagined she could see through my disguise, that I would be discovered, thrown out of the Court, tried and burnt at the stake, the common punishment for impostors, intruders and heretics. But I managed to hold my stance and was relieved when at last she spoke, her voice deep for a woman and her words prolonged in syllables.

"So, John Palmer, do you wish to see my sadly misinformed cousin, who once I cherished and gave presents of silver and gold, only to be so arrogantly rejected by an insolent child as then she was. And thus, because of her young years, I chose to ignore her stubborn ignorance but I should then have realised she would not budge as now Feckenham discovers, after going to great lengths to procure a conversion out of her, that she sees the error of her ways and realises the true faith."

"You will have undoubtedly been advised, my sovereign lady, that I am a humanist and merely wish to talk with the Lady Jane on that score, that perhaps she will regard you as so fair a Queen, that her apartments are comfortable and fitting for one of royal blood and that you deem to make her last days on earth as well ordered as you can. I will, I feel sure, discover that to be the case, Ma-am, and I am humbly grateful for your kind permission in allowing my visitation to her."

"I suppose, John Palmer, I should be grateful that you feel she is worth the time and effort on your account but I suspect there are other reasons why you come and that is mainly why I wanted to see you. Rather than allowing one of my subordinates to see you, I wanted you to be quite clearly advised of the extreme measures I have taken to avoid Lady Jane's demise, which, clearly she brings upon herself, does she not?"

I replied with another question: "Given new findings, could you not resolve to pardon her?"

"You are obviously referring, John Palmer, to her resolve, that pig ignorant protestant, not wanting to be Queen in my stead, taking the throne illegally, that she was tricked by the scoundrel John Dudley into the belief that was best for her country? A girl of such strong determination, so forthright, so stubborn. Where were all those characteristics when the loathsome

148

Northumberland persuaded her to accept the crown, which was lawfully mine? There is clearly no excuse for ignorance, and she was succumbed to the inevitable."

"But she is so very young, Ma-am, and so very talented. It would be a sad loss in the eyes of our Lord, would it not?" I saw her expression fill with anger and thought I had overstepped the mark, realising her staunchness to her faith, that she would only see if the Lord would recognise only Catholics in her version of heaven, but she calmed again and continued adamantly.

"I think not. Her misguided faith is set. God only accepts the true faith, the Catholic principles and I abide in them for the true good of our country. Although I was reticent to caste a severe punishment to those who seek to steal the throne away from me, Simon Renard was right to advise me that I must dispose of any threat which would send my father's kingdom into the abyss, that the righteous and only way forward is with the advancement of Catholicism, the only true way, John Palmer, Humanist. By the power invested in me, my faith and my God require that I am Queen for the foreseeable future and indeed through Simon Renard the Lord has trail guided me. I shall thus only reconsider pardoning Lady Jane if she deems to convert and I hope you, as a humanist, will make her see sense. This is the way you could save her head, John Palmer, and I confirm, the only way. Your visitation is therefore approved for this reason, that the people will see and realise I, as their beloved Queen, have actively tried to help her save her own life."

I felt sick and confused and realised her mind was set and my efforts to change her were quite useless.

CHAPTER SEVENTEEN

Edward Vere agreed to see me the following day and took great lengths to ensure my disguise was convincing. He produced a beard made from real human hair to match the dark brown colour of my own hair with a camouflaged cloth backing and a solution with which to adhere it to my face. He showed me how to carefully remove the beard by dabbing the edges with heated water and delicately peeling off, making it reusable. But as a precaution he made a second identical beard. He demonstrated how my eyes could be made to look quite different with the use of light marking pads soaked in a dye, which could simply be washed off. He supplied me with a set of clothes fitting a man somewhat heavier than myself and supplied various pads with strings attached explaining how I should apply them to the waist, shoulders and thighs. It was all part of the general disguise.

I had a slight Norfolk accent, being born in that county. Edward suggested I practice to adjust the accent, talk with a lower pitch. Since I was a boy I had been enthused by accents and have often mimicked some of my bowling friends who come from the southern counties. But my favourite was the Devonshire accent, which, to my amusement, has often caused strangers to ask from which place in Devon I had come. So the accent was the easy part. Not so easy was the adjustment to my voice, but with tireless practice I reached an attainable pitch, which delighted Edward. During the following three days I paid hourly visits to him. I will always be indebted to him for his patience and resolve for he has done me a great service indeed.

Roger and I agreed, and definitely Edward himself, that, in his own interest, it was better he did not know my true identity or the reason I required his services. His involvement if discovered would be enough to send him to the scaffold.

On 29th September 1553, accompanied by Roger, I made my first call by appointment to the Tower and was greeted by Sir John Brydges who instantly recognised my consort and offered a hearty welcome. Roger introduced me as John Palmer and afterwards left to undertake some business in the city.

There was a chill in the air, which I felt despite all the padding around me. A dense mist rose from the river and the huge wall of the Tower glistened in the residue of the dampness there and the presence of ravens made it seem quire eerie. It truly was a fearsome place. As I approached the postern gate, a guard approached me, and, on announcing my business, I was asked to wait until the Lieutenant of the Tower came. I checked to ensure my beard was secure and felt a little uneasy as the tall lieutenant looked down at me, taking the letter of appointment firmly from my hand. But he offered a broad smile, returned the letter and escorted me to the Gaolers Lodge, a three storey brick terraced building with three dormer rooms set in the roof. I was informed, the Lady Jane and her attenders occupied the upper storey and the dormer rooms. In contrast to the neighbouring Beauchamp Tower, the building was not unlike a typical town house. To its right, past Beauchamp Tower was the Royal Chapel of St. Peter ad Vincula, which Jane was permitted to use for her daily prayers.

I hardly noticed the area marked by four short posts set into Tower Green aside the chapel. I did not even want to think about it. It was the place where a scaffold was erected when an execution was ordered. I felt if I set my mind on Jane's pardon, given with the Queen's blessing, with God's help all would be well for her. We had arrived at the gaoler's lodge as the Lieutenant spoke:

"Mr. Partridge is in, Sir. Just knock three times and you will be welcomed."

I gave a sigh of relief. The first part of my new experience had been successful and my confidence was boosted. Hopefully, soon, I would be with Jane again.

I was greeted by a tall middle-aged, balding well-built man with a welcoming smile. He shook my hand warmly and I felt immediately at ease. He was not at all how I imagined. His manner was gentle but firm.

"You must be John Palmer. Well, Sir, you are a little early. We are having our lunch but you are welcome to join us, come in." He had a deep rich voice and I traced a northern dialect

It was almost as if I were being welcomed into an ordinary home, not that of a gaoler. It was a humble place with heavy furniture. He showed me through a door where I caught sight of a woman whom Partridge introduced as his wife, Mary. She, unlike her husband, was small, petite but her wide blue eyes and open smile greeted me with enthusiasm.

"Mary, go and bring a bowl of stew and some ale for our guest. I'm sure he would welcome it."

His generosity surprised me. I expected an austere welcome. But I was more surprised by a third person who sat at the dining table. I caught sight of her as I passed fully into the room.

"This will be the Lady Jane, Sir, who honours us with her presence at the dining table today." Then he turned graciously to Jane. "This is John Palmer, my Lady."

The moment I saw her I wanted to go to her and take her into my arms. But realising my predicament, and not prepared, I took heed to discipline my natural reaction, but Partridge must have noticed my surprise.

"The Lady often dines with us, Sir. She is a prisoner, yes, but a very privileged one and her presence here is most welcome."

Jane looked up with a hearty smile, beckoning me to join her at the table and take an empty chair next to her. I felt sure, at such close quarters, she would realise who I was and prayed, if she did, she would not reveal it.

"John Palmer. I have thus been advised by Roger Ascham you will be calling upon us this morn and I heartily welcome you. I take enthusiastic heed to the purpose of your visit and look forward to our conversation."

I acknowledged and thanked her for her kind welcome in my well rehearsed tone of voice to which she responded:

"You remind me of somebody but my mind retracts. Life here is daunting and the mind becomes stale, so kindly make allowances."

I was relieved to note she was in such high spirits and assumed Queen Mary must have pardoned her. I had expected her to be depressed and at her wits end. After the meal she left the table to return to her rooms and whispered I was welcome to see her as soon as I had finished my refreshment.

When Jane left the room, Partridge turned to me with a wondrous expression advising me of Jane's remarkable stance. "You would not think that this fair young Lady was, for a short a time, our Queen, that she is here awaiting Queen Mary's pleasure, that she could lose her head. She is a brave girl indeed and does much for the soul."

Partridge explained that the Lady frequently joined them for lunch and they heartily enjoyed her company. That it was their opinion she was innocent of any treason and should immediately be pardoned. He groaned that the remaining prisoners were atrocious, degraded men who would do anything to save their skin. But the Lady was quite the opposite.

He lamented, "If I could convince her that it would be in her interest to convert her faith she would stand in good stead of being pardoned." He advised that Dr. Feckenham called every day and pleaded with her so to do "but she will have none of it".

"Alas, that is not why I have come," I advised. "I am bound by Her Majesty not to discuss religion or politics."

Partridge nodded, understanding me. I was relieved to learn Jane had a sympathetic gaoler.

"Well, Sir, the Lady will be ready for you. I will direct you to her rooms and will take you to see the others later. Some, including the Dudley brothers, have less accommodating lodgings in Beauchamp Tower. They are not under my jurisdiction you understand. My place is here. But as head gaoler I have the authority to guide you into that foreboding place."

It was expected I would be visiting the other prisoners during my time there, so my time with Jane would be limited.

I followed him up some twisting stairs to the second floor when he knocked at the door to the right. "Lady Jane's waiting women have smaller attic rooms above. Mrs. Tylney will be in attendance whilst you are here," he stated and, indeed, Elizabeth Tylney opened the door.

"Welcome, Sir, The Lady is ready to see you."

I was directed into an adjoining room where Jane relaxed on a small couch. She looked out of place there, remembering the size of the rooms and the luxurious furniture at Bradgate. The plain plastered walls were hung with arras. A carved oak table stood in the centre of the room. I recognised Jane's red prayer book placed opened upon it. Velvet-covered seats were placed in the deep embrasures of the windows. It appeared that everything had been done to lessen the rigour of her confinement there. In one corner of the room stood a familiar writing desk and high stool with her grand collection of books neatly placed upon the shelves above, the same cherished piece of furniture she had in her room at Bradgate.

A strong aroma of lavender greeted my nostrils and that of a fine white English rose placed in a stone vase near the windowsill.

"The kind Lieutenant of the Tower brings fresh pickings every two days and asks me to place them in the Lady's room," whispered Mrs. Tylney.

Jane greeted me once more with a wondrous smile and bid me to be seated opposite her, then she asked Mrs. Tylney to leave her with her honoured guest.

Jane did not immediately reply when I bid her good morning. Her whole expression seemed to query my presence. Then suddenly, her whole face lit up.

"I would recognise that mole anywhere," she gasped with excitement. "It is you isn't it! It is John Aylmer, my beloved school master?"

I might have known I could not fool this highly intelligent young woman. I'd forgotten about the revealing mole on my left cheek. I simply nodded in the affirmative as she continued to lavish my presence with words of praise.

"When we met downstairs I could not help but think it may be you, John. It is so good that God has found a way for you but you must be careful, you must tread warily. Although Mr. Partridge is sympathetic he is loyal to our Queen. It is better my attenders are not informed because, although I trust them implicitly, we wish not to incriminate them. Your disguise is splendid. I do not think they will perceive it to be you. Maybe it would be better, though, if I adjust the collar of your coat thus…"

She lifted my collar to hide the mole, which, although slight, was better hidden. She spoke quietly with some difficulty, occasionally covering her mouth with her hand, as if to control the volume of her words.

"It is so good to see you, John. I have prayed for this moment, never believing that it would ever be possible to be answered. But how, apart from the disguise, did you manage to come here? Pray not you have succumbed like Dr. Harding? Excuse me, Sir, that is an impertinent question, I know a man so deep in conviction would never convert."

She stretched over and placed her hands upon mine looking apologetic. I assured her that my faith was and would always remain unaltered and explained how and why I was there. The official reason interpreted as being to see her and the other prisoners in the name of humanism.

"It is good that I have such distinguished allies when I am in such a ghastly predicament. But I have written to Queen Mary who will surely recognise my truly unfortunate circumstances and pardon me."

I so dearly wished I could have had the confidence she attained. But I decided to put this into the back of my mind. I was there not to depress her but to cheer her. Yet, despite my brave efforts to hide my true feelings and my deep, deep sorrow and sympathy for this woman I could not hold back the tears and found it impossible to speak.

"Truly, your disguise reminds me of how trees alter their garb come the changing seasons, from the budding and blossom of spring into the maturity of summer and the shedding of the autumn fall, till winter shows their starkness. I have often thought, compared with the garb we wear, how different it can make us be.

"Do not lament for me, my dearest friend. You are more than a mere friend we know," Jane said cheerfully, "but rejoice with me that I have been so profited by your guidance as to be able to bear my present dilemma with resignation.

"It is autumn again, the colours are golden, trees all around I see from my window ready to shed their summer clothing and stand there naked in the chill of winter. How strong and hardy they are. How different are we who defy the Winter chill and put on our winter garb and then, when the warmth of Spring and Summer come along, we shed again whilst the trees dress up with their trinkets of buds which become leaves and new seedlings."

It was like my love for her: The buds of speculation developing into the leaves of the awakening, a new romance to share and our feelings for each other growing into fruition.

The clothes she wore, the scent of woman, tempted me to give of my love complete. Then the falling of the leaves and I saw the real woman and the seed of life passing, I feeling part of her, our love completely fulfilled.

Her words helped me to subdue my emotion and suddenly my words gushed out telling her I rejoiced heartily with her and would gladly persuade myself, that my guidance had contributed in however slight a degree to her present composure, but truly her resilience came from a higher source than any on earth.

"It is your piety," I humbly continued, "not your wisdom that sustains you. The Lord watches over you so lovingly and though I have pointed out the way to eternity it is merely through the great countenance of our Lord himself. Your name will surely be a future beacon and a guiding star to the whole Protestant church."

"Heaven grant it!" exclaimed Jane, fervently. "God will forgive your deviousness by disguise, John. It must have caused some conflict for I know you to be such an honest man. But you will cause me to secure my faith at a time when bitterness creates doubt and I do so confess I have wondered why a just Lord puts me to the test."

She told me that, though she was a prisoner, she was still treated well. She and her loyal attenders were all comfortable and well fed. That she was blessed in having so loyal a company around her and least she should thank the Queen's Majesty for that.

Would that such a woman, who had been Queen, be thankful for small mercies? She seemed to have lost the arrogance, which sometimes showed since when she married. It was as if she accepted her part too well.

I was appalled to learn her mother had paid no heed to her since her imprisonment. I assumed she blamed her daughter for the fall in her social standing because she would not follow her footsteps to convert to Catholicism as, indeed, all her contemporaries had done.

Her father kept his distance, too, but Jane felt he had plans to dethrone the new Queen by devious means and this concerned her because, if he failed and his plot be discovered, he would certainly hinder her cause and he, too, would find himself a prisoner in the Tower.

She poured out her thoughts to me. If she were capable of hate she would truly despise the actions of the late Duke of Northumberland who had conspired, even with King Edward himself, her tenuous path to the throne. That he had so convinced Edward that it was right and he should put his signature to such an illegal document. The fact that he and his stock had used her, that the significance of all that was in Northumberland's note, was still utmost in her mind and she could never forgive her father for failing even to discourage him, knowing full well his intent.

"It is mainly due to Northumberland and his stock that I am in this predicament but, even so, I should have never agreed to be Queen over Mary. That is an offence truly inexcusable and I must take my punishment whatever that may be."

It was wonderful to be with her again, to share our thoughts. Our hands met upon the small, wooden table between us. That her tenuous position there in the Tower fastened me to her every move, to know and hear as much of her in so limited a time, not knowing if I would be seeing her again. She was mercifully in the hands of Queen Mary who could act any time with devastating consequences, who could forbid my further planned visits during the days to follow.

My time with her was drawing to an end. The question in my mind had to be asked. It seemed to me that Jane was resigned to her presence there.

"Have you thought more about the note?" I whispered. "If you were to divulge its content, you could well be out of this place."

"Forget it!" She snapped fiercely in such a way that I had never known before. But I urged that it was crucial that the Queen should know of Northumberland's devious schemes, enticing her to accept what he contended was a legal crown, that it would become obvious.

"I trust you implicitly, John, that you have not divulged the existence of such a note, yet I fear that another knows of its existence."

"How could that be?" I asked uneasily. "I have not mentioned it to anybody. As much as it has been difficult for me, I would never break my promise to you, my beloved."

"Truly, I accept that and know indeed that you would never destroy the trust I have in you. It is simply that I overheard something I could not fully decipher when exercising in the courtyard recently. But of course the mention of a note could have referred to a thousand and one things and I am prone to be paranoid these days. Heaven forbid I have been known to talk in my sleep, so who knows. I must simply trust in God that no harm will come of it if it is known.

"I will never cause sentence of death upon my own father, and you, John Aylmer, should positively honour my decision. It is with a dull and disappointed heart I bid thee farewell and remind you of your promise that the note is never spoken of again."

She turned away from me. I was completely lost for words. She and I had always been on good terms. But in my stupid attempt to save her soul I should have known better. She would protect her father no matter what.

She would not agree to see me when I called the following day. I feared the worst, that I should have held my tongue, forced to say what I did because of my deep concern. I asked Mr. Partridge how she was. He observed she was deeply depressed and was suffering sickness, having said she would not be joining them for dinner. She had never refused to see me before when she was feeling poorly. Indeed she would welcome my company more during such times. I spoke to Mrs. Ellen who understood her mistress's health problems and nervous debility only too well. She maintained that besides the Lord only one man could cheer her now and that was her tutor John Aylmer who could see her no more. At this point I naturally longed to advise Mrs. Ellen that I was he but immediately dismissed the thought.

I paid my second visit upon her husband, Guildford, the next day in Beauchamp Tower. I needed to gain his confidence in order to complete my humanism essay that day. My first visit had ended abruptly, for this weak and dismal character, beset in his own sorrows, pleaded that I speak to his cherished Majesty the Queen Mary that he played no part in the devious plans of wishing harm upon her. That marriage to that despicable girl Jane was forced upon him, the fact that he was not pronounced King and that he chose not to be so, proved that he should not be linked to Jane's atrocious acceptance of the position, which she knew was rightfully her Majesty's tenure by birthright and affixed by her honourable father, King Henry VIII.

I left him abruptly after having advised the reason I was there did not give me authority to approach the Queen unless she summoned me so to do. I was not in the position to put my opinion to Her Majesty. He called me a liar and feared I was just a spy sent to him in no good measure, that I would attempt to discredit him by means foul. I was therefore surprised when he agreed to see me again this day but soon realised he would talk to anybody who may be in a position to save his soul.

"Should you not be asking me if I would convert my faith to please her Majesty? For I would surely do so, unlike my bigoted wife who would do nothing for me by refusing to convert herself. The monk Feckenham regularly visits her but never pays heed to me. I have never had the opportunity to change my ways, for I am never asked. Surely you can pass my wishes to the honourable Queen Majesty. Would she put you down for that, Sir?"

When I replied my instructions were not to delve into religion or politics he openly wept and complained that the devil would never let go, that he was doomed.

"Well brother Robert is seeing her, he will have tough words with her, you can be sure. It is not simply about sacrificing herself, but me, too, and, indeed, I am not ready to sacrifice my soul for such paltry matters," Guildford scoffed. "If the Queen Majesty refuses to accept my willingness to accept her faith, it is probably because of my selfish, thoughtless wife."

"But your wife sees her faith as the be all and end all, Guildford," I said carefully.

"To the expense of her beloved husband?" he protested. "Should not one's kin come before anything else? My so-called wife, who refuses to see her husband, is more content to fraternise with the lieutenant of the Tower. I see her through my window, every morning, walking in the courtyard with him. Then he disappears inside with her. I can imagine what she thus shares with this tall handsome figure. I know she thinks of me as a despicable imp who is of no use to any woman. She is truly a witch and deserves all that is coming to her."

I shared a few thoughts with him and managed to calm his degenerating soul before I left. I assured him that it would be most unlikely for Jane to do anything uncouth at this time. Certainly, she was absolutely obsessed in her devotions to her maker. But I could not help feeling sad for him. If Jane was of right mind, I feel sure she would wish to talk with him, to assure him that she meant him no harm. He was a year younger than she but mentally she was more than that. He was still a boy but she was a fully mature woman. I realised that the pair were so different from each other and understood why Jane could never accept him as a husband.

I was glad that she had obviously befriended the lieutenant of the Tower. Poor Guildford's imaginings were misguided but understandable.

Before leaving I left a note with Mrs. Ellen instructing her to pass it to her mistress. I explained, I truly regretted having upset her, apologised and trusted she would see me the following day. Upon my arrival the next day,

Mrs. Ellen informed me that her mistress was in no mood to see anybody. I was at the end of my tether. Having gone to such great lengths to secure these meetings with her I felt she was no longer interested in me. It was so unlike her.

I paid my usual visitations on the Dudley brothers. Guildford continued to slander his wife in no uncertain terms. I felt truly sorry for him, this very young man with a boy's heart who was seemingly void of courage. I worked hard to find the right words to help him. But he was truly a lost soul, resolute that his days were limited, relating terrible recurring nightmares of the headsman coming down with his axe, taking off his head. Yet, he still lived, the world was spinning around him as his head rolled off the scaffold. Then he awoke screaming.

"The only way you can help me, Sir, is to inform Queen Mary of my plight, that she may be sympathetic and give me the pardon which truly should be mine."

I simply had to inform him that I would do my utmost knowing full well that I was in no position to deliver such a message or gain the Queen's council.

"If it was not for that bitch Jane, I would not be in this loathsome predicament, that she truly accepted the position of Queen even though she claimed it was not hers. She knew what she was doing and will be rightly condemned but I had no doing with it."

"Then you must write a letter to Her Majesty, Guildford. Simply explain how you feel and graciously seek her pardon," I advised speculatively.

"I have already done so three times and she does not heed me," he snapped. "She will always think of me as that tramp's husband. If only she knew. Jane is no wife to me, Sir. She may deny me of herself, yea, her passion. But she cannot deny a passion shared with her darling lieutenant who is the only person in the world who seems to care for me. I wonder if she knows he comes to my bed. I know he goes to hers. She knows that to fall with child may save her neck awhile but I have no such advantage. She takes heed to this now knowing she may die. So, watch your virtue, John Palmer. She would even try the monk I would be bound, no wonder she is so popular."

Guildford's slandering words astounded me. I was dumbfounded and he noticed.

"There, John Palmer. She is not the sweet innocent being you may think. I could tell you a few home truths about her 'beloved' tutor with whom she has been intimately associated. Not my words but her nurse's. Now she is unable to have him she turns to my lover. She truly is a loathsome witch."

I felt myself pressed to comment but had to remain silent knowing he was lying about Mrs. Ellen.

"And her, the bitch that she is," he continued, beside himself now, "saying she would not see me because it would interfere with her devotions to her Maker. Yet, it appears the Lieutenant is of no such interference. Look, even as I speak she strolls with him in the courtyard."

He pointed through the barred window in his cell and sure enough it was they. Sir John Brydges, the tall lieutenant was walking upright, turning to Jane as they talked. Jane's head looked down, her hands clasped behind her.

I needed verification of Guildford's accusation.

"Has the lieutenant thus informed you of his intimacy with Lady Jane?" I enquired gently, not wishing to give away my true emotions, but immediately realising what a stupid question it was. Perhaps, because of Jane's recent attitude towards me, that she had refused to see me, I had reservations. It was obviously very unlikely that, in the event the lieutenant was intimately connected with Jane, he would let it be known. His position, least his life, would be threatened by such a disclosure. If it were true, which I very much doubted, it would be a secret between them.

"He has no need. I know the aroma of her body lotion. When he comes to me after he has been with her I know it. Only Jane would use that horrendous concoction of which I never approved. She maintained it was good for the spots caused by her nervous debility. Have you not noticed, Sir? Did you not notice today?"

I told him I had not seen her today or yesterday.

"Then you are safe from her, Sir. She is obviously content with her lieutenant."

"But do you not mind sharing him with her?" My intrusion into personal detail was wholly spirited in my search for more clarification than that he had offered. If Jane was having intimate relations with Sir John Brydges, it would truly be against the grain of the Jane I had known for so long.

"You ask stupid questions, Sir. Then you would not understand. It is different for me. A sort of vengeance if you wish. I want her to know that he finds my body much more appealing."

"He has told you this, Guildford?" I again enquired wistfully.

"He has told me, he has never known anything so good and that says everything, Sir. I believe, he goes to her because he truly feels sorry for her."

"Nonsense!" I snapped, forgetting myself.

Guildford turned away from the window and caught me in his glance. "You really think so and you are a humanist? Is not that what humanism is all about, caring and sharing and being concerned? Or perhaps you had the same intentions as darling lieutenant but he has got there first. Poor John Palmer. But you can still try. Even the lieutenant has his limitations. Of that I am fully aware."

In the heat of the moment I was about to explode. I felt I had been grossly insulted. I was forced to listen to his slandering and lies about Jane because of my false position and believing he was mentally disturbed. But this

159

insult to who I really was, John Aylmer, was gross and I wished only to cause him bodily harm. I managed to control myself and hastily made my departure, but knowing he had been very aware of my reaction. I would have to tread more carefully in future.

That night I could not sleep. This time it was not because of Guildford sharing Jane's bed but Guildford's insinuation about Jane and the lieutenant. But if it was true, even though I could not accept it, perhaps there was a certain truth in what Guildford had suggested. I pondered with the notion that, perhaps, Jane had discovered some quality in the lieutenant, which aided her depressing predicament. I was thinking in terms of mental satisfaction, not bearing to believe anything else. Jane was woman of great moral beliefs and her long and close relationship with me had proved such. The rest of what Guildford said was absolute nonsense. Jane would never fall to that. I could not believe anything else lest my conscience told me I, too, was slandering her name. Yet, the doubts were there. Guildford's words constantly sounded in my mind. They would not disperse.

I desperately needed to see her the following day and hoped she would see me again after the absence of two days. I prayed that it should be so with every ounce of good motive I could render, casting other thoughts finally from my mind, which my Lord would not wish to hear. I eventually found peace of mind in sleep.

The next day, my journey to the Tower was in vain. Partridge informed me that Her Majesty had proclaimed Lady Jane and the Dudley brothers must stand trial and further visitations were thus prohibited.

CHAPTER EIGHTEEN

Fortunately, my life was busy having taken new post as Archdeacon of Stow in the Diocese of Lincoln, in 1553, succeeding Dr. Draicot, recently deceased. The post was held in for a while during the reign of Queen Mary Tudor. There was much work to be completed in the diocese. Despite my deep concern about Jane during the time she awaited trial, I took comfort from her great strength in handling her predicament and trusted the Lord would help her.

Roger Ascham strongly advised that my position at Stow was extremely tenuous. Although the new Queen had proclaimed sympathetic overtures for the Protestants, their future was not clear. Mary was prone to the advice of Simon Renard who discussed banishment of the Protestant and other religious orders to make way for a true Catholic regime, which, he argued, would be best for England as it was for France.

Roger maintained his diplomatic contacts and was highly respected in aristocratic circles. He was thus my mentor in all things appertaining to the present state of the crown and government and how that would affect the people. He had already assumed that Mary would confiscate the Protestant buildings as she had already done with Bradgate House, which was now unoccupied.

He strongly advised I should flee from England until possibly Elizabeth was Queen. He feared Mary would not prove to be a popular Queen because of her Spanish connections and her proposed marriage to Prince Philip of Spain, sure to create unrest in her French domain and probable hysteria at home.

He feared, too, for the Lady Jane, that Simon Renard had already strongly urged the Queen to execute her and Guildford Dudley despite her earlier resolution that she would not take this step. The trial at Guildhall was purely a cosmetic operation, that she should be seen to be a fair and just Queen. But that the findings were inevitable, that Lady Jane accepted the crown despite her doubts and that was treason enough.

"I must give you bad tidings, John," Roger advised. "There is no chance for Jane or, indeed, Guildford. When the trial is over there may be some time before the execution and Mary may grant us further visits upon the sentenced prisoners, so I completely understand your reluctance to flee until after the execution. But, then you should do so with haste, I know that the ruthless Renard will press her to burn heretics. High ranking Protestants and other non-Catholics will be on her list. You are truly a brave man, John, and I know you would not flee with cowardice in your heart. But, in my opinion, when Elizabeth is rightfully crowned Queen, your place at Stow will accord great worth. You will be needed with your body complete, John. You will be no use without it. Therefore to flee is the logical thing to do."

Roger's findings were deeply depressing, but I was grateful he was truthful. I pondered a discussion with him regarding Guildford's accusations and Jane's refusal to see me, but assumed what Roger's advice would be to put that aside, that their lives were truly precious and weak souls like Guildford would attempt anything to save himself.

Of course, he would say that and I would agree. There was no need to ask.

I wrote to Jane signing my letters as John Palmer but received no response. I assumed all correspondence was being held back pending the trial period and this was the reason. If only I could have left her on our usual friendly terms and I had not disturbed that in her mind, which was sacrilege, namely her father's life. I think, too, she was disturbed by my observations in that which she had made known to her court when she was briefly Queen, that she would bestow the death sentence on those who were unwilling to convert their faith to Protestantism. She had also later been heard to express this bigoted expression and she would know I would never condone such drastic measures. For once we were at loggerheads with one another.

But the time of her trial had ended. Although I could not be present, I was there to hear the predicted verdict on November 14th 1553 that Jane and Guildford were found guilty of treason. The sentence was pronounced by Chief Justice Morgan. They should be burnt alive or beheaded.

My prayers had been in vain. I wrote to Jane once more as John Palmer and urged her to reply. I could not bear to think of how she had taken the awful sentence of death and felt she would need any amount of counseling now. I paid another visit on Roger in this vein, that he might be able to arrange something in his capacity as Queen Mary's Latin secretary, that he might approach the Queen, suggesting, now the trial was over, she may allow John Palmer to visit the convicted prisoners again.

He vowed he would try his best and promised to advise me of any news. The days went by but on the second Monday following the trial I received a letter from Jane via Roger whom she had asked to give to me under the guise of John Palmer. I knew immediately it was imperative I saw her at the earliest. The letter began stating her case as being a desolate miserable woman, grievously tormented with a long imprisonment and how each day slowly passed. She wrote, that God had let her down, that he delays and delays her overdue departure from that horrible place.

She concluded: "My Lord and Saviour has always been for me a strong tower of defence but He seems to have abandoned my sinful being. How long will He tarry? I have prayed that I am His work ship, created in Jesus Christ. Then why cannot He release me forever?"

I immediately replied stating I hoped to be seeing her soon but in the meantime to understand that our Lord knows best when she should be delivered unto Him. Whilst there is life perhaps her Majesty may issue a pardon otherwise why does she leave it so long?

Another two days passed and I feared the worst, that Queen Mary would not allow further visits upon Jane. But my fears were in vain. The following day I heard from Roger who advised that further visits were granted twice per week and I know such permission was granted because of Roger's great influence with the Queen.

I was glad to receive the services of Edward Vere again who did an excellent disguise. I was once again the lamented John Palmer and hastened to the Tower to arrive by the hour of two in the afternoon.

Again, Sir John Brydges greeted me, this time in serious mood: "Things do not look good for Lady Jane Dudley. I fear the Queen will soon have to make a decision in accordance with her advisors, that the prisoners should not be pardoned."

He spoke in a daunting tone and was obviously saddened by Jane's dilemma.

The gaoler, Partridge, also looked glum as he quietly ushered me to Jane's quarters. Mrs. Ellen received me and beckoned me to where Jane sat on the window seat. She simply lifted her right hand to greet me, then warmly interlocked it with mine. I handed her a solitary red rose, a token of the deep affection I felt for her. As she took it, her eyes said everything as she held it close to her bosom.

Just for what seemed a moment we were both locked in an unexplainable trance, as if frozen in a moment of time, as if knowing each other's innermost thoughts. The hand that had greeted me came out to stroke the side of my face this time, she was looking up at me, and her whole expression said that she wanted me as much as I wanted her, in every way. Then she glanced down again, to the single rose she held in her other hand:

"It'll be next to my heart, dear John, a token of our very special relationship. It is so wonderful that you come to see me. That you excuse me for my intolerable behaviour when last we met and the content of my recent letter."

I looked at her with concern and her reaction clearly indicated the response: "Worry not, John. I have realised how foolish I was to doubt our Lord. Of course, He knows best and I fear not whatever the Queen's pleasure will use to be rid of me. Whenever my end will come, I heartily look forward to it and prepare for it. I am but as mortal as any human and so must die. I know I will die alone, as do we all. Some have fair warning, others not, 'tis the way the Lord chose. I have had overdue warning but when the time comes, God will not make me further suffer; I feel that. Although I go alone, I will have my God with me."

I was pleased enough Jane had cleared her head of any doubts regarding her faith but what she was saying complied with her studies in

163

Platonism. We live to die. That life is merely a rehearsal for death. This belief feigned any popularity she may have gained with the people who were often upset by this philosophy. By the same token I feared that she was accepting her demise too well and lightly suggested to her that she should write to Queen Mary and relay her thoughts.

"I shall never beg for pardon, John. Not unto her Majesty's conditions, whether I received a pardon or not.

"I think you ought to write to the Queen," I said diligently. "She is the only person who has the power to issue a pardon and, despite your feelings and your trust in the Lord, He would want you to take steps to procure your life which is all but natural. The survival of all species is paramount to the purpose of our Lord."

She looked at me and, for a while, said nothing. She turned her head and peered through the window bars. Then she spoke about the birds in the trees and the fact she had seen two squirrels gathering the last of the fallen nuts for the winter.

" 'Tis true, John, what you say. Each day the wild creatures strive to procure their existence, but they have the freedom to do so. Apart from my daily exercise in the privy garden I am stuck in this man-made pile made from clay and timber. I walk with Sir John, which, at least, helps my mind and body be exercised. He has an active mind and, although we often beg to differ, we have some very interesting conversations."

I particularly noted what she said about John Brydges, remembering how Guildford translated it, and I felt absolutely certain that her version was the real truth of the matter. I spoke about the idea of her writing to the Queen again. She proposed that she pen it in my company and we spoke on certain matters, how they would best be put to the Queen. She repeated, she would not beg for a pardon. She simply wanted the Queen to hear her story as it came truthfully from the heart. Her first words admitted her fault, that she would not expect any pardon or forgiveness from the Queen. But she let it be known that she had listened to those who, at the time, appeared to be wise and have now shown themselves to the contrary, having had the audacity to give to others, that which was not theirs. She continued that she was ashamed to ask pardon for such a crime and trusted God as to the outcome.

I suggested that she should tell the Queen of her reaction when, without notice, she was informed she was the new Queen at Syon House and put it that she was not wholly responsible for the actions which were put upon her that day.

She made two attempts, which she rejected and told me she would later complete the letter and send it the following day and heartily thanked me for my invaluable assistance.

She said how glad she was that the Queen permitted her still to write to her many beloved correspondents, that the person she had befriended as Lady

Mary when she was a child still had the grace to show some mercy, despite the time, when visiting Mary at Newhall with her parents, the then Lady Mary had just cause to smite her.

"I was in the chapel there with Lady Ann Wharton," Jane recalled. "I was surprised when Lady Ann stood on the alter and curtsied. I thought perhaps Lady Mary had entered the chapel and asked her if that was why she curtsied.

"The Lady Ann very patiently advised me on how one should behave in that holy place and that she would advise Lady Mary that I should undergo confirmation there.

"I was appalled when she told me how they eat bread and drink wine in representation of that being the body of Christ. I declined to do such a thing. It was terrible to believe that one so gifted as the Lord Himself, who made each and every one of us, should in Jesus, be made by a baker and a wine brewer."

When Jane discussed this with Lady Ann, the practice of giving communicants the bread and wine was rigorously practised in the Christian church. King Henry had been brought up a Catholic and the new learning was in its infancy. Katharine Parr's friend, Lady Anne Askew was sent to the stake for suggesting Christ's body was not bread. Similarly, a woman from my county in Kent, called Joan Boacher, preached that Christ did not take flesh from the Virgin Mary. He only passed through her body as water flows through a conduit and not participating anything of that body. She was thus imprisoned for a year, and then burnt at the stake when she refused to relent.

Perhaps Lady Jane had simply reacted like a child would. Yet the view she then held remained unaltered for the rest of her life.

"You were young at the time," I eased. "I expect the Lady considered that."

"Nay, Sir, because she was aware of the rhyme Prince Edward wrote and which I repeated whilst there: *Not with our teeth his flesh to tear, Nor take blood for our drink, Too great absurdity it were so grossly for to think.*

"I was badly beaten by my mother for those horrendous things I said to the Lady Ann who was quick to advise Lady Mary. I would not at all be surprised if she still remembers my outburst to this day."

"Perhaps she is too taken up with her marriage plans to King Philip of Spain, Jane. You will have heard that this betrothal is not a popular one with the people because of the country's indisposition with Spain."

"I have indeed, Sir, and even now, a condemned woman, I have my doubts if even she will survive as Queen for very long. These are troublesome times, indeed, and I will leave them all behind."

Jane neither looked sad or happy. When the time came to bid my farewell, I said I would see her again in four days when I hoped she may have some response from the Queen.

As I left the building I looked back and saw Jane waving at the window and she seemed to be unaware of her present position. I made for Beauchamp Tower to see the Dudley brothers but was informed that the Queen had forbid further visits upon them.

At the end of January, 1554 Roger informed me of some devastating news. Jane's father, Henry Grey, had joined forces with an ally, Thomas Wyatt, in a rebellion to remove Queen Mary from the throne because of her planned marriage to Philip of Spain and the feared consequences of this Catholic betrothal. Most Englishmen hated foreigners, least the Spanish. Sir Thomas Wyatt was a gentleman from Allington in Kent. Roger continued to say he stood not a chance for the timing was wrong.

Roger doubted Henry's integrity in joining the rebellion proclaiming it would be far better if he waited, until such a time that a stronger opposition could be mustered together in the country. I suggested that perhaps his true motive was to free his daughter by Mary's expulsion but Roger, praising me for such wholesome thoughts – that he would expect nothing less from me – went on to explain that the uncouth Henry Grey cared not for his daughter's predicament, hard as that may seem, but more for his own.

"It is assumed, his wife, Lady Frances, backed him all the way, having complained so about the degradation of her status in the confiscation of her lovely country mansion at Bradgate Park. They clearly do not do their daughters justice, John."

They had been forceful and active. They had spent a great deal of time out of doors and led a healthy, busy life. This obsessive routine was sometimes too strenuous for their daughters, of whom much was required, with the result that both, Katherine and Jane, would suffer from nervous exhaustion to the irritation of their parents.

Roger was right, by February 2nd Wyatt's revolt was crushed before he could properly organise his huge army and both he and Henry Grey were captured.

One thing immediately occurred to me. The content of the note hidden by Jane at Bradgate was no longer relevant so far as her father was concerned. He would surely, along with Thomas Wyatt, meet the executioner on Tower Hill. Ironically, his actions would also convince Queen Mary that Simon Renard was right, that she should immediately set a date for Jane's execution.

I desperately needed to contact Jane, to talk to her about the note and the changed circumstances. But that now was out of the question. She would naturally be aggrieved by her father's senseless act and what that would mean, but surely she would wish now for the contents of the note to be known to Queen Mary. I felt certain the promise I made regarding the note was no longer appropriate, that she would want me to collect the note and immediately pass it to the Queen. But I was in turmoil. I needed Jane's verification of this. I needed to know for sure that my assumptions would meet with her absolute approval.

There was no way of contacting Jane and I feared her time on this earth was growing short. I wanted to believe her reply would be in the positive. I had no idea of the whereabouts of the hidden note but I would search and search until I discovered it.

Early the following morning I made headway post–haste on my reliant stallion, Rob. He had been accustomed to the road via Fosse way from Stow to Bradgate but the road to Bradgate from London was unknown to us both. I would need to make directional enquiries on my journey.

I estimated the journey would take approximately three days allowing for rest stops.

The morning of Saturday 3rd February was bleak and damp and a low hanging mist made it heavy going for Rob but he enjoyed a good gallop and I was confident he would not let me down. We stopped at some watering places occasionally and I lunched at an inn, which stabled Rob with a good helping of hay. There was even a blacksmith on hand, which was just as well, because Rob needed two replacement shoes. In an hour we were on our way again as the day brightened and the mist disappeared. The first day we made a good thirty-two miles according to the landlord of the Craybrook Inn where I spent the first night in a comfortable room and Rob in a good stable. It would not be long before we reached Bradgate when I hoped my mission would be accomplished.

After a further night's stopover we reached the County of Leicestershire and on into Groby on Monday evening 5th February, thanks to the Lord for good weather. I was soon in the familiar surrounds of Lyn Ford. I instantly recognised a familiar face, that of William Briggs, a stout fellow with a ruddy complexion who served time in the great mansion as a stable lad when I was there in my youth. He greeted me and invited me to share refreshment and stay overnight with him and his good wife, Vera.

"You live in Lyn Ford now?" I asked William when we sat down at his table.

"These three years past," he replied. "His Grace wished to extend his boundary and we were told to go in no uncertain terms. The old village was levelled because, we heard, the duchess felt it was not right her aristocratic guests should have to pass through the village on the road to the mansion and suffer the unpleasant experience of noting the way we peasants live.

"But he did not get away with it that easily, he was 'obliged' to provide alternative accommodation for us and several others here in Lyn Ford. Like his father, the 2nd Marquis of Dorset, who moved twenty-nine villagers from the original Bradgate village, but his reason was that he wanted more hunting grounds.

"There has been no third attempt to build Bradgate village, His Grace has seen to that.

"Now Bradgate House is derelict. Queen Mary has seen to it also that

167

all the trappings have been removed in numerous cartloads but only a week ago. There is nothing there now, everything has gone and we do wonder what will become of the place if and when the Master and Mistress will return."

"I doubt that, following what has recently happened," I said. Although William and his wife knew about the demise of Jane they were unaware of the news regarding her father and were deeply saddened. William commented that, although the Lady Jane was unknown to them because of her disposition, they had often spoken with her father who always enquired after their health. William said he did not much care for Jane's mother, though, who would never give them her time when passing by in her luxurious carriage.

"She was always too good to speak with commoners like ourselves. That was all too clear. But why do you come, Sir, if I would not be too bold in enquiring? There is nothing at Bradgate now, just the shell of that which once was. The park is still as it was, though. At least our new Catholic Queen has seen fit to leave the deer and other stock in the charge of Farmer Robert Wills, who receives a pardonable wage for the purpose."

Robert Wills was Mary Ellen's betrothed.

"Yes, I remember Robert when he was last at Bradgate, but I thought he had tenanted another farm near the village."

"That is so, but when the mansion was confiscated. Robert had the opportunity to take up the lands as tenant farmer. He has done quite well for himself and employs three assistants."

"Good for him. In reply to your question, William, I simply wish to revisit Bradgate for old time's sake. I have served many a sermon in the Chapel and plan to tender prayers there for remembrance and thanks for the happy times I remember." This being but part of the truth given, it was prudent not to mention the rest, of course.

"Well, Sir, you are fortunate in that, as far as I know, nothing has been taken from the Chapel. I daresay it is a matter of time our Catholic Queen will require to change all that is Protestant there. So, you have come in good time. She apparently refutes a caretaker's presence there, even just to keep the place tenable, so it will be a lonely place. But even so, in respect of such a beautiful place, Robert Wills keeps an eye on the building, as we all do from time to time."

In the morning I thanked William and Vera for their kind refreshment and taking me in for the night of which I was well in need. Like all commoners they were keenly aware that times would drastically change under Queen Mary's rule and prayed the future would not bring strife and bloodshed.

I reached the familiar wide cobbled road out of Lyn Ford and soon noticed the high towers of Bradgate House looming up before me. I spotted a number of fallow deer in the large park and rabbits quickly scurried into burrows as Rob and I approached.

I also was pleased to encounter Robert Wills and it was good to talk with him once again. I handed to him the message from Mary Ellen.

I remembered my promise to Mary Ellen and during our conversation he was pleased and anxious to talk about Mary with whom he regularly corresponded. I diligently praised him for his patience in waiting for the opportunity to marry Mary.

"She is a woman worth waiting for," I said. "She has been a great comfort to Lady Jane of late."

"She certainly is that, Sir, and I will wait forever if need be. Everything is ready and waiting for when her services are no longer required."

"I am glad indeed, Robert. She has been a great comfort for Lady Jane."

I had no need to press further regarding Mary Ellen's fears.

It seems, Mary Ellen's concern about Robert falling off, because of the waiting to marry the woman he loved, were fortunately unfounded

Robert advised that I could enter the house through the old kitchen entrance and wished me well but not to expect too much of that which was once so fine a house.

As I made way for the house, everything seemed the same as I had remembered. There was no indication that anything had changed. On reaching the house, however, I immediately noticed the absence of the window coverings and a large iron bolt and hinges secured the main entrance gate. I found the kitchen entrance to the side of the house, camouflaged by heather and gorse. I was glad Robert reminded me of this entrance, otherwise it would have meant my clambering over one of the lower walls, for I was determined, by means common or foul, to enter the house. At this time, I considered nothing in the world was more important than discovering the note Jane had hidden there.

I linked Rob to a tree and ventured through the small entrance, hacking the overgrowth aside with the assistance of a small branch torn from the tree.

Immediately, as I reached the other side of the wall, I sensed an overwhelming calm. The formerly well-kept grounds were sadly neglected and overgrown. The grassed area, on which I often practised bowls with my contemporaries, was covered in ridges of moss and wild flora. But, even now, it was difficult to accept the house was empty. I imagined hearing all those sounds of the past. The clattering kitchen pans and crockery as the cook and kitchen maids prepared dinner for numerous staff and guests and set the large lengthy dining table with enough utensils adequate for several courses. Horses and carriages drew up to the main door to deliver high-ranking guests. I heard of the duchess' voice as she greeted them and the mingling of numerous voices inside the great hall. It was all part of that which was once Bradgate House. But it was no more. I found my way inside via the tradesmen's entrance, one part of me expecting to see the familiar objects inside but the other, remembering what William had said. He was sadly right. Only a few damaged relics and cutlery remained, scattered upon the large scullery table where food was once busily prepared at all times during the day.

Just absolute silence, all those sounds gone, just the memories remained. As I ventured further through corridors into the banqueting hall I felt so small, just me and the Great House, something that could never have been before. It was an eerie dreamlike experience, yet still, the tranquillity remained. I have no idea how long I spent just standing there in the centre of the great hall, looking around, remembering the scurry and flow of the house, attenders and the servants, the scullery maids, the cleaning women, ensuring everything was as it should be, lest the Lady Frances would soon come down upon them.

I remembered how there was always an abundant supply of water, which emerged from a man-made lake on high ground north of the house, designed by the first Thomas Grey, the present duke's grandfather. An outlet from the River Lyn, by way of a dam, supplied flowing water, which flushed the drains by linking channels under the house and turned the water mill there. I could just hear the water flowing beneath as I stood there, something I never heard when the house was occupied, too much was always going on. The sweetest water I have ever tasted emerged from a natural spring to the rear of the house.

But remembering my mission, I shook my head and instinctively knew where I would start my search. I climbed the stairs and headed for the family's living quarters, specifically Jane's rooms. She spoke about removing mortar between bricks. How well had she disguised them afterwards? Would there be any indication of damaged plaster or brickwork? I worked out a methodical plan in my head and commenced my search in the area of the corner tower where Jane resided during daylight hours. But firstly I went to the master's study, remembering that was where Jane discovered the partly burnt note in the hearth. I crouched down and wiped my fingers across the hearth, imagining I was Jane picking up the note, about to throw it back into the cinders once burning there, her curiosity getting the better of her, opening it, reading it. How would she have felt at that moment?

I imagined her thoughts: "What shall I do with it? Let it burn completely in order that it will not get into harmful hands of those who would seek some vengeance on my father and Northumberland, or keep the information safe from harm's way inside my head? But the note was written by Northumberland and does not directly involve my father. Perhaps one day I may have need of it, for the ruthless Northumberland works in twisting ways and its content could prove useful for some purpose yet unknown. He has surely taken an unnecessary risk to deliver this note to my father, as much as father was careless not to have secured it's complete destruction. That being so, fate has accorded I discovered the note for reasons I do not yet know. I will then hide it in a safe place where only I will know."

It was almost as if they were Jane's real thoughts, dispelled at that time and coming into my mind. Now I elevated my thoughts hopefully to discover where she might have hidden the note, certainly not in her father's room, but perhaps in hers? I made way for the southeast tower again and stood there, quietly looking around.

But what was I doing there? Would it please Jane? Questions, and more questions in my mind. But there could be no hope of preserving her father's life. But she may not be aware of the trouble Henry Grey has made for himself. Even if she were aware of his forthcoming execution, would she still condone my search in that which was once the privacy of her residence? I spoke out loud the questions I needed Jane to answer, hoping some sort of miracle would take place that some form of mind transition could emerge between us.

"Please, Jane, help me. What should I do? Would you wish that I found the note? Would you guide me to it? The secret place in the mortar where you have placed it, in a leaden container you said, so small as to be easily hidden, deep inside the aperture between two corner bricks. Is it in the corner of your bedroom? Your study room, where? Give me some indication, Jane. By your mind let God transmit a message to me in this place which was your home, the place where we shared many a happy hour in study and consolation".

It seemed so long ago, yet as I spoke, the place being so lacking in life and spirit, it could have been a hundred years past.

I stood there, frozen, willing a message to come to me. But then something happened within my being. It was not that which I had hoped. It was something much, much more that shook my soul. The frame of my body seemed to vibrate and spin. Then calm again. It was a strange eerie calm. I simply perceived that poor Jane knew she was doomed. I felt I was feeling that which she was feeling through the closeness of our souls, that which had brought us spiritually close. That soon Jane would be dead.

Something told me I must leave the house and return to London at the earliest.

My feelings were correct. On calling upon William Briggs for refreshment before my return journey, he broke the news to me, the dreaded news that everybody expected that had just arrived by messenger in Lyn Ford. Jane and Guildford were to be executed on the 9th February! Jane must have known the day after my departure for Bradgate!

"'Tis right," William told me. "We know the Lady Jane was not popular in the country, but here in Lyn Ford, well she lived in our immediate surroundings, and we do feel somewhat akin to her, not meaning to be disrespectful to our new Queen, but we cannot understand why a so quiet and refined girl could have committed such treachery that merited execution."

I told him, I agreed whole heartedly and trusted he would pray for Lady Jane that the Lord himself would know the truth and He alone would show mercy unto her soul.

"Did you discover what you wanted up there, Dr. Aylmer?"

William caught me unawares. How could he know? I assumed he was simply making reference to my reminiscences.

"I realised the emptiness of the house yet still a certain ambience remained there, especially in the chapel."

"Did you see a young lad up there, lurking around? Once or twice Robert has told me of his presence there that he was seen to be looking for something but I dare say he was simply looking for any valuables to pilfer. He always scarpers hastily enough when seen."

"Really, William. Tell me, have you seen him too?

"Only once and he seemed to have something in his hand, looking at it intently but then, realising my presence, he was off. I often wondered what it was that interested him so much. I did give chase to see what the lad clutched in his hand, what it was he had apparently stolen, but when I did catch up with him he opened his hands to show me he had nothing and my guess is that he must have thrown it into the swift flowing river. When I questioned him further he was away again and I knew his young legs were too much for me to challenge further."

I wondered if the lad did find the note, was it that he was looking at it contained in its leaden casket. But I had no option than to return to London at the earliest possible moment. Nothing else seemed important now, except to return and see Jane for the last time. I bid William and Vera farewell.

Yet, I knew even the magnificent Rob would find this a difficult journey. We were fortunate, indeed, to make the outward journey in three days, even in good weather, but it was turning colder and there was a hint of snow. It was already three in the afternoon on 6th February. Executions were always performed early in the morning. Even without rest stops, it would be too much for Rob. But I resolved that even if I could not make it in time, I would at least be nearer to the woman I loved. Why, Lord, did you resolve I should be so far from Jane at this crucial time? But of course His reasoning was for the sake of that which must be presumed best. I was to find that such imprudent questioning of my Lord was in vain when, wretched and tired, I finally reached London early in the morning of the 10th February and saw my beloved friend, Roger Ascham.

"I can see you know of the proclamation, the time Jane must die, John", he announced on my arrival, ensuring my loyal stallion was stabled, watered and fed and that I received refreshment.

"I thought she would be dead by now, Roger. In fact I understood the execution was set for yesterday."

"She has received a pardon for three days given by the Queen who would have it from Dr. Feckenham that she needs the time to reconsider converting her faith. But I hear that Jane has scorned the monk, that she never asked for a pardon on those terms, certainly not a pardon for her life. Albeit, her Majesty would ever presume the Lady Jane to convert if she did not receive a pardon. That she would wish to go to her Lord in the true faith adorned by the Queen.

"Feckenham is astounded by her deep presence of mind. She confirms she is ready to face death patiently and in whatsoever manner it may please the Queen to appoint. He expressed deep emotional feeling to me when describing the events of his final visit with Jane. How he found her on her knees fervently in prayer asking her Lord to grant her strength for their encounter. When she finished she arose and fixing her eyes upon him, said firmly: 'I am ready, Sir. I pray you question me and spare me not.'

"He immediately proceeded to question her on the articles of her faith. We know him to be a man of profound learning, well versed in the subtleties of scholastic dispute. He tried in every way to confound and complex her and proposed the most difficult questions to her.

" 'My faith is strong that I shall never resolve to convert whether or not the Queen will pardon me. I was bound by absolute loyalty to Lady Katharine Parr and her learning, and also to my tutor who has taught me so well, sire.'

" 'But, Lady Jane, your life is at stake, a life so young for I know if you would consent to convert our Queen will submit and pardon you. Please, please trust me that I know she feels strongly that because too you are of the royal blood line.'

" 'I shall never change my mind no matter how you try Dr. Feckenham, would you change yours?'

"He felt awkward and remained silent.

" 'Of course, you couldn't so please respect my faith and, with the same respect, inform the rightful Queen that I shall not. If she so chooses to kill me, then she must, but the consequences will be hers because truly our Lord will take this into account on her judgement day or do you really believe, Dr. Feckenham, that maybe she feels all protestants of the New Learning are witches and devils and that will excuse her of such atrocious acts?

" 'Why do you spend so much time with me? I suspect the Queen bends on the news that you would report to her of my submission to her wishes.'

"The discussion went on for several hours, during which Jane sustained her part with, what Feckenham admitted, admirable constancy, never losing a single point, but retorting upon her opponents questions when he was unable to answer, showing such powers of argument, such close and clear reasoning and such wisdom of the tenets of her own faith and of his that he was baffled and astounded, that one so young had absorbed so much knowledge. She matched his long and eloquent address with equal length, repeating her allegiance remained constant and unmoving with the dear departed Lady Katharine, that apart from her own feelings she would not stoop that low to dispel all that she stood for.

" 'Sometimes, Lady Jane, the Lord knows and respects, as mere humans we have to make sacrifices that are most times hard. Sometimes we need to weigh up our own feelings against those who may love us. I know of your love, Jane. I feel it but would never condescend to discover who shares it, although I have a good idea. I am merely saying that, perhaps, it would be better for you to save your life, to use that precious life to achieve something everlasting and wonderful in the eyes of the Lord, that in initiating your early departure you deprive Him and the world of what you can surely offer. You are a highly intelligent girl, of that we are all acutely aware and you can offer so much, Lady Jane. Please, please reconsider your decision. The Lord would surely forgive you, one so young too.'

" 'Then I would have to live the rest of my life in utter torment, knowing I had cheated death. That is precisely how I see it, what you are suggesting, to pretend I have submitted and condescended to convert. That is absolutely atrocious, Dr. Feckenham, and, knowing you are a man of God, I will deem that I have misunderstood you and you will thus leave me now to continue my own path in worship. I am ready. I begin to truly understand the life I have lived to die and now accept I must die to live in another place as our Lord chooses.

" 'If I thought your suggestion was to pretend, I would be so angry that you even assume that such a scheme would be acceptable to me.'

"Her expression changed from the calm ordered girl to that of anger and she ordered that Feckenham leave immediately, perhaps with even more eloquence and fervour concluding that she had lived by the Protestant faith and would continue so until she died.

"She swore to him that she had no time for the controversy between the two religions any more. All she sought was the peace to ready herself for death. Feckenham was surely influenced by Jane's gentleness and honour and asked that she may allow him to accompany her to the scaffold, to which she consented."

Roger Ascham continued: "Poor Guildford requested if he could meet Jane before their execution, and the Queen consented adding that she hoped it would be some consolation to them both. But Jane refused, announcing that it would disturb the holy tranquillity with which they had each prepared themselves for death, that her presence would weaken rather than strengthen him. She is set for death, John, and nothing can change that. She will be executed in the morning of the 12th of February."

Roger's words were quiet and slowly pronounced, yet came as no surprise to me. It was what I would have expected of Jane.

"You would like to be in her presence before she meets her maker, John?"

Roger was talking speculatively. This was something more than ever I could have imagined. Only her family and Dr. Feckenham were likely to sustain Queen Mary's permission at this time.

He noticed I was puzzled. "I have thus arranged for your final visit, in disguise of course, and, if you so wish, you can attend the execution, John."

I was overwhelmed. My words could not come. Of course, I had to see her again, assuming she would wish to see me.

Roger read my mind. "I am fortunate to be in good favour with the Queen at this time. She seems to think my work has everything to do with Catholicism and, of course, it has, but it also has as much to do with all that is religion, all that is philosophy. There can be no barriers. You will understand this, John. You will know."

"You have no need to explain, Roger. I understand fully and have no doubt. You are clearly in the enviable position that will steer you from harm's way. You are a diplomat indeed and thank the Lord the human race is blessed with those like you, who by their actions resolve to bring out all that is best in the human kind. I feel proud to know you, Roger. I guess it is my turn to embarrass you now but I am so amazed by your deliverance of good news, I cannot but help myself."

Roger would have none of it. He said he was simply glad to be of assistance. "In the morning, after a well-earned rest, I have arranged for Edward Vere to come down from Cambridge and he will arrive later in the day."

He would turn me into John Palmer once more before I travelled to the Tower. Although my journey would be the saddest in my life, I strangely felt at one with God. I was so happy that, with Jane's blessing, I could see her before her short journey to the scaffold.

Sir John Brydges quietly acknowledged me on my arrival at the Tower.

"Just another day, Mr. Palmer, and such a fine Lady will be lost forever," he said bleakly. "It is good she has friends at a time like this, for there are not many who pay her homage, yet she is so graceful a woman, blessed with a calm I have never before encountered within these prison walls. It is as if she welcomes death."

He paused for a moment and closed his head to mine, whispering in my ear: "It will come forth one day that Jane is truly innocent and has been grossly mistreated. If I were religiously inclined I would certainly back the Lady Jane. I will not relish her departure from these walls tomorrow morning."

I acknowledged the lieutenant and commented that, whatever our faith, we should all pray for Lady Jane tomorrow. I was soon with the Partridge's whose comments were similar to the lieutenant's.

"I have never felt so bad about the horrible fate awaiting one of my prisoners. Something is not right about this one. Lady Jane and her husband, being so young to meet finality of their lives. They are surely not responsible for what has been perceived of them, that which only the penalty of death suffices. Tomorrow will be a heavy day for us both," he said turning to his wife who was already in tears.

"Perhaps, she will be grateful you have come, Sir", she said, wiping her cheeks with a handkerchief. "Poor, wretched girl, she does not have many friends. Only those so called who have used her for their own ends."

Partridge cautioned his wife warning her that such words spoken could be the end of her. I remarked, they needn't have any fear on my account, for my feelings were theirs. That Lady Jane was the victim of those who sought selfishly their own ends, leaving her to face death.

It was as if the couple wanted to talk more but realised their position. Partridge knew about the Duke of Suffolk's recent attempts to overthrow the Queen and loathed such actions, which had surely influenced the Queen to forego any pardon for Lady Jane.

"Now he, too, will go to the scaffold. But we have ventured not to tell Lady Jane of this and, as far as I understand, all those who have come into contact with her these past few days, since we learned about her father's demise, are of the same opinion, that we should keep this tragic news away from her."

Partridge, of course, was hinting that I did, too, knowing well it was not his place to advise me one way or the other. Although I full appreciated the good intent it occurred to me, even at this late hour, that such news, tragic as it was, would persuade Jane that her secret note should be read to the Queen, that her precious life could still be saved.

But, for this moment, I could not be sure that Jane would even see me. Partridge asked me to wait until he returned from Lady Jane's quarters. He would let her know of my arrival.

Moments later he appeared at the foot of the wooden stairs in the hallway where I waited. He looked overwhelmed, not sad, not happy but something in between. He turned to me, started to speak, but then froze. He turned to his wife who was near to me in the doorway. His head went down upon her shoulder and he openly wept. His wife looked up at me with eyes opened wide, her hand gently patting his back.

"What is it, beloved? Is the Lady all right, why do you behave so?"

I held my breath, one half of my mind telling me of her refusal to see me, even now. I braced myself for the bad news as Partridge slowly lifted his head from his wife's shoulder and humbly apologised for his behaviour.

"I think not, Mr. Partridge." I said soothingly. "These are obviously trying times for you. I am aware of your good relationship with the Lady which was so apparent when last we met."

There was a half-smile on his face now and Mrs. Partridge calmed as she saw it, too. "How is she?" I continued not knowing what to expect. First the tears and now the smiles.

He eventually found his words and spoke gently to both of us. "She is surely a saint. You would think she was going to her wedding and not her death tomorrow," he said bleakly. "She looks more like a Queen than when she sat upon the throne. She greeted me heartily and her small open face was aflame. She is happy that you are here, Sir, and asked that you give her five minutes when she will gladly see you."

I immediately understood Partridge's reaction. Jane's happy mood would have been understandable if the Queen had decided to pardon her but, obviously, Partridge himself would be among the first to know of this. Then why, on the last full day of her life, would Jane react so? I would soon know the answer.

Again, as the time before, Elizabeth Tylney opened the door of Jane's rooms and greeted me. She looked solemn but welcoming. I entered and she passed and made her exit, closing the door behind her.

I looked towards the window and saw Jane in the white spread of midday sun flowing through the window. I could barely encounter her features as the sun made me squint. Whether it was the thought of her ultimate passing or a signal from the Lord, I will never know, but the moment froze and then, quite gently and slowly, the figure moved away from the window. It was as if her spirit was visualised in a canopy of bright glaring white mist in preparation for her imminent departure from this world.

I cannot put into words just how I understood why Jane was in good spirits at this time. But it was all there in the charisma of this remarkable young woman. Not simply a human soul embodied by flesh and blood, derived to meet the needs of our tenancy on earth. This was indeed the preparation of the passing of life from this place to another. Now the spirit would embody the material body and eventually leave it to replenish the earth from whence it came. No need for the body in the next place. The spirit was practically transportable to another time and another place. The place I ventured would be heaven for Jane and I considered that her short stay in this world would meet all the requirements set by the good Lord.

Yes, I completely understood why Jane was happy.

Her voice was soft and her presence was absolutely calm. Her nervous debility, the shaking of the head, the flicking of eyelids was absent. The manner in which she conducted herself generally was consistent of the Jane known to me in the past. This was a young woman ready and waiting for her maker and almost longing to take the journey without further delay.

My concern about the news of her father and what should she do about the note were no longer significant. I soon realised that Jane would stop at nothing to meet her maker the next day, that He had finally called upon her soul after so many days waiting. The early prison days, awaiting the Queen's pardon, later those days when she knew not if she would be eventually pardoned. Then the final days, one day being told she and Dudley would be executed the following morning, then another three days given by the Queen, following Dr. Feckenham's request that the couple needed more time to prepare themselves for their maker. Not that a late decision by Jane to convert to Catholicism, as desired by Her Majesty, would now make any difference. Certainly, I learned later her death was imminent and notwithstanding amendment. The chance for a pardon promoted by Feckenham had long passed.

"My beloved schoolmaster," Jane cried. "And I thought I had driven you off forever, that I would never see you again after my recent despicable treatment of you, then you stubbornly return again and again and especially now, for I have the Queen Majesty's assurance I will be absent after the hour of ten tomorrow, that I once foolishly ventured not to see you on recent occasions. What a foolish woman I was. But all that has passed now, good Sir. Although I cherish the dwindling hours, my life here is almost ended and I will soon meet my just and Holy Lord, I still will sadly miss you, whom I have so dearly loved and cherished, whom I have shared body and soul complete, and secretly wanted so to do. All my secrets mean nothing to me now. Nobody on earth can do me more harm than I have already encountered. No person can venture to execute me a second time for that which I have done wrong. But I would that no harm come to you. I am assured by my good friend, Sir John Brydges, who has loyally stood by me during my trying days in the Tower that the spies and ears, known to have haunted the cells during the past, have all gone. My good ladies have the wisdom to know that your presence here is very special indeed and there will be no disturbance. We can talk freely, for the first time ever, since I have known and discovered I loved you as a woman loves a man. You are the contrary to the last person who visited, another of my unwanted family who has abscond to Catholicism, Robert Dudley, the *'fine standing'* man who is five years senior to Guildford and a person whom once I admired. No more indeed, I would have imagined he had more stamina than to succumb to the Queen's *'true faith'* as she would have it. He had the audacity to visit me in order to blackmail me in feeling guilty, because of my stubbornness in implementing the death sentence to Guildford as well as myself.

" 'Jane, my beloved sister in law, I have been granted special permission by our sympathetic Queen to leave my cell to try and make you aware of your possible pardon if you do convert as she has said I will be pardoned shortly.' "

Jane said, she angrily responded: "Do you have the audacity to think if the Monk Feckenham, with all his cunning and charisma, was unable to gain my agreement you will?

178

"He knelt before me and I instantly reminded him that I was no longer Queen, so he had no need, but I realised his idea was to please me.

" 'I have been prisoner long enough, why sacrifice your life so virile and so young to be a martyr?'

" 'You plainly have no idea, do you Robert? You have thrown away your conscience to save your soul and you think I would do the same? I rule you in contempt of all those who have supported you and you will gain nothing from me. Go, tell your brother that this day I feel stronger and closer to the Lord than ever before and I will never forsake Him. My faith remains strong and secure and forever constant until the axe man chops of my head!'"

She looked up at me and I could see it in her eyes, despite the anger she had raised with Robert, it made her realise how confident and happy to remain faithful to her beliefs.

She beckoned me to come to the window and asked that I looked in the direction of the chapel. I was horrified to see that work had commenced on the building of the scaffold on Tower Green. I quickly came away from the window and could not bring myself to face my beloved, so strong, so courageous.

"It matters not, John. Do not be concerned. At least my journey to the Lord will be short. Be assured, I am of good heart and joyful stance in readiness for my journey tomorrow. Be also assured that your coming has completed the request of my prayers lately. That now you are here and tomorrow, immediately after you have slept, immediately you must go, too. Flee to another land where you know you will be safe, John, for Mary's advisor will grant you no mercy and will surely find a way of burning you as a heretic. You will surely not be safe in this land until Elizabeth reigns, which, surely, she will. I instinctively know she will. She will make a better Queen than ever I could. She is made to be a Queen.

"But I will be there to watch over you, dear John. My prayers to our Lord have this arranged. So we shall always be in touch, John, if you wish to contact me I will know and I will be there in your head. We are as mortals in this world, most are unable to understand what life is and what comes after life. That is why I have joyfully read the many works of the great philosophers to which I owe you much, for it was you who introduced me to Plato. I knew and understood the meaning of my life on earth in those early days at Bradgate, John, when you so gently taught me. You have been my true angel as well as my schoolmaster. If it were not for you, today I would be the wretched figure of a rejected human being, fearsome of what is to come, not knowing what true faith is. I surely pray for all those poor souls who meet their maker in this mind but trust the Lord will be fully aware of their shortcomings, and they will mercifully be given another chance in preparation to properly qualify to meet their maker."

Jane was resolute. I had never before felt so humble in her presence.

179

Indeed, I had played a big part involving her in the work of the philosophers. I considered I was well versed, especially in the doctrines of Plato and Socrates, which generally concurred with my religious beliefs. I am of the same opinion as that of my contemporaries that both Greek thinkers, who lived well before Christianity, were part of God's mission to prepare the theoretical foundations for the coming of the Christ figure. Of course, Jane and I had enthusiastically shared these opinions since the Bradgate days.

But Jane was no longer simply a student. In many ways it became clear to me that she had discovered aspects in Plato, for instance, of which I was unaware. Perhaps we all see and learn different aspects of what those learned men really meant. From Jane's point of view it seemed to me uncanny that she, whose life was deemed to be short, accepted the theory that our tenancy here on earth was meant to be a preparation for death, that we are all sentenced to that certainty which is death. That, indeed, what we do with our lives and how we behave is all but part of a test in preparation for another life after death. Jane had truly devoted her life to the ways of the Lord and the teachings of the Holy Bible. Now here she was, fully equipped in mind and spirit, to have served her sentence of life and present herself wholly to the Lord.

She took her bible from the windowsill, clasped her small hands to form a cradle on which the book rested and paused in deep meditation. Then she looked up at me, her face full of brightness, those wonderful brown eyes that truly were the windows of her soul, because something was coming through which I cannot begin to put into words. But when she spoke in a soft but distinct tone, her thoughts were transferred to me.

"I am truly blessed that I am permitted access to my wondrous books, to replenish my soul with the readings of Socrates by Plato. For he, too, was sentenced to death, albeit for poisoning the souls of his scholars. The circumstances were, of course, different and he was not so young as I, but he was duly rehearsed for death and it was easy, so easy for him to accept. Jesus, of course, knew, too, and he was well rehearsed. So you see, John, you need not be concerned. I will stand on the scaffold tomorrow and thank the Lord for the life I have had. I will cherish my journey into His kingdom. They can dispose of my body in which way they think fit but, no matter, we know flesh and blood for what it is, purely a form by which our souls can cope in a material world yet is always destructible. Destruction of the soul would be another thing but, God willing, I go with soul intact and nothing can destroy that."

In the past we had spoken much of the soul. Jane was fascinated by it. She vigilantly held the view that if we lived a life according to the scriptures, our souls would go forth unharmed, yet fully replenished by the goodness which expands from the experience of life on earth, yet always accepting humans were vulnerable to the temptations of the devil, as she had been, most prominently in accepting the role of a sovereign. She asked for compassion in her prayers, that her soul be restored for presentation to God.

I put it to her that my belief was that she had nothing to worry about on that score, compared with many who had scarred their souls to such extent that God would feel inclined to exclude them forever from entering His kingdom. But God is merciful and Plato, who knew nothing of Christianity, concluded that our souls could be restored within another life form. It was reincarnation, another chance to restore the soul scars of a former life. All of this, of course, had been discussed in detail between us many times. But at this time it was more meaningful than ever it was in the past. She thanked me for my confidences, which she said, gave her full spirit. She even joked about how God would look immediately referring to my false beard, which she thought, suited me.

"Perhaps when you are Bishop, John – as I know you will be – you should grow a real one."

As we spoke with each other, there were times when we did not. Sometimes the silence, the utter silence, when yet we both seemed still to be in conversation. It was as if we were frozen in time and space. She was so happy and joyful. I had never known her to be so exuberant.

She told me she had written to her parents and her sisters and, although they had not replied or come to visit her, she forgave them, understanding they had to tread carefully under the regime of the Queen. She was glad Dudley's brothers had been pardoned but sympathised with Dudley whom she felt did not deserve to die.

"But in reality, Jane, who deserves not to die more than you?"

"Please do not upset yourself, John. I was meant to die, that was meant to be. It is my destiny, of that I am now fully aware. Even if I was unaware of the seriousness of my meek acceptance of the crown, I accepted it. Even now, fully understanding the misdoings of Northumberland and his stock, and how I was tricked into acceptance, in the end I did accept and, with my faith in God, I should have found the strength to deny it, knowing that the true wearer should be Mary Tudor."

Strangely, I was in her world. The main purpose of my visit, to help her during this terrible time, to come to terms with everything, made me feel redundant. She needed no help from me. She needed not a messenger of God when she was in direct contact. I felt truly humble. Although my faith in God was complete, I could only have delivered the message I felt was in accordance with the true wishes of God. I still had so much to learn. I felt I must now regularly pray and thank the Lord for the lesson I have learned today.

I felt I had been with her for hours and mentioned to Jane I feared the time was right for my departure.

"Fear not, John. The good lieutenant allows me freedom on this my last day and it is the Queen's wish. He is a good man and will accompany me tomorrow to the scaffold. He has truly touched my heart but I have known for a long time that only one man can take it as our Lord will take my soul tomorrow. That is you, John Aylmer, my beloved schoolmaster."

I had never experienced such intense closeness to the soul of this remarkable young woman as then. Oh, how foolish was I ever to imagine there was any truth in Guildford Dudley's remarks concerning Jane and the lieutenant.

She continued: "We still have much to ponder in good spirit and the time is nigh. I must render to you the real Jane Grey who has been stifled. Besides which, you have only been here for a small hour and there are thus three more I can easily endure with one who is my dearest companion in the life I have known."

She closed to me. I was glad she was given such freedom. But the room looked bleak enough. All such things removed upon which she could do herself some harm.

"You will have noticed I have just this simple but comfortable couch and a wooden chair and table as is the rule for all sentenced prisoners here. Those who will find strange satisfaction in the method of my departure would not wish to be disappointed by my taking my own life. If I were inclined I would find it difficult enough. Even the windows have been barred should I wish to jump to my Maker. I find merriment in all this, John. I am not afraid any more. I shall give them what they want to see, but I shall give them good tidings as well. I have already written my farewell speech which has been well rehearsed."

She told me that she had also written to her father who also was now held prisoner in the Tower. I knew the reasons why he had been detained only two days before but assumed Jane was not aware of the true deed and the consequences, that he, too, would meet the executioner at the Queen's pleasure. Although, she did mention that her father's imprisonment did not help her cause, if that is what was intended in the crime committed. I did not wish to distress her further with the truth and hoped she would be unaware of it. Even to this day I believe she knew not the circumstances of her father's imprisonment, that in the same month he would also be executed for his involvement in Thomas Wyatt's ill-timed uprising.

I was pleased, too, that she had written to her sister Katharine but she did not mention her mother in her note. She told me she had also written to those correspondents who had served her so well with the outstanding knowledge, without which she undoubtedly would have found this last day much harder to bear.

" So many, including you, John Aylmer, have subscribed to that and I am overwhelmed with a certain peace."

"I am informed, Jane, that the Queen's chaplain has talked with you, no doubt to offer religious counsel and persuade you to convert to his faith?"

"I like the man well," Jane said. "He is a truly good man and means well. Dr. Feckenham came for the last time this morning, knowing I would be so bold, that he could not make a Catholic out of me. I told him, before the Queen delayed my execution for three days, that I am ready to face death patiently and in whatsoever manner it may please the Queen. It would truly be hypocritical to wonder aimlessly from one faith to another like the weak Dr. Haddon and the late Duke of Northumberland. I have no time left for the controversy between the two religions, John. All that I require is the peace to ready myself for death. It would seem that Dr. Feckenham misconstrued my meaning regarding my reference to time and returned two hours later that day, having spoken with the Queen and gained a reprieve for myself and Guildford of three days for further spiritual enlightenment. I heartily scorned him despite his good intentions, but he had failed to understand me. He comes on the Queen's instigation, I know that, to persuade me to convert. This does not mean that a pardon will be given, simply that her majesty is concerned that I meet the Lord given the true faith."

My heart was bursting with sympathy for this poor unfortunate soul. I prayed for a miracle, that the new Queen would repent and render an unconditional pardon in knowing Jane was plainly innocent of any crime.

It was as if Jane read my thoughts. Even now, although tears glistened on her pale cheeks, she offered a radiant smile and spoke so sweetly and clearly.

"Try not to be sad for me, John Aylmer, for these are tears of joy and gratitude that I have truly been blessed by our Lord with His teachings through you and your guidance, too, in showing me the way attributed by those fine philosophers, particularly Plato who understands the reason for life and death and the part we all play.

"I believe Dr. Feckenham has finally absorbed the reasons why I accept my punishment tomorrow without fear in my heart but with joy. He asked if he could be present and I gladly welcomed him. I really do believe, John, he has cause to question his own beliefs after our discussions. He realised my disapproval in going to the Queen to seek a reprieve with the notion that it is what I wanted for myself and for Guildford, poor Guildford. And she concluding that three days would be sufficient for our spiritual enlightenment. She means well, I understand that, but, alas, she is unable to recognise the real truth. I seek a better life in eternity and asked that I may be left to make my own peace with God."

I comforted myself into a chair facing Jane. I was no longer tense and fraught with the thought of how I would ease Jane's most awful dilemma. I looked full into her wide brown eyes not being able to quite apprehend why she was not alarmed or concerned about her imminent end. God! She was so young, so vibrant and complete. How could the Lord allow this to happen to one so very learned and wise? She rested with both hands clasped upon her lap. My hands went to them, found them. They were so small nestled in mine. I closed my eyes and suggested we pray together. She nodded so sweetly and closed her eyes. We did not utter a word. Our prayers were in our minds, each of us knowing what we must ask. It was as if an angel passed over, tranquillity equal to that I felt at Bradgate. The Lord was truly with us that day, easing the way for Jane. Oddly, I felt Jane had nothing to lose but everything to gain, and then she spoke, so softly.

"Yes, my beloved schoolmaster, our Lord comforts me in this fearsome place. I once questioned his reason for dealing with me so severely. I have sinned as all human beings do and could not understand why a punishment so final was necessary. But that is because I am mortal in this life, because life is a rehearsal for death and the immortality that follows. I look forward to immortality, that I will suffer the torment of this world no more. I do feel for those like yourself who have given so much, but hope you will resolve, in memory of me, to live your life as I have seen you live it, as the very likeable, nay loveable, joyful human being so full of esteem, wit, humour and energy. Without you, John Aylmer, I swear, I could not have taken these last hours so easily."

"No, Jane. It is the Lord not me," I corrected.

"Yes, but it was you who has always given the best of yourself in tutorship and persuasion in the teachings of our Lord. So please do not be despondent, for one day you will join me in Heaven...." She paused for a moment, then smiled and continued, "Who will put me to task if I waver, who will guide me? Even the Lord must have His limits and will call especially on those who have preached upon earth."

"For selfish reasons, Jane, I am truly grateful for the reprieve because I would not have been able to see you before..."

I could not finish the sentence. It was too painful even to think of it. I wanted to tell her of my return to Bradgate but realised it was of no significance now. Her memories of Bradgate must remain untarnished. She would not wish to learn of its demise and neglect. I perceived she would not wish to be reminded of the hidden note.

"Before my death, John," Jane said completing my sentence. "You have no need to hide the word. Death is simply the call of the Lord, is it not? Others will join me. I will not entirely be alone and so the world goes on. New lives will enter to begin the great rehearsal for the hereafter. If they do not get it right, in accordance with the way our Lord has shown us, then they will surely return to do it all over again, perhaps in a different body, I know not, but with the same tarnished soul. I really do believe that is so."

"Of course you do, Jane. You are so brave, so very brave. The Lord will truly take account of your trials and tribulations upon this place. That He, through Queen Mary, has blessed you with a short reprieve."

"A short reprieve for a short life, John. He surely does work in mysterious ways and I am, despite earlier respites, that I had the audacity to question our Lord in letting me suffer the torment of another three days, I am now eternally grateful that He did so, because it is good that I, too, meet you once more before death.

"I must tell you that our Queen also permitted Guildford to see me for one last time yet. Respecting her reasoning I was bound to reject the meeting. Taking into consideration Dr. Feckenham's dismay and, apparently, Guildford's broken heart it would be hypocritical for me to allow that to happen. I do not love Guildford or have any liking for his stock, but I do not seek revenge on Guildford for that. He was probably as much coerced, as was I into the devious schemes of his father.

"We are so different in every way, and such a meeting would truly hinder the pathways we tread. We have absolutely nothing in common, least our God who he has blasphemed more times than not."

Then again, after I had given her the red rose, our eyes met again and it seemed our very souls were as one again. I now knew for certain just how very much in love I was with her now and I also knew her feelings were the same.

She beckoned for me to join her, to be seated next to her on her small comfortable couch. Before Jane I had never been quite so physically close to this remarkable Lady and the vibrancy of her being set me afire. Without reservation my heart said it was absolutely right to kiss her on the mouth. I immediately pulled back and stood up, apologising for my outrageous behaviour at this time and seeking her pardon.

"You, John Aylmer, need not seek pardon on my account. Your kiss is most welcome even if it were unfinished. We have both known our deep affection for each other. You, in your way, have indicated this many times to the masked Lady Jane. I have stifled it behind that mask so many times but once, that wonderful time I know we both remember so well. But now the mask is departed. I can heartily render body and soul unto you. No longer need it matter about social standing for soon I shall be departed and it will be of no consequence to God because we both know in his eyes we are all the same. I am sure our Lord would not cast aspersion in the circumstances of this unmarried pair for, truly in my heart, I am joined only to you. My marriage to Guildford was never complete for, in accordance with my beliefs, I could never join souls with one I could not love."

"You have only once loved completely, Jane?" I asked gently and remembering what Guildford had said about her and Sir John Brydges.

"I have John, with you and then I knew how love really was. The best thing that has ever happened in my short life is to have known and loved you, your encouragement and devotion in my quest for learning the scriptures and the works of the great philosophers, least my correspondence with many great scholars.

185

"But, perhaps more important than that, although each go together, you John Aylmer, you are truly the very best, simply you! It was you who introduced me to my happy and joyful learning and it is simply you I love with all my heart, with all my being, and with all my absolute soul. So, please be seated and complete that kiss for which I have secretly craved for again."

"You have loved me for that long?" I asked taking the place beside her.

"I have probably loved you most of my life but as I grew up I discovered how an adult felt about being in love. Please, be silent now, John, and finish the kiss. My time is short indeed, this must be the once only joining of our souls, our hearts, our…"

My lips had found hers. Her response was instantaneous and warm. The kiss was soft, gentle. I felt her hands clasp together behind my head as the kiss continued. She did not want me to stop. Her fingers opened and ran though my hair in circular motions. The kiss grew deeper now.

"I love you so very much, John," she whispered when the kiss ended. "I have never felt such love and affection. My whole being warms and tingles to your touch. Please, do not stop. Please, show me your true love in order that our hearts, minds and bodies combine."

It was so right, so natural being with her. My fingers instinctively fondled her neck. She raised her chin to induce another kiss as I traced the line of her neck upwards until I reached her lips once more. She made soft sounds revealing her pleasure as we continued, sounds, which expressed her joy.

I whispered so softy into her ear: "I will be with you forever. My soul will combine with your own as if we be one. Mere words cannot tell the strength of my love for you. My darling, you are all and everything to me."

We looked closely into each other's eyes, hers full of love and compassion. It felt so right with her. We belonged to each other and she closed to me again. Her lips once more found mine and she clasped my hand guiding it to her bosom. I felt that which I had longed for so long, those full firm breasts, which seemed to swell to my ardent caress.

"Please, sweet John… Please, now… I need you so much, I ache for you!"

Then we were both removing fervently each article of clothing until we stood there, appraising each other.

Now, we could not stop ourselves, systematically enjoying the thrill and excitement of exploration. The kissing, touching, which were accompanied by the sighs and whispers of two people so deeply in love with each other.

Then I knew there was no foundation in what Mary Sidney had assumed, that indeed sweet Jane was pure and untouched.

I felt I should tell Jane about my time with Mary Sidney, but in my mind it was not the time or the place, and there could be no other time or place now as her remaining hours on earth were short.

What really mattered is what had just happened between us was with complete love.

Our love was spiritually and passionately rekindled in her bedchamber. When the time came for our sad farewell, I simply said I would be close to her in the morning. My dear friend Roger Ascham had arranged even that. Tears filled her eyes but she told me not to be concerned, because the tears were as much for the joy of having shared freely and completely our true love. She said she would be content enough in the company of her maker, her other great love who would be watching over her. I closed to her once more, my hands clasped tightly behind her small form, then a final kiss.

"Farewell, my beloved schoolmaster. Tomorrow you must be gone from here. You must flee for your life and I will wait in God's good stead for the time when you will join me."

I silently parted company, turning as I reached the door. My eyes focussed on hers, then I gently closed the door behind me.

Sir John Brydges accompanied me from the building as I turned, looked upwards and saw Jane waving. The scaffold was almost complete but as we passed the labourers paused and turned away.

"She is a very brave young woman, such that I have never known before in these circumstances, John Aylmer," the lieutenant said as we neared the exit gate

I shuddered realising he knew my identity. I would surely be detained. But a kindly smile soothed my concern. "Your beard, Sir. It has slipped. Better adjust it before you go through the gate, the guard will surely notice."

His tall presence shielded me as I quickly put my disguise into place. Why was one of Queen Mary's most loyal attenders not taking action against me?

"Do not be disturbed, Sir. I have known from the start of your visits. There is only one person in the world who could rekindle our Lady Jane for whom we both share so much affection. I have no religious tendencies, Sir. In my steering I feel that is best. But our Lady has caused me to question my antagonism of God. Yet if there is a true God, why would He let Lady Jane die?"

"Perhaps her time on earth was destined to be short," I replied. "God's need for her is in another place, another time maybe."

The lieutenant, looking down at me, just smiled as if he wanted to believe that.

"Be on your way, Sir, and make an early sailing before the Queen catches you!"

That night passed so slowly. I could not find the release of sleep. I wanted to be awake this night, Jane's last night, to experience the spark of life every second, every minute and hour in the knowledge that I was still sharing this earth with the one I love. Those last hours were too precious to squander in sleep.

My mind constantly focused on Jane, laying there on her bed, awaiting death in the morning. I tried to imagine how she would be feeling but knowing that was impossible. I consoled myself knowing that she was in constant touch with her Maker and, being the kind of woman she was, she would be calm, tranquil and at peace with the world that had treated her so cruelly. Yet, it was as if she was in contact. Her thoughts reaching mine, constantly appealing to me not to wait a second longer to accomplish my arranged journey to the continent away from the clutches of Queen Mary, who would surely have me burnt at the stake if she discovered my true identity. That special feeling of our bodies and souls joined still remained and 'tis true, I pined because it could never be repeated.

I simply asked her to forgive me, that not even because of my own life could I venture forth and make for the safety of the continent whilst she still lived, but I vow she did not receive my thought because she was immersed in the prayers of our Lord. I joined her in those prayers and when they finished I felt she had found the slumber to when she was no longer awaiting death. And when she awoke, the Lord would constantly be at her side to comfort her. She had no need of me now. She would soon be in the hands of her Maker. Yet, I felt still that I could not yet abandon her, not until after her soul had departed her body.

I was there in the crowd again, witnessing Jane's execution. Moments before she had so bravely addressed her audience, pale and dry eyed wearing a black gown, telling them that she was wrong to accept the crown: "The fact, indeed, against the Queen's highness was unlawful, and the consenting thereunto me, but touching the procurement and desire thereof by me or on my behalf. I do wash my hands in innocence, before God and the face of you, good Christian people this day."

Of course, she was innocent. In her trial this innocence was queried in so much that it being well known she was an intellectual and so being, must have known the illegal proclamations issued by Northumberland and his corrupt council. But Northumberland was devious to the extreme and I am fully assured that Jane had no prior knowledge of his plans.

But now it seemed she had momentarily envisaged the true nature of the most horrid and cold execution, for that confusing moment, when after she had been blindfolded, she could not find the block. She lost control of herself when she screamed the scream of terror and fear. I could take no more. Those on the scaffold stood like statues whilst Jane fumbled, her arms and hands reaching out in every direction. I ran to the steps, which led up to the platform and quickly found a way through those who stood up there – and to Jane. I took her wrists and gently guided them. She found the sides of the block and was quiet again. Just beside her I saw her red prayer book, which she must have dropped earlier. But more significantly I noticed something peeking out between the pages. Closer examination revealed it was the red rose I had given to her. I knew because it had the same notepaper bound finely around the stem, which I had carefully endorsed with words of love. At that moment, as if by fate, a gust of wind caught the delicate dry petals and they disappeared into the surrounding trees.

"Farewell, my beloved. We will meet again when we will both be free souls," I said. I just felt she knew I would be with her until the end.

In the quietest of whispers she said: "Thank you, my schoolmaster," and found the aperture in the block, her slim neck easily fitting between. I caught the glance of the axe man, the whites of his eyes just staring into mine. But his nod was enough to tell me he would make it quick, as if he realised and understood this complete stranger, who had appeared before him, was someone special. Had he heard my whispers with Jane? I will never know.

I turned and made for the steps when I heard her last words ring out: "Lord, into thy hands I commend my spirit" in such clear diction I knew she was again with her maker. I reached the ground. I could not bear to watch and instantly made my exit. In a second I heard a thud and a chant from the crowd below mingled with the screams of Jane's waiting women behind me. Several large ravens scurried around me. My head was whirling and I seemingly imagined a second thud but cast it from my mind. I knew Jane had gone forever. I fled into the chapel before my departure and dropped to my knees, crying to God that she would now be truly safe. My tears came in torrents, the absolutely horrid demise of that sweet wonderful so strong innocent girl

Soon I had reached the stable where my horse was ready. I mounted to leave when Mrs. Ellen quickly approached me and raised her right arm to reach my hand.

"God bless you, Sir, for being with Jane. I knew you would be there. But you must be away in all haste. I have heard that our Queen has knowledge of your identity."

"As indeed do you. You must also escape." I advised

"I have known all along, for Jane would react to no body the way she would react to you. God bless her soul, that she now at least be in peace. Now away with you, Sir, and I hope we will meet again.

"And thank you, Sir. God has been good to me. At least some happiness has come out of all this. Robert took heed of the message I asked you to give him. Now that poor Jane needs me no more, he will have my hand in marriage."

"When Elizabeth is Queen, then we shall all meet, again," I cried.

She held her handkerchief to her face and held her hand high waving goodbye. "God speed!" she shouted over the sound of Robs gallop.

CHAPTER NINETEEN

I spent the next four years safely in exile, along with many of my Protestant contemporaries, who conscientiously held on to the reformed religion.

I wanted to keep busy, to offset the trauma in my mind following the death of poor Jane. I resided in Strasbourg and afterward in Zurich at Helvetia where, in peace, I followed my studies. I befriended Dr. Peter Martyr who was the late King's reader in divinity at Oxford and attended his lectures. We both instructed promising young students in good literature and religion.

I was often asked about my tutorship of the Lady Jane. Some still referred to her as the late murdered Queen. John Fox was busy collecting material for his Martyr logy and was keen to communicate with me regarding the brilliant lady. He was enthused to set up a chronological record of Jane's personal items and portraits that had been painted. I mentioned, she was reluctant indeed to sit for such but those that were commissioned were probably, along with many other belongings, destroyed by the hapless Queen Mary.

I felt honoured to do so and presented him with a letter she had written to Dr. Harding during her imprisonment in the Tower, which I had published. She had spoken to me of her disgust regarding her former tutor's conversion to Catholicism, but never so much as described in the letter. This came from the heart, clearly showing how deeply she felt about her faith. She wrote the letter shortly after receiving the news about Dr. Harding's conversion and seemed to have later softened her views. I had always tried to mellow her in this regard, explaining that God would see fit to judge no matter what our opinions were. But the letter did show that Jane carried hate in her heart which was truly expressed in her letter to the "chicken hearted" man because of his dramatic conversion *"that she could not but marvel and lament his case."*

She had remembered him in her early childhood as a devoted Calvinist, a 'lively' member of Christ as she put it but he had defected to the *"imp of the devil"* and *"belonged in the stinking and filthy kennel of Satan"*. In her eyes he was a *"wretched and unhappy man resisting his maker and neglecting the word of the Lord which he had taught her so implicitly and thoroughly."* She went on to pound him with a barrage of texts from the Old and New Testaments before asking him to repent before it was too late.

Although I have come to the conclusion that Jane exceeded her opinion of Dr. Harding, I understand how she must have felt when she wrote the devastating letter. She had the ability to render harmful accusations upon those whom she felt had badly let her down. But this was a part of Jane, which, I have to acknowledge, was unknown to me. Whether she chose not to share such obtrusive opinions with me because of my standing, or what I was to her,

I do not know. Reading the letter, it almost seems that she was not the author, that something, I know not what, had infiltrated her mind. But it gave good account of how she had felt at times during her imprisonment and indeed deserved publication as record of how utterly devoted she was to her faith.

If John Fox were minded to make any memorials of her, nothing would be worthier of his pen.

Dr. Harding indeed had bitterly complained to the new Queen of the disrespect shown to Jane in allowing her body to remain unattended for so long upon the blood drenched scaffold, almost as if she expected a hoard of the Towers Ravens would become like vultures and dispose of the remains. And the disgrace that it was still there four hours after her execution and noted by the French Ambassador who could not believe his eyes, stating the French would never act so uncivilized. Of course, it was all to do with the Queens instruction to the effect that no Protestant would ever again be buried under the floor of the Chapel Royal of St. Peter ad Vincula here.

I am truly relieved I did not witness this atrocity, otherwise I would surely have committed my fate to Queen Mary's indulgence and have joined the many other so-called heretics who were so cruelly and slowly burnt at the stake. I could not have held back my disgust and would have complained to the ends of the earth that, no matter what the Queen thought, Jane deserved the respect at least to have been properly attended and buried afterwards.

But the very embittered Bloody Queen was to meet her end and would be adjudged not by me but by her maker. Karma ensured her life was miserable and true love did not come her way.

News swept the continent in 1558 that Queen Mary Tudor was dead. No great sympathy was shown, especially by the non-Catholics. She had already become known as the merciless Bloody Queen for all the atrocities committed in her reign and her marriage to Philip of Spain was very unpopular. Significantly, she did not keep her word in stating at the beginning of her reign that she would allow Protestants to follow their faith unhindered and that all sympathy would be shown thereto.

England was about to change dramatically when the very popular Elizabeth took the throne and I was joyful to return to my homeland again.

She welcomed and invited me, along with my contemporaries who had returned from exile to court, and praised us for our fortitude and good sense and advised it was no cowardly act to flee from England when that "abominable" half-sister of hers took the throne.

"I, myself had to make certain mindful sacrifices for she would have cut even her own half-sister's head off," Queen Elizabeth scowled. "We had to think of England's future and the important part we would imminently play. I will need your absolute trust and support, gentlemen."

In her role as head of the Church of England she advised each of us of our new positions and told me I would be Archdeacon of Lincoln.

191

I was both proud and delighted she had seen fit to present me with so dignified an archdeaconry as Lincoln and I would cherish my new position.

We spoke tenderly about Jane and the Queen said she was the most intelligent and religious girl she had ever known. But she added that perhaps that was her downfall because we all knew to what depths Mary Tudor had degraded herself in her obsession to be rid of any person with royal blood who may threaten her crown.

"I have the people to thank for my life, Dr. Aylmer, for without their support I, too, would have joined the others in the vaults of St. Peter ad Vincula. She dared not execute me, lest she lost her head, too".

"But I have heard it said, Your Majesty, that Lady Jane's body was not buried there because she refused to convert. Mary Tudor wanted only Catholics buried there," I submitted.

"That is despicable but, if true, typical of Mary," the Queen sighed. "If only Jane could have made herself more popular. She had the charm and grace but her introverted disposition was her great downfall. Yet, ironically, if she had taken a permanent hold of the throne then I would not have been Queen, which, I must declare, is important to me. I feel, too, and I know Lady Jane felt the same because she who was my cousin, unlike my half-sister who was not a direct descendent of my lamented father, I feel the crown has now found its rightful owner."

"The Lord has His ways," I responded. "I do believe Jane would have proudly delivered the crown to you because she never felt comfortable with it. It is a pity that your half-sister was the next in line as your father's first daughter."

"Clearly, Dr. Aylmer, and how brave was the young girl to accept his ways with such conviction upon the scaffold, that she could easily and so calmly read that long sermon without any sign of nervousness."

Queen Elizabeth looked the part and, although she had a formidable personality, I felt happy and secure in her company. Indeed, I was convinced that in as much I revered Jane, she was, by her own admission, not of the right calibre to rule the land. Truly, I think Jane would have preferred Elizabeth to be Queen instead of Mary. Perhaps, because of her execution the life threat on Elizabeth was curtailed. If Mary had taken the advice of her council to dispose of Elizabeth because of her threat to the Monarchy, she would have found a way to do so. But having already executed Jane, who had royal blood in her veins, she settled for pardoning her half-sister. By her marriage to Philip of France she hoped for an early successor to the throne and banked on the Catholic Monarchy surviving after her.

But God thought otherwise and I discovered Jane's death was not in vain

When I bowed farewell to the Queen and took my leave, I looked forward to further discussions with this elegant lady. Being with anyone who knew Jane so well aroused a feeling of kinship.

Less than one month at Lincoln I received a letter from another who was close to Jane.

It was an invitation from Mr. and Mrs. Robert Wills to meet them at their home in Lyn Ford. It did not immediately register who Robert Wills was, but then I remembered Mary Ellen. Happily, they were now married.

"We realise, Sir, having recently taken your new position, you may not be able to travel to Bradgate again and we feel it is perhaps unethical of us to ask such a thing. But we can promise you will be interested in what we have to say, something of the nature that only word by mouth can tell."

I immediately returned the letter and made plans to pay the Wills a visit the following week.

I was very curious to learn what it was they had to tell me which necessitated my presence at Lyn Ford. I would have been happy to visit anyway and give my heartfelt belated congratulations. I fully intended to visit Bradgate again when the opportunity was right, in sweet memory of Jane and my happy days there.

However, it was not to be as arranged and I hastily wrote to Mary and Robert delaying my visit for a further week. The Queen announced that she would be making visits on her clergy in certain areas and Lincoln was one of them. Already, she was displaying her great enthusiasm to keep in personal contact and take order of her kingdom and it's people.

During her visit she honoured me with her presence in my humble lodge for a light meal and told me she remembered me more as an uncle figure than Lady Jane's fine tutor and that she still recalled those vibrant days at Chelsea Palace, when Katharine Parr was 'a Queen so fitting' and where she last saw me.

I wanted to know if she had any thoughts about Lady Jane and took it upon myself to ask. She looked at me with a forlorn expression, which made me wonder if I should have asked. She was an intelligent Queen and she knew immediately that my question meant something more than just a casual enquiry.

"My dear schoolmaster, that is what she called you, isn't it? You must remember that my half-sister Mary, as much as I, cherished our days at Chelsea Palace when my father was still alive. The dear, dear Katharine Parr was as much a substitute mother to me as she was to Jane. But as Queen, Mary was trapped and was continually pressed by her formidable advisors to be rid of those who would threaten the Catholic throne. As much as she respected me and Lady Jane and, knowing in her heart we were both innocent of any treason her company would imply upon her, she was obliged to be rid of us. For my own part, I was indeed fortunate and all such accusations were dropped. I also had the people behind me. Jane did not. She was simply a pawn in the hands of that atrocious, power hungry Northumberland, and in marrying his son, as she was obliged to do, did herself no favours at all. Being a member of the hated Dudley family was enough to dispel any respect the people may have had for Jane, those that had known her, that is. She showed no interest in her subjects and was submerged within her own circle. That was her eventual downfall."

The Queen paused for a while and then continued with a softer voice, perhaps sensing despair in my expression.

"Have no fear, Doctor Aylmer. She was strong in faith and you know that. But she could never have made a successful Queen. Everything was against her. Hard as it may seem, she is better where she now is. Take heart from that, for I truly know your deep feelings for her soul departed.

"Instead God has chosen me and I have every reason to believe He had good reason for that. I will do my utmost to serve Him and our country the way I know best. I will have no hunger for power to forestall my better judgement."

I shall always remember what Queen Elizabeth said and her feelings that Jane was now in the best place. It installed within me a wonderful warmth.

A week later, however, I was free to take the time to travel to Lyn Ford and hopefully, if the weather remained fine, to visit Bradgate, too.

My worthy steed, Rob was growing older but still had the substance to carry me on my journey. On my arrival late the following day I was given a hearty welcome from Mary Ellen and her new husband Robert who stabled and fed my mount.

She proudly showed me around her new abode, which, she said, Robert had taken great heed to prepare before the wedding two years gone.

"I am so fortunate, indeed, to have had a second chance at marriage and with a wonderful man like Robert. He has been wonderful in helping me cope with life after the dear Lady Jane. Mrs. Tylney died, you know. She had a troublesome heart at the end. I believe it was the shock of all that bloodshed. We hated Queen Mary for all she had done. Now we have Queen Elizabeth who, I am sure, will prove to be a wonderful Queen. I should imagine you are joyful to return to England again, without the fear of Bloody Mary. I am sorry, Sir, calling her that, but most people do. They were pleased to see the end of her, even though that may sound wicked in your eyes. I could never forgive her for that, what she did to Jane. It was a despicable horrid deed."

I chose to give a comforting smile and completely understood Mary's feelings.

"But Mary Tudor suffered because of her actions," I eased, seeing the tears which she attempted to avoid. "She encountered a very unhappy life and did not have a happy marriage. Now she will be adjudged accordingly and all those she cruelly killed will be present as witness to her atrocious deeds."

She looked up at me. I remember how she had done before when we both took the stroll at Bradgate, when she was concerned about Robert.

"I will call you Mary now and your husband Robert. No need to be formal with each other anymore, especially as this is your home. But now you

194

have something to tell me, something you said could only be told by word of mouth?"

Mary hesitated for a moment as Robert entered, returning from the stables. Then we became immersed into talking about his progress at Lyn farm and how he still attended the position of caretaker at Bradgate House.

"We have heard word that the surviving Grey family will soon be returning to the great house and I expect there will be all haste then to put the old place back to rights and there will be much to attend to. I manage to keep the chapel presentable at all times in accordance with the late Queen's wishes and those of Queen Elizabeth."

Robert spoke briskly. He was a matter of fact man, sturdy and full of energy, obviously happy and contented sharing his life with Mary. He spoke with a stammer in his voice, which I put down to the excitement of the occasion.

"Never spoke with an Archdeacon before," he said after a pause. "Hope, you can understand me."

I nodded with an encouraging smile.

Mary brought me up to date with the news of Jane's sister, Katharine. How sadly her marriage to Lord Herbert was quickly annulled and how utterly distressed she was that her father-in- law procured this because the marriage became an embarrassing connection, she being the sister of the woman executed for treason.

"Apparently, Lady Frances Grey astonished everybody when she married again three weeks after her husband's death," Mary continued in a disapproving tone. "She married a young man fifteen years her junior called Adrian Stokes. You will remember him, he was a member of her own household at Suffolk House and had no high rank which, considering Lady Frances's position, took everyone by surprise because it was so uncharacteristic of her. She now lives quite near at Beau manor near the village of Woodhouse and her youngest daughter, Mary, is there, too. But we know nothing of how Mary is."

As the afternoon passed into evening my hosts brought me up to date with the happenings during the years I had been in exile. But I realised one question still remained unanswered.

I suspected the reply must have been to do with Jane. There was so much I wanted to know but felt reluctant to ask of Mary because she attended the execution and, as one of her serving ladies, was expected to assist in removing the body afterwards.

I wanted to know everything. Was it a straightforward execution? Hopefully, Jane did not suffer a painful death. I distinctly remember hearing the sound of a second fall of the axe as I was obliged to hastily depart, knowing that I had done everything possible within my power to be there until the final moment. For four years I constantly heard that terrifying second thump and the groans of the observers. The execution had been kept so secret that nobody knew, except the witnesses and Mary Ellen was one of them. But how could I ask her, no matter how delicately, how carefully. It wouldn't be the thing she would wish to recall.

"You must be hungry for it is already seven o'clock," Mary said arising from her bench and departing the room. "I will immediately go to the kitchen and prepare a hearty meal to nourish us all for the day ahead."

She left me in the company of Robert who was plainly pleased I had come.

"Mary still honours you as much as always, Sir. She has cried so many times over Jane. If the execution and aftermath had been straight forward, it still would have caused so much sorrow and distress but...well, the way it all went must have been like hell on earth for all those who loved Jane."

My mind numbed for a moment, I did not want to accept what Robert was saying.

Did Jane suffer a horrible painful death? Surely not. Our Lord would surely not be so cruel. The girl had already suffered enough even though she appeared to take it all so calmly.

I simply had to ask the inevitable question: "Why was it not straight forward, Robert?"

"You do not know, Sir? Dear Lord, I do humbly apologise."

"Please do not blame yourself. How could you have known? But you must tell me now. And before Mary returns."

For the following five minutes I was imagining things, which, in my worst imaginings, I could never have envisaged. Things heard that explained why the late Queen was so castigated by Mary Ellen. Robert spoke quietly, almost as if he had been there, sharing the experience.

"Mary and Elizabeth Tylney were horrified when the axe man had to come down a second time, having not done the job properly the first."

"Oh No...No!" I cried. One part of my mind wanted not to hear any more but the other... I had to know if Jane suffered.

"That man knew what he was doing, Dr. Aylmer. I feel certain of that. The Lady having so slender a neck, it should have been easy. But she refused him her gown in reward for a clean end to her life. When he held out his hand to take it, she scorned him and handed the gown to Mary who has it to this day."

At this point Mary returned from the kitchen with a parcel wrapped in an embroidered bag. Her expression informed me that she was quite aware of our conversation.

"I am sorry, dear," she said looking at her husband. Then, turning to me she continued: "I could not help but hear if not the words but the tone of Robert's voice. It is only right you should know what happened."

Then turning again to Robert: "Do not despair, dear. I will not break down this time, not in Dr. Aylmer's company, for his strength of mind will guide me through."

She made herself comfortable in her chair, clasped her hands together in her lap. Told me, the dinner was simmering in the pot, paused, then looked downward.

When she looked up again her expression had changed. She said she had a duty to perform and faced me open eyed.

"The first time... When Lady Jane was down there, kneeling over, her head over the block, I watched the executioner lining himself up and lifting the murderous weapon high above his head, at full arm's length, hands clenched tightly around the shaft.

I cried out for him to hurry in my mind and let that be an end of it, for Lady Jane's sake. He seemed to be holding that axe high in the air for ages, as though he was having some difficulty in making the obligatory movement. That is probably why he got it wrong, as much as he was not rewarded, I shall never know. But this is what you will want to know, Sir, and I will tell it with my heart that it be the absolute truth as I witnessed it. I feel certain, Lady Jane was rendered unconscious by the first blow, even though it did not severe her head. She made no noise, not even a whimper. She must already have been despatched to her Lord. I saw the swift movement of the axe come down. I placed both of my hands against and pressed my face backwards not bearing to see it, but my head lurched forward and I saw the blade slice one side of her neck.

"It was awful, fearful. The crowd groaned and stared at her head rolling to one side as if held by elastic. But the axe man rapidly made another swing to properly sever the head. But fear not, Sir. I know she was already gone, I just know it."

"I feel sure God would have made that so, dear Mary, and I am grateful that you so bravely told me of this,"

"But that is not only the shame of it, Dr. Aylmer. We were forbidden to remove the body. The crowd dispersed and Sir John Brydges, looking bewildered, told us the Queen had ordered that there would be no more Protestant burials in the Royal Chapel. But Dr. Feckenham had managed to gain the Queen's counsel and was presently attempting to persuade her to change her mind on this occasion.

"But we later heard that she would have none of it, that the body should be secretly transported and buried in un-consecrated ground.

"I must tell you that the body was laying at the scaffold four hours later and only after a complaint from a the visiting French ambassador was permission obtained for its removal. But, despite Dr. Feckenham's most earnest endeavours, the Queen maintained her decision that Lady Jane should not be buried in the Royal Chapel and that be an end of it!"

I was astounded by this news but not particularly surprised because of

197

the rumours that had been circulating, but I was not aware of the long delay before the body was removed from the scaffold. Then I noticed a certain calm in Mary, watched her turn to Robert and smile.

"If it hadn't been for Sir John Brydges and Robert, Lady Jane's request may never have been fulfilled."

Mary must have noticed my puzzled expression and said she was about to explain all. That this was what they had to tell me in utmost secrecy.

"Truly, if it had not been for the Queen herself, Lady Jane's body would never have reached its final resting place. The place only I knew she wanted that to be. But she assumed, because of her nobility, she would be buried in the Tower chapel.

"At least there is a certain happy ending to her story, Dr. Aylmer, and tomorrow we will take you there, to see her burial place, not far from here. She will love that. She will know that we are there to pray for her soul. And who could better deliver that prayer than her beloved tutor. God be blessed that you have come, Dr. Aylmer. It has made my day and I know tomorrow will make yours.

"Now 'tis time for dinner. I shall go and fetch the utensils first. Here, Sir, open this small parcel and you will see inside something precious indeed."

As Robert watched I opened the parcel and there to behold was Jane's black velvet gown.

Robert suggested, her good friend and governess should keep it in memory, not of that horrible day but that she wore it when she was going home to her Lord God.

"A treasure indeed," I gasped, delicately brushing the soft velvet.

"But the biggest treasure of all, Sir, is what we shall see tomorrow."

I slept well that night. Although Jane had gone forever I was near to the place I knew her best, the place where she was born.

Mary served each of us a bowl of hot oats in the morning, ready to make our journey.

Robert prepared a horse and carriage and soon we were off towards Bradgate.

"I remember travelling this road so many times with the three sisters, Jane, Katharine, and Mary in one carriage, her parents in the leading carriage as we started those long tiring journeys to other counties," Mary said calmly. "It did not seem that long ago, weeks more than years. If only we had known then what would become of the Lady Jane. But if we had, there was nothing we could have done about it."

We soon approached the boundaries of Bradgate Park and Robert made no move to change our route. We stopped at the familiar iron gates I remembered so well and Robert stepped down from the carriage and, taking with him a large key, put it into the lock and turned the key. Soon the gates were open, Robert was back in his driving seat and we were riding into the park.

"But why do we come here?" I queried. "Not that I object. I always love to come to Bradgate and fully intended to during my visit in these parts. You have known this, of course. That is why you bring me here."

"Well, yes, Sir - in a way. But we have a very special purpose for bringing you here today."

My mind swam. It could not be true. I shouted it out.

"Jane is here? She is buried here?"

Mary smiled profusely. "Right here in Bradgate Park, Sir. She always said she would like to be buried here during those awful last days in the Tower. She could never believe that it could happen but now, in heaven, she will know."

"Near the house, Mary, near the house?" I asked excitedly.

"You will see, shortly you will see," Mary calmed.

"But how did you manage to bring her body to Bradgate?" I asked.

Robert replied: "I had arranged to go down to collect my betrothed. Her services were no longer required, so I took down the horse and carriage. I was told of the terrible way Jane's body was to be disposed of, in un-consecrated ground in a thick wood away from the Tower. It was to be removed during the night when it could not be seen. It was then that the idea occurred to Mary.

"Sir John Brydges himself arranged for the body to be properly embalmed and placed in a small round oak cask. When it was dark, I was given permission to enter the Tower and pick up the cask.

"It took us the whole of four days to travel back to Bradgate. The weather was bad, the wind was howling and it poured most of the time. Yet that never seemed to matter. It was as if God himself was guiding Jane back home to where she belonged and we were well replenished at every rest stop. As if the Landlord at each Inn realised our purpose and made great heed to ensure our warmth and comfort with lashings of good hot food. When we arrived here at Bradgate Park Mary had another one of her ideas..."

Now Mary took over the conversation: "The Family carriage was left in the Bradgate stable. Robert had kept it in good order, should it be needed again. Beautifully polished it was. Just fitting for Jane's last journey into Bradgate, back to the place she was born. Robert un-harnessed the horse and rode it to the house soon to return with the black and cream carriage proudly displaying the fine coat of arms of the House of Grey each side. Sadly yet joyfully we transferred the casket from one carriage to another and finally made our way to the spot to which we have now come."

I saw a circle of oak trees on a small slope then realised where we were. It was where we, Mary, Jane and I, picnicked on that fine summer day before her wedding and where her favourite pet was buried.

Mary caught my eye and shared my absolute joy.

"Yes, it is here she wanted to be buried, Sir. In the ground consecrated by you, in this tranquil lovely place surrounded by her favourite trees, near to Henry, her white retriever. In her belongings we discovered Henry's collar. She must have loved the creature so dearly. We buried the collar with her. We thought that was the right thing to do."

The tears came in plenty that day, Samuel. But we all cried tears of sadness and joy.

Before finally leaving Bradgate for the last time I wanted to take a final look at the empty house. I just stood back to take in a panoramic view from the front, then walked a little nearer towards the courtyard. Mary and Robert waited for me as I recalled those happy, wonderful times with my dear, dear Jane.

Then something caught my eye in the top window of the corner tower where Jane studied. My mind was surely playing tricks, I saw her there waving to me as she always did upon my departure from Bradgate. The sun was hanging low but sent a beam of light flashing through the moving branches of oaks behind me, picking out a shadow in that place. I remember how she told me how much she enjoyed the view, looking over the small chapel roof and onto the sweeping countryside beyond.

I really felt she was there, waving to me for the last time. I realised I was responding and as I lifted my hand into the air, a whisk of wind caught the leaves of oak behind and made the tiny shadows dance around the tower head. She was happy now. An indescribable force overwhelmed me. I felt that her spirit was, for that brief moment, joining mine in harmony. There was something so very special about my Lady Jane, my so very much loved and cherished Jane… "I love you, Jane."

Certain tranquillity followed. The silence was overwhelming as I felt her lips so gently touch mine, then whispers in the branches of the trees as now the breeze blew, they were saying: "And I love you, my beloved schoolmaster, and will await you in another place, another time for forever but in your life you will honour me by letting your faith guide you as it truly has guided me, and be not guilty to fall in love with another if that is what God has planned for you."

She was with me at that moment, complete as we had never quite been before. I knew what she wanted me to do, that history would discover in time the true story.

"For Mary Tudor and her advisors have been sure to destroy almost everything that belongs to me, my portraits and many of my letters referring to the new learning…."

I felt the question burning in my mind, the note she had hidden but she was almost gone now. I felt that she had good cause for it to remain secured and did not let my question be asked. If it was to be found, God would ensure that but one last question remained:

"How would you wish to be remembered and the truth explained, Jane?

"Write it all down in the chronicles of your mind that the vibes will in future be properly translated in a time when the world will wish to search for the truth and England of her past."

I lost her form, just the shadows remained, but I felt exhilarating warmth and a feeling of wellbeing. It was as if Jane was telling me all is well with her and be not too saddened by her sudden departure. That nothing is lost but all is gained in the heaven of God.

But was it a dream or was it for real? I distinctly saw her in the tower, looking out for me as she oft times did to welcome me when I came to Bradgate.

"But I am spirit now, my beloved schoolmaster, suspended here for a short time, enough to transmit my thoughts to you and then my task is complete. I have no further reason to stay. The time is nigh in the eyes of the Lord."

"You do know how deeply I love you, dear Jane, and why forever I had to hold my feelings and emotions to myself?"

"John, when we made love in my cell I realised your passion and your total love and God told me that it was so and you are my guardian angel."

I went from there a far exalted man feeling that God indeed had His reason to prematurely take Jane from the world and Bradgate, that she was now out of harm's way in perfect peace. The tears I had earlier shed were now redundant as I felt the urge to shout up at the heavens, thanking the Good Lord for saving Jane from further perils she may have encountered in those violent times.

I returned to where the horse and carriage stood and joined Mary and Robert for one last prayer.

We prayed and thanked the Lord for his mercy and fulfilling Jane's wish.

Jane was gone from our lives forever but never from our thoughts.

"God be with you, Jane, now and forever more."

I returned to Bradgate, still curious about the note but never found any trace of it. I searched many times, almost feeling its presence hidden somewhere in the pile in a leaden casket between the mortar which I believe was near to Jane's apartment, yet every time I felt I was certain to discover it when I felt a brick was loose, and there was a cavity behind, there was nothing. Wherever it was, Jane had made quite sure it was well concealed.

I concluded that Jane possibly did decipher from the salvaged remains of the message more details regarding Northumberland's devise. Perhaps she was aware of his intention to use her as a political pawn. There was something she never divulged to me in this context. The mystery must remain. But somewhere in the ruins of Jane's childhood home in Bradgate Park, lest it was discovered and thrown away by the young lad seen to be running form the scene, the casket will surely eventually be revealed...

***

Samuel closed the manuscript and looked at his father.

"Father, your story is a treasure to behold."

But there was no reply. After a 'feverish distemper,' the Bishop John Aylmer, beloved schoolmaster to Lady Jane, peacefully passed away at the 'good old age' of seventy-three on June 3, 1594 at his palace in Fulham, London.

His rehearsal for death was accomplished, but not without some labour given to his disposition in the Protestant Church under Elizabeth's reign. When he became Bishop of London he was sometimes harsh on Popish divines bent to overthrow the gospel. He later offended the Queen in that he committed a certain Thomas Cartwright and other purists to prison, stipulating the authority so to do was warranted by her majesty.

Some confusion arose when the Queen denied this, even if it was true and for reasons of her own, she did not want this to be generally known.

By all accounts she was about to expel him of his Bishopry but he died first.

But that is another story.

He married a 'matron from a fine family' called Judith and sired seven sons and three daughters.

Jane's note has never been discovered in the House at Bradgate, which is now in ruins.

Perhaps Jane and her schoolmaster have now come together again.

THE END

CPSIA information can be obtained at www.ICGtesting.com
Printed in the USA
LVOW082320050212

267205LV00007B/48/P